Capture Creatures™

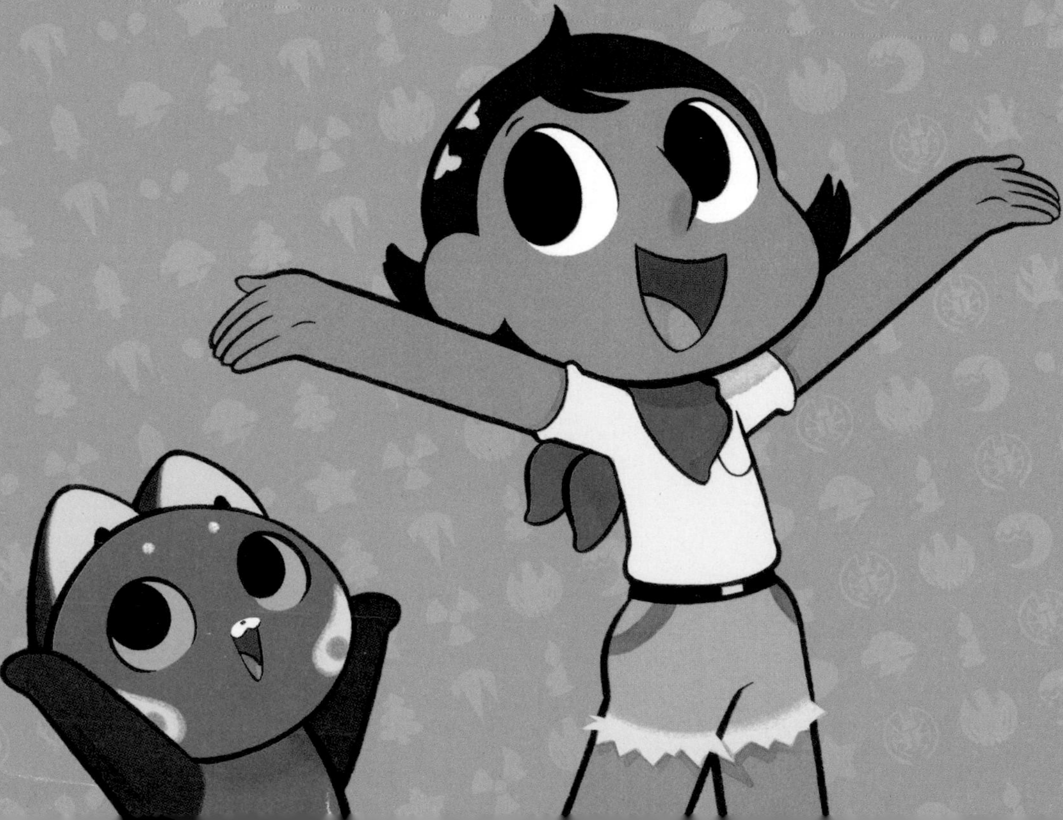

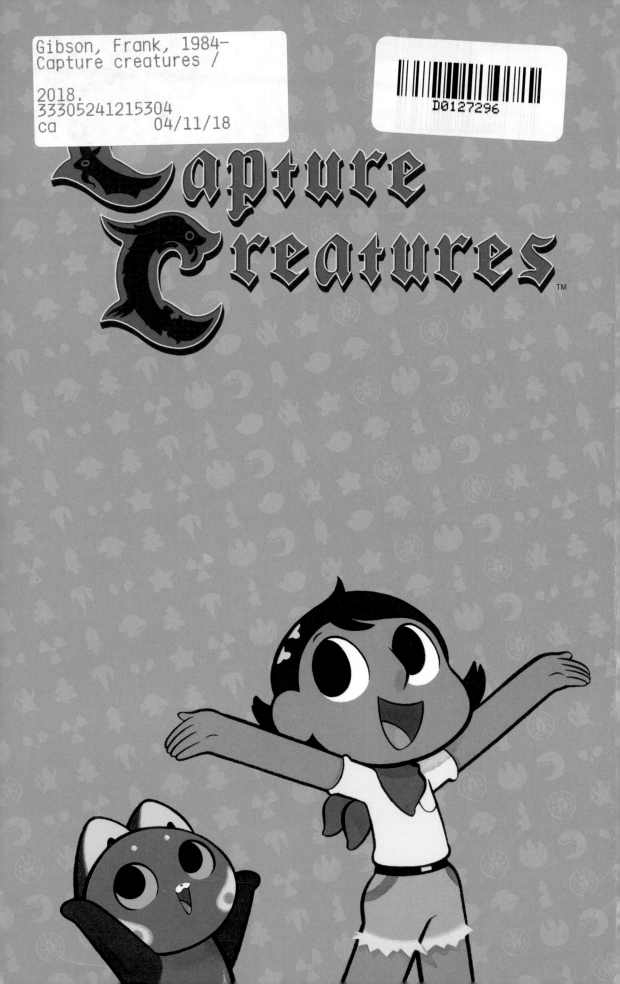

CAPTURE CREATURES, February 2018. Published by KaBOOM!, a division of Boom Entertainment, Inc. Capture Creatures is ™ & © 2018 Frank Gibson and Rebecca Dreistadt. Originally published in single magazine form as CAPTURE CREATURES No. 1-4. ™ & © 2015 Frank Gibson and Rebecca Dreistadt. All rights reserved. KaBOOM!™ and the KaBOOM! logo are trademarks of Boom Entertainment, Inc., registered in various countries and categories. All characters, events, and institutions depicted herein are fictional. Any similarity between any of the names, characters, persons, events, and/or institutions in this publication to actual names, characters, and persons, whether living or dead, events, and/or institutions is unintended and purely coincidental. KaBOOM! does not read or accept unsolicited submissions of ideas, stories, or artwork.

For information regarding the CPSIA on this printed material, call: (203) 595-3636 and provide reference #RICH – 771144.

BOOM! Studios, 5670 Wilshire Boulevard, Suite 400, Los Angeles, CA 90036-5679. Printed in USA. First Printing.

ISBN: 978-1-60886-798-1, eISBN: 978-1-61398-469-7

Created by

FRANK GIBSON & BECKY DREISTADT

Script by

FRANK GIBSON

Pencils by

BECKY DREISTADT

Inks by

KELLY BASTOW

Colors by

TRACY LIANG (CHAPTERS 1-2)
JOSEPH BERGIN III, LIN VISEL,
& BECKY DREISTADT (CHAPTER 3)
KATY FARINA (CHAPTER 4)

Letters by

BRITT WILSON

Cover by

BECKY DREISTADT

Designers

GRACE PARK & KARA LEOPARD

Assistant Editors

MARY GUMPORT & SOPHIE PHILIPS-ROBERTS

Editor

SHANNON WATTERS

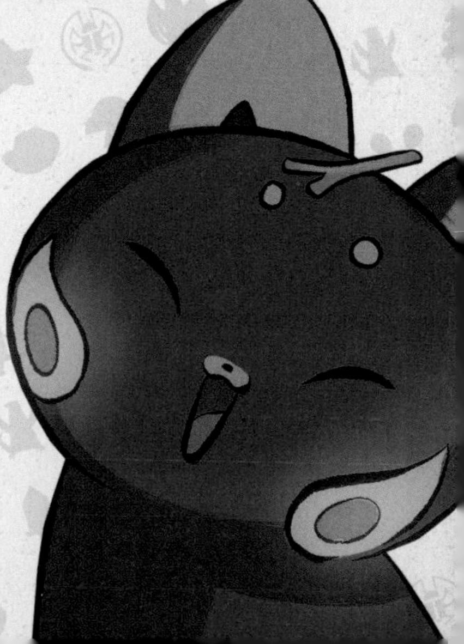

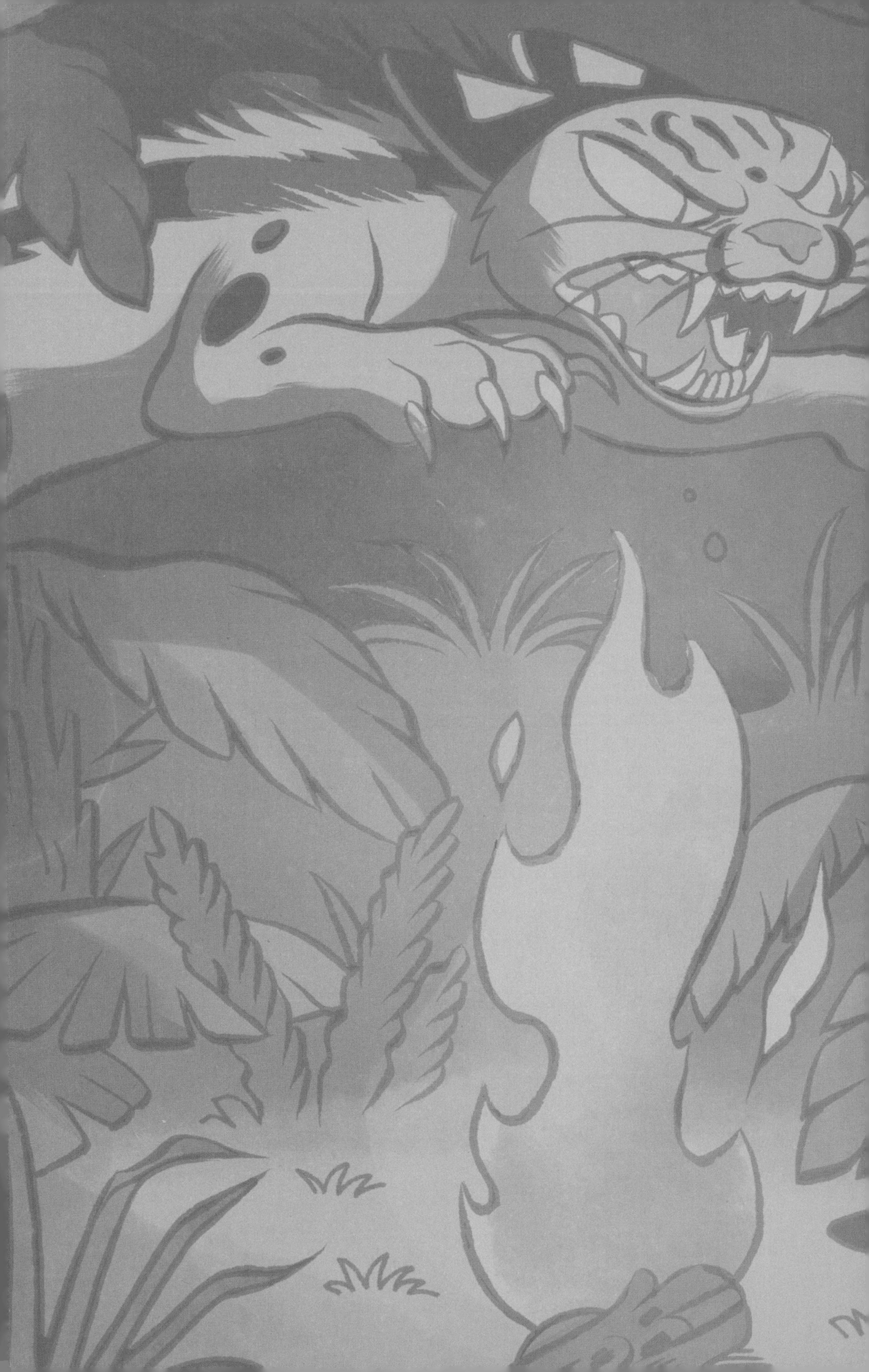

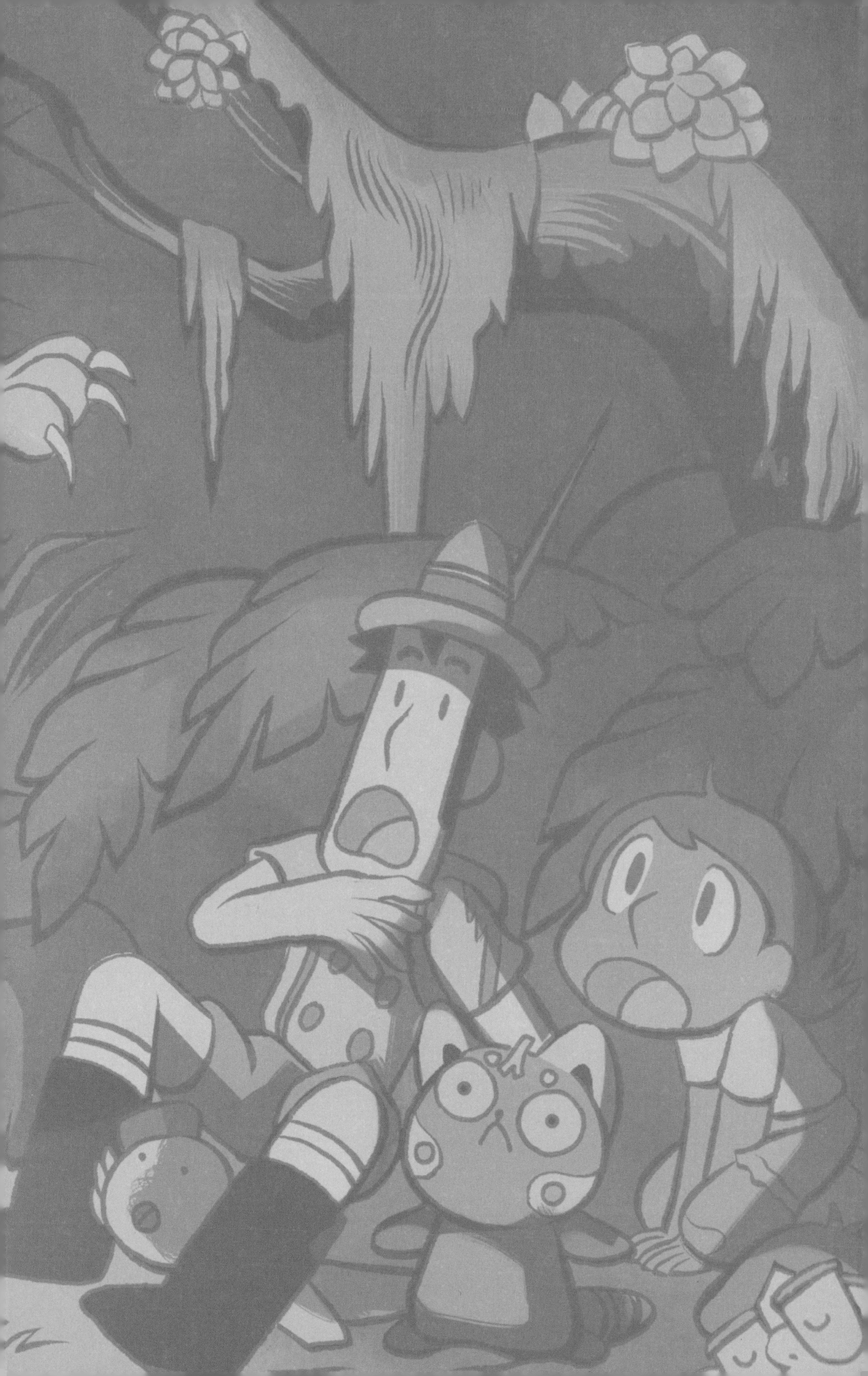

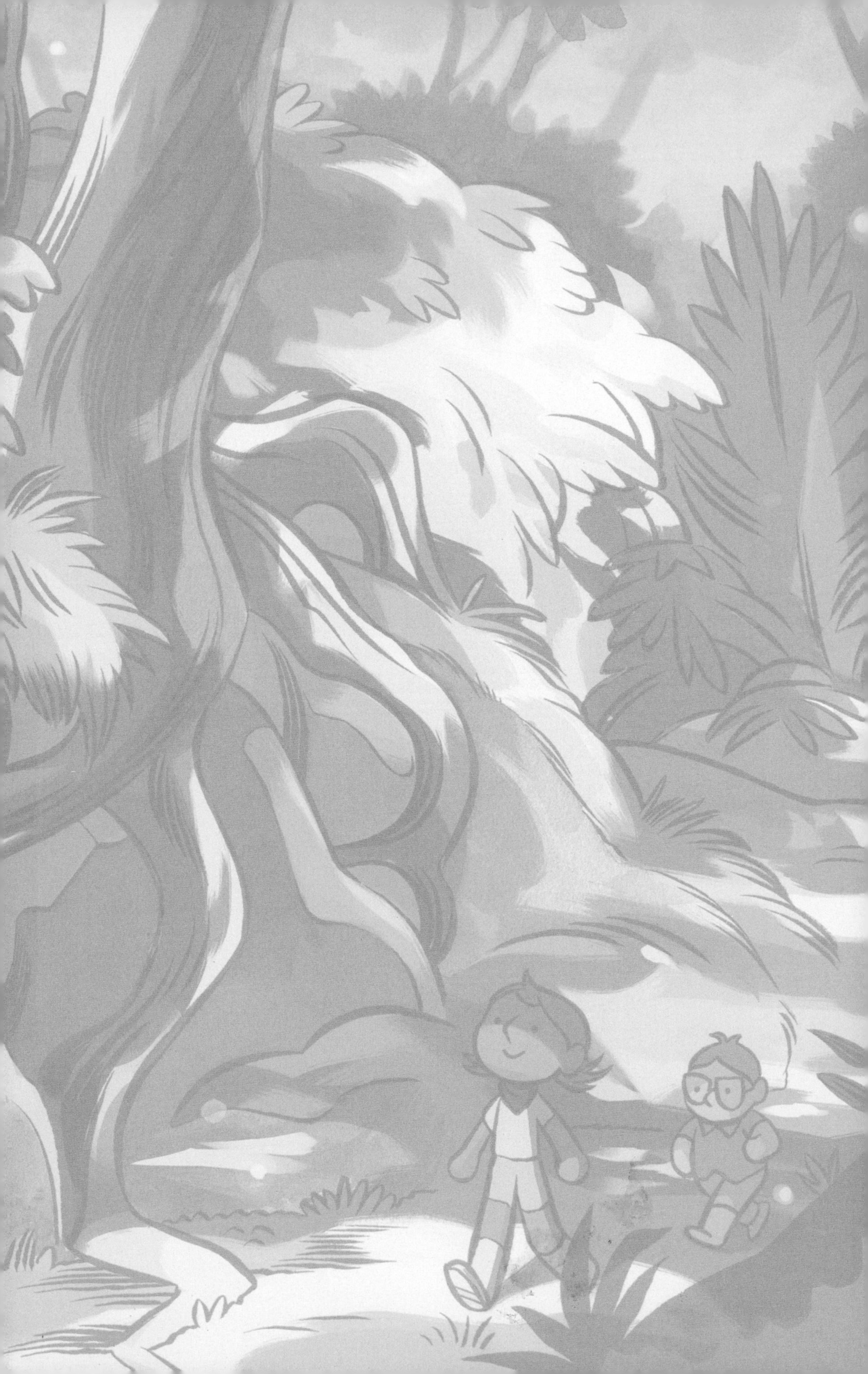

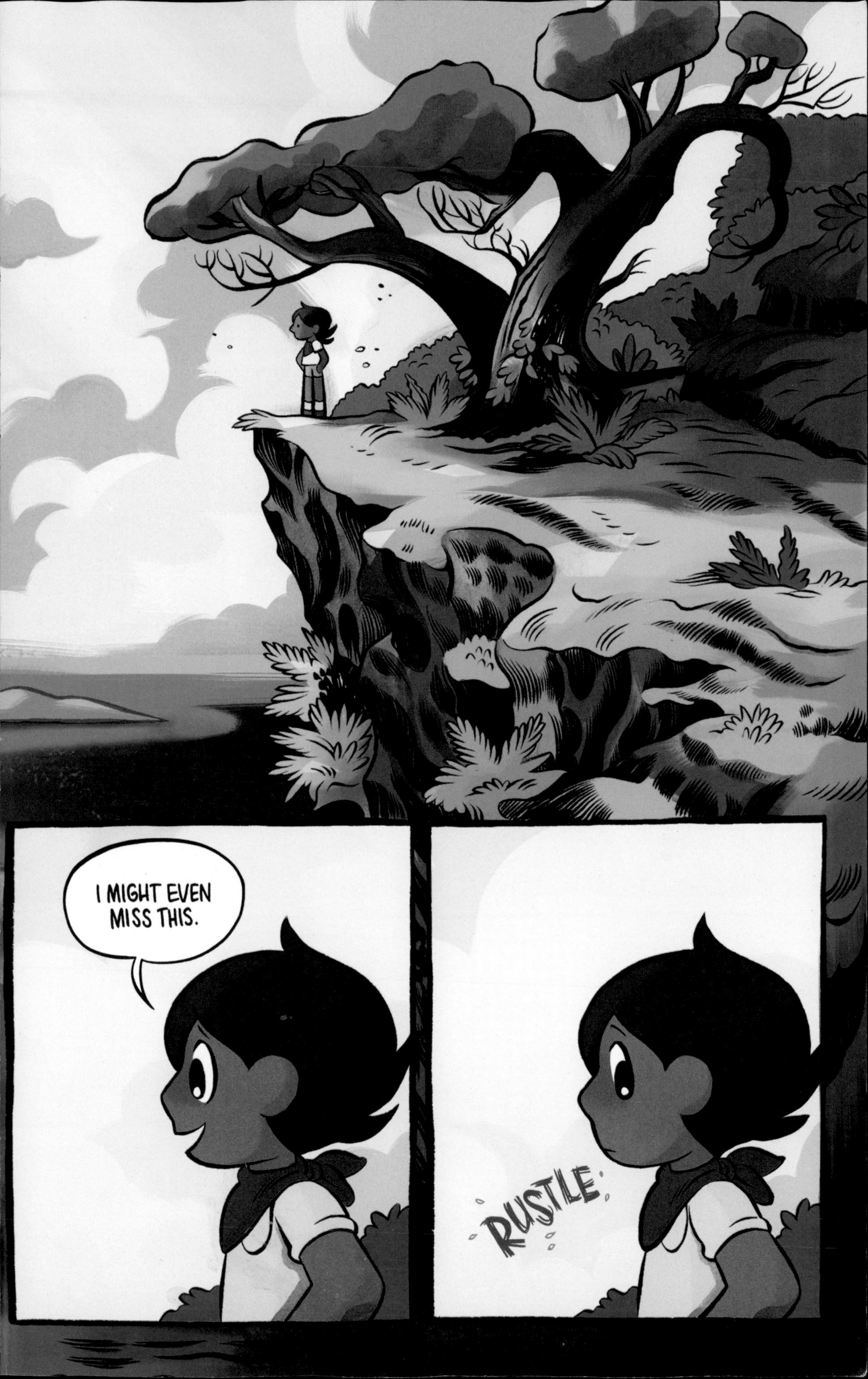
I MIGHT EVEN MISS THIS.
RUSTLE

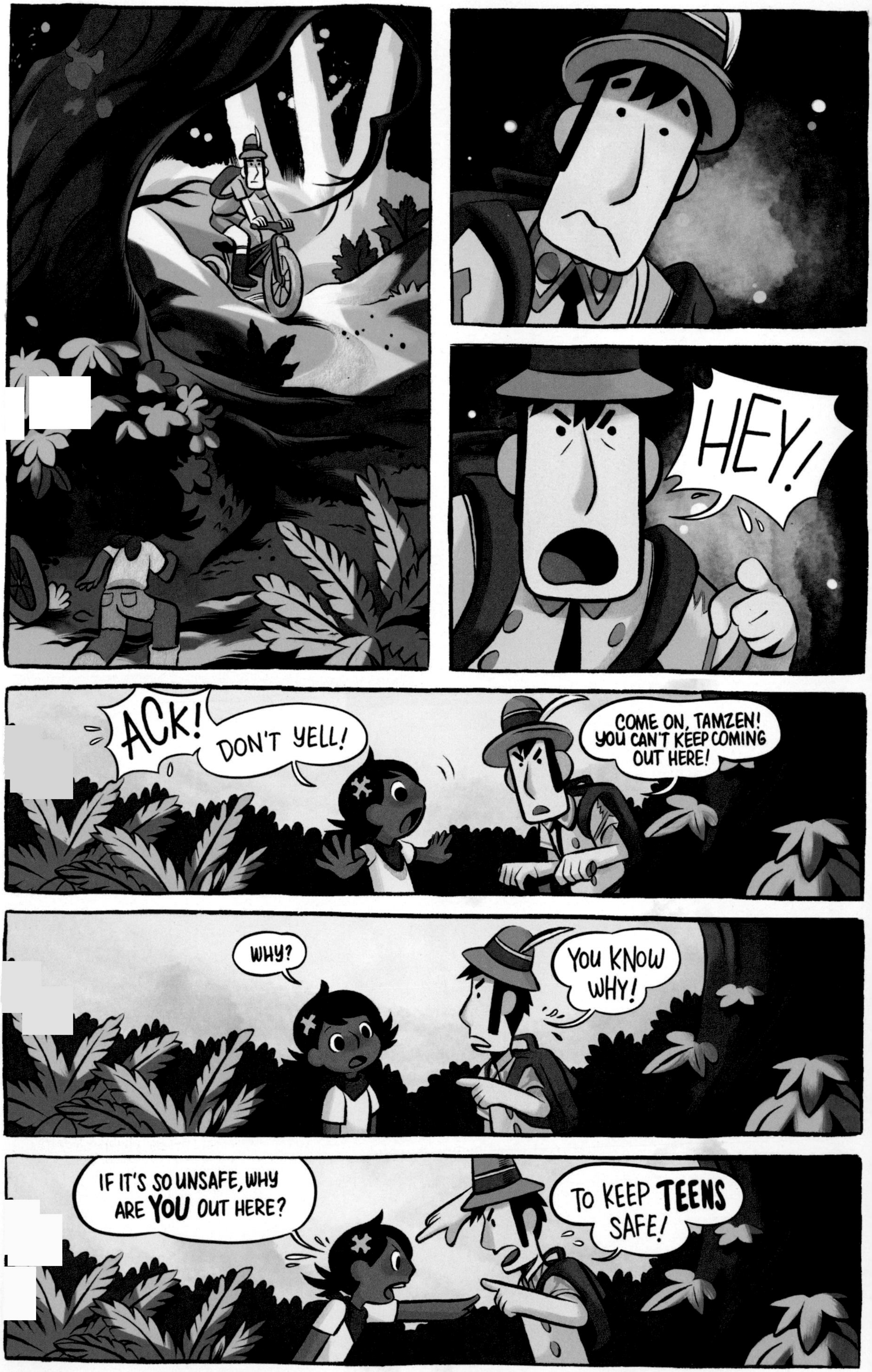
HEY!
ACK!
DON'T YELL!
COME ON, TAMZEN! YOU CAN'T KEEP COMING OUT HERE!
WHY?
YOU KNOW WHY!
IF IT'S SO UNSAFE, WHY ARE YOU OUT HERE?
TO KEEP TEENS SAFE!

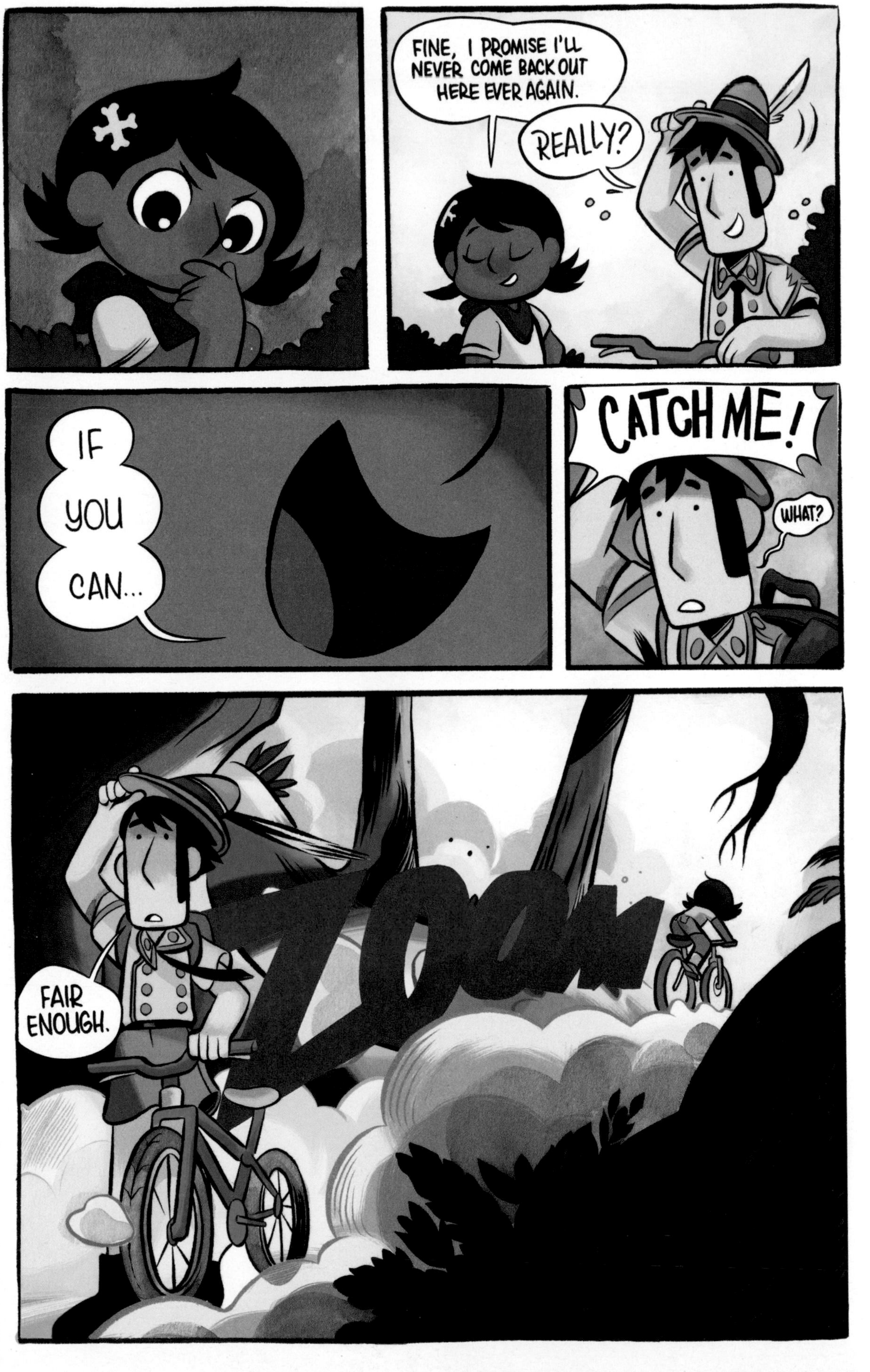
FINE, I PROMISE I'LL NEVER COME BACK OUT HERE EVER AGAIN.
REALLY?
IF YOU CAN...
CATCH ME!
WHAT?
ZOOM
FAIR ENOUGH.

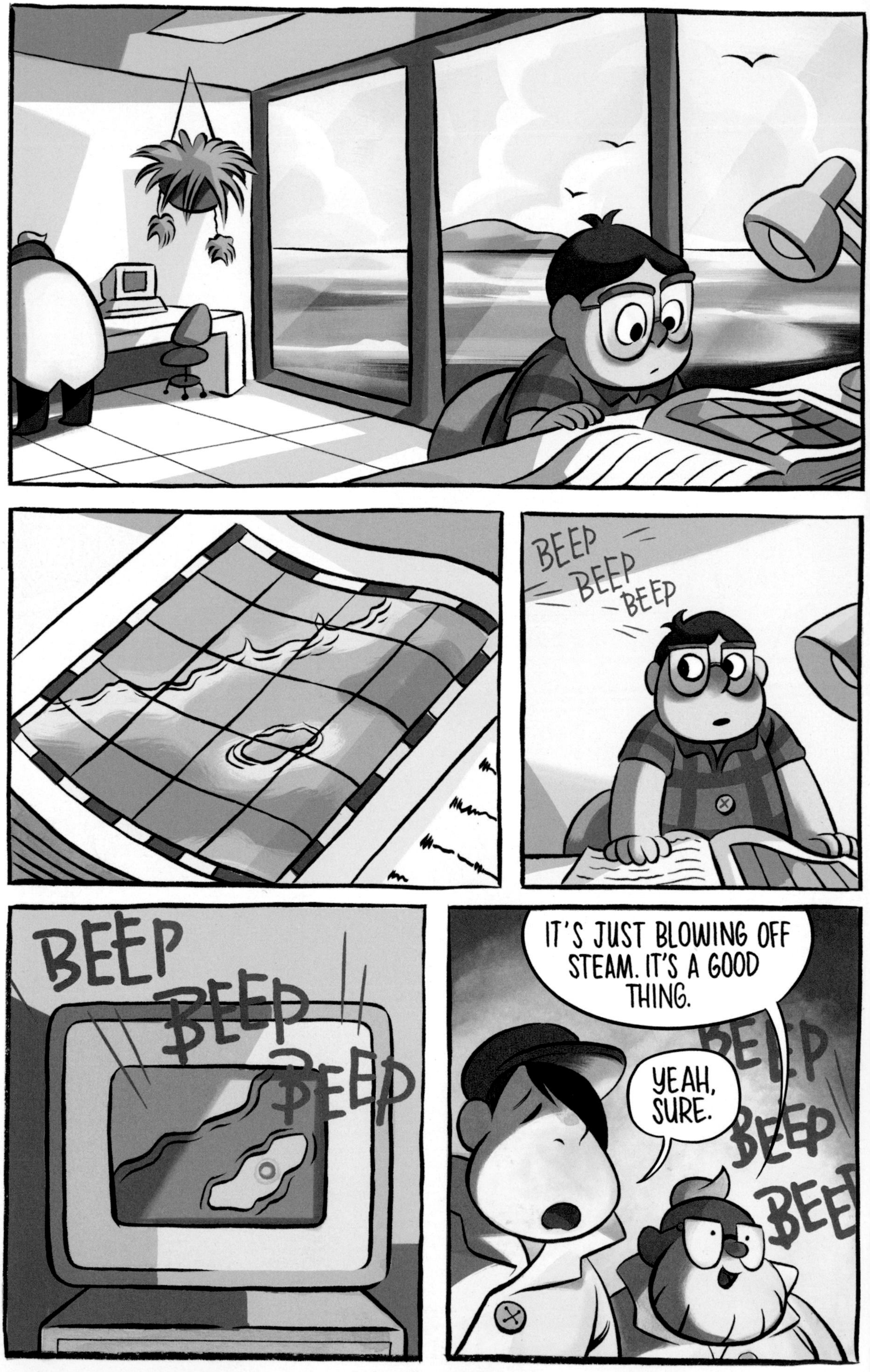
BEEP
BEEP
BEEP
BEEP
BEEP
BEEP
IT'S JUST BLOWING OFF STEAM. IT'S A GOOD THING.
YEAH, SURE.
BEEP
BEEP

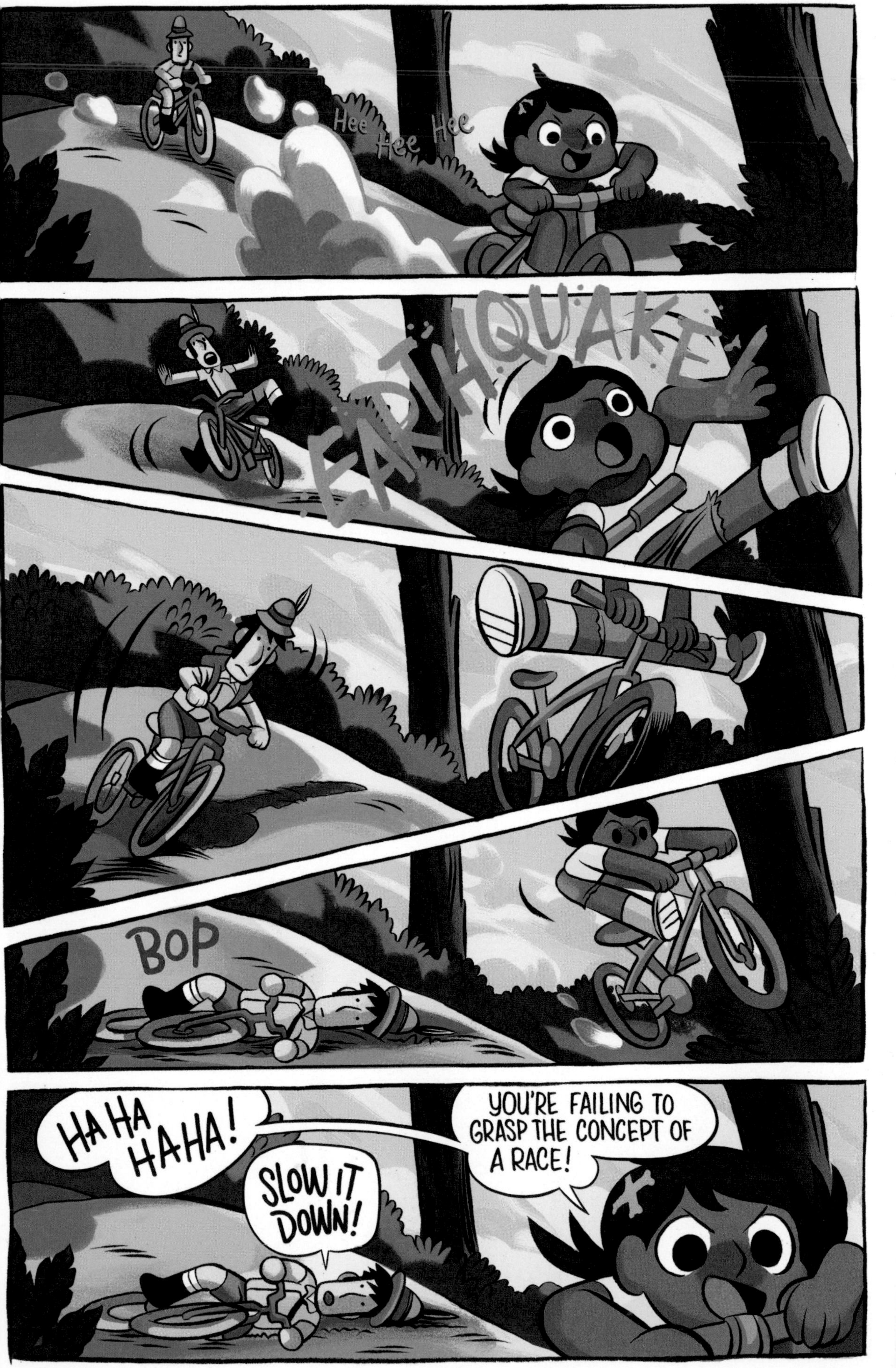
Hee Hee Hee
EARTHQUAKE!
BOP
HAHA HAHA!
YOU'RE FAILING TO GRASP THE CONCEPT OF A RACE!
SLOW IT DOWN!

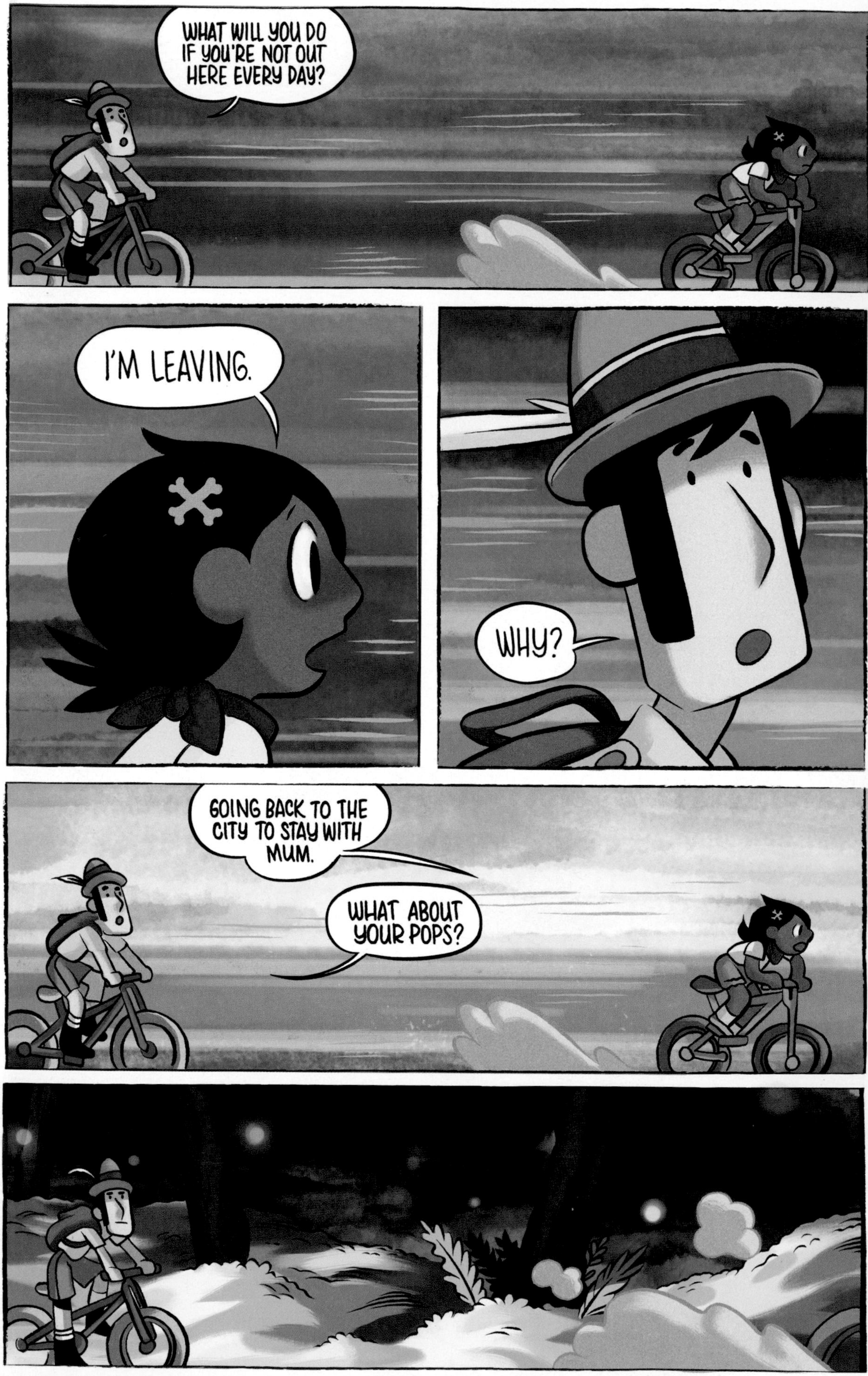
WHAT WILL YOU DO IF YOU'RE NOT OUT HERE EVERY DAY?
I'M LEAVING.
WHY?
GOING BACK TO THE CITY TO STAY WITH MUM.
WHAT ABOUT YOUR POPS?

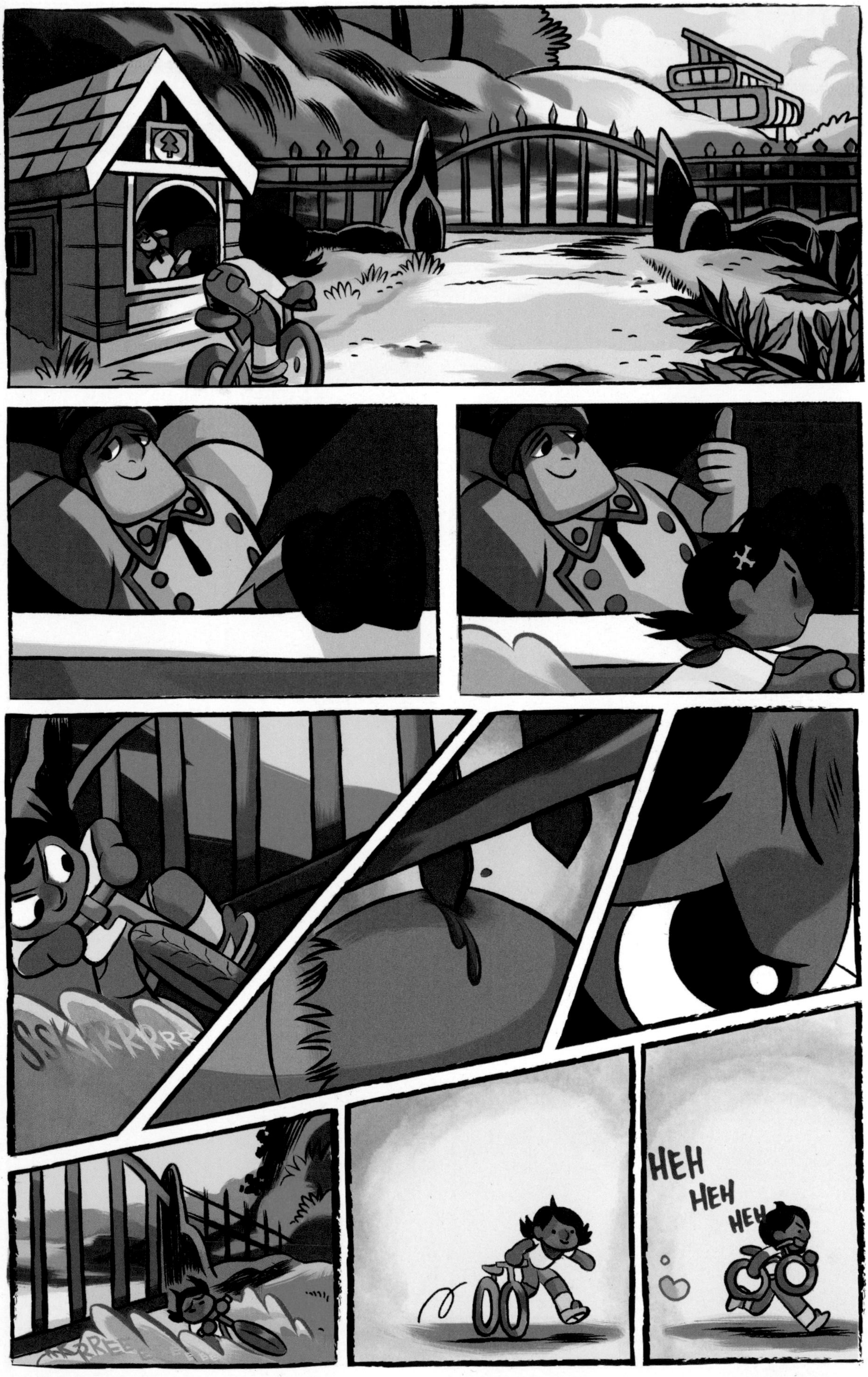
SSKRRRRRR
HEH
HEH
HEH

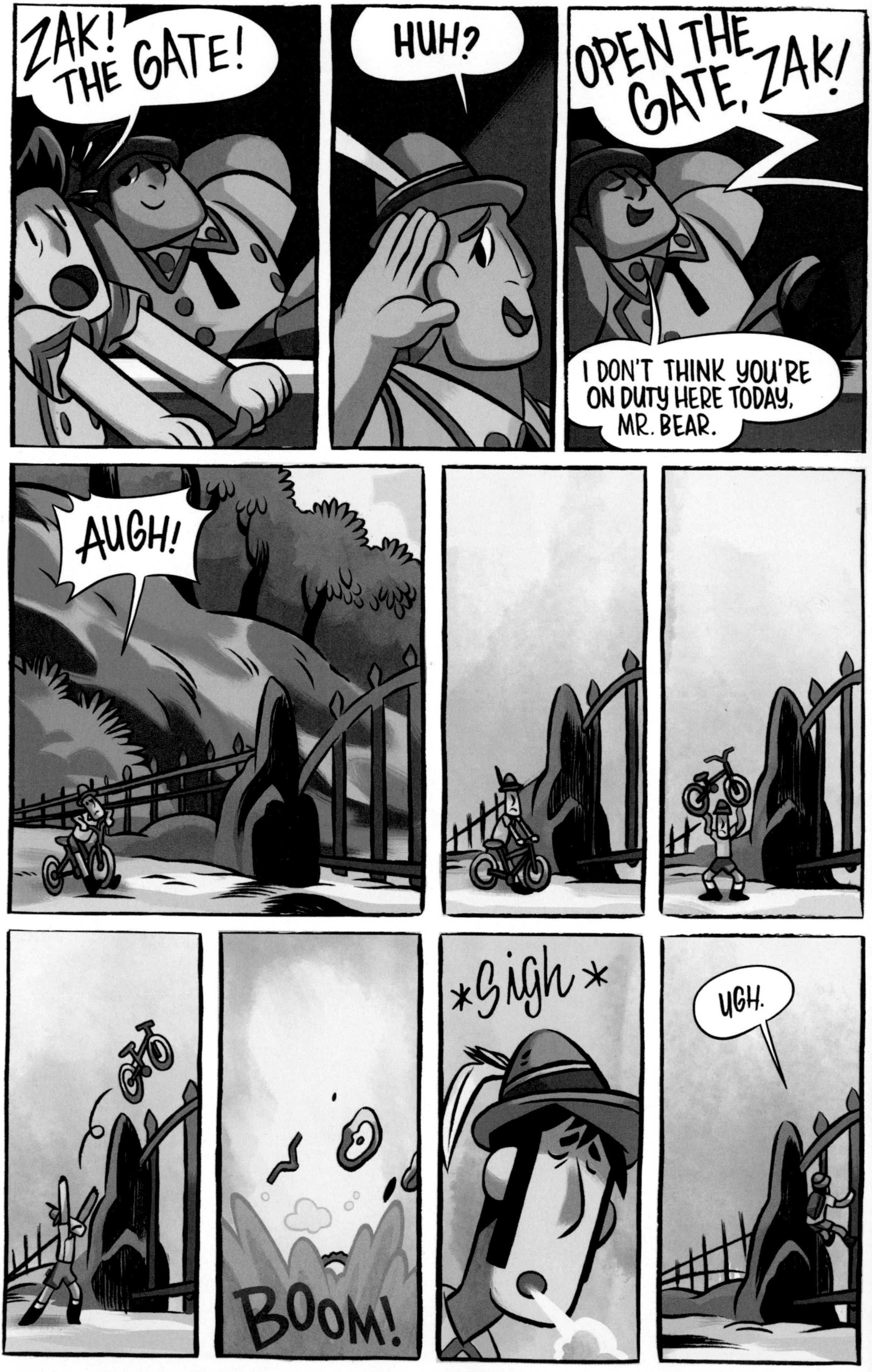
ZAK! THE GATE!
HUH?
OPEN THE GATE, ZAK!
I DON'T THINK YOU'RE ON DUTY HERE TODAY, MR. BEAR.
AUGH!
BOOM!
Sigh
UGH.

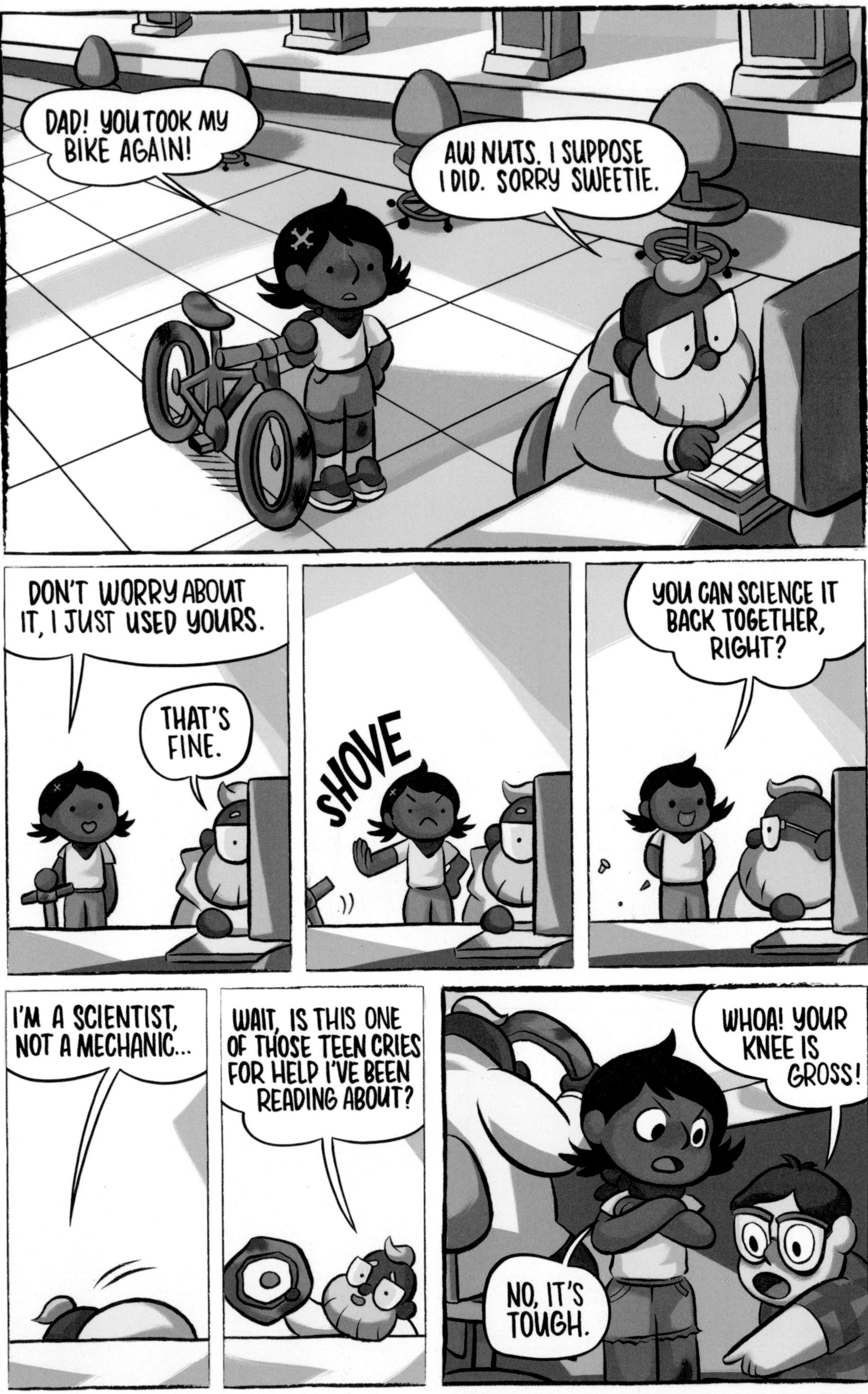
DAD! YOU TOOK MY BIKE AGAIN!
AW NUTS. I SUPPOSE I DID. SORRY SWEETIE.
DON'T WORRY ABOUT IT, I JUST USED YOURS.
THAT'S FINE.
SHOVE
YOU CAN SCIENCE IT BACK TOGETHER, RIGHT?
I'M A SCIENTIST, NOT A MECHANIC...
WAIT, IS THIS ONE OF THOSE TEEN CRIES FOR HELP I'VE BEEN READING ABOUT?
WHOA! YOUR KNEE IS GROSS!
NO, IT'S TOUGH.

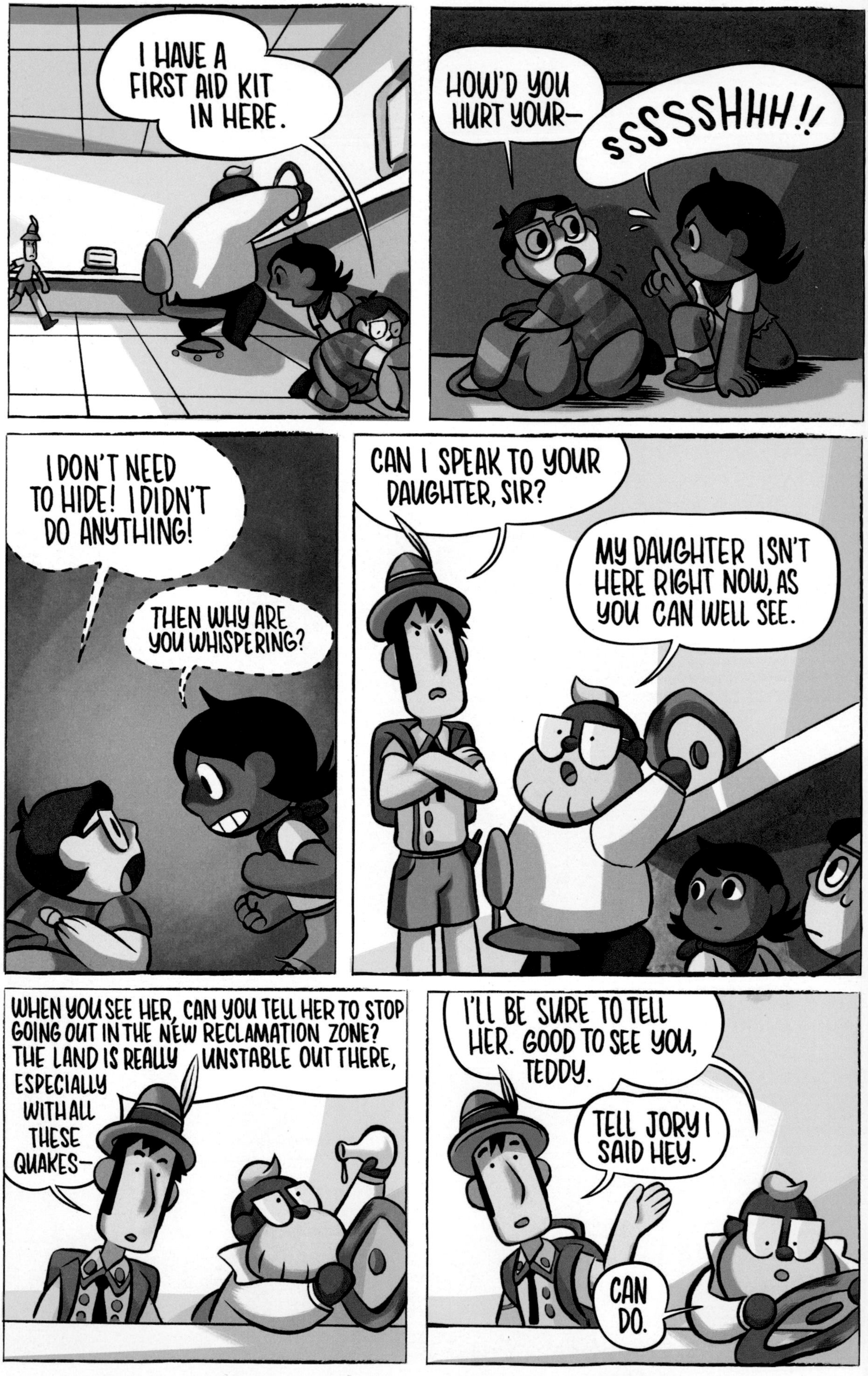
I HAVE A FIRST AID KIT IN HERE.
HOW'D YOU HURT YOUR—
sSSSSHHH!!
I DON'T NEED TO HIDE! I DIDN'T DO ANYTHING!
THEN WHY ARE YOU WHISPERING?
CAN I SPEAK TO YOUR DAUGHTER, SIR?
MY DAUGHTER ISN'T HERE RIGHT NOW, AS YOU CAN WELL SEE.
WHEN YOU SEE HER, CAN YOU TELL HER TO STOP GOING OUT IN THE NEW RECLAMATION ZONE? THE LAND IS REALLY UNSTABLE OUT THERE, ESPECIALLY WITH ALL THESE QUAKES—
I'LL BE SURE TO TELL HER. GOOD TO SEE YOU, TEDDY.
TELL JORY I SAID HEY.
CAN DO.

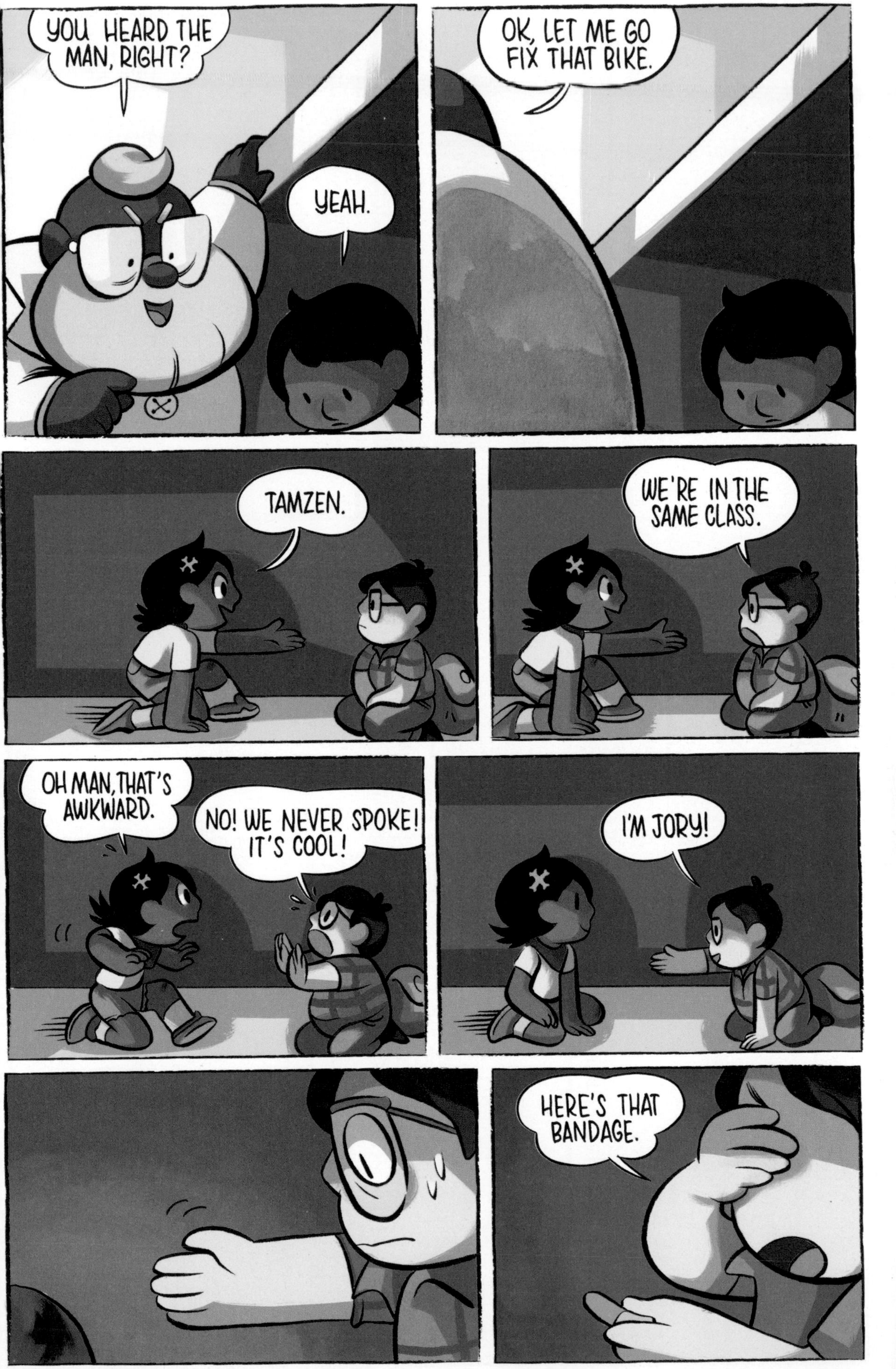

YOU HEARD THE MAN, RIGHT?
YEAH.
OK, LET ME GO FIX THAT BIKE.
TAMZEN.
WE'RE IN THE SAME CLASS.
OH MAN, THAT'S AWKWARD.
NO! WE NEVER SPOKE! IT'S COOL!
I'M JORY!
HERE'S THAT BANDAGE.

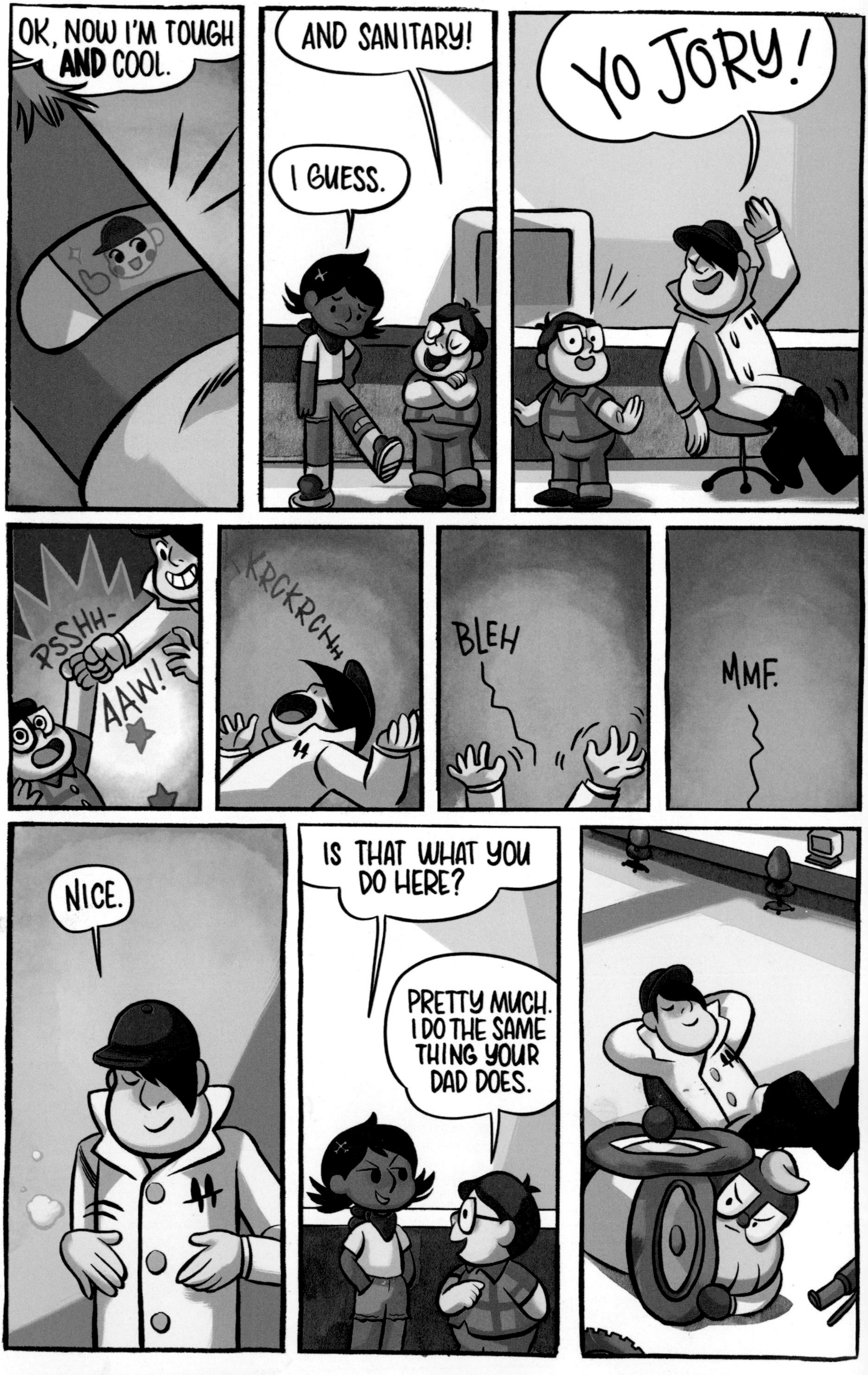

OK, NOW I'M TOUGH **AND** COOL.
AND SANITARY!
I GUESS.
YO JORY!
PSSHH-
AAW!
KRCKRCHH
BLEH
MMF.
NICE.
IS THAT WHAT YOU DO HERE?
PRETTY MUCH. I DO THE SAME THING YOUR DAD DOES.

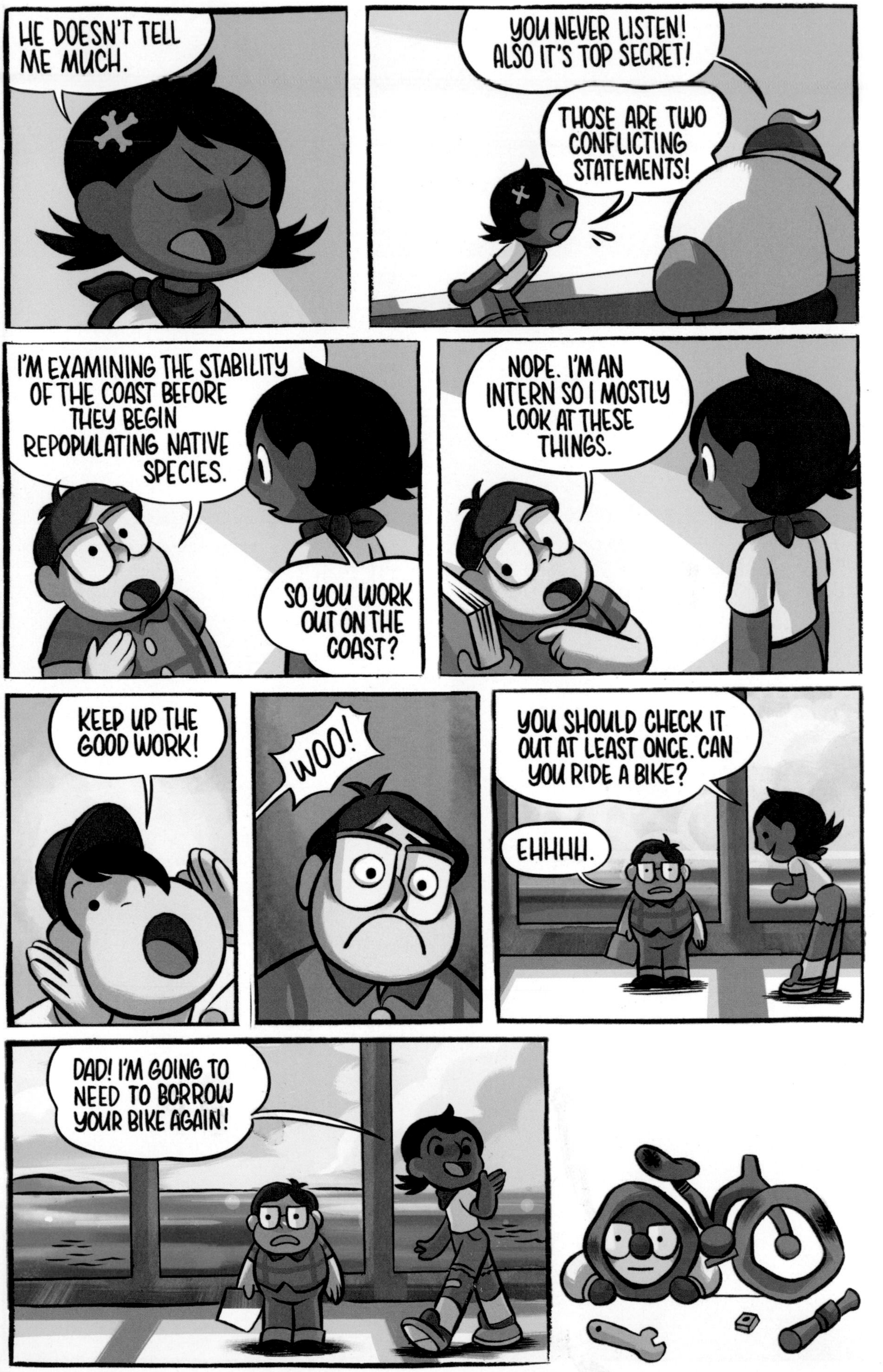
HE DOESN'T TELL ME MUCH.
YOU NEVER LISTEN! ALSO IT'S TOP SECRET!
THOSE ARE TWO CONFLICTING STATEMENTS!
I'M EXAMINING THE STABILITY OF THE COAST BEFORE THEY BEGIN REPOPULATING NATIVE SPECIES.
SO YOU WORK OUT ON THE COAST?
NOPE. I'M AN INTERN SO I MOSTLY LOOK AT THESE THINGS.
KEEP UP THE GOOD WORK!
WOO!
YOU SHOULD CHECK IT OUT AT LEAST ONCE. CAN YOU RIDE A BIKE?
EHHHH.
DAD! I'M GOING TO NEED TO BORROW YOUR BIKE AGAIN!

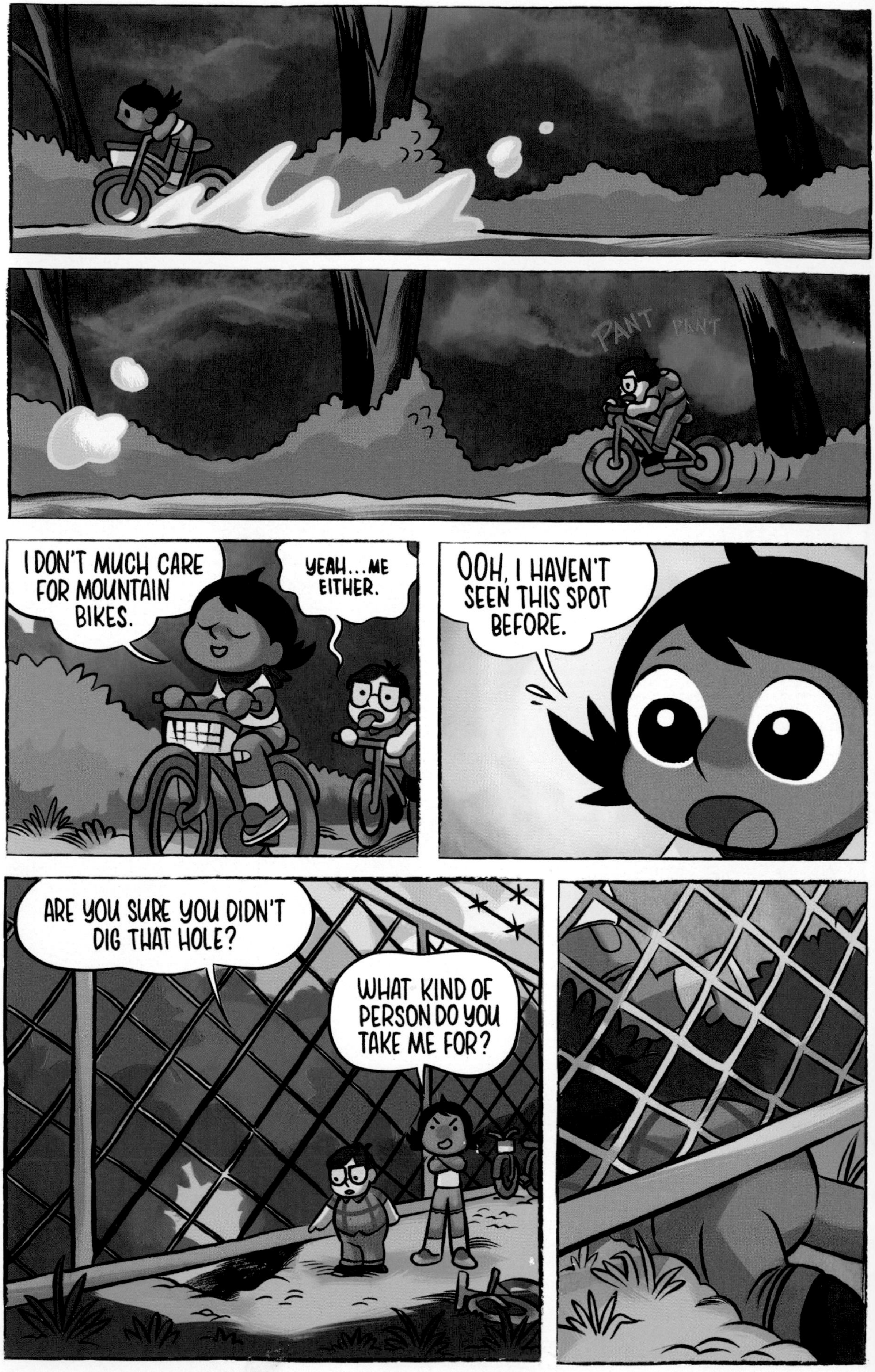
PANT PANT
I DON'T MUCH CARE FOR MOUNTAIN BIKES.
YEAH... ME EITHER.
OOH, I HAVEN'T SEEN THIS SPOT BEFORE.
ARE YOU SURE YOU DIDN'T DIG THAT HOLE?
WHAT KIND OF PERSON DO YOU TAKE ME FOR?

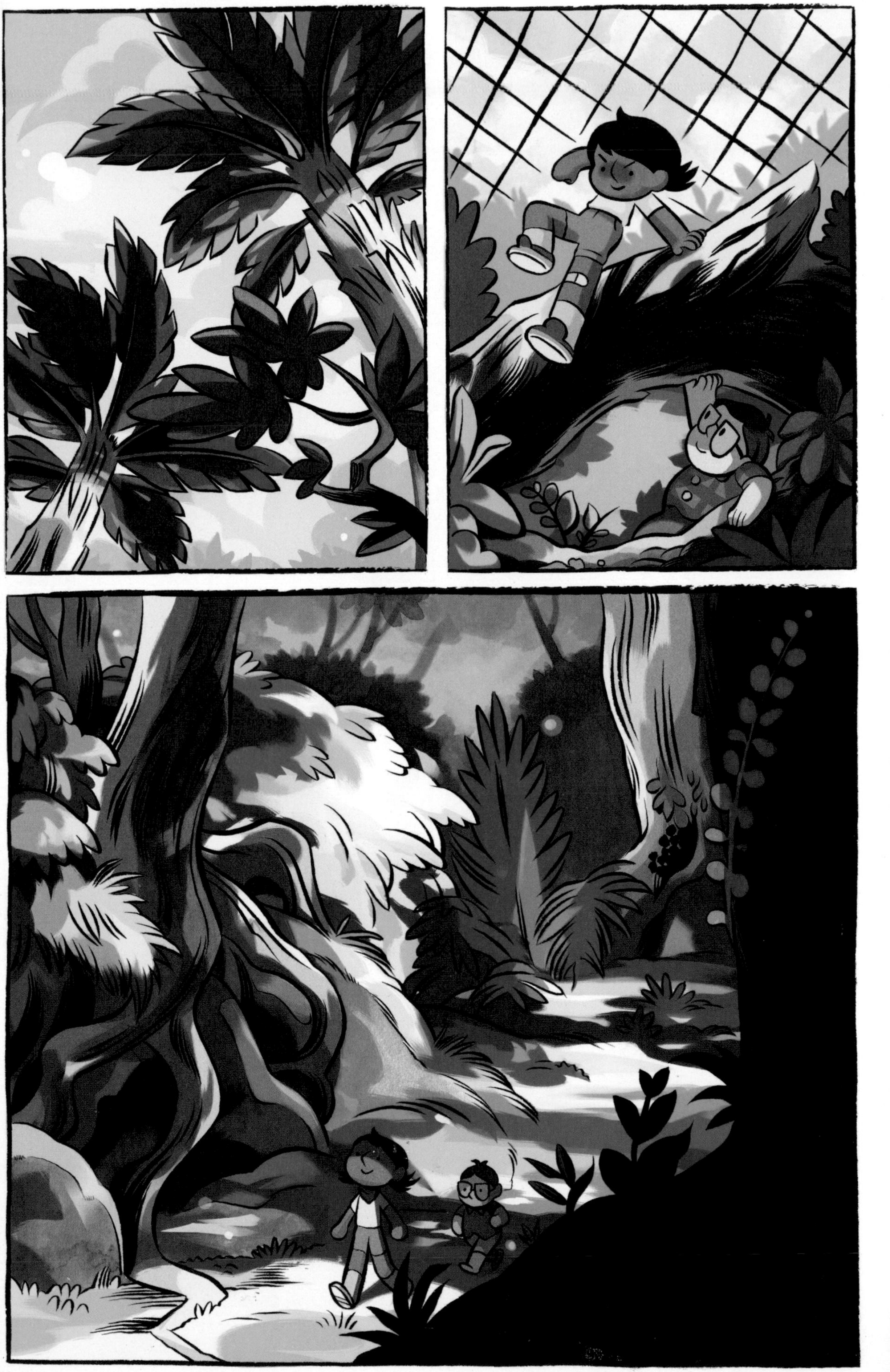

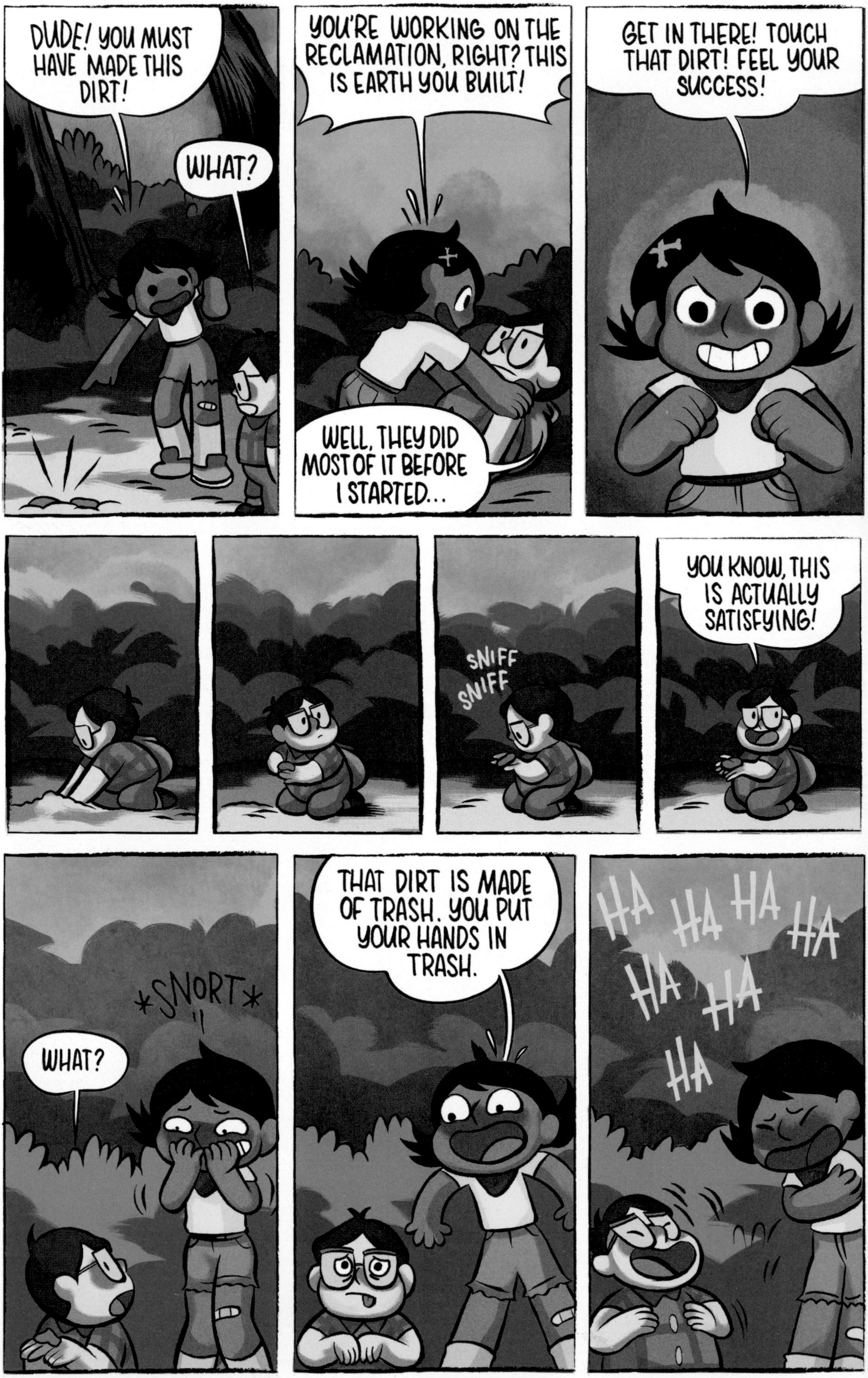

DUDE! YOU MUST HAVE MADE THIS DIRT!
WHAT?
YOU'RE WORKING ON THE RECLAMATION, RIGHT? THIS IS EARTH YOU BUILT!
WELL, THEY DID MOST OF IT BEFORE I STARTED...
GET IN THERE! TOUCH THAT DIRT! FEEL YOUR SUCCESS!
SNIFF SNIFF
YOU KNOW, THIS IS ACTUALLY SATISFYING!
SNORT
WHAT?
THAT DIRT IS MADE OF TRASH. YOU PUT YOUR HANDS IN TRASH.
HA HA HA HA HA HA HA HA

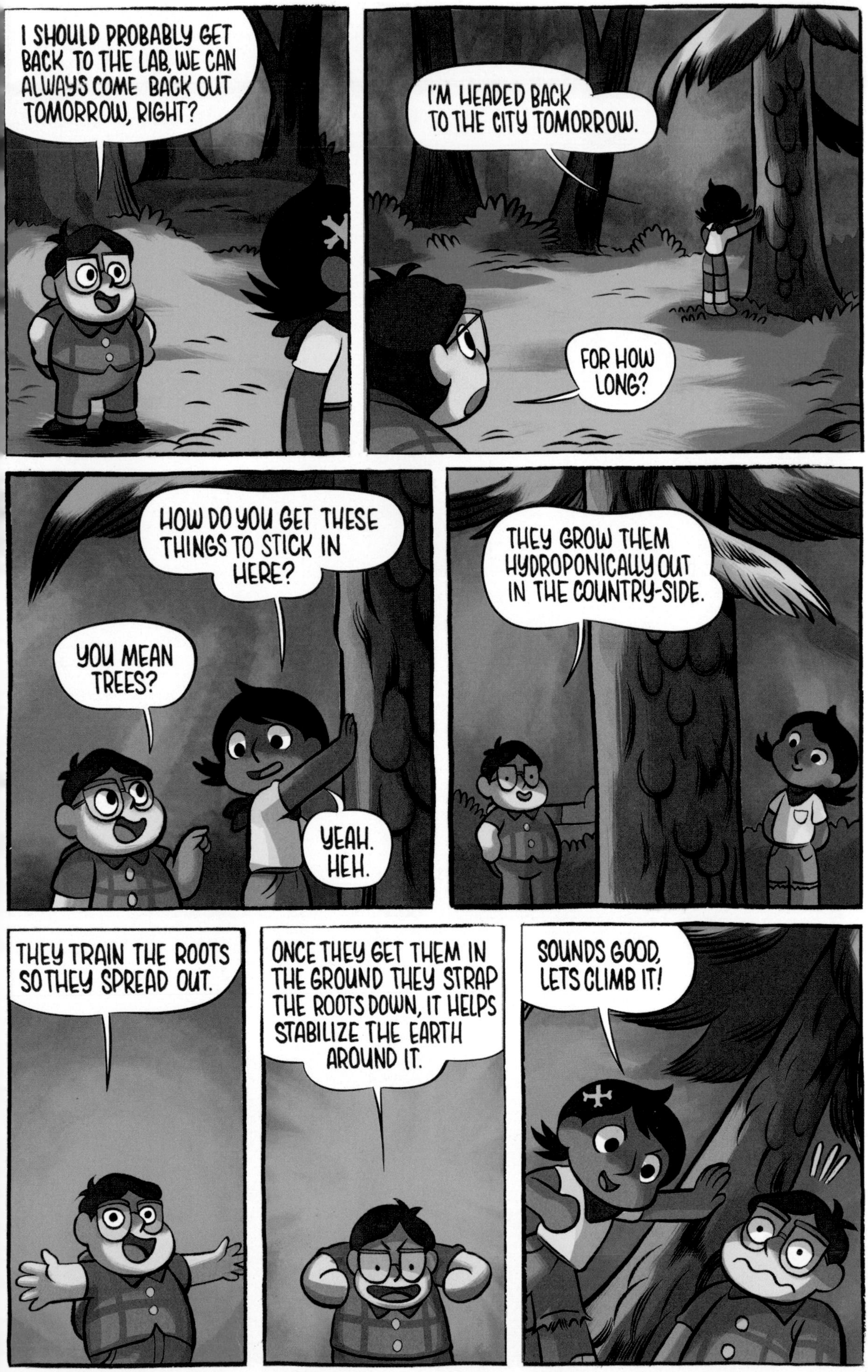
I SHOULD PROBABLY GET BACK TO THE LAB, WE CAN ALWAYS COME BACK OUT TOMORROW, RIGHT?
I'M HEADED BACK TO THE CITY TOMORROW.
FOR HOW LONG?
HOW DO YOU GET THESE THINGS TO STICK IN HERE?
YOU MEAN TREES?
YEAH. HEH.
THEY GROW THEM HYDROPONICALLY OUT IN THE COUNTRY-SIDE.
THEY TRAIN THE ROOTS SO THEY SPREAD OUT.
ONCE THEY GET THEM IN THE GROUND THEY STRAP THE ROOTS DOWN, IT HELPS STABILIZE THE EARTH AROUND IT.
SOUNDS GOOD, LETS CLIMB IT!

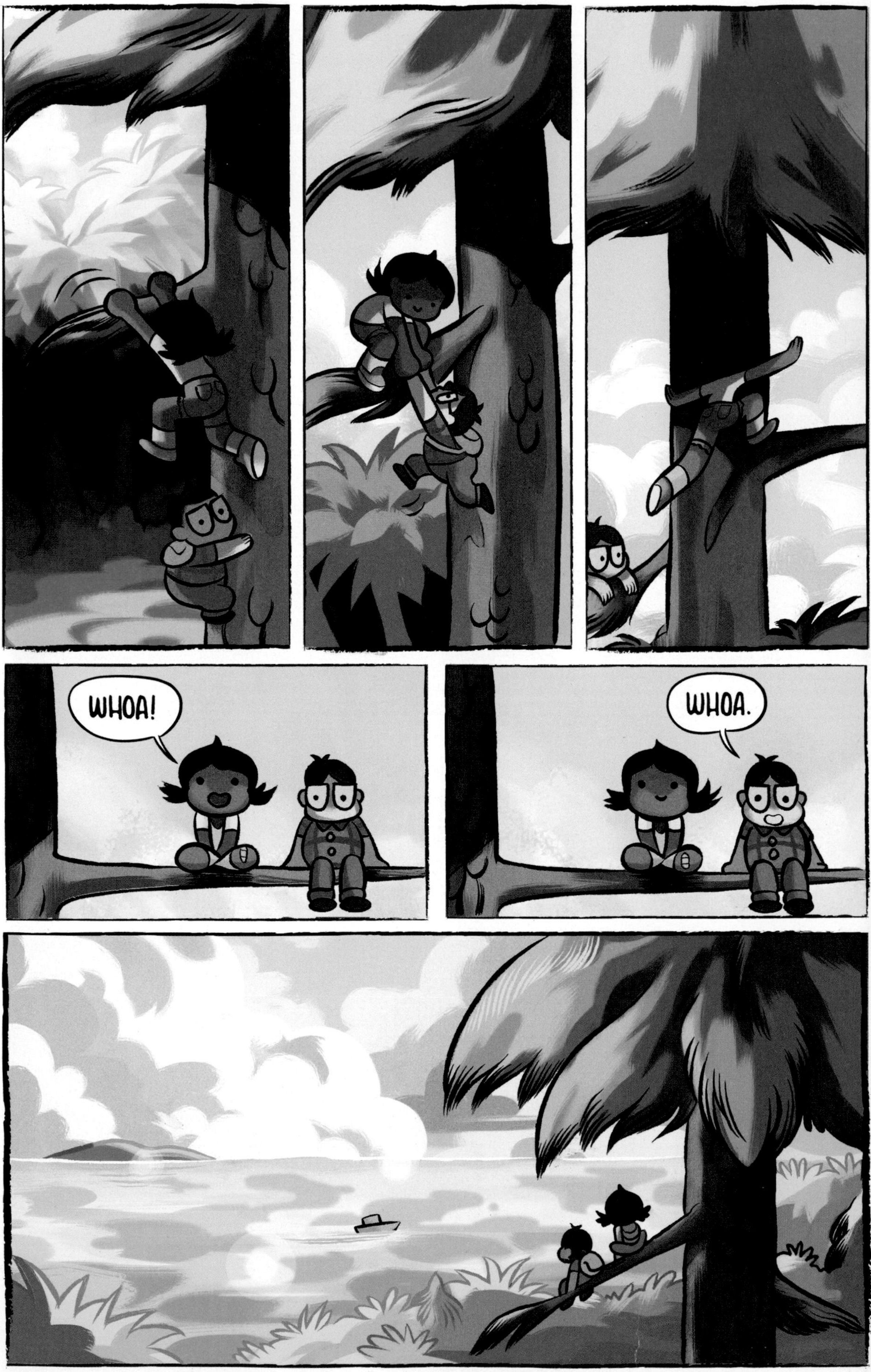
WHOA!
WHOA.

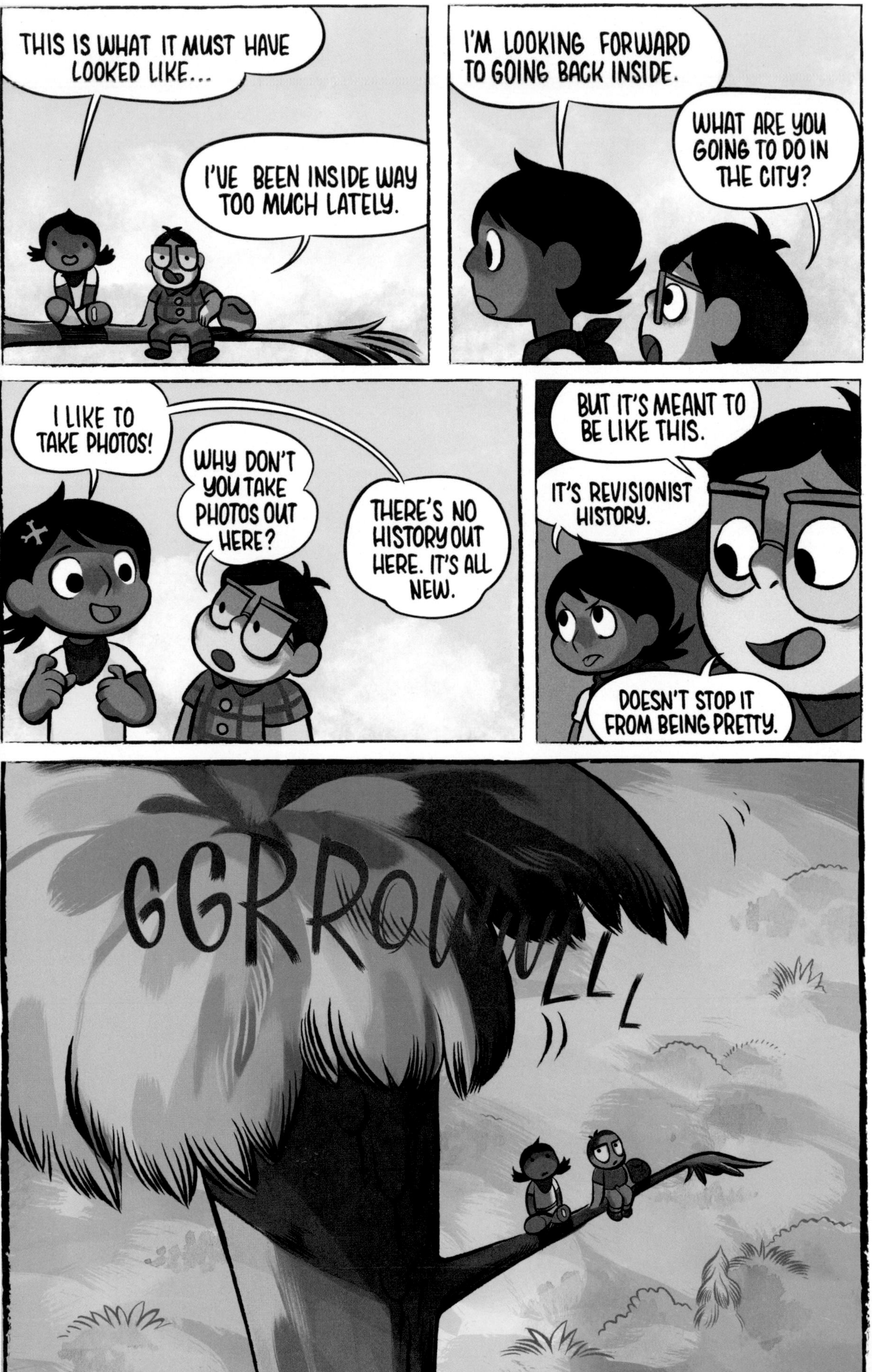

THIS IS WHAT IT MUST HAVE LOOKED LIKE...
I'VE BEEN INSIDE WAY TOO MUCH LATELY.
I'M LOOKING FORWARD TO GOING BACK INSIDE.
WHAT ARE YOU GOING TO DO IN THE CITY?
I LIKE TO TAKE PHOTOS!
WHY DON'T YOU TAKE PHOTOS OUT HERE?
THERE'S NO HISTORY OUT HERE. IT'S ALL NEW.
BUT IT'S MEANT TO BE LIKE THIS.
IT'S REVISIONIST HISTORY.
DOESN'T STOP IT FROM BEING PRETTY.
GGRROWWLLL

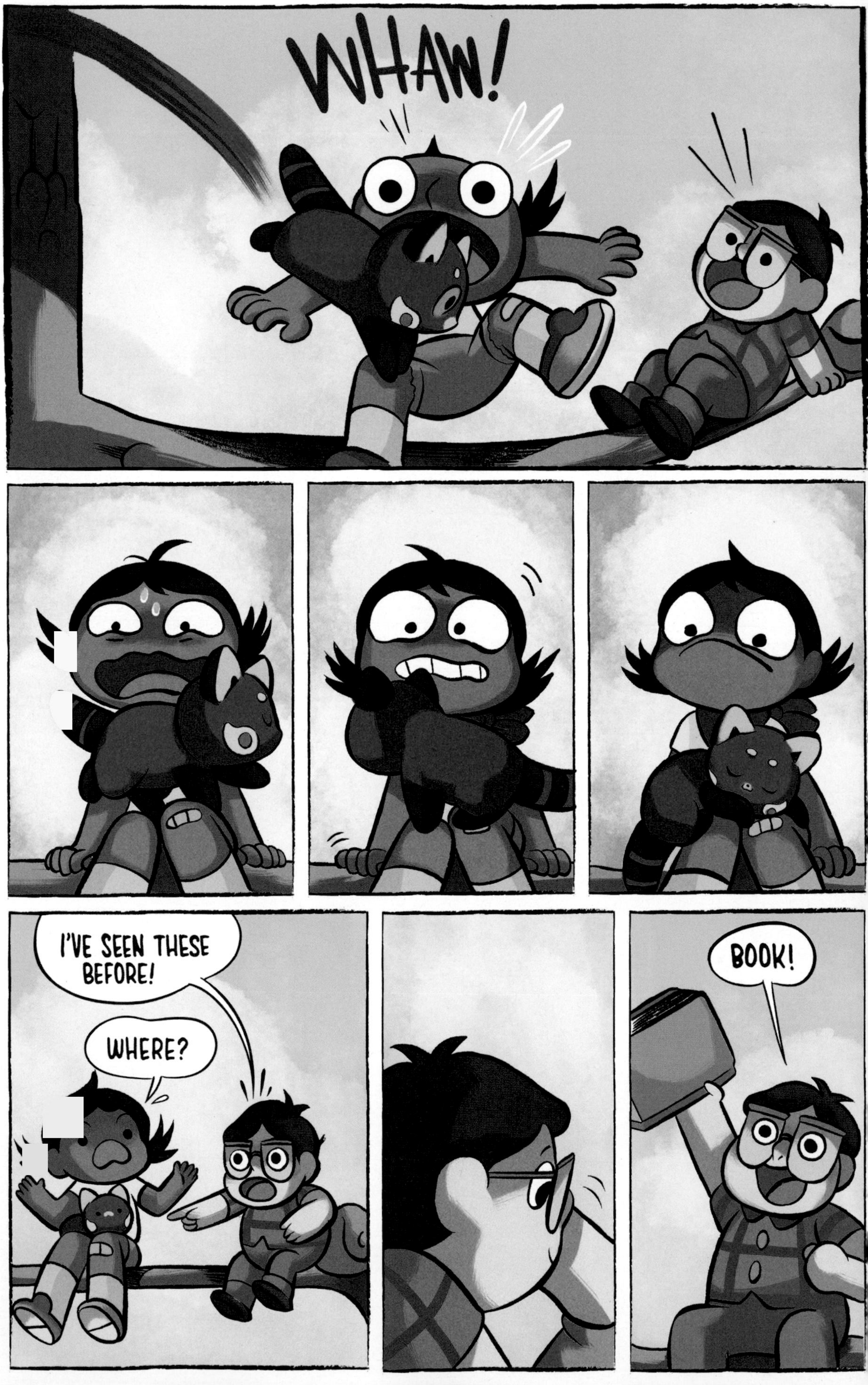
WHAW!
I'VE SEEN THESE BEFORE!
WHERE?
BOOK!

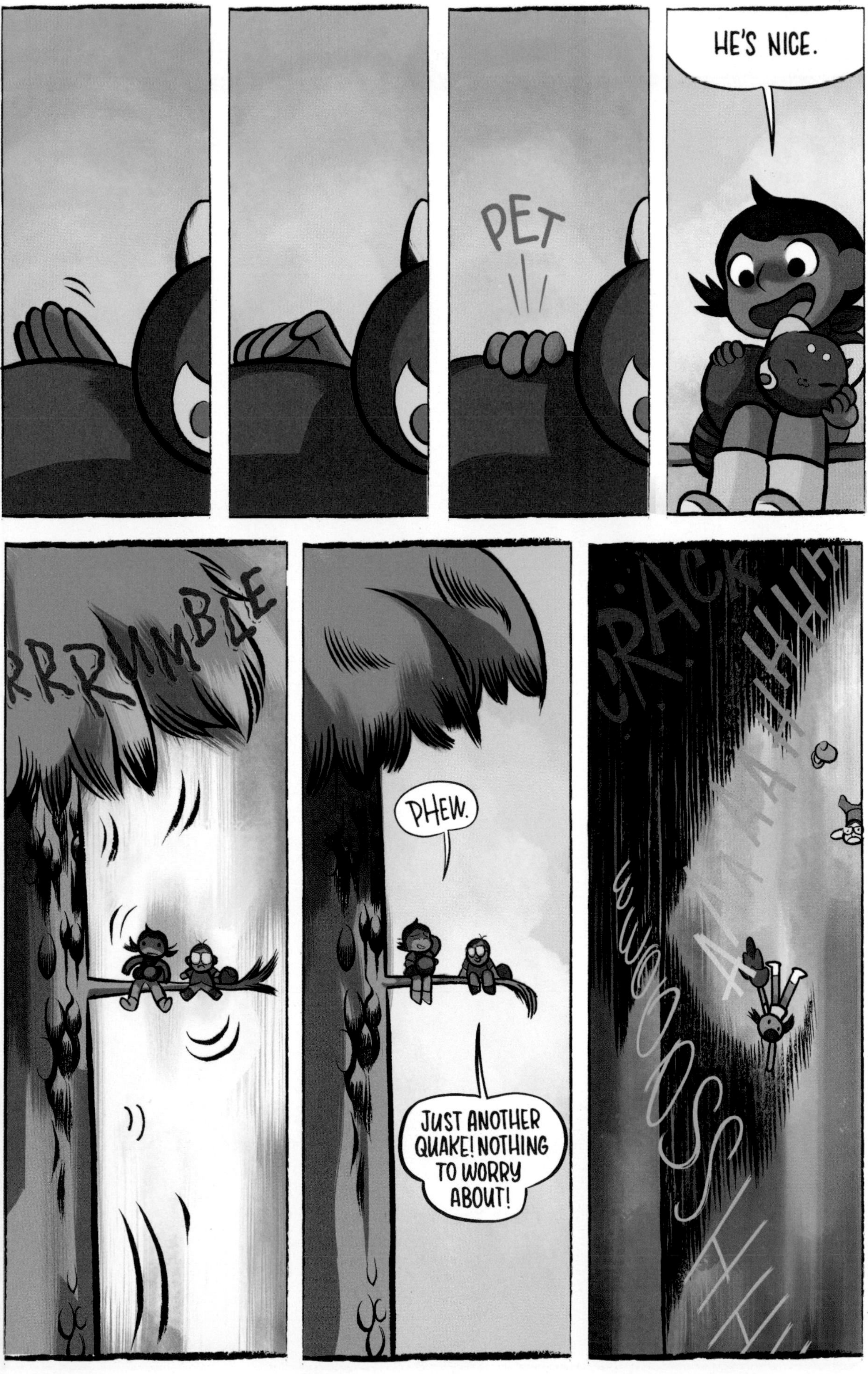
PET
HE'S NICE.
RRRUMBLE
PHEW.
JUST ANOTHER QUAKE! NOTHING TO WORRY ABOUT!
CRACK
AAAAHHHH
WWOOOSSHHH

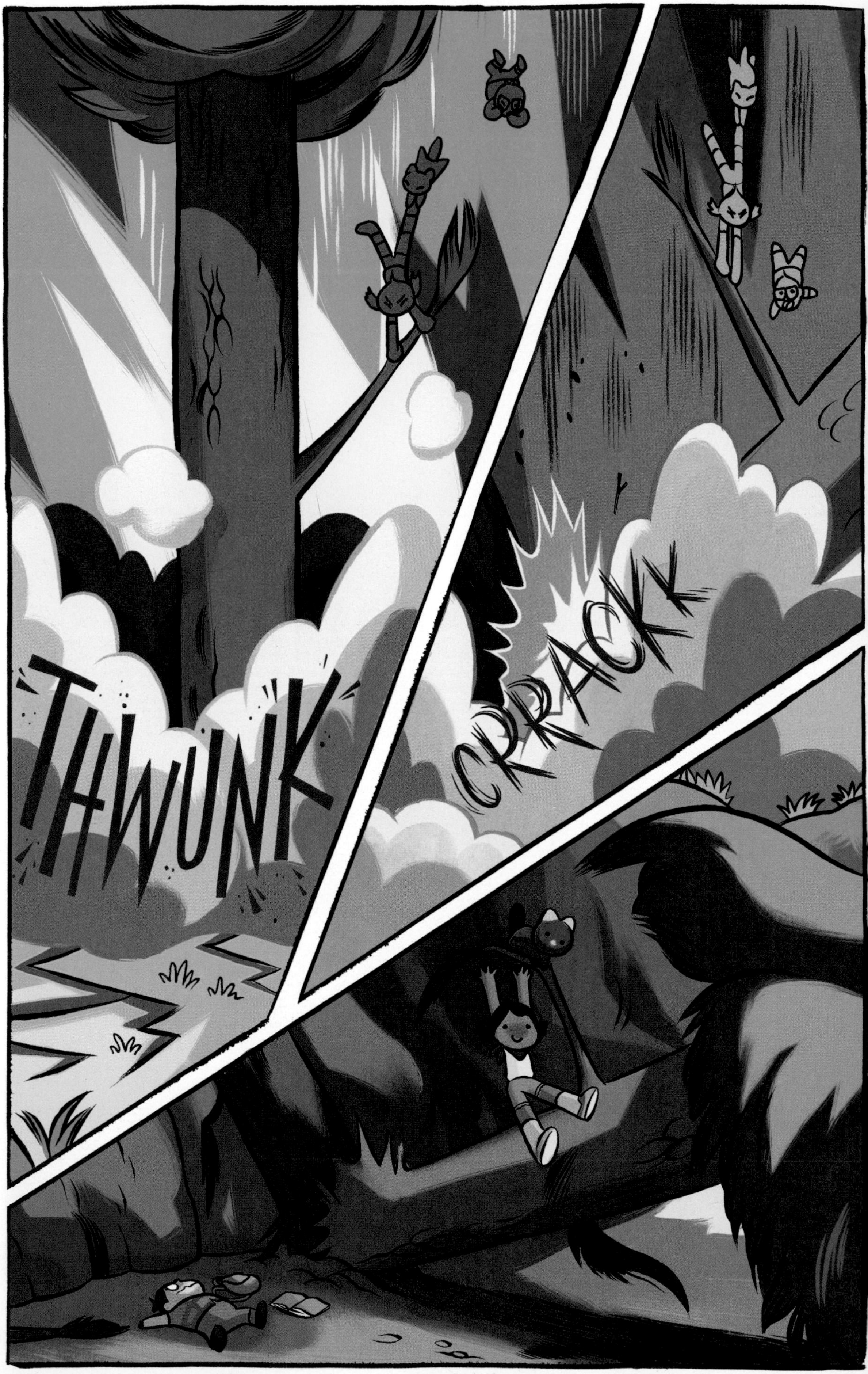
THWUNK
CRRACKK

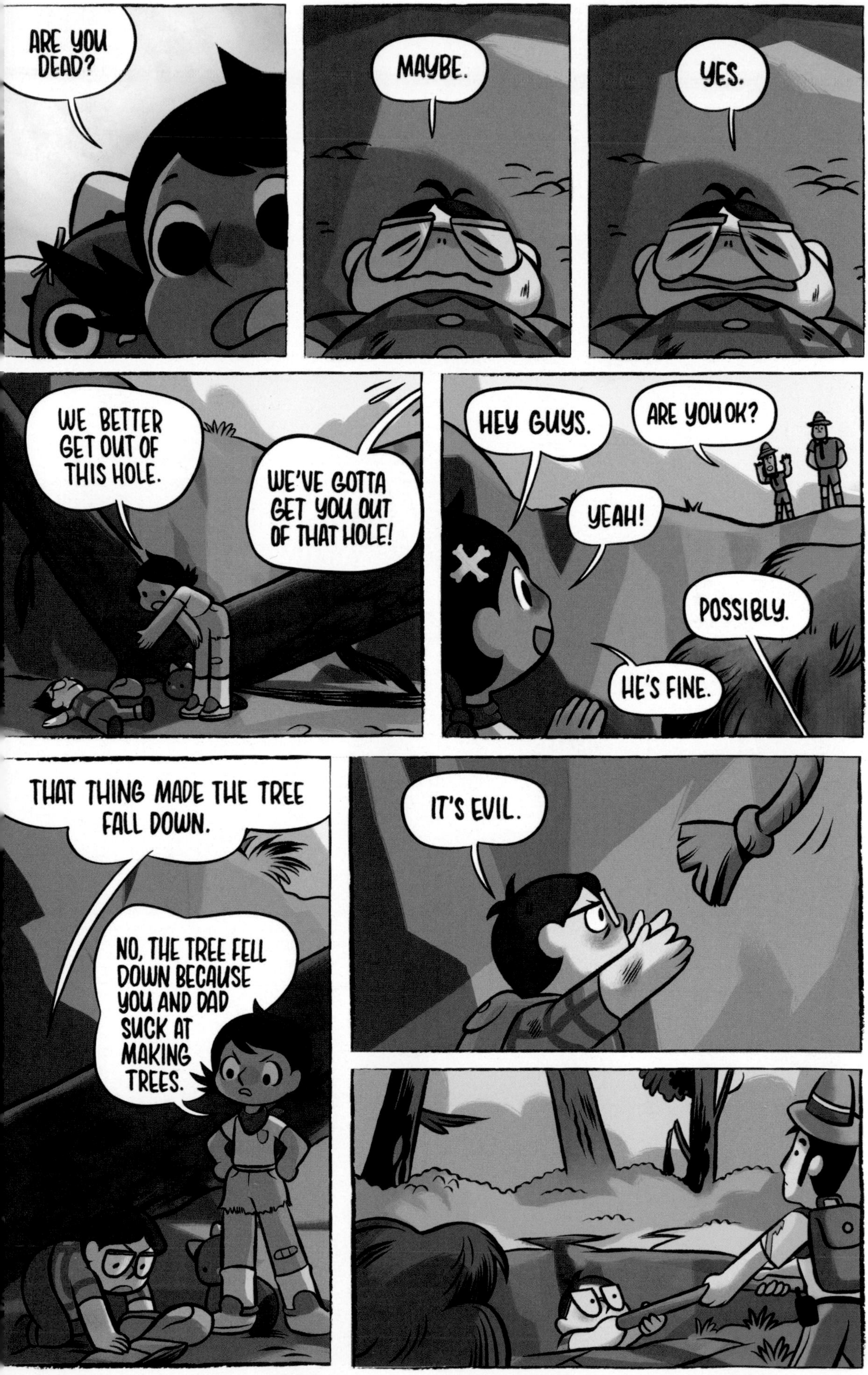
ARE YOU DEAD?
MAYBE.
YES.
WE BETTER GET OUT OF THIS HOLE.
WE'VE GOTTA GET YOU OUT OF THAT HOLE!
HEY GUYS.
ARE YOU OK?
YEAH!
POSSIBLY.
HE'S FINE.
THAT THING MADE THE TREE FALL DOWN.
NO, THE TREE FELL DOWN BECAUSE YOU AND DAD SUCK AT MAKING TREES.
IT'S EVIL.

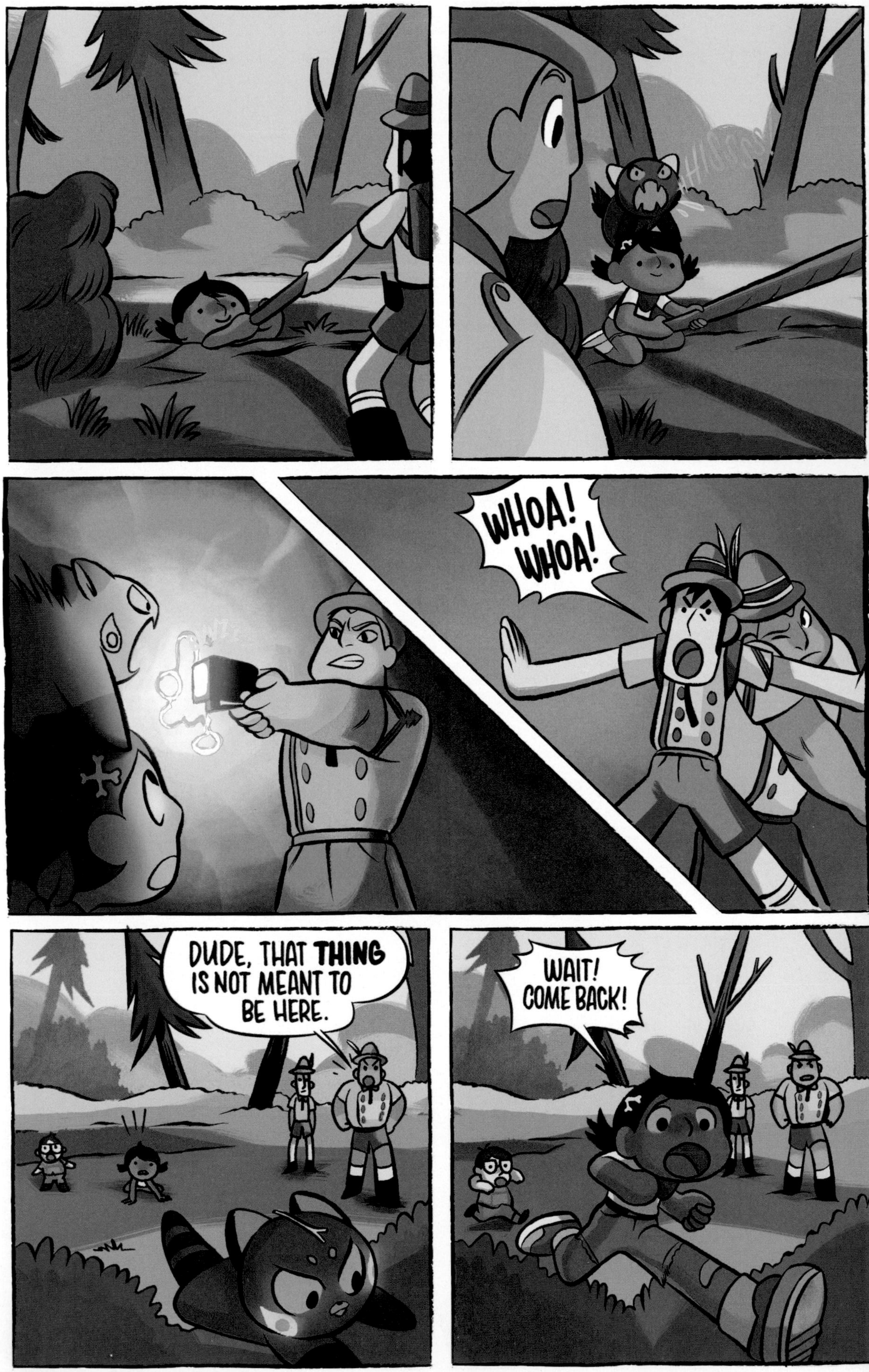
WHOA!
WHOA!
DUDE, THAT THING IS NOT MEANT TO BE HERE.
WAIT! COME BACK!

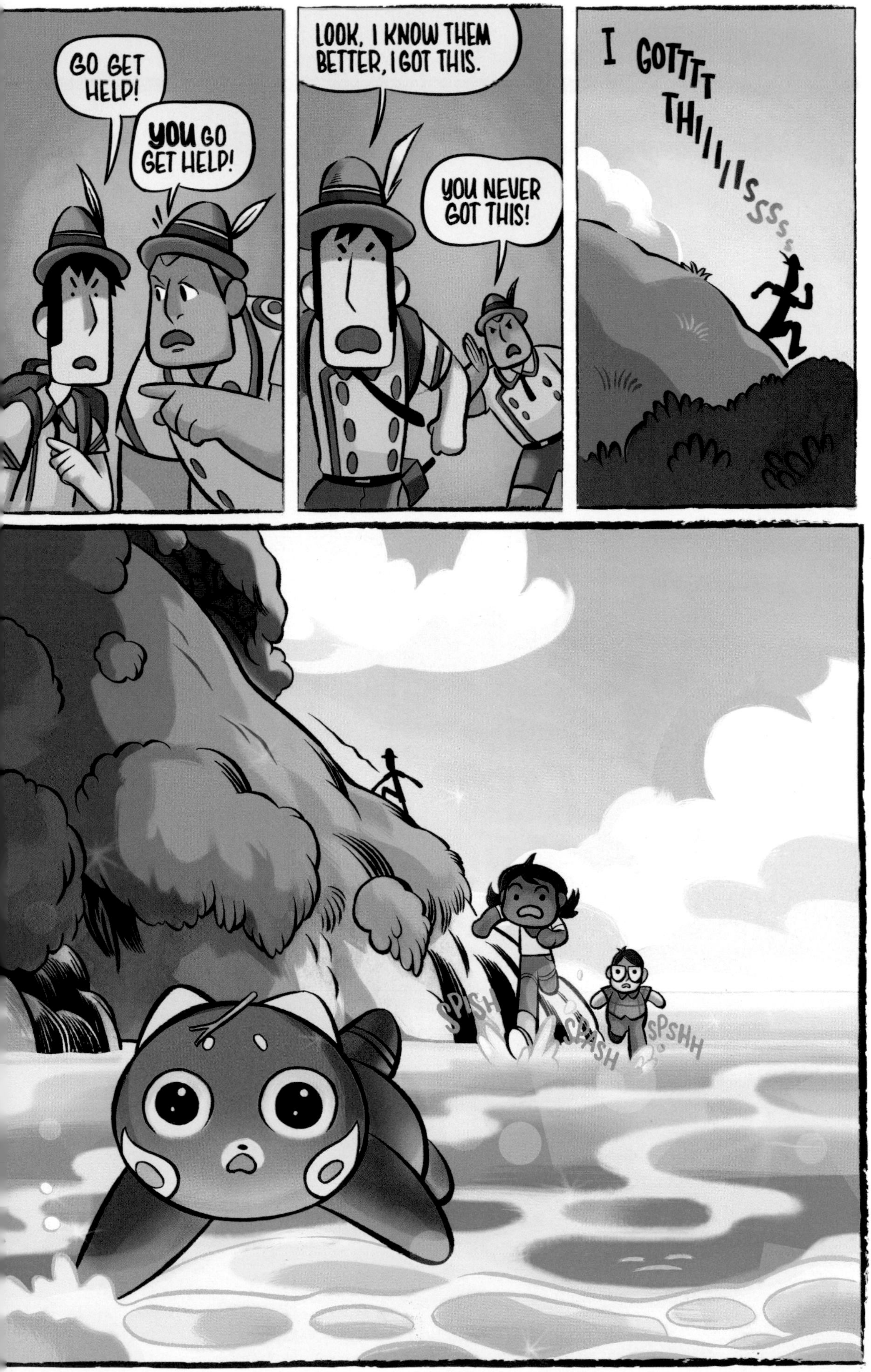
GO GET HELP!
YOU GO GET HELP!
LOOK, I KNOW THEM BETTER, I GOT THIS.
YOU NEVER GOT THIS!
I GOTTTT THIIIIISSSSS
SPSH
SPASH
SPSHH

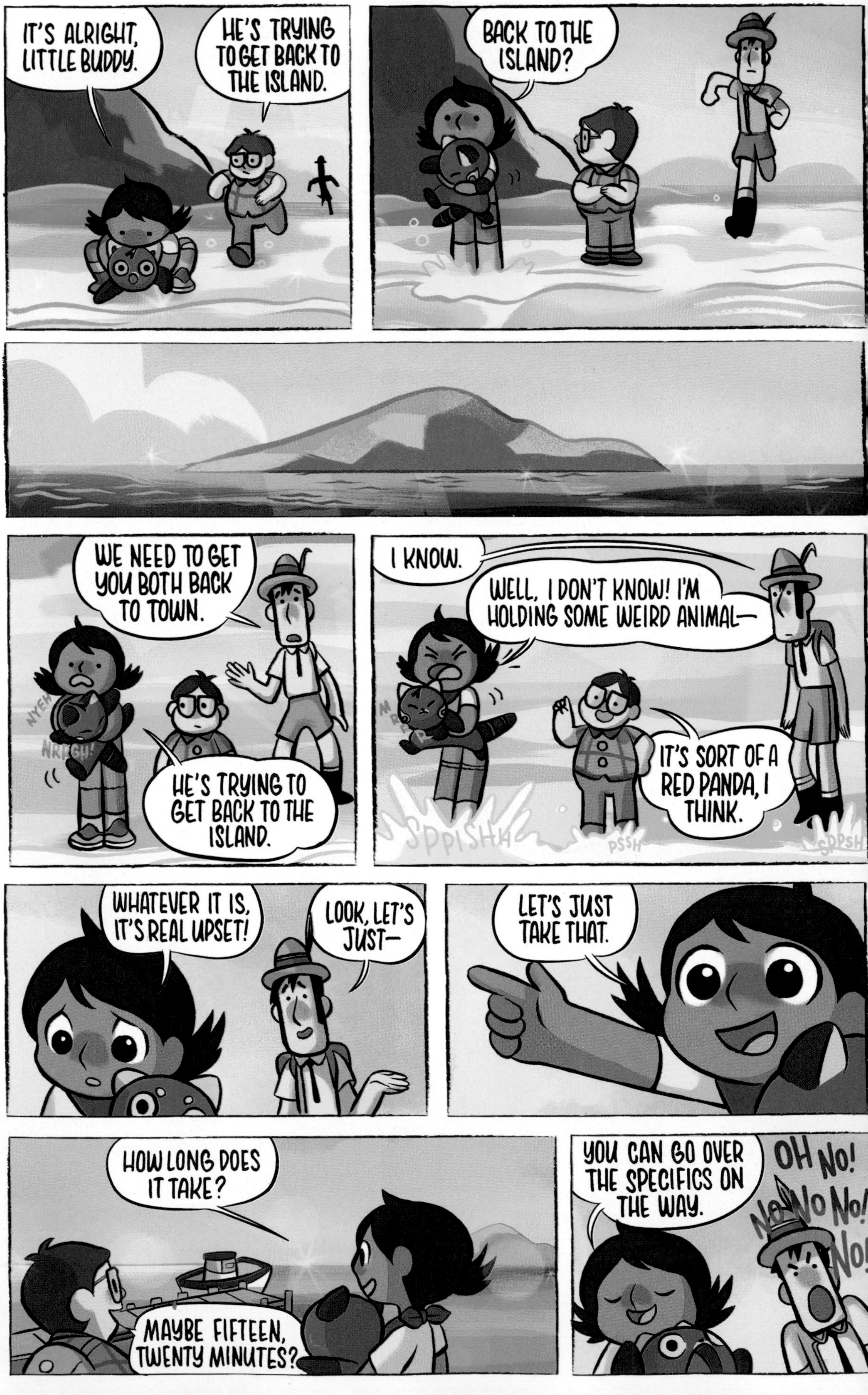
IT'S ALRIGHT, LITTLE BUDDY.
HE'S TRYING TO GET BACK TO THE ISLAND.
BACK TO THE ISLAND?
WE NEED TO GET YOU BOTH BACK TO TOWN.
NYEH
NRRGH!
HE'S TRYING TO GET BACK TO THE ISLAND.
I KNOW.
WELL, I DON'T KNOW! I'M HOLDING SOME WEIRD ANIMAL—
IT'S SORT OF A RED PANDA, I THINK.
SPPISHH
PSSH
SRPSH
WHATEVER IT IS, IT'S REAL UPSET!
LOOK, LET'S JUST—
LET'S JUST TAKE THAT.
HOW LONG DOES IT TAKE?
MAYBE FIFTEEN, TWENTY MINUTES?
YOU CAN GO OVER THE SPECIFICS ON THE WAY.
OH NO! NO NO NO! NO!

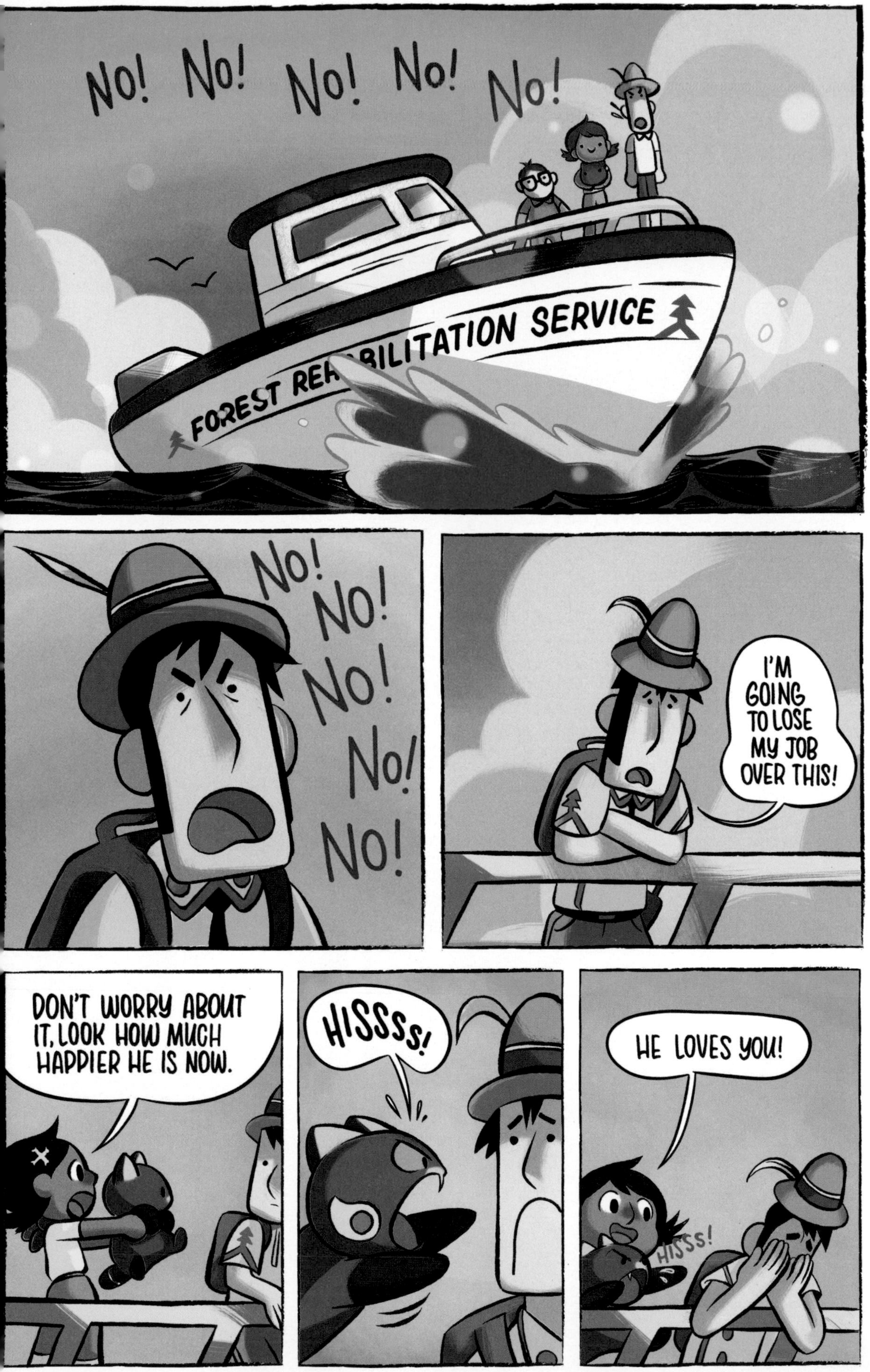
No! No! No! No! No!
FOREST REHABILITATION SERVICE
No! No! No! No! No!
I'M GOING TO LOSE MY JOB OVER THIS!
DON'T WORRY ABOUT IT, LOOK HOW MUCH HAPPIER HE IS NOW.
HISSSs!
HE LOVES YOU!
HISSS!

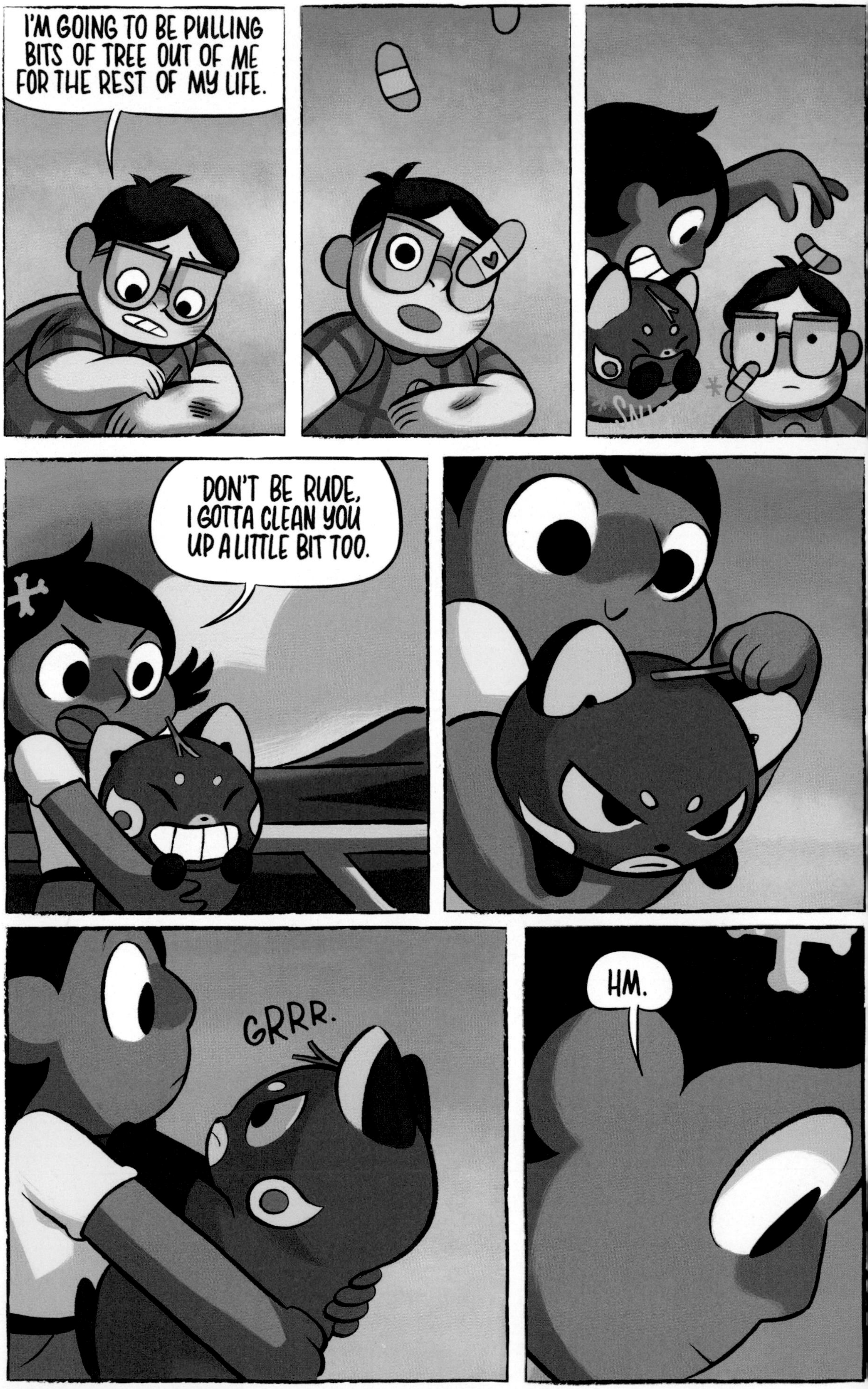
I'M GOING TO BE PULLING BITS OF TREE OUT OF ME FOR THE REST OF MY LIFE.
DON'T BE RUDE, I GOTTA CLEAN YOU UP A LITTLE BIT TOO.
GRRR.
HM.

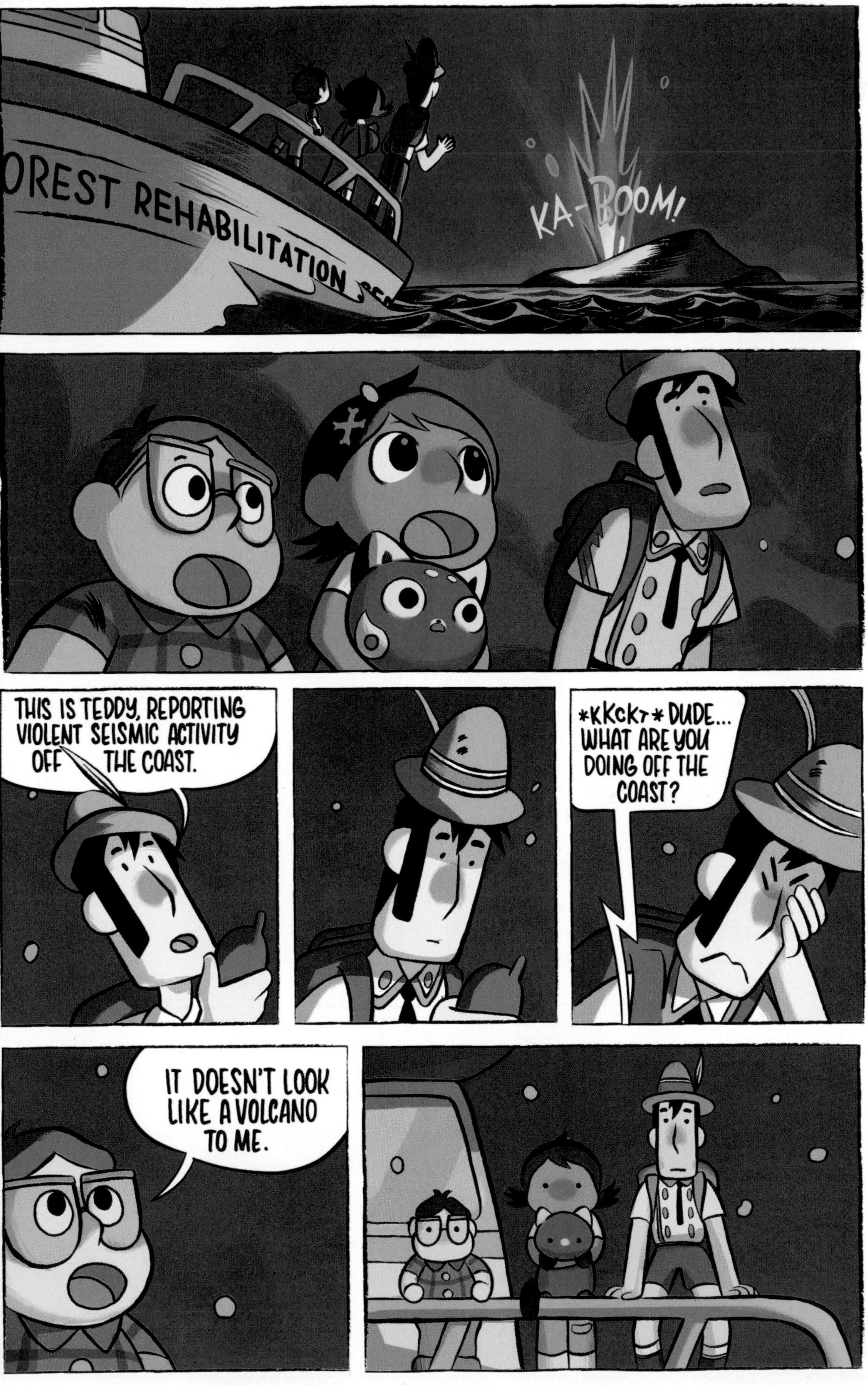
OREST REHABILITATION
KA-BOOM!
THIS IS TEDDY, REPORTING VIOLENT SEISMIC ACTIVITY OFF THE COAST.
KKCKT DUDE... WHAT ARE YOU DOING OFF THE COAST?
IT DOESN'T LOOK LIKE A VOLCANO TO ME.

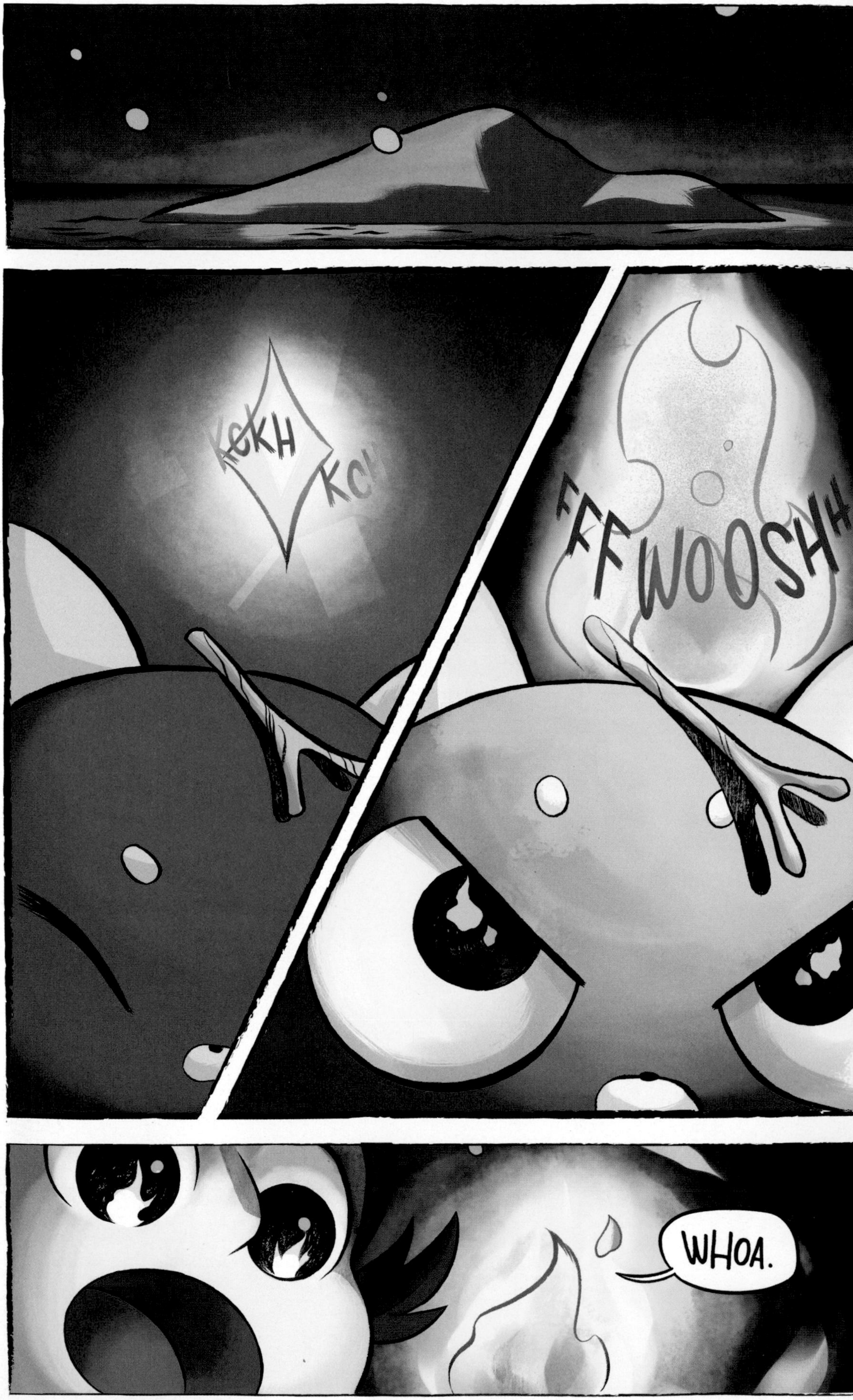
KCKH
KCH
FFWOOSHH
WHOA.

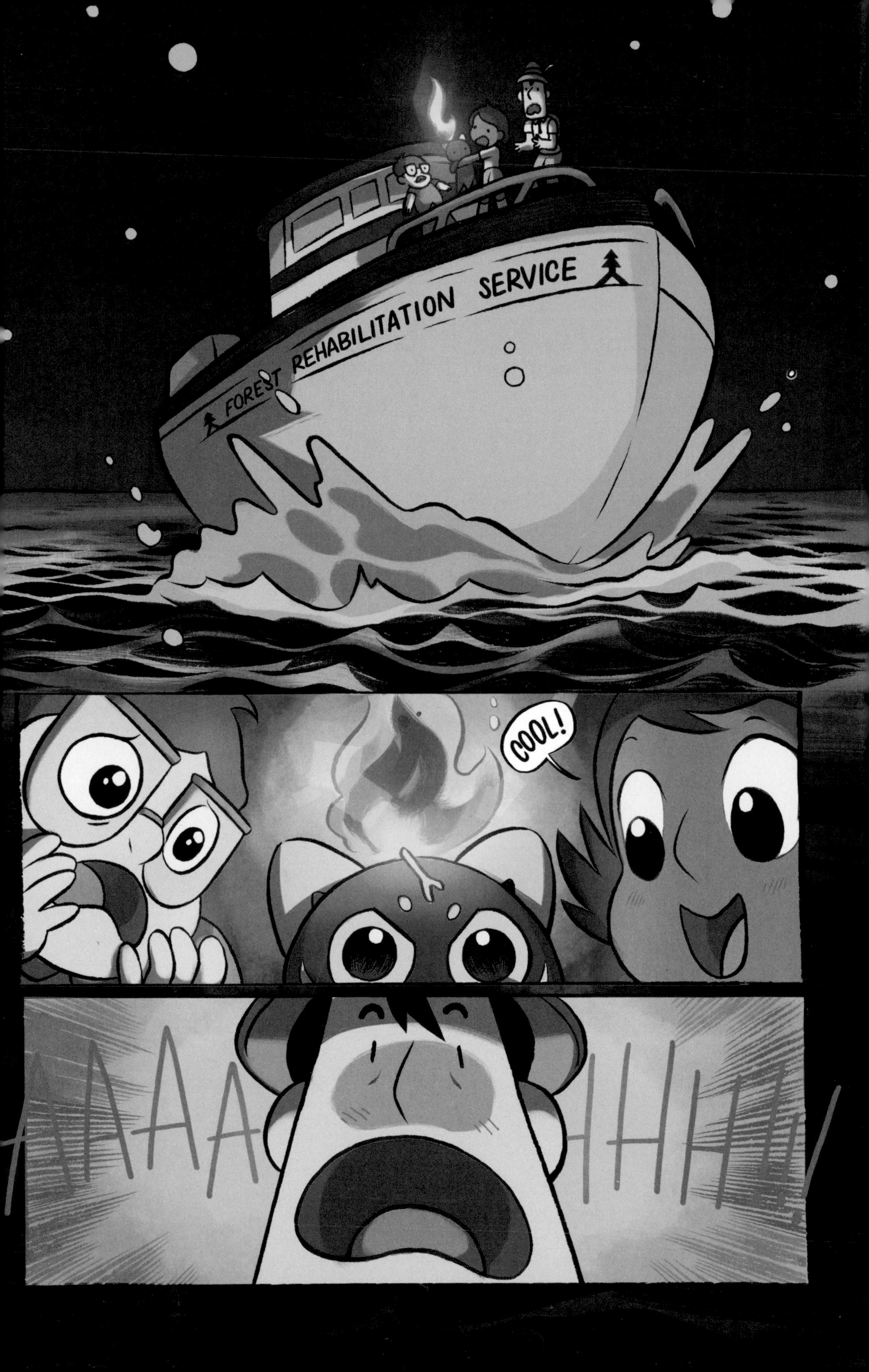
FOREST REHABILITATION SERVICE
COOL!
AAAAHHH!!

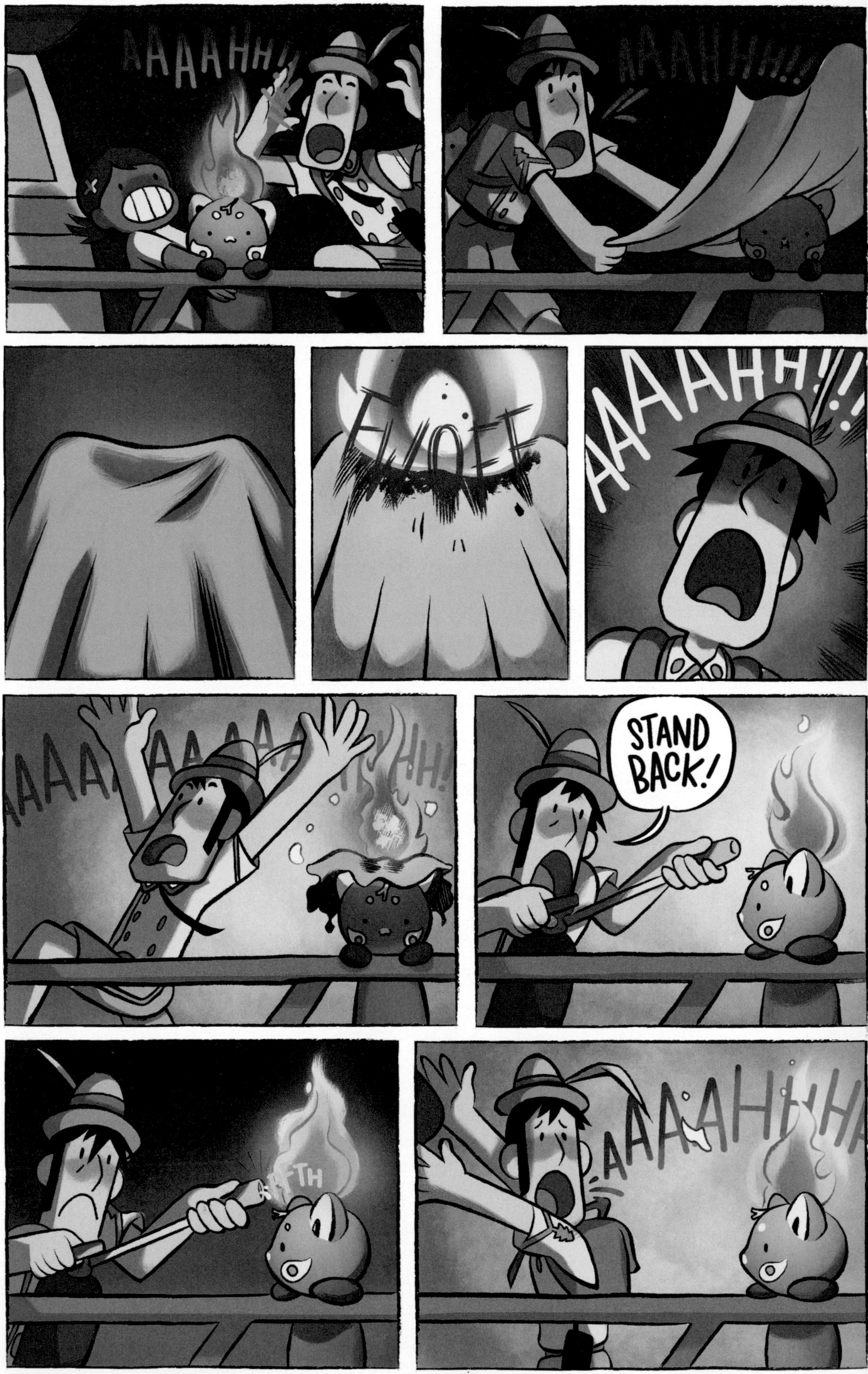

STAND BACK!

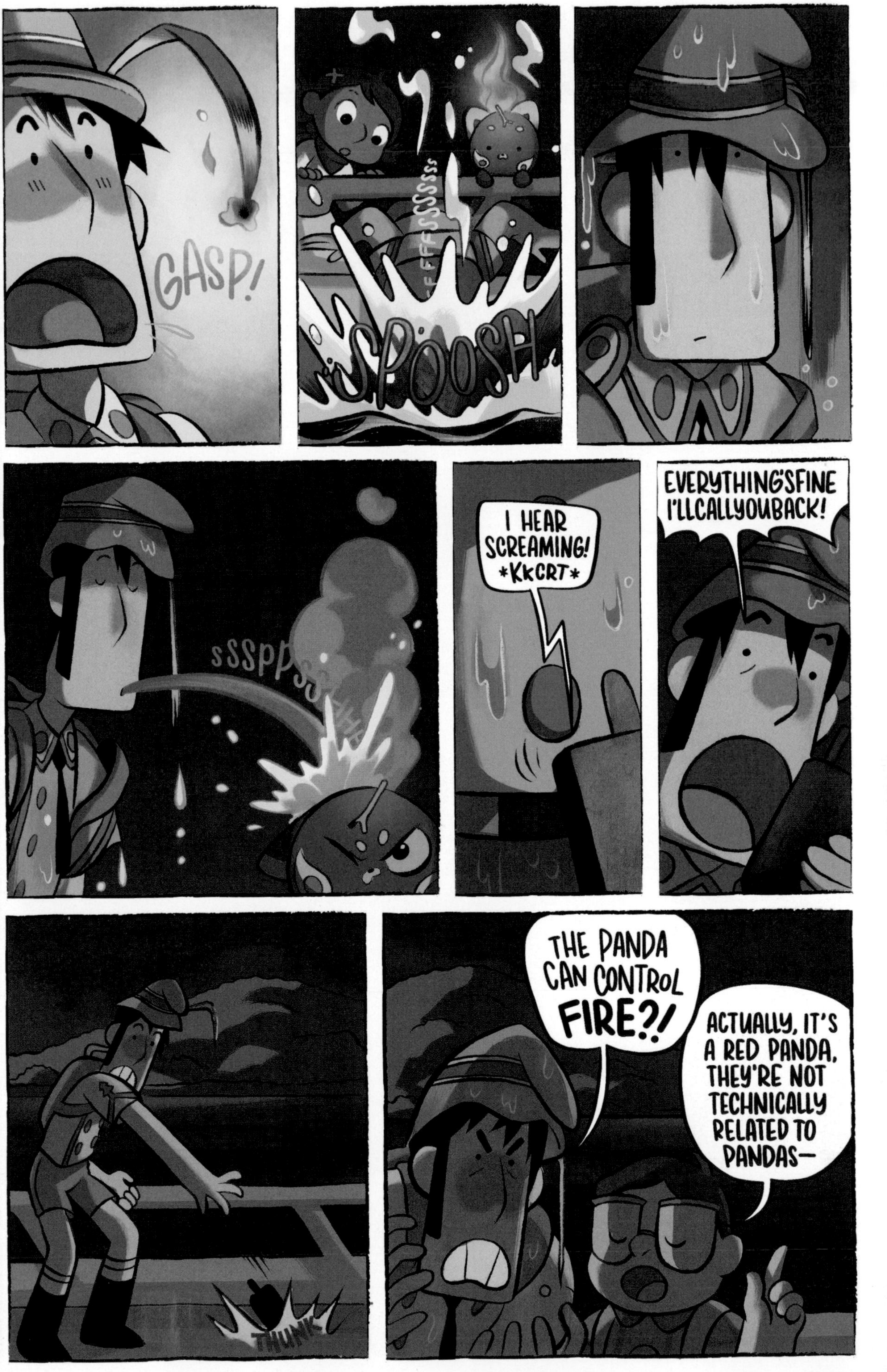
GASP!
FFFSSSSSSsss
SPOOSH
SSSPPSS
I HEAR SCREAMING! *KKCRT*
EVERYTHING'SFINE I'LLCALLYOUBACK!
THUNK
THE PANDA CAN CONTROL FIRE?!
ACTUALLY, IT'S A RED PANDA, THEY'RE NOT TECHNICALLY RELATED TO PANDAS—

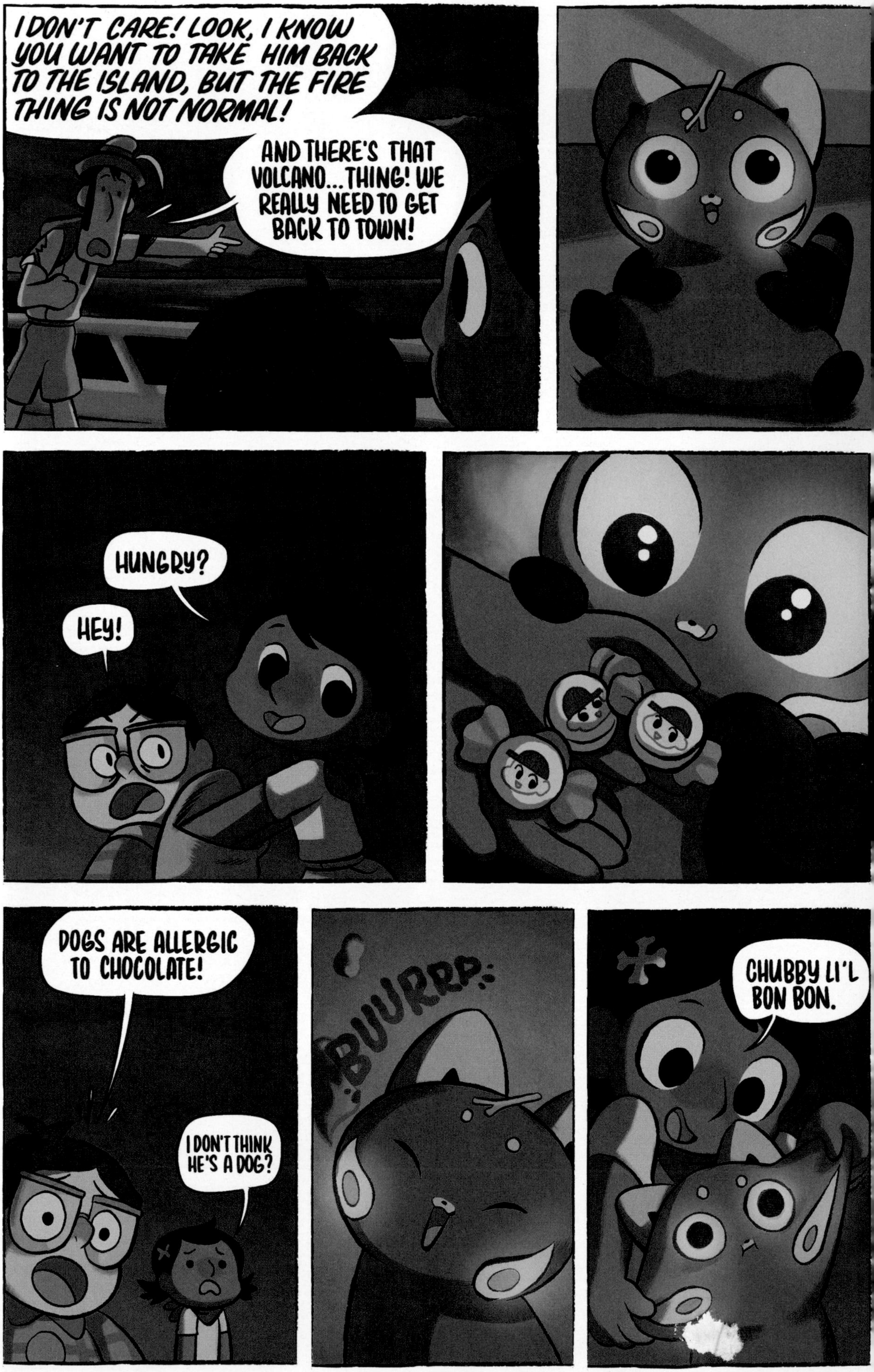
I DON'T CARE! LOOK, I KNOW YOU WANT TO TAKE HIM BACK TO THE ISLAND, BUT THE FIRE THING IS NOT NORMAL!
AND THERE'S THAT VOLCANO...THING! WE REALLY NEED TO GET BACK TO TOWN!
HUNGRY?
HEY!
DOGS ARE ALLERGIC TO CHOCOLATE!
I DON'T THINK HE'S A DOG?
BUURRP
CHUBBY LI'L BON BON.

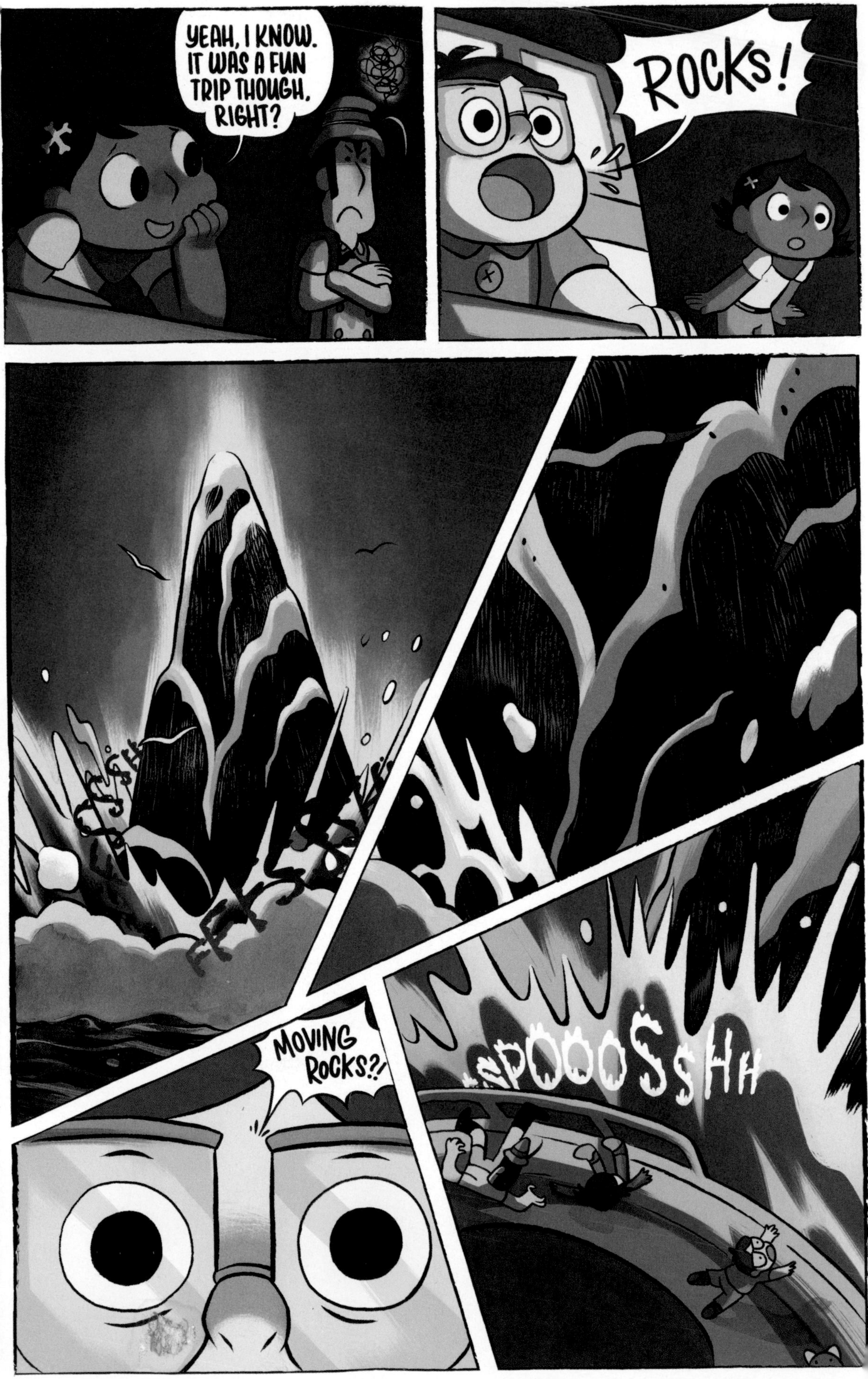
YEAH, I KNOW. IT WAS A FUN TRIP THOUGH, RIGHT?
ROCKS!
MOVING ROCKS?!
SPOOOSSHH

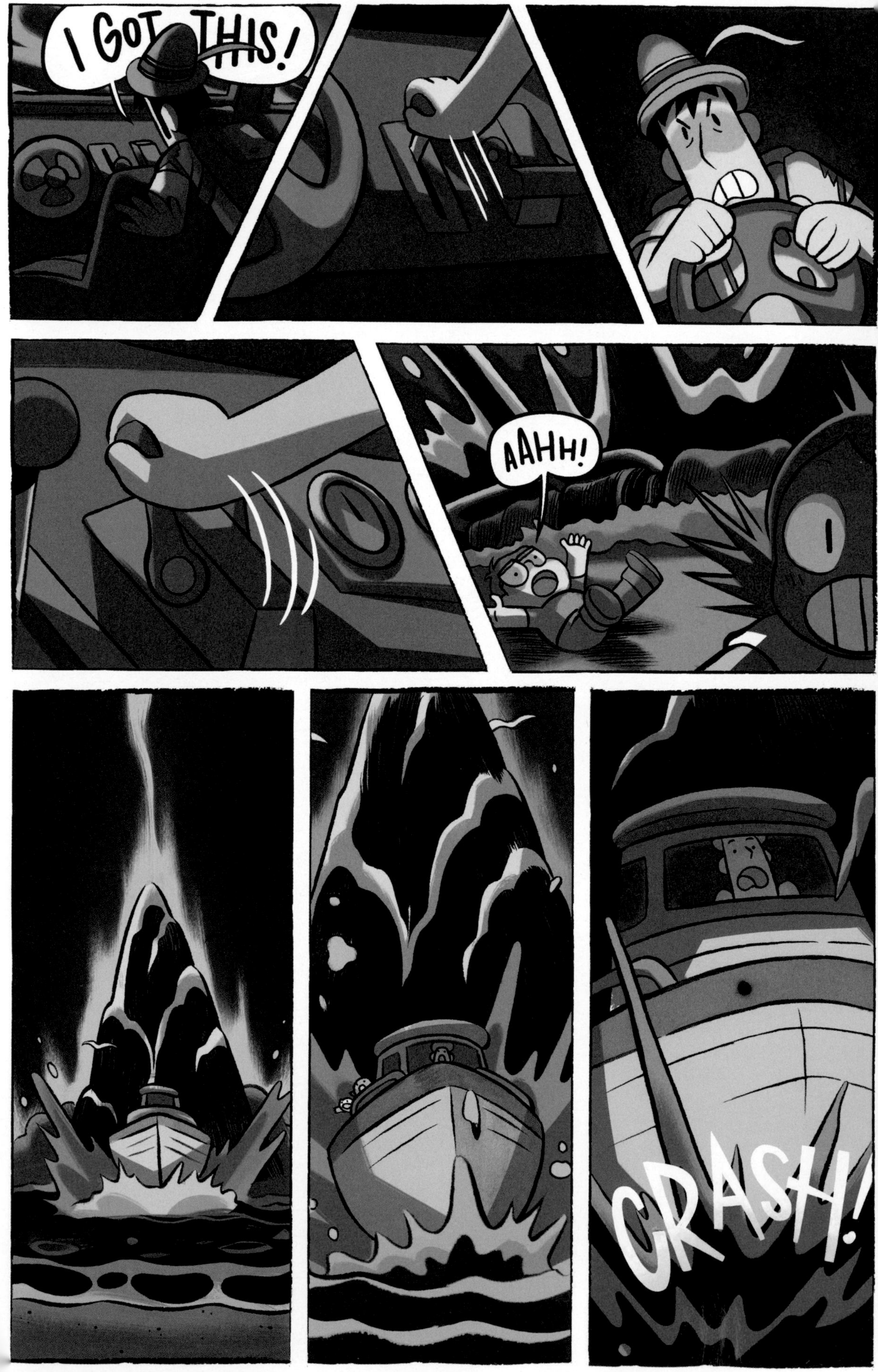
I GOT THIS!
AAHH!
CRASH!

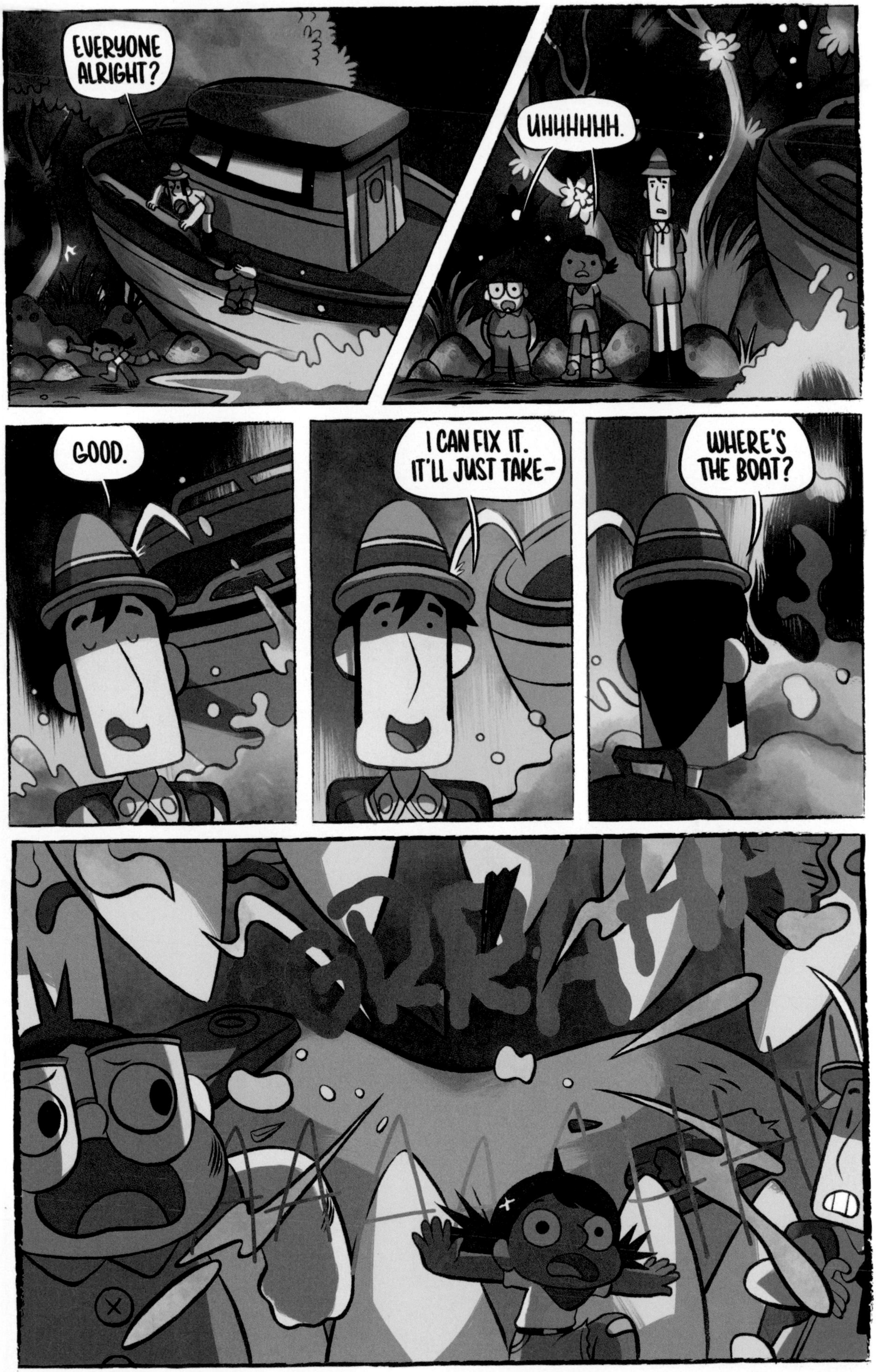
EVERYONE ALRIGHT?
UHHHHHH.
GOOD.
I CAN FIX IT. IT'LL JUST TAKE-
WHERE'S THE BOAT?
GRRAHH
AAAAAHH

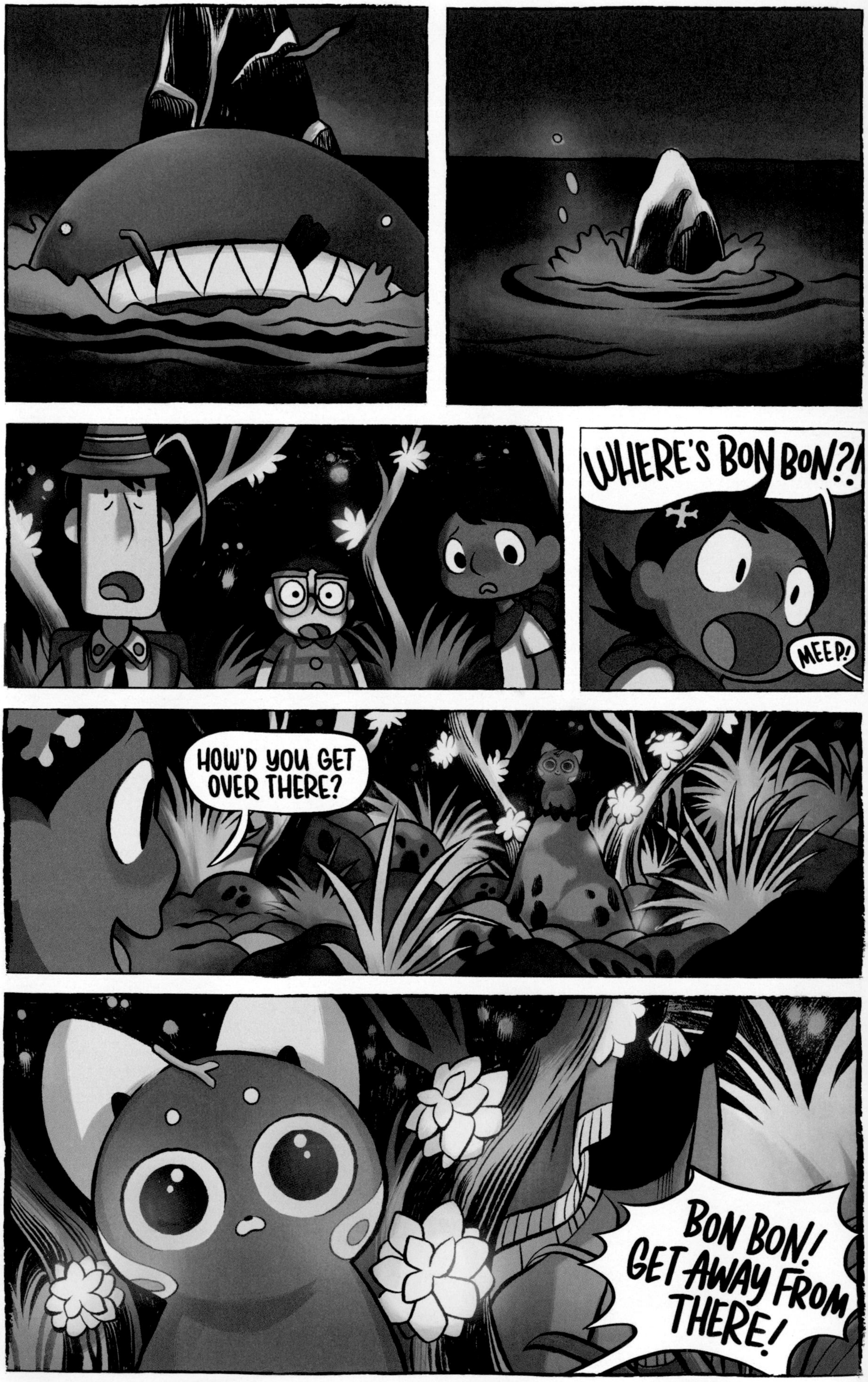
WHERE'S BON BON?!
MEEP!
HOW'D YOU GET OVER THERE?
BON BON! GET AWAY FROM THERE!

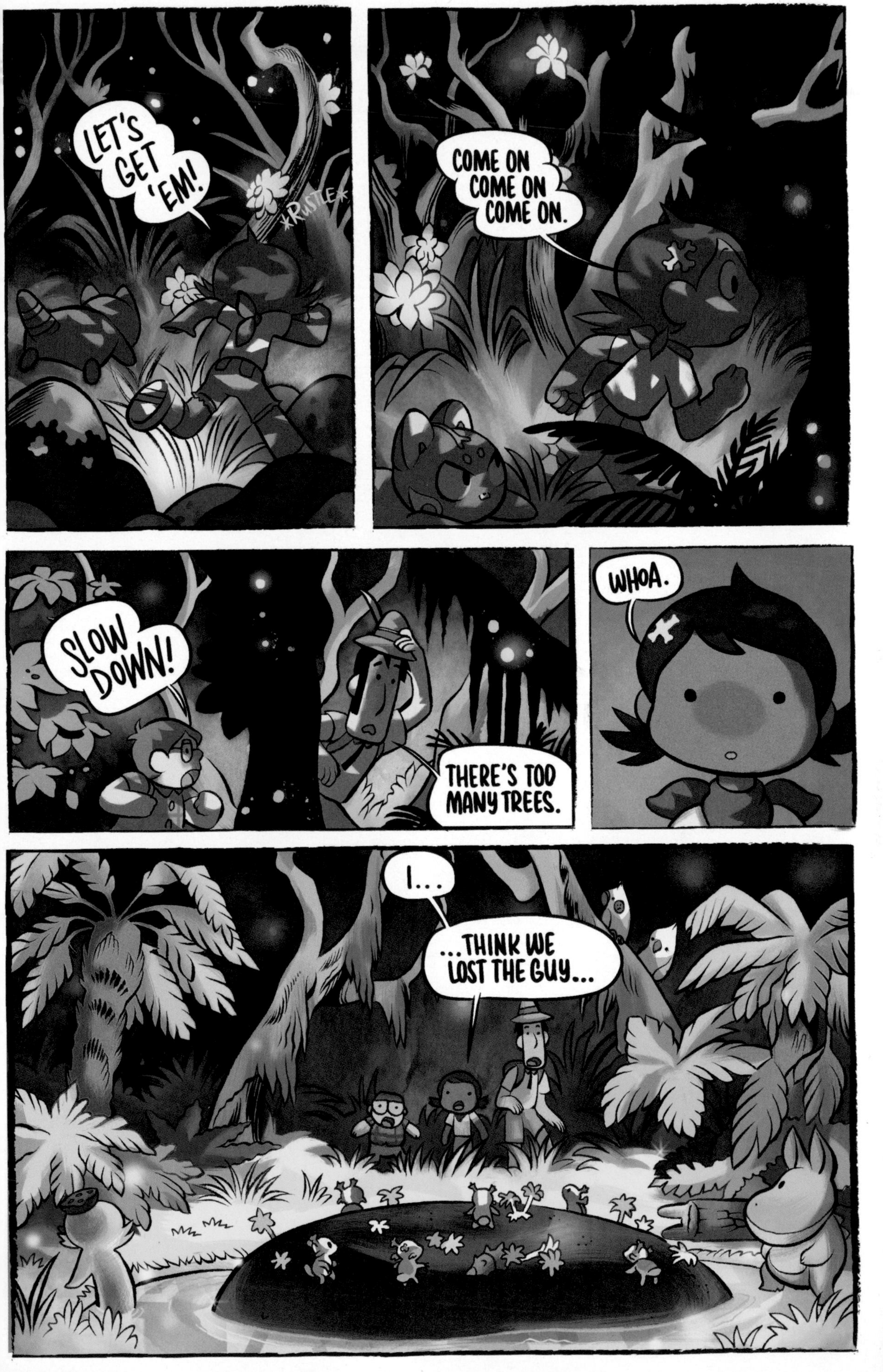
LET'S GET 'EM!
RUSTLE
COME ON COME ON COME ON.
SLOW DOWN!
THERE'S TOO MANY TREES.
WHOA.
I...
...THINK WE LOST THE GUY...

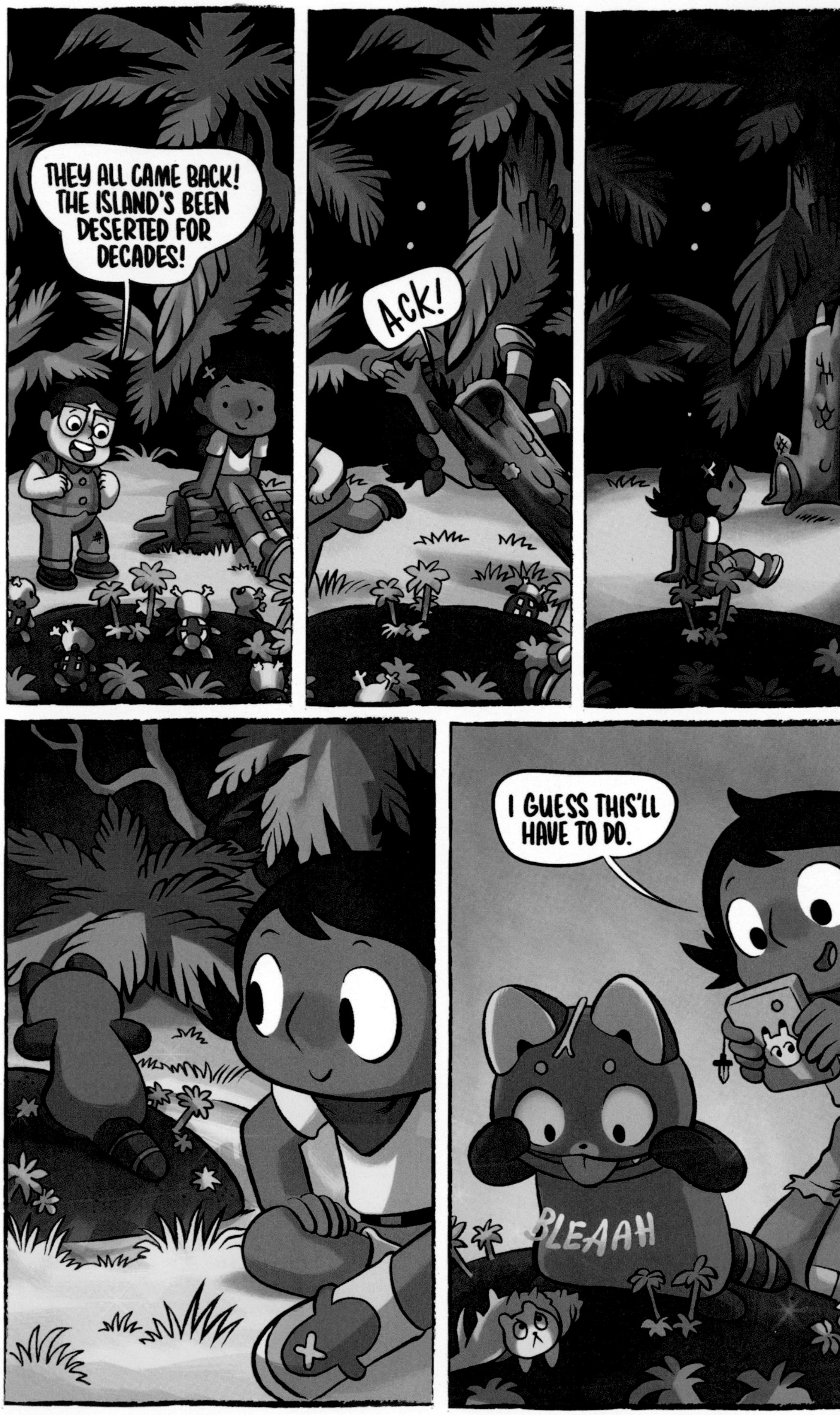

THEY ALL CAME BACK! THE ISLAND'S BEEN DESERTED FOR DECADES!
ACK!
I GUESS THIS'LL HAVE TO DO.
BLEAAH

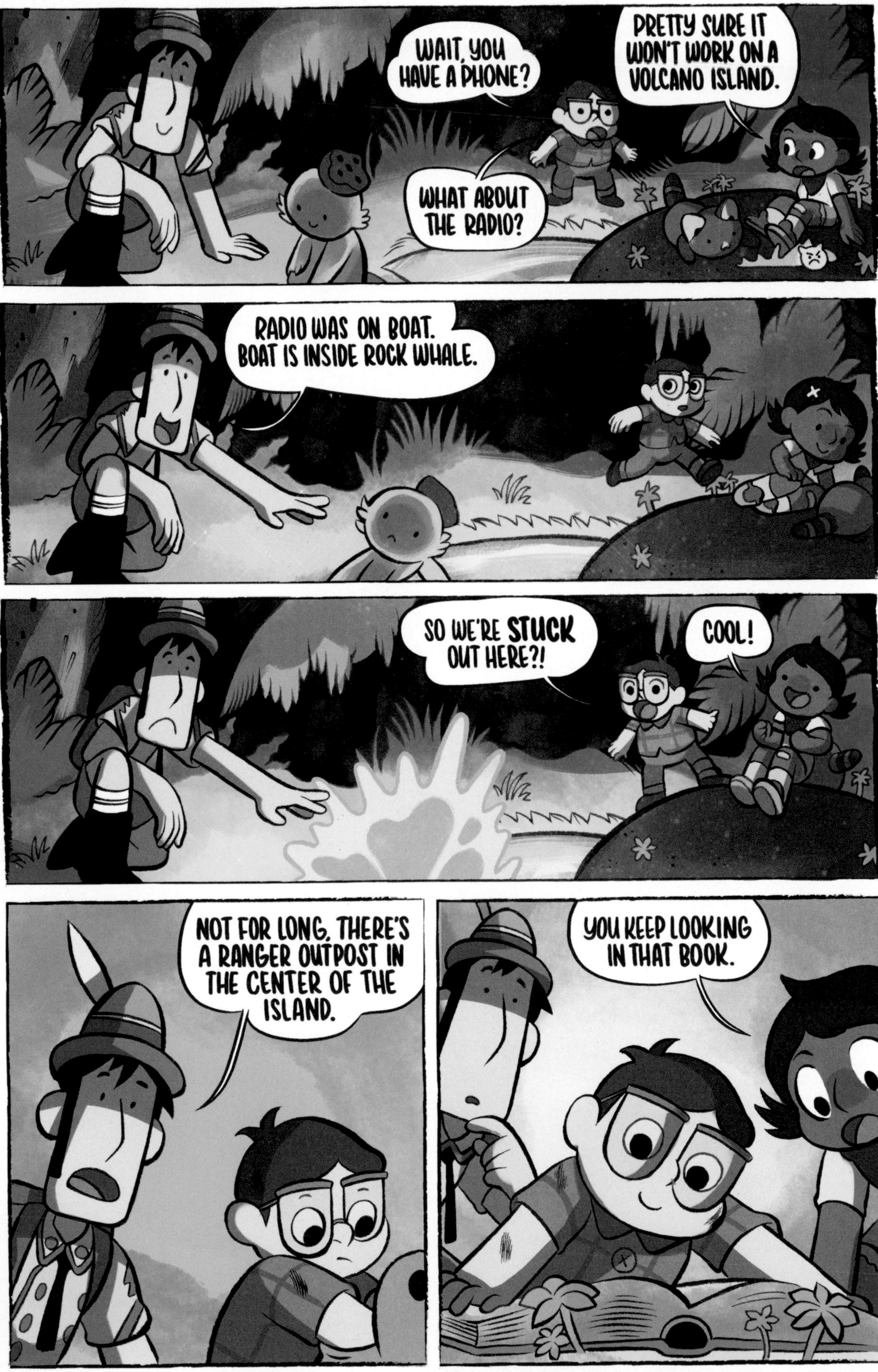
WAIT, YOU HAVE A PHONE?
PRETTY SURE IT WON'T WORK ON A VOLCANO ISLAND.
WHAT ABOUT THE RADIO?
RADIO WAS ON BOAT. BOAT IS INSIDE ROCK WHALE.
SO WE'RE STUCK OUT HERE?!
COOL!
NOT FOR LONG. THERE'S A RANGER OUTPOST IN THE CENTER OF THE ISLAND.
YOU KEEP LOOKING IN THAT BOOK.

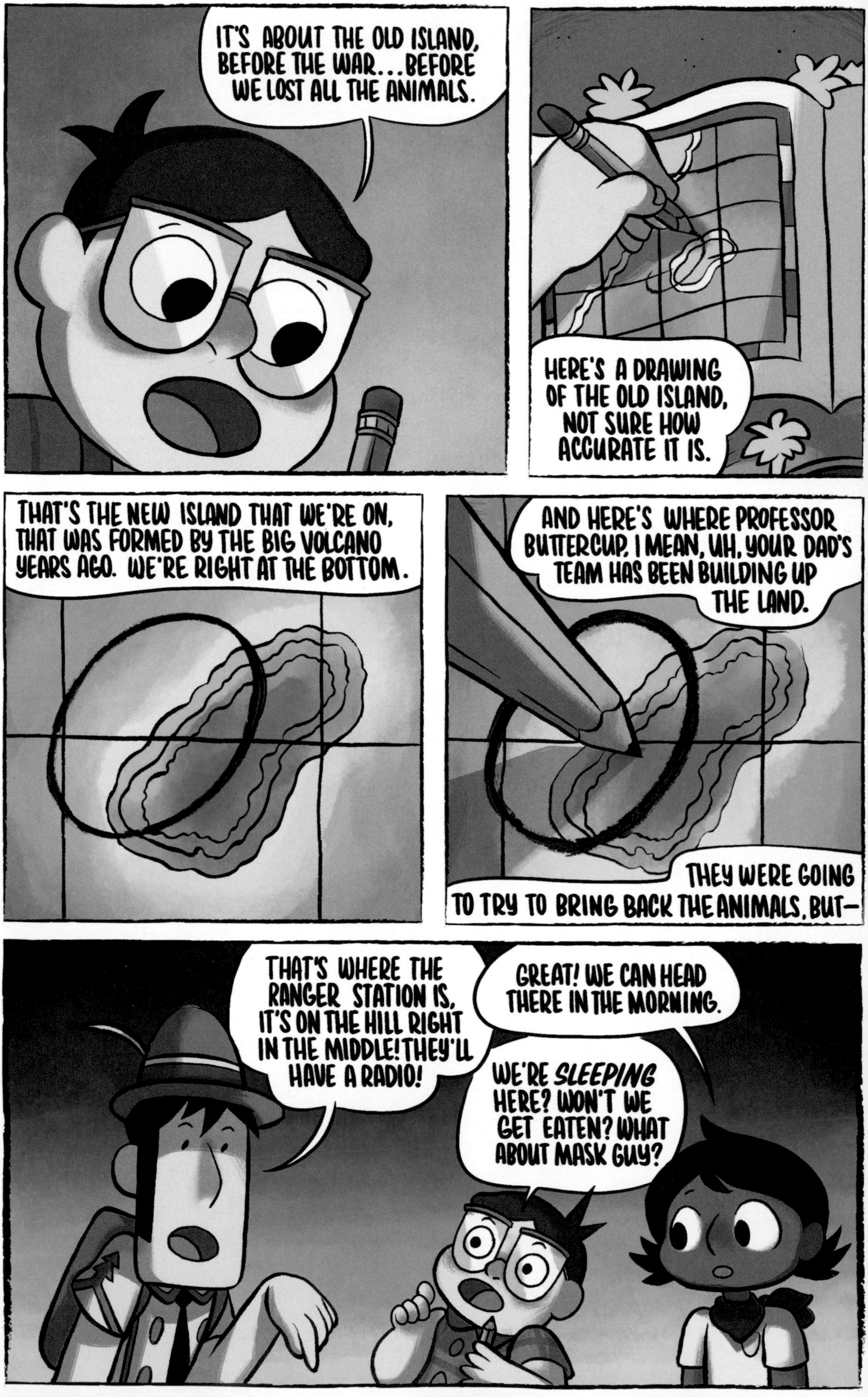
IT'S ABOUT THE OLD ISLAND, BEFORE THE WAR... BEFORE WE LOST ALL THE ANIMALS.
HERE'S A DRAWING OF THE OLD ISLAND, NOT SURE HOW ACCURATE IT IS.
THAT'S THE NEW ISLAND THAT WE'RE ON, THAT WAS FORMED BY THE BIG VOLCANO YEARS AGO. WE'RE RIGHT AT THE BOTTOM.
AND HERE'S WHERE PROFESSOR BUTTERCUP, I MEAN, UH, YOUR DAD'S TEAM HAS BEEN BUILDING UP THE LAND.
THEY WERE GOING TO TRY TO BRING BACK THE ANIMALS, BUT—
THAT'S WHERE THE RANGER STATION IS, IT'S ON THE HILL RIGHT IN THE MIDDLE! THEY'LL HAVE A RADIO!
GREAT! WE CAN HEAD THERE IN THE MORNING.
WE'RE *SLEEPING* HERE? WON'T WE GET EATEN? WHAT ABOUT MASK GUY?

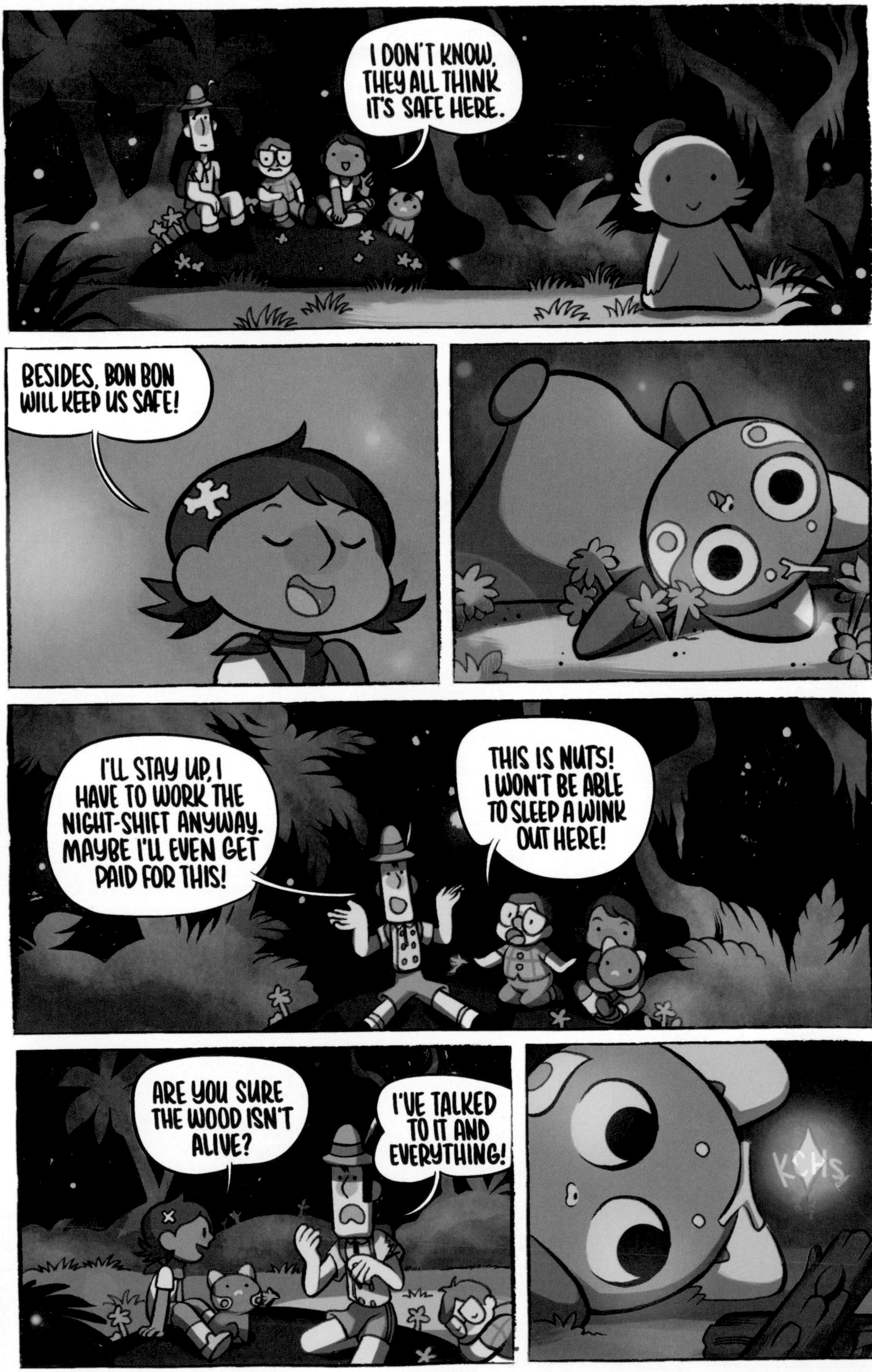
I DON'T KNOW, THEY ALL THINK IT'S SAFE HERE.
BESIDES, BON BON WILL KEEP US SAFE!
I'LL STAY UP, I HAVE TO WORK THE NIGHT-SHIFT ANYWAY. MAYBE I'LL EVEN GET PAID FOR THIS!
THIS IS NUTS! I WON'T BE ABLE TO SLEEP A WINK OUT HERE!
ARE YOU SURE THE WOOD ISN'T ALIVE?
I'VE TALKED TO IT AND EVERYTHING!
KCHS

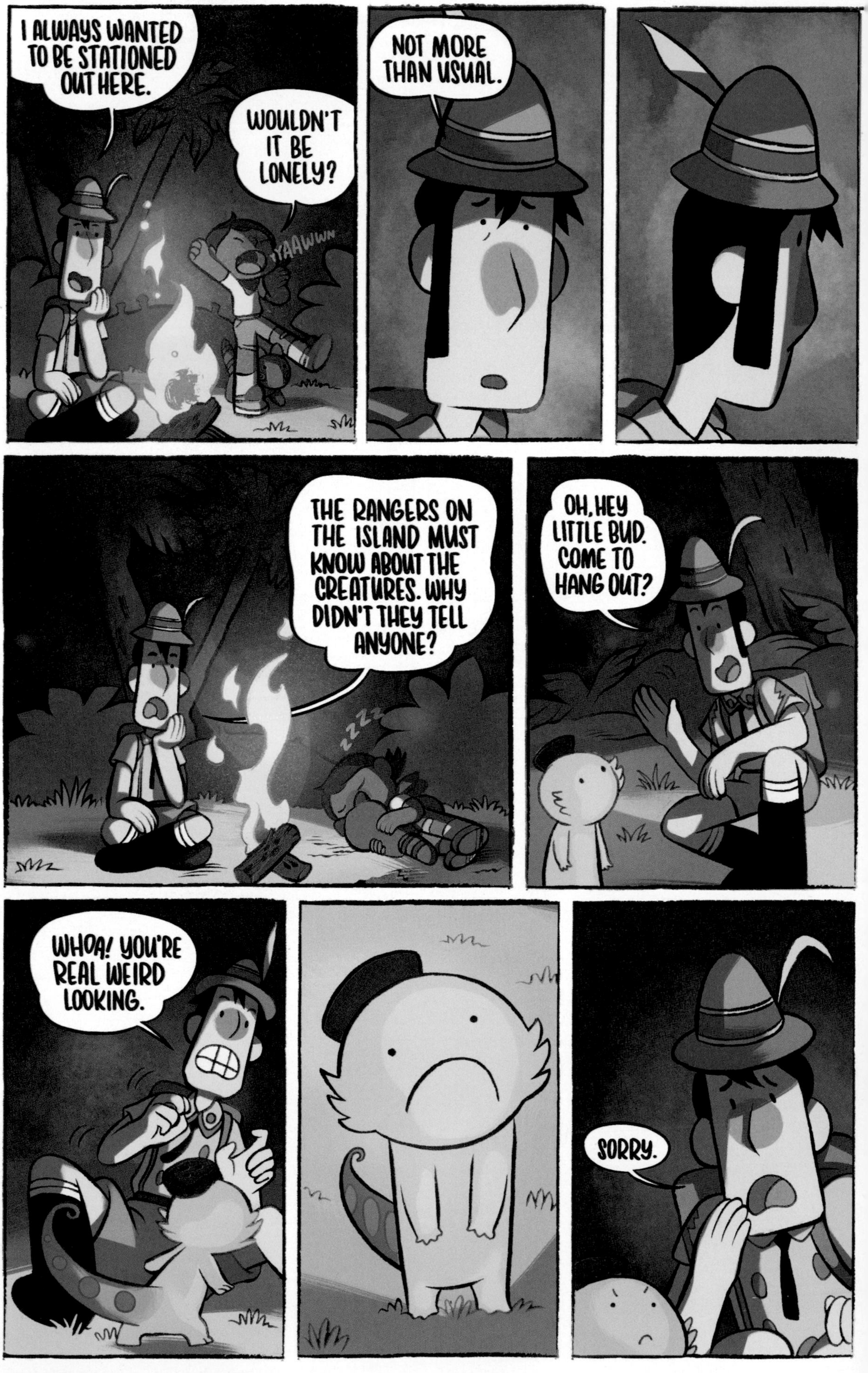
I ALWAYS WANTED TO BE STATIONED OUT HERE.
WOULDN'T IT BE LONELY?
YAAWWN
NOT MORE THAN USUAL.
THE RANGERS ON THE ISLAND MUST KNOW ABOUT THE CREATURES. WHY DIDN'T THEY TELL ANYONE?
ZZZ
OH, HEY LITTLE BUD. COME TO HANG OUT?
WHOA! YOU'RE REAL WEIRD LOOKING.
SORRY.

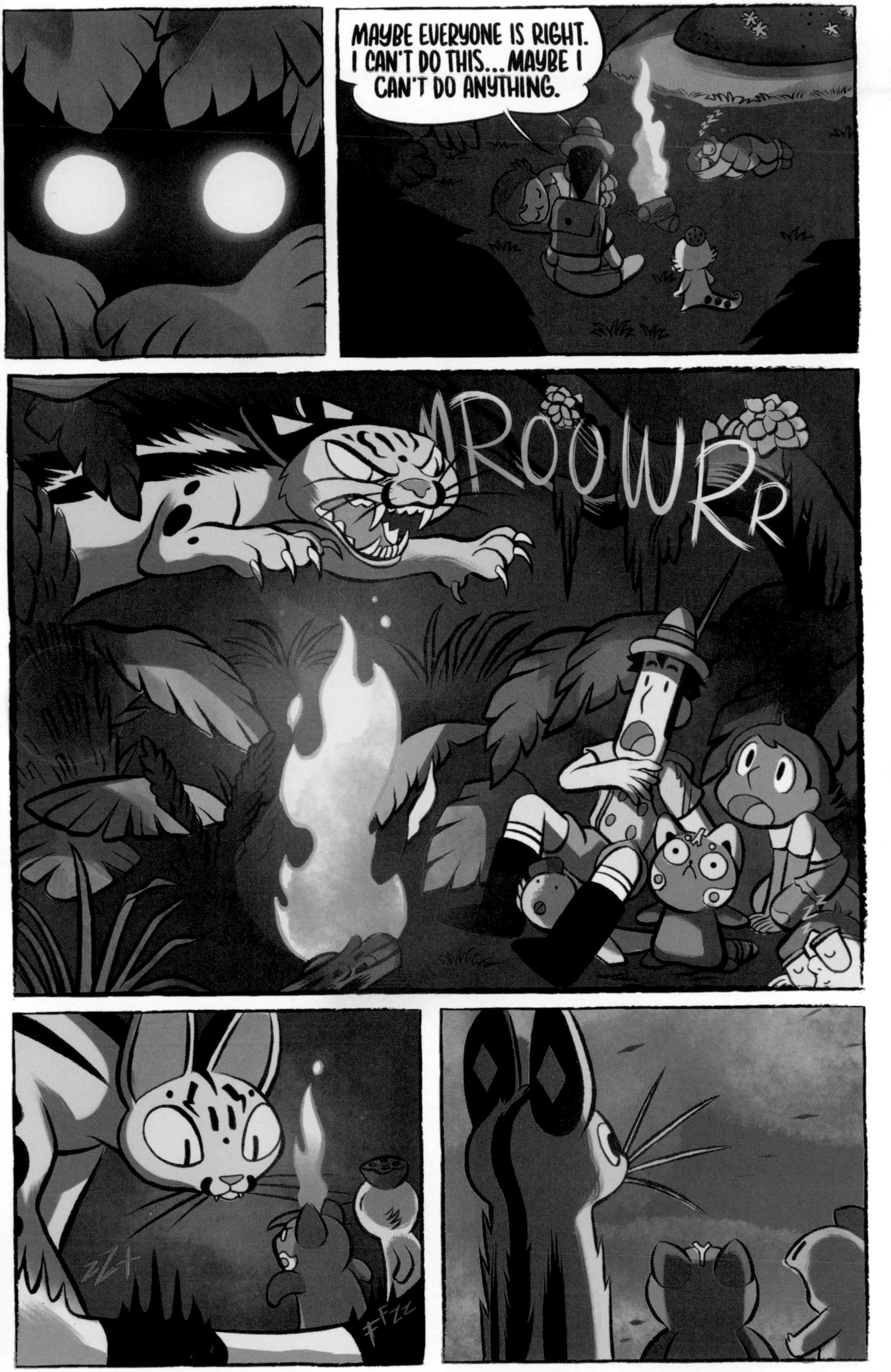
MAYBE EVERYONE IS RIGHT. I CAN'T DO THIS... MAYBE I CAN'T DO ANYTHING.
MROOWRRR

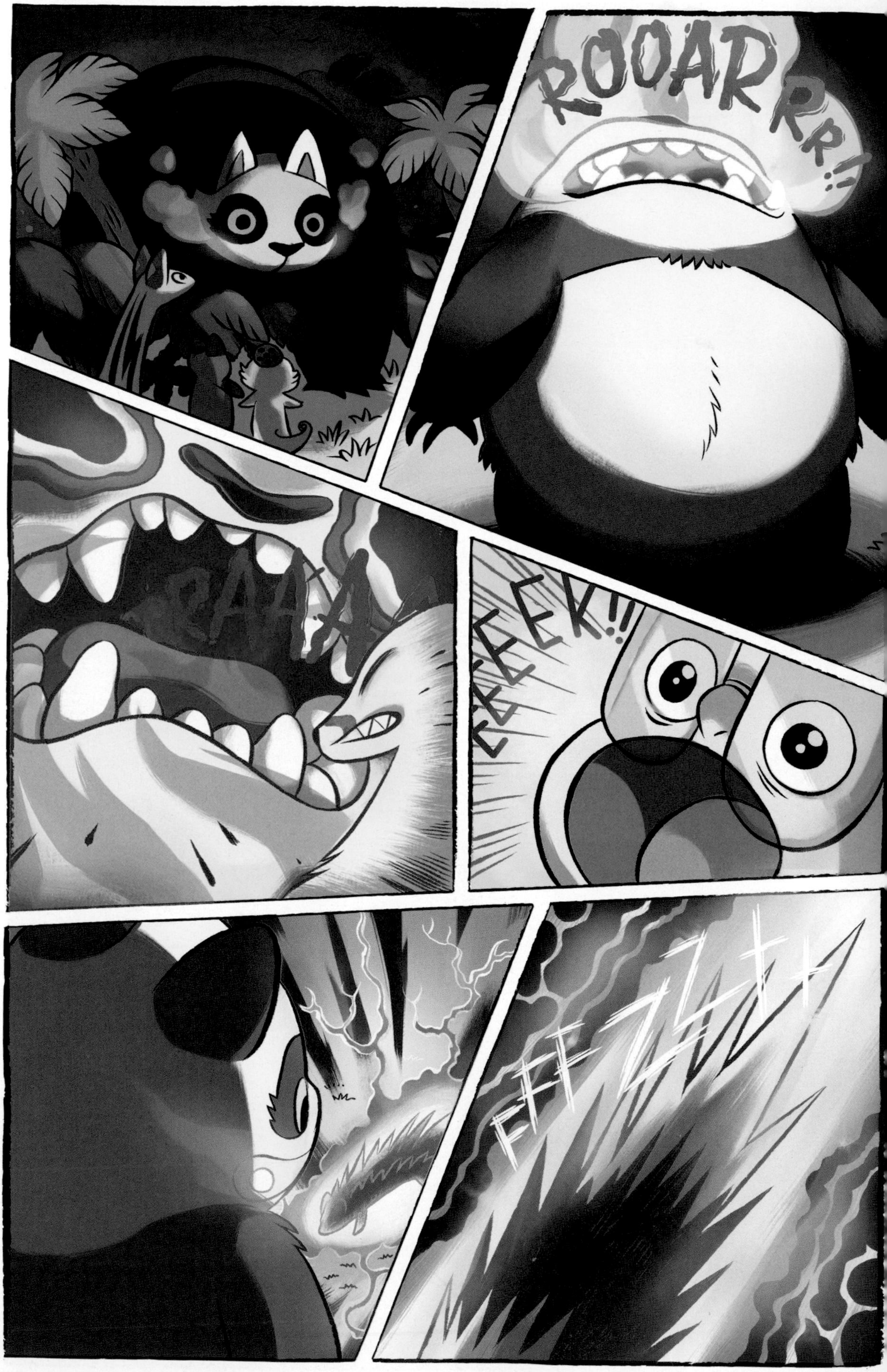
ROOARRRR!!
RAAA
EEEEEK!!
FFFZZZTT

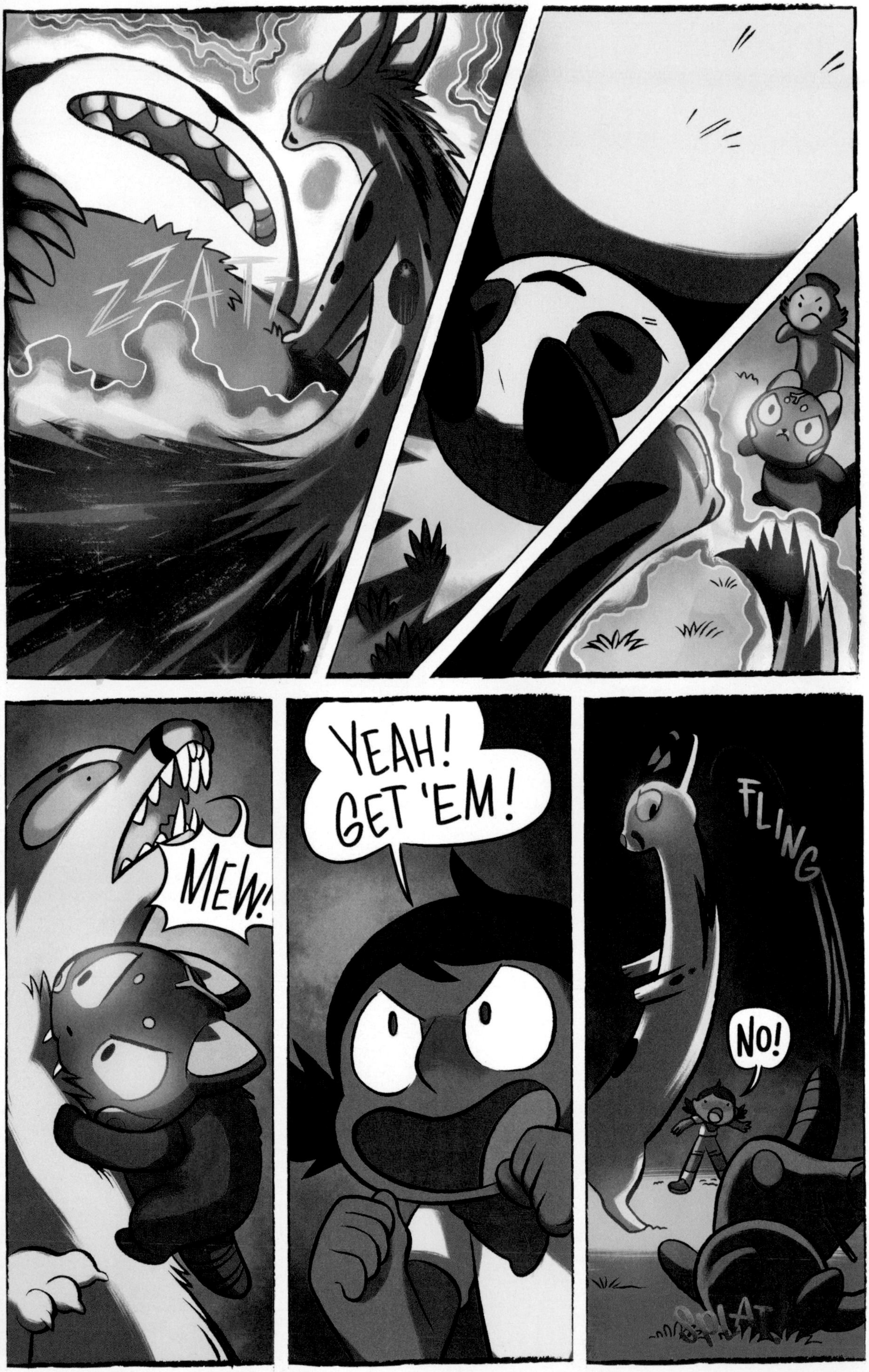
ZZATT
MEW!
YEAH! GET 'EM!
FLING
NO!
SPLAT

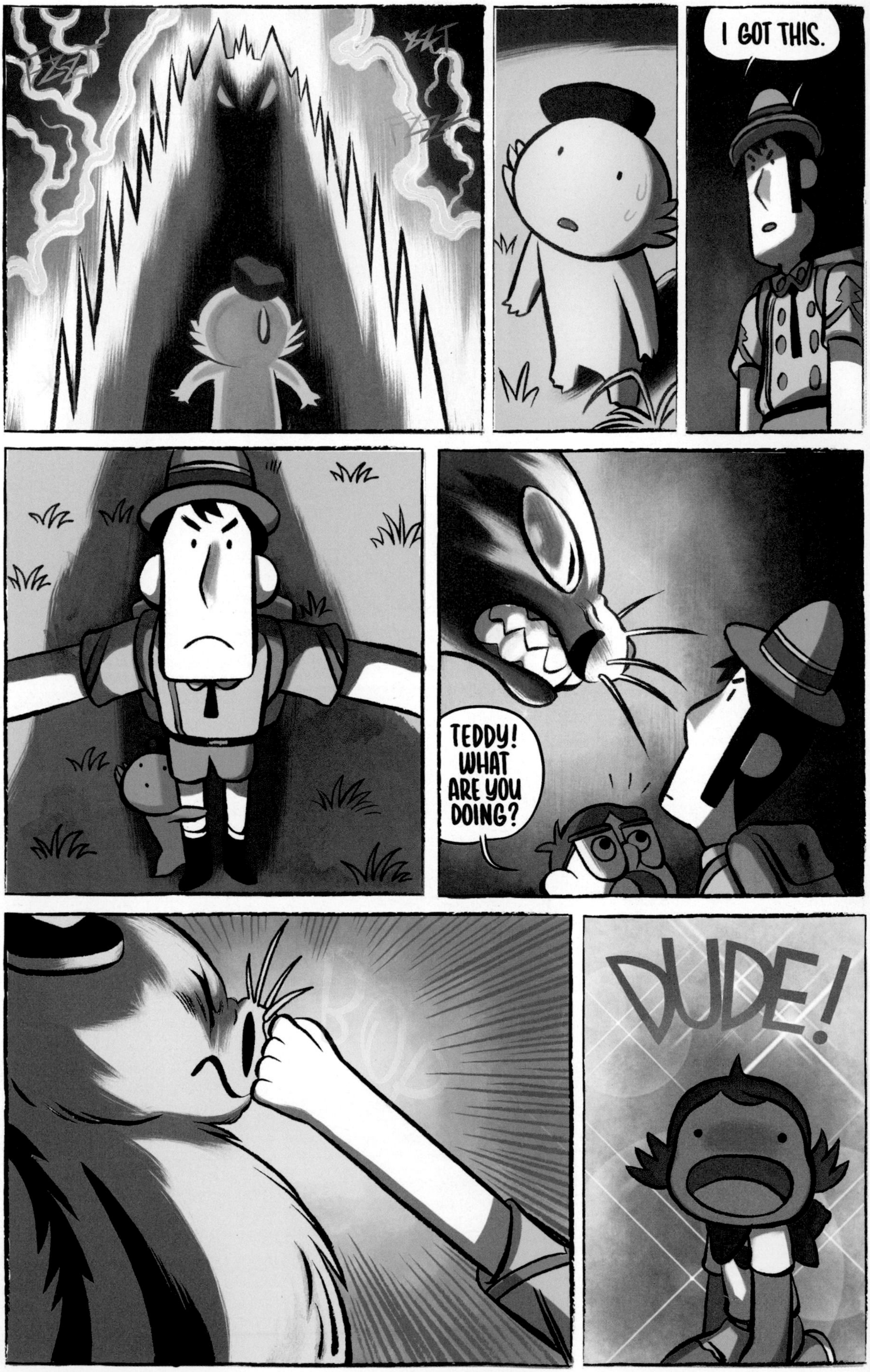
I GOT THIS.
TEDDY! WHAT ARE YOU DOING?
DUDE!

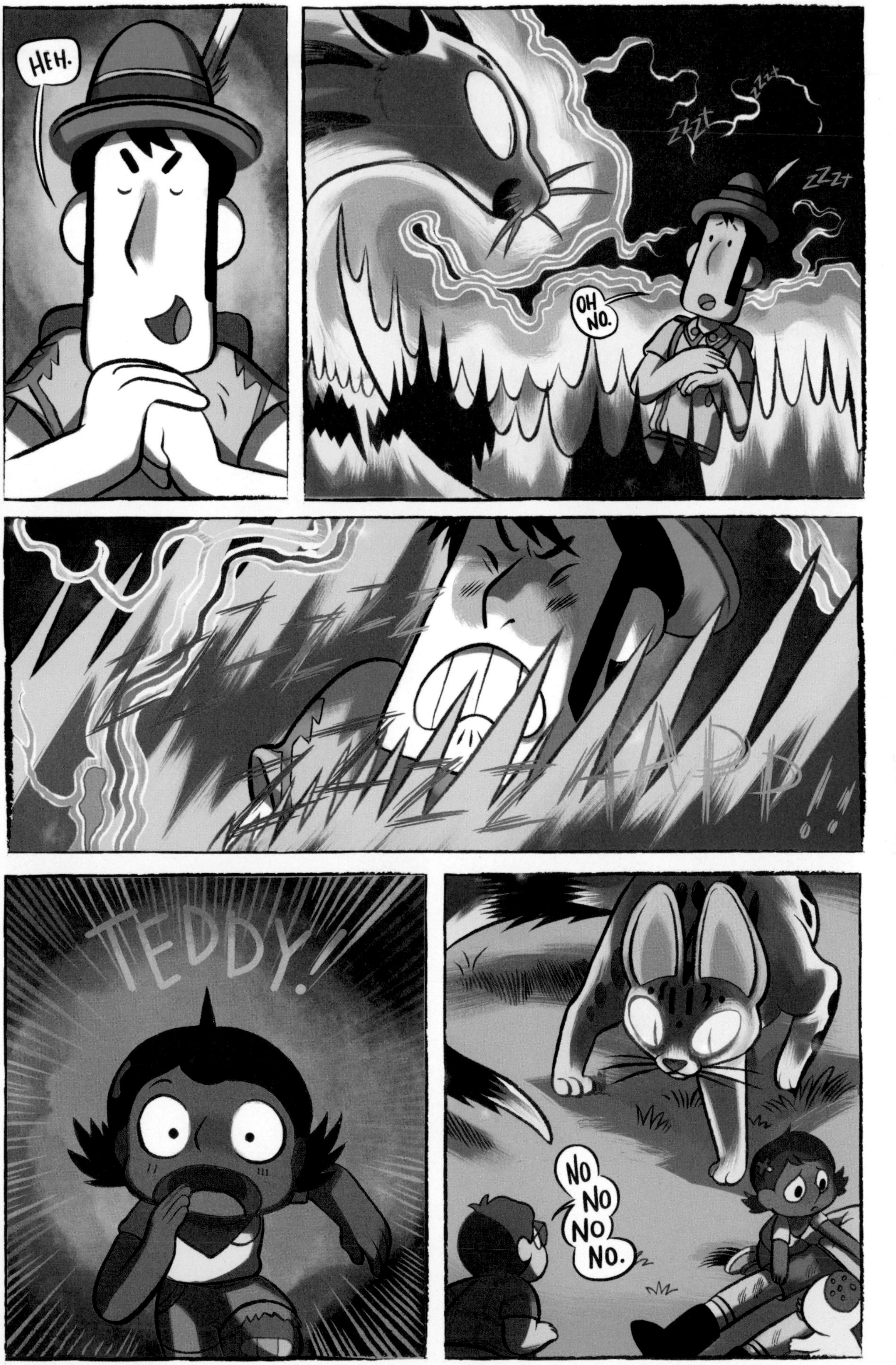
HEH.
ZZZT
ZZZT
ZZZT
OH NO.
TEDDY!!
NO NO NO NO.

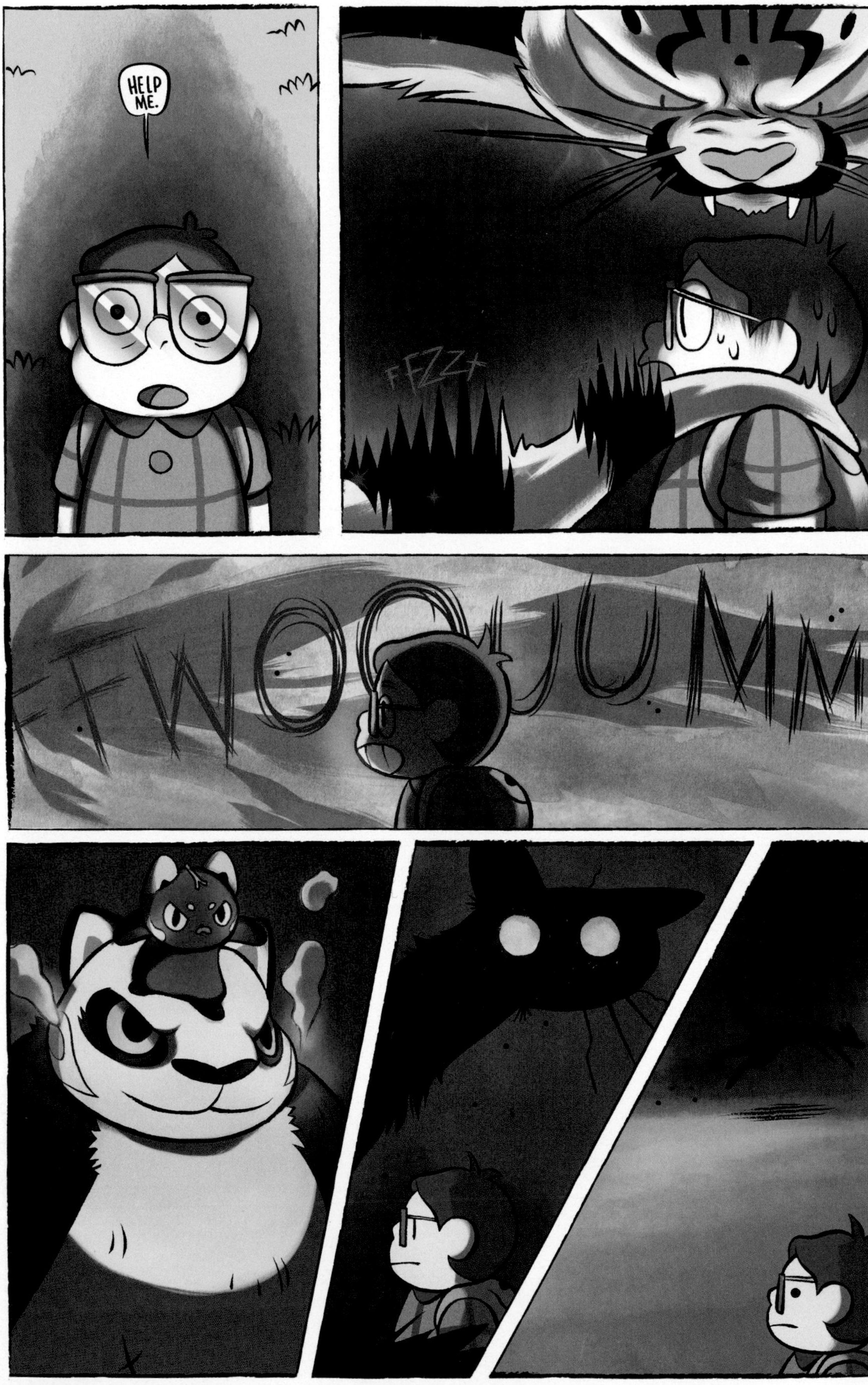
HELP ME.
FFZZT
FWOOOUUMM

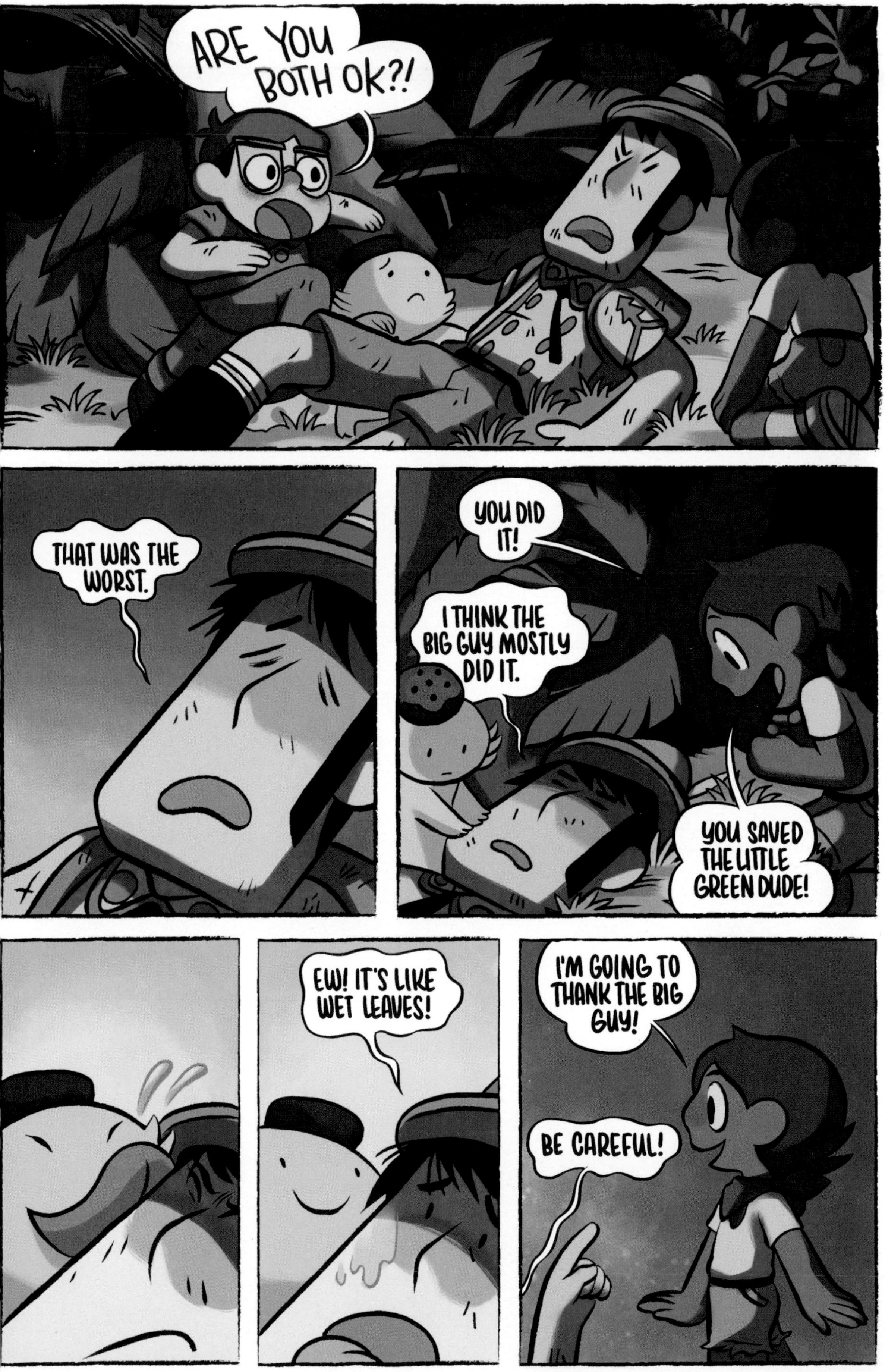
ARE YOU BOTH OK?!
THAT WAS THE WORST.
YOU DID IT!
I THINK THE BIG GUY MOSTLY DID IT.
YOU SAVED THE LITTLE GREEN DUDE!
EW! IT'S LIKE WET LEAVES!
I'M GOING TO THANK THE BIG GUY!
BE CAREFUL!

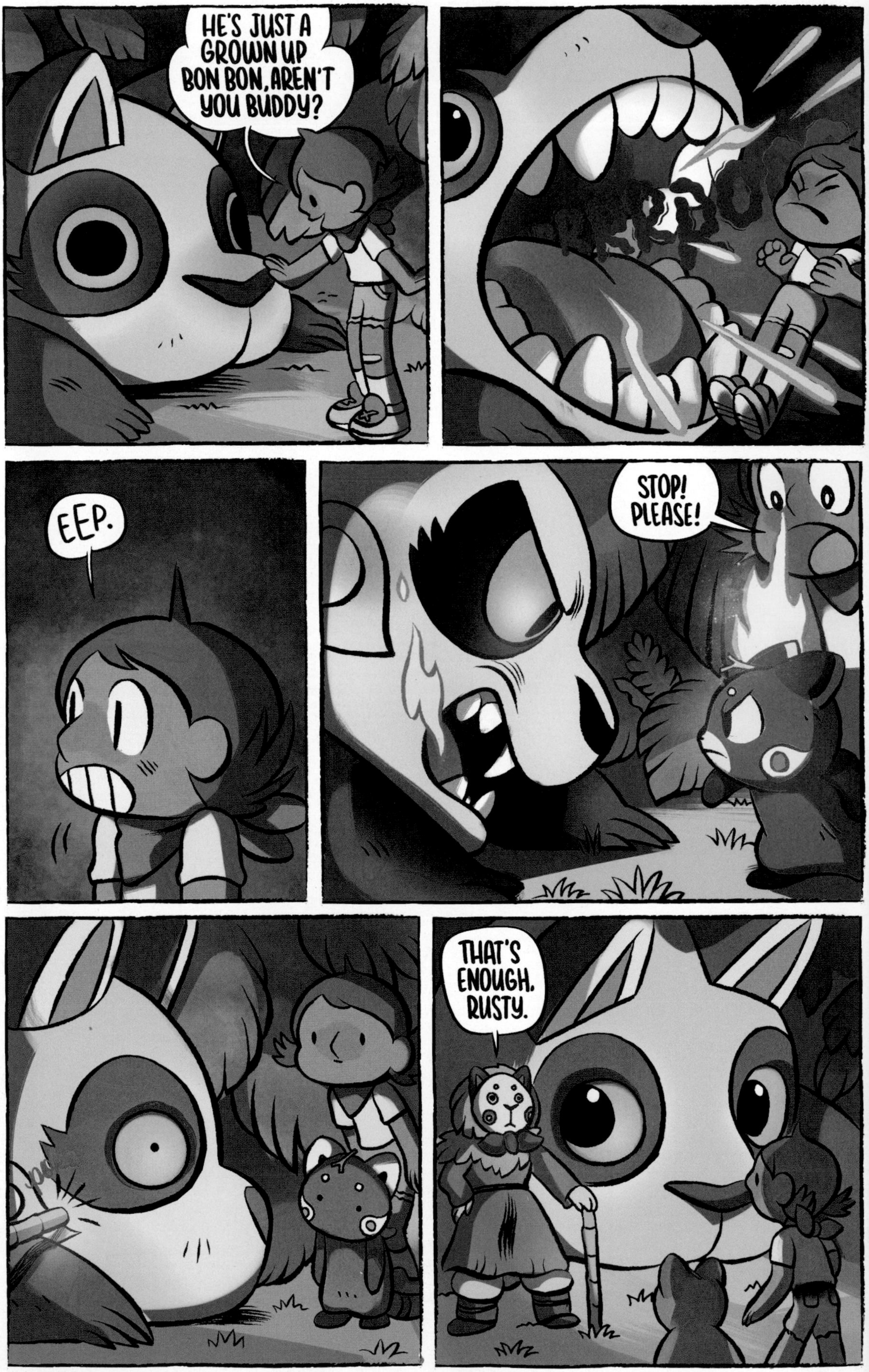
HE'S JUST A GROWN UP BON BON, AREN'T YOU BUDDY?
EEP.
STOP! PLEASE!
THAT'S ENOUGH. RUSTY.

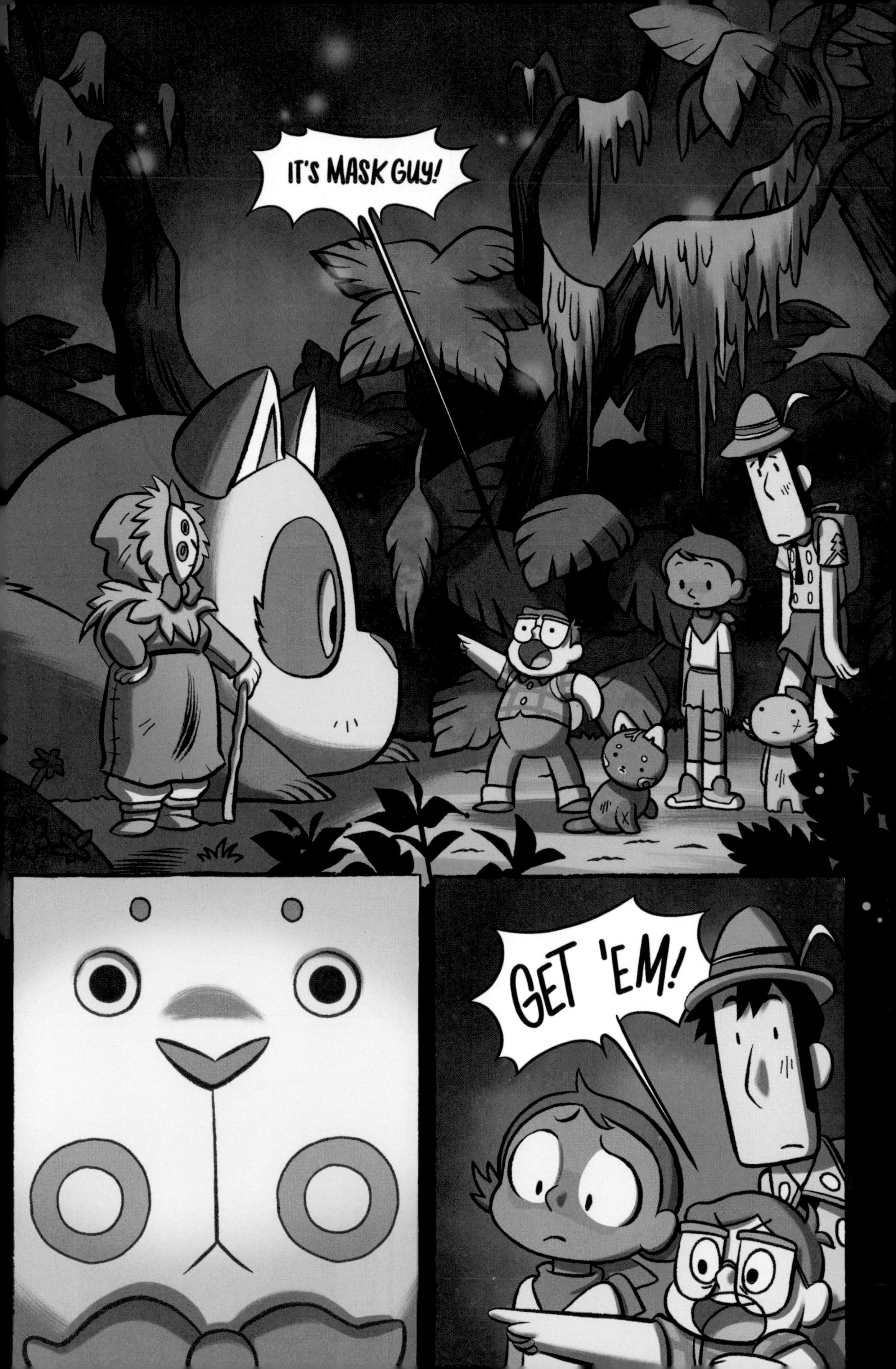
IT'S MASK GUY!
GET 'EM!

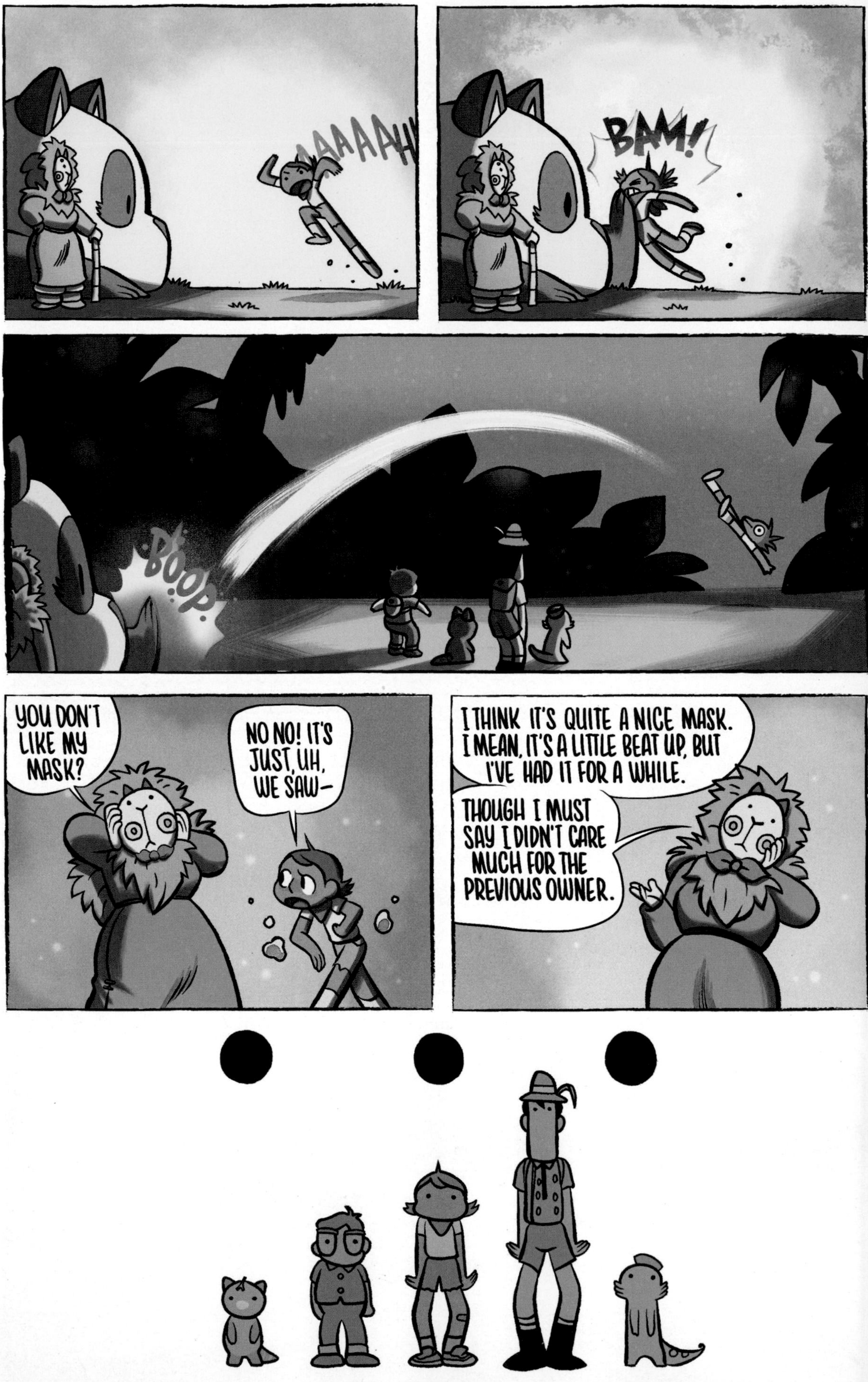
AAAAAH
BAM!
BOOP
YOU DON'T LIKE MY MASK?
NO NO! IT'S JUST, UH, WE SAW-
I THINK IT'S QUITE A NICE MASK. I MEAN, IT'S A LITTLE BEAT UP, BUT I'VE HAD IT FOR A WHILE.
THOUGH I MUST SAY I DIDN'T CARE MUCH FOR THE PREVIOUS OWNER.

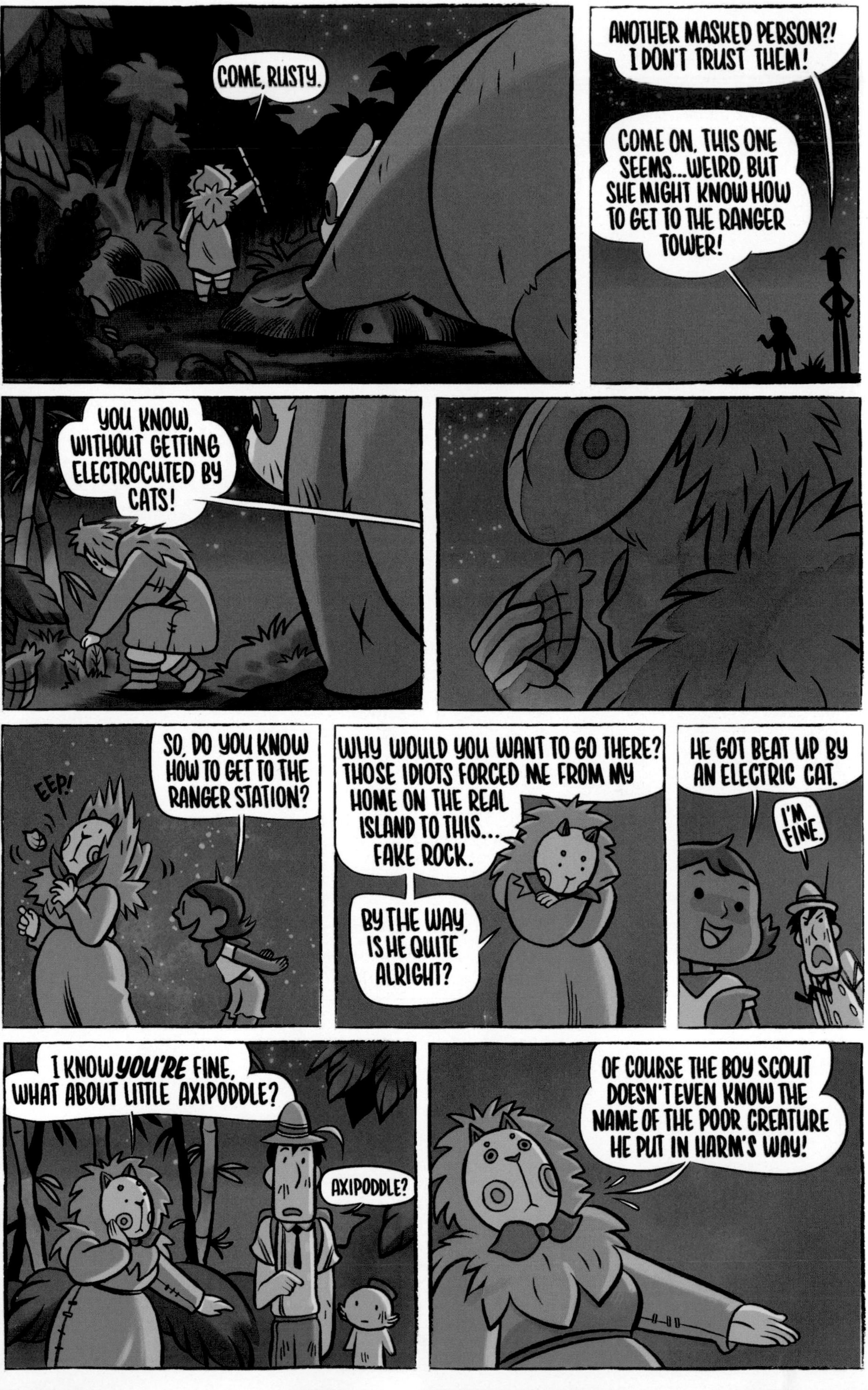
COME, RUSTY.
ANOTHER MASKED PERSON?! I DON'T TRUST THEM!
COME ON, THIS ONE SEEMS...WEIRD, BUT SHE MIGHT KNOW HOW TO GET TO THE RANGER TOWER!
YOU KNOW, WITHOUT GETTING ELECTROCUTED BY CATS!
EEP!
SO, DO YOU KNOW HOW TO GET TO THE RANGER STATION?
WHY WOULD YOU WANT TO GO THERE? THOSE IDIOTS FORCED ME FROM MY HOME ON THE REAL ISLAND TO THIS... FAKE ROCK.
BY THE WAY, IS HE QUITE ALRIGHT?
HE GOT BEAT UP BY AN ELECTRIC CAT.
I'M FINE.
I KNOW YOU'RE FINE, WHAT ABOUT LITTLE AXIPODDLE?
AXIPODDLE?
OF COURSE THE BOY SCOUT DOESN'T EVEN KNOW THE NAME OF THE POOR CREATURE HE PUT IN HARM'S WAY!

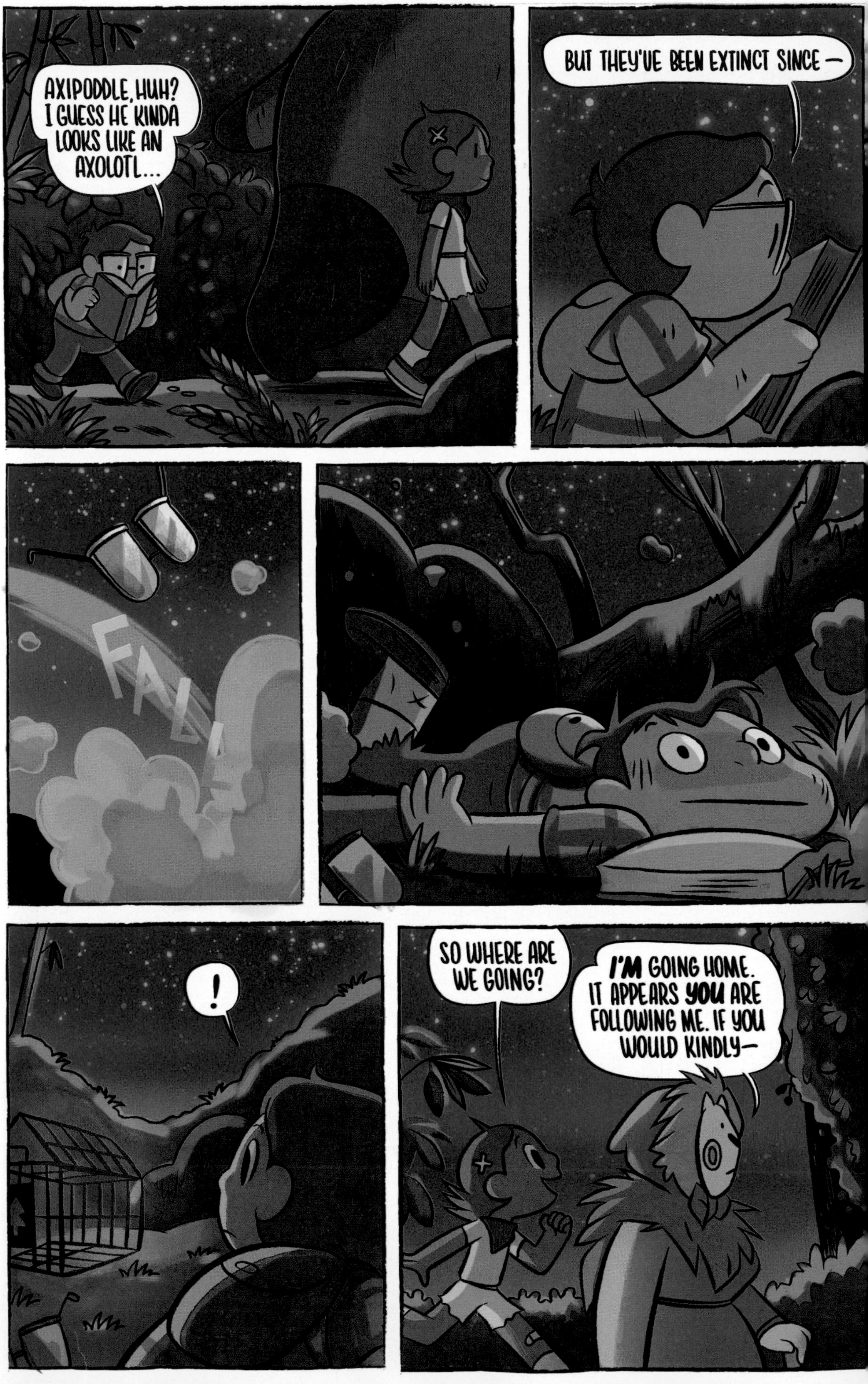
AXIPODDLE, HUH? I GUESS HE KINDA LOOKS LIKE AN AXOLOTL...
BUT THEY'VE BEEN EXTINCT SINCE—
FALL!
!
SO WHERE ARE WE GOING?
I'M GOING HOME. IT APPEARS YOU ARE FOLLOWING ME. IF YOU WOULD KINDLY—

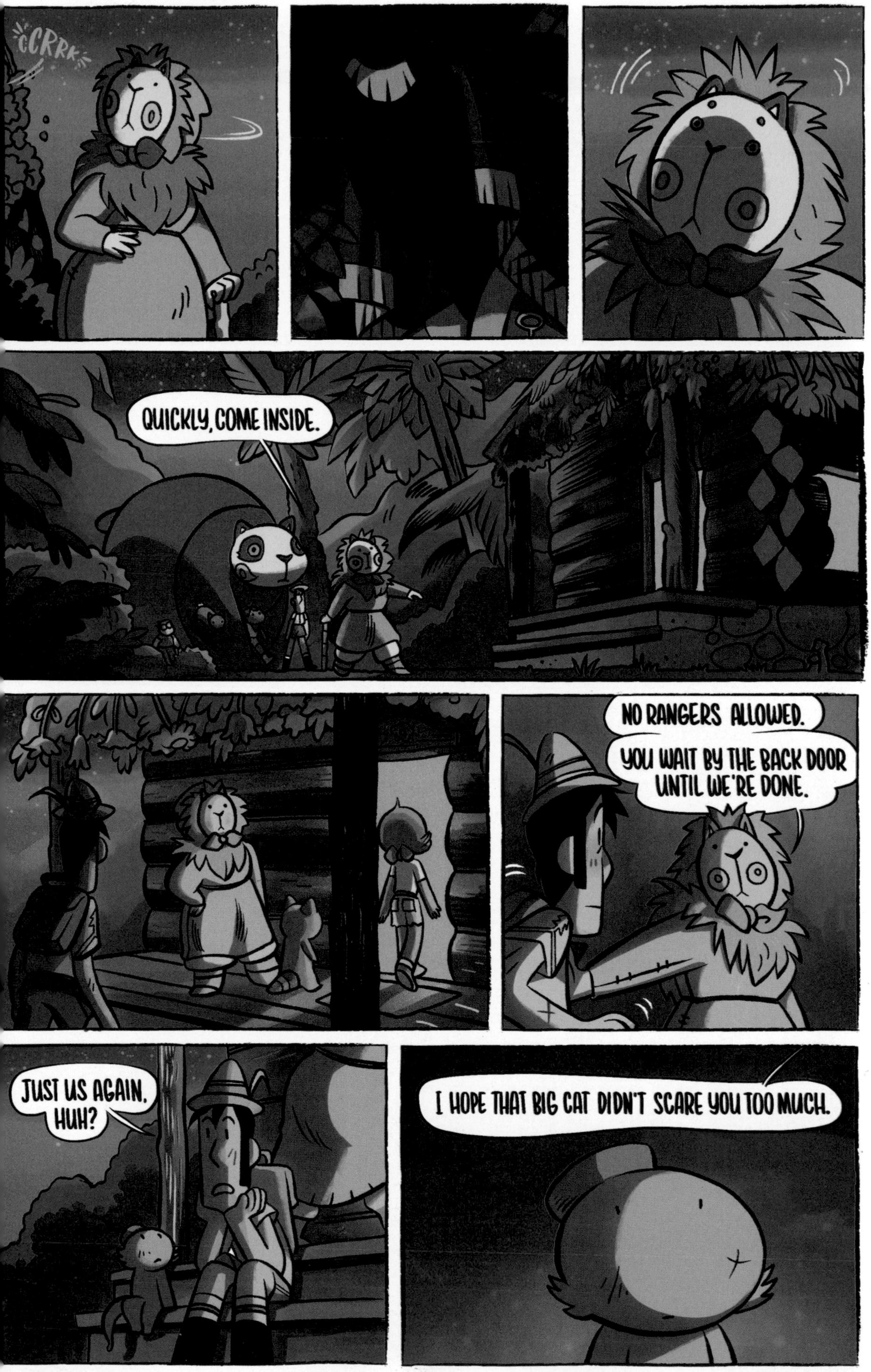
CCRRK
QUICKLY, COME INSIDE.
NO RANGERS ALLOWED.
YOU WAIT BY THE BACK DOOR UNTIL WE'RE DONE.
JUST US AGAIN, HUH?
I HOPE THAT BIG CAT DIDN'T SCARE YOU TOO MUCH.

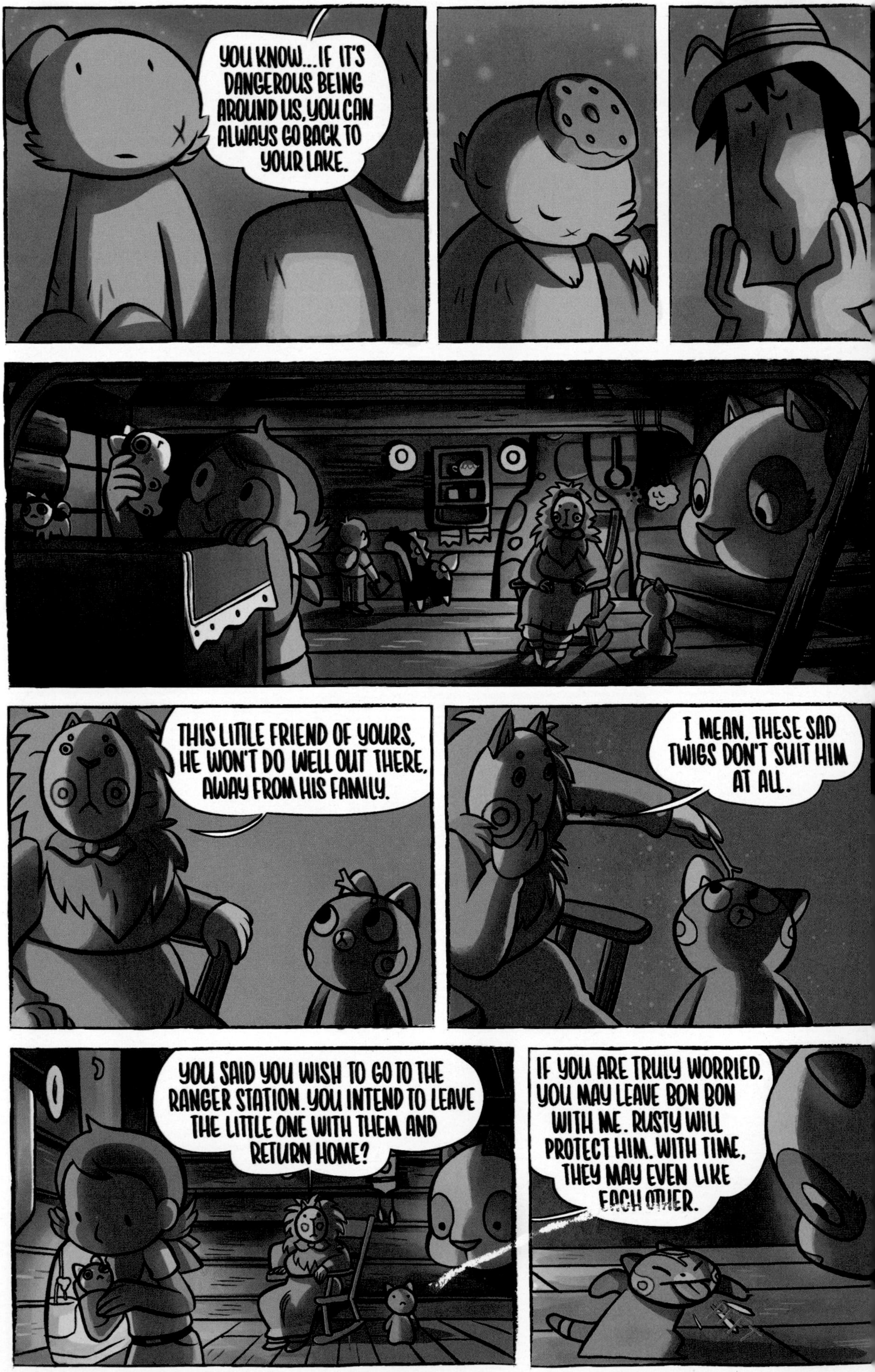
YOU KNOW... IF IT'S DANGEROUS BEING AROUND US, YOU CAN ALWAYS GO BACK TO YOUR LAKE.
THIS LITTLE FRIEND OF YOURS, HE WON'T DO WELL OUT THERE, AWAY FROM HIS FAMILY.
I MEAN, THESE SAD TWIGS DON'T SUIT HIM AT ALL.
YOU SAID YOU WISH TO GO TO THE RANGER STATION. YOU INTEND TO LEAVE THE LITTLE ONE WITH THEM AND RETURN HOME?
IF YOU ARE TRULY WORRIED, YOU MAY LEAVE BON BON WITH ME. RUSTY WILL PROTECT HIM. WITH TIME, THEY MAY EVEN LIKE EACH OTHER.

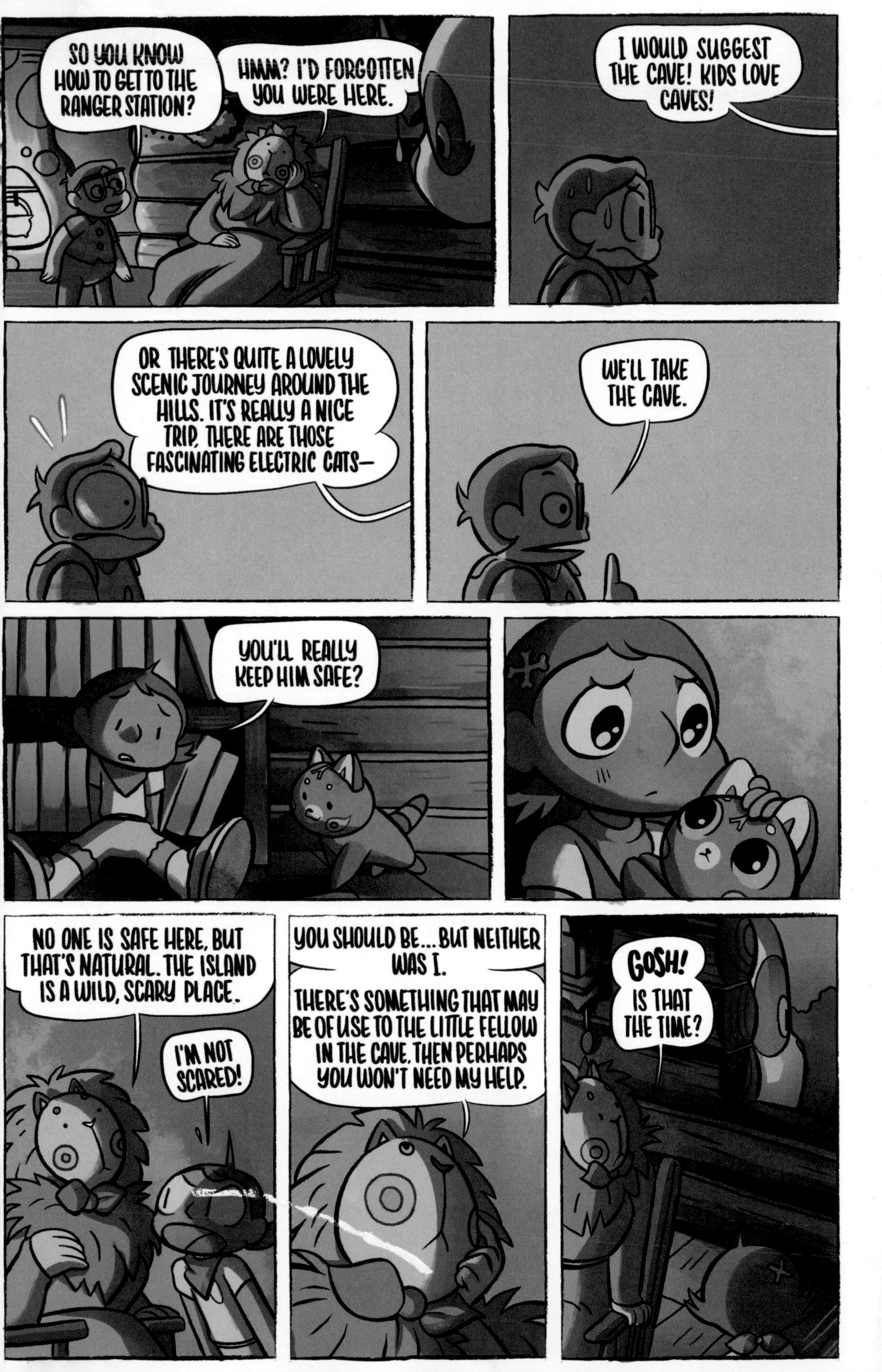
SO YOU KNOW HOW TO GET TO THE RANGER STATION?
HMM? I'D FORGOTTEN YOU WERE HERE.
I WOULD SUGGEST THE CAVE! KIDS LOVE CAVES!
OR THERE'S QUITE A LOVELY SCENIC JOURNEY AROUND THE HILLS. IT'S REALLY A NICE TRIP, THERE ARE THOSE FASCINATING ELECTRIC CATS—
WE'LL TAKE THE CAVE.
YOU'LL REALLY KEEP HIM SAFE?
NO ONE IS SAFE HERE, BUT THAT'S NATURAL. THE ISLAND IS A WILD, SCARY PLACE.
I'M NOT SCARED!
YOU SHOULD BE.... BUT NEITHER WAS I.
THERE'S SOMETHING THAT MAY BE OF USE TO THE LITTLE FELLOW IN THE CAVE, THEN PERHAPS YOU WON'T NEED MY HELP.
GOSH!
IS THAT THE TIME?

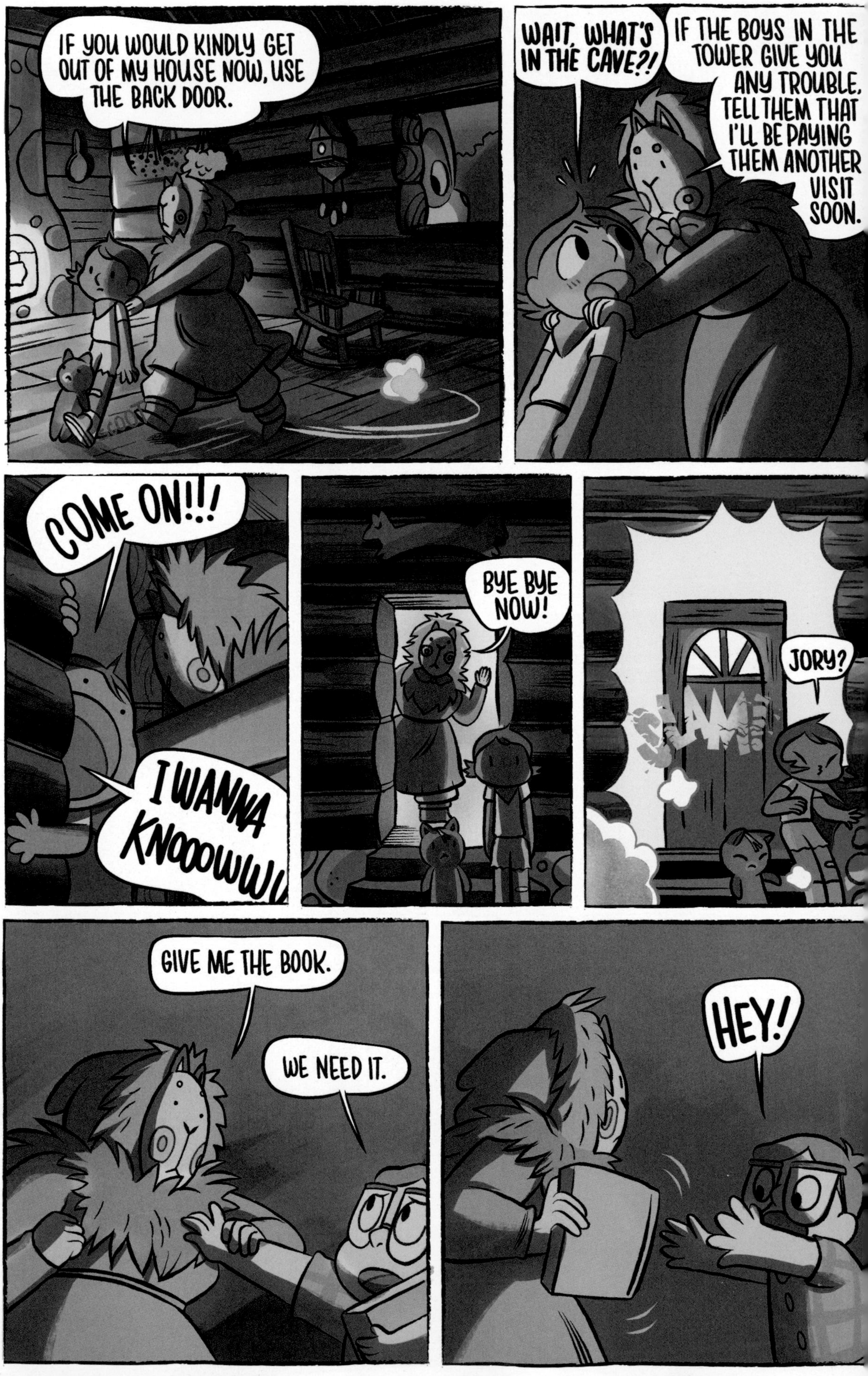
IF YOU WOULD KINDLY GET OUT OF MY HOUSE NOW, USE THE BACK DOOR.
WAIT, WHAT'S IN THE CAVE?!
IF THE BOYS IN THE TOWER GIVE YOU ANY TROUBLE, TELL THEM THAT I'LL BE PAYING THEM ANOTHER VISIT SOON.
COME ON!!!
I WANNA KNOOOWWW
BYE BYE NOW!
SLAM!
JORY?
GIVE ME THE BOOK.
WE NEED IT.
HEY!

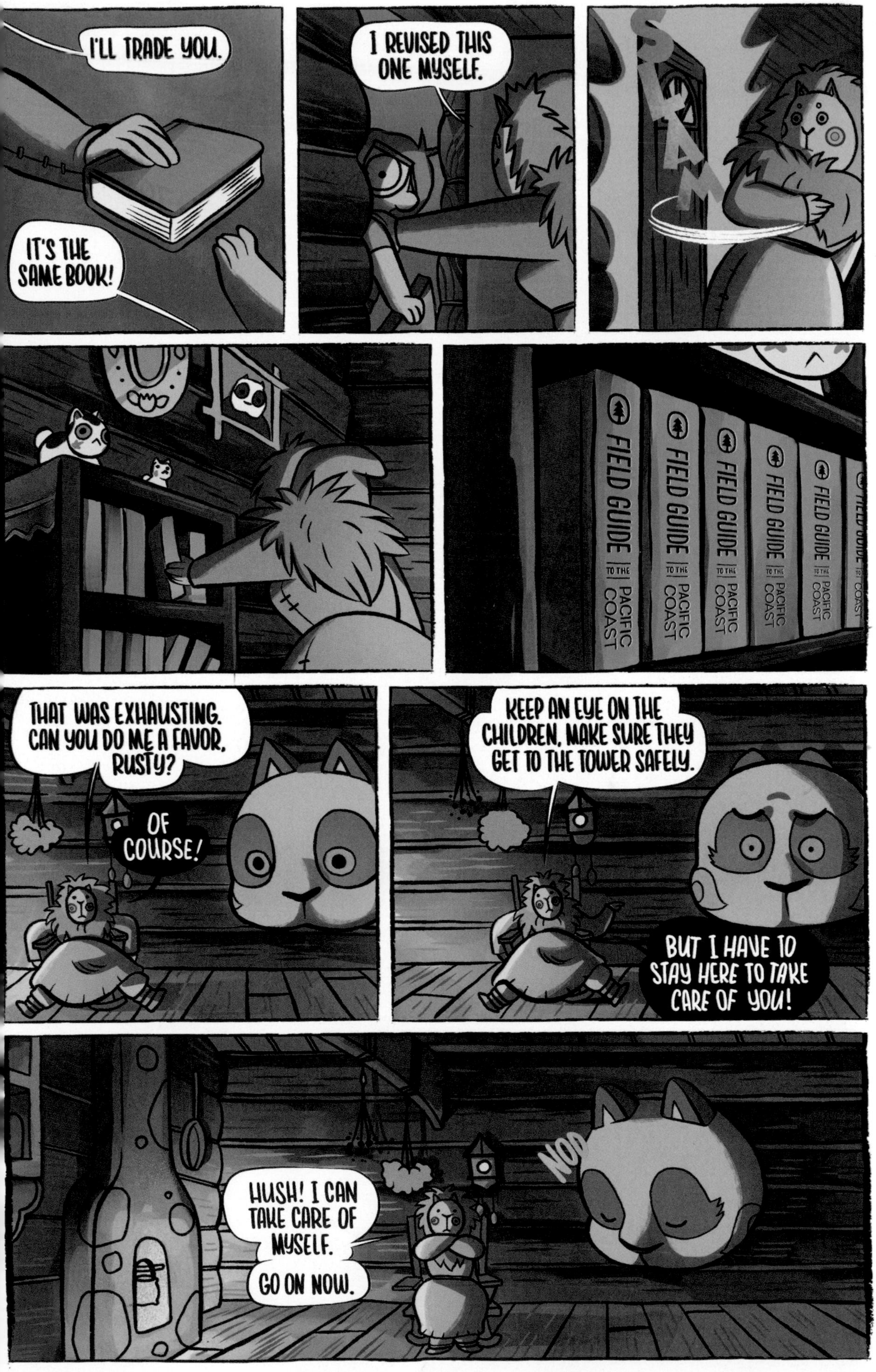
I'LL TRADE YOU.
IT'S THE SAME BOOK!
I REVISED THIS ONE MYSELF.
SLAM
FIELD GUIDE TO THE PACIFIC COAST
FIELD GUIDE TO THE PACIFIC COAST
FIELD GUIDE TO THE PACIFIC COAST
FIELD GUIDE TO THE PACIFIC COAST
FIELD GUIDE TO THE PACIFIC COAST
THAT WAS EXHAUSTING. CAN YOU DO ME A FAVOR, RUSTY?
OF COURSE!
KEEP AN EYE ON THE CHILDREN, MAKE SURE THEY GET TO THE TOWER SAFELY.
BUT I HAVE TO STAY HERE TO TAKE CARE OF YOU!
HUSH! I CAN TAKE CARE OF MYSELF.
GO ON NOW.
NOD

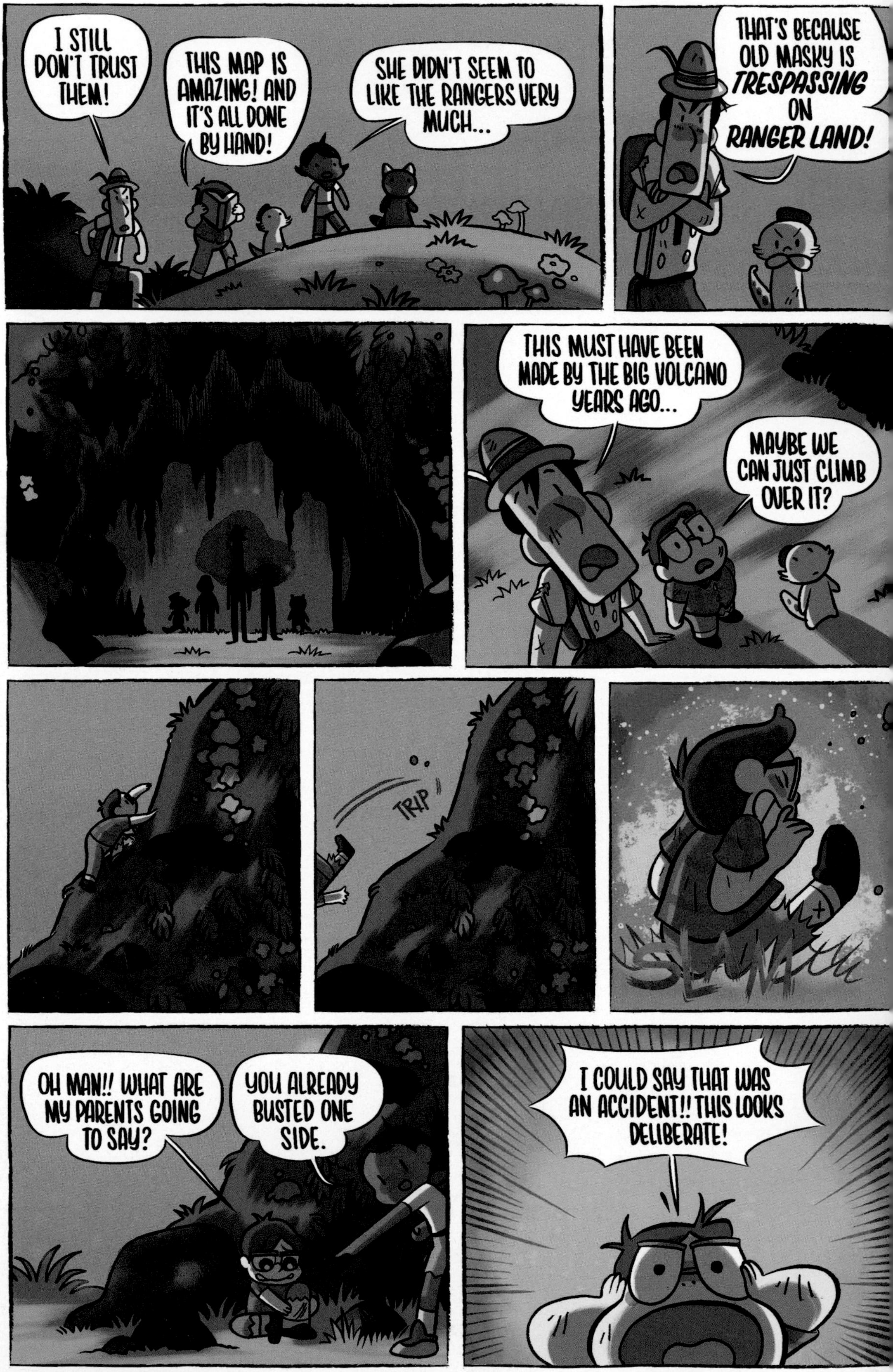
I STILL DON'T TRUST THEM!
THIS MAP IS AMAZING! AND IT'S ALL DONE BY HAND!
SHE DIDN'T SEEM TO LIKE THE RANGERS VERY MUCH...
THAT'S BECAUSE OLD MASKY IS TRESPASSING ON RANGER LAND!
THIS MUST HAVE BEEN MADE BY THE BIG VOLCANO YEARS AGO...
MAYBE WE CAN JUST CLIMB OVER IT?
TRIP
SLAM
OH MAN!! WHAT ARE MY PARENTS GOING TO SAY?
YOU ALREADY BUSTED ONE SIDE.
I COULD SAY THAT WAS AN ACCIDENT!! THIS LOOKS DELIBERATE!

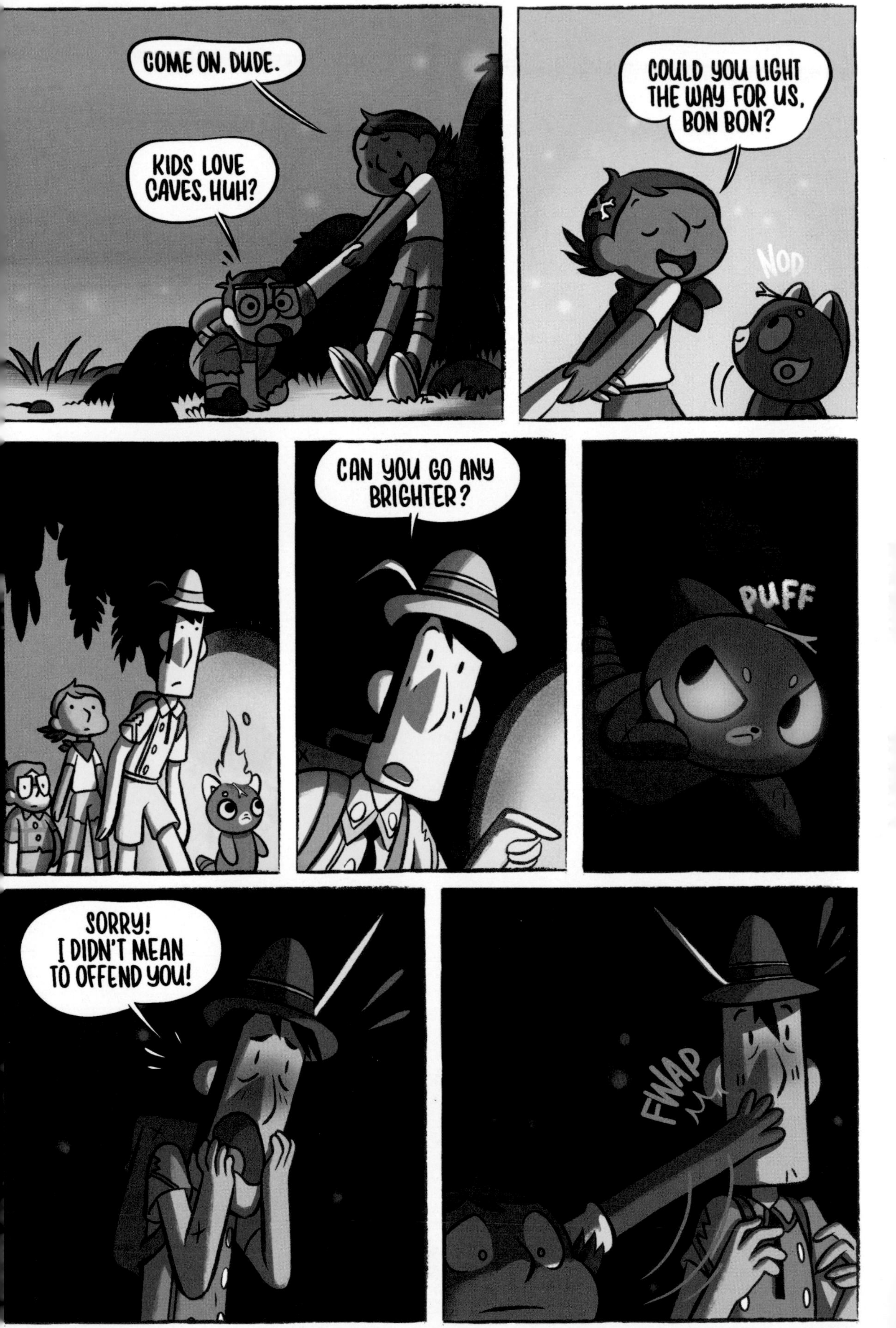
COME ON, DUDE.
KIDS LOVE CAVES, HUH?
COULD YOU LIGHT THE WAY FOR US, BON BON?
NOD
CAN YOU GO ANY BRIGHTER?
PUFF
SORRY! I DIDN'T MEAN TO OFFEND YOU!
FWAP

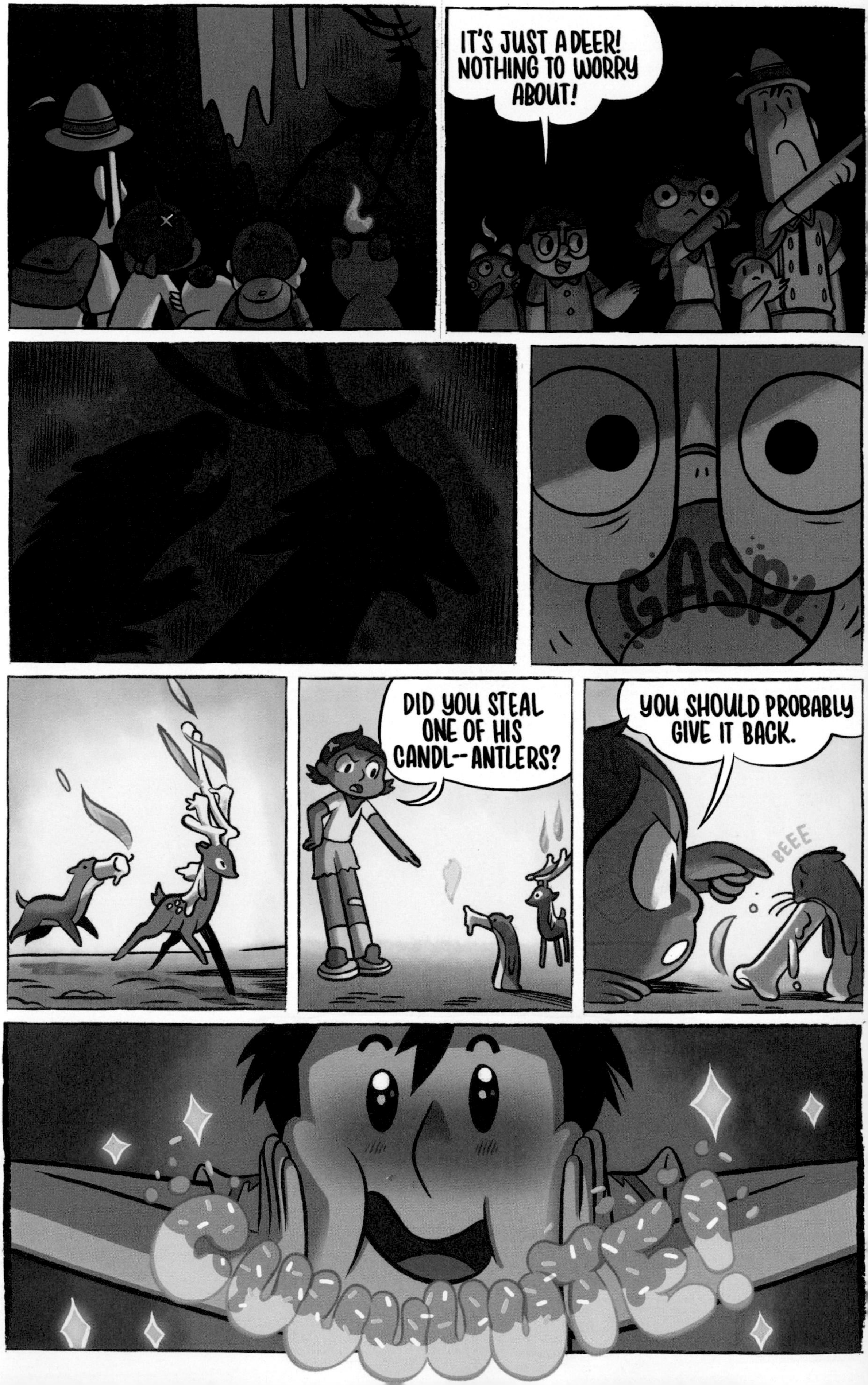
IT'S JUST A DEER! NOTHING TO WORRY ABOUT!
GASP!
DID YOU STEAL ONE OF HIS CANDL--ANTLERS?
YOU SHOULD PROBABLY GIVE IT BACK.
BEEE

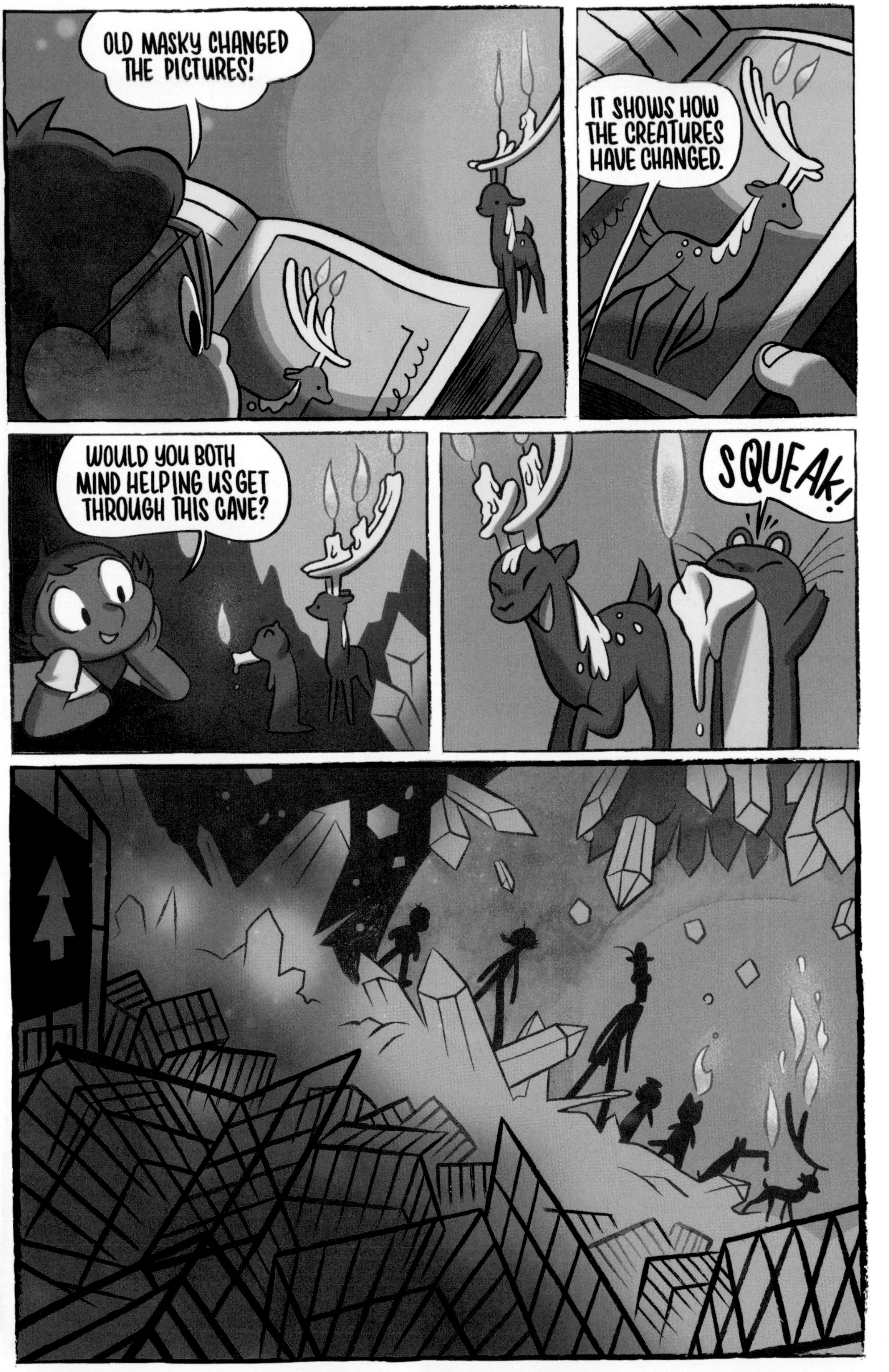
OLD MASKY CHANGED THE PICTURES!
IT SHOWS HOW THE CREATURES HAVE CHANGED.
WOULD YOU BOTH MIND HELPING US GET THROUGH THIS CAVE?
SQUEAK!

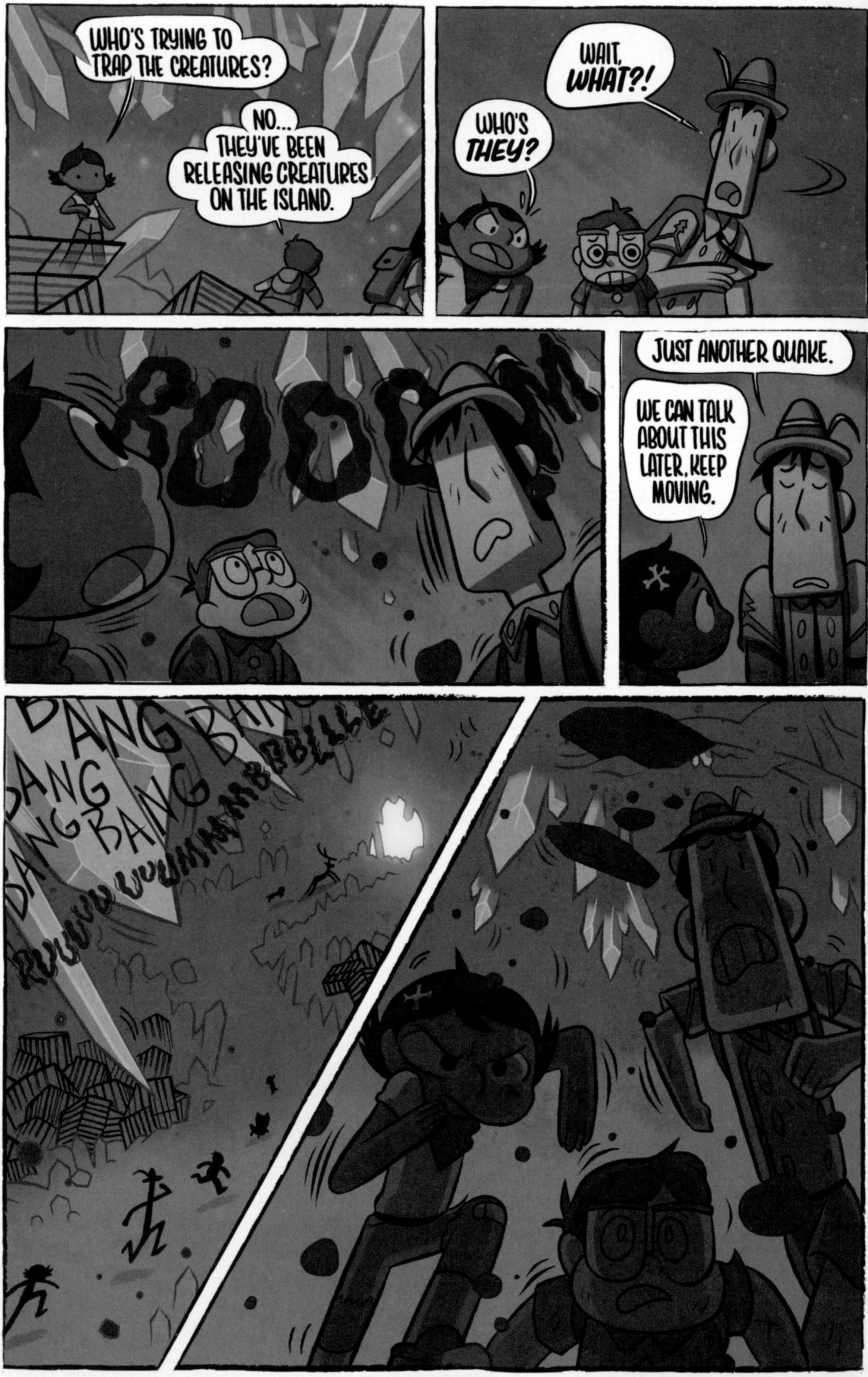
WHO'S TRYING TO TRAP THE CREATURES?
NO... THEY'VE BEEN RELEASING CREATURES ON THE ISLAND.
WAIT, WHAT?!
WHO'S THEY?
JUST ANOTHER QUAKE.
WE CAN TALK ABOUT THIS LATER. KEEP MOVING.

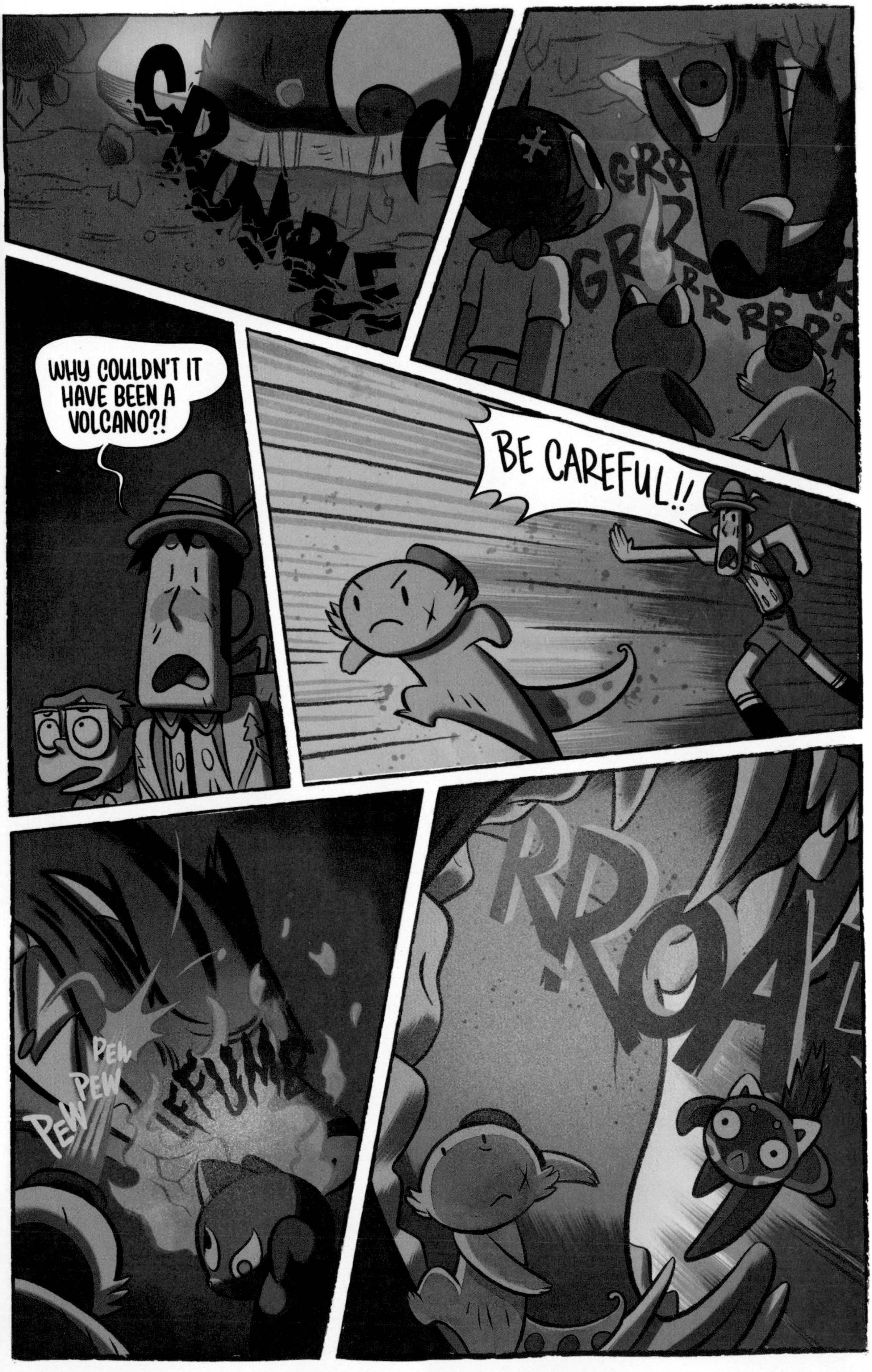
CRUMBLE
GRR
GRR
GRRRRRRR
WHY COULDN'T IT HAVE BEEN A VOLCANO?!
BE CAREFUL!!
PEW
PEW
PEW
FWUMB
RROA

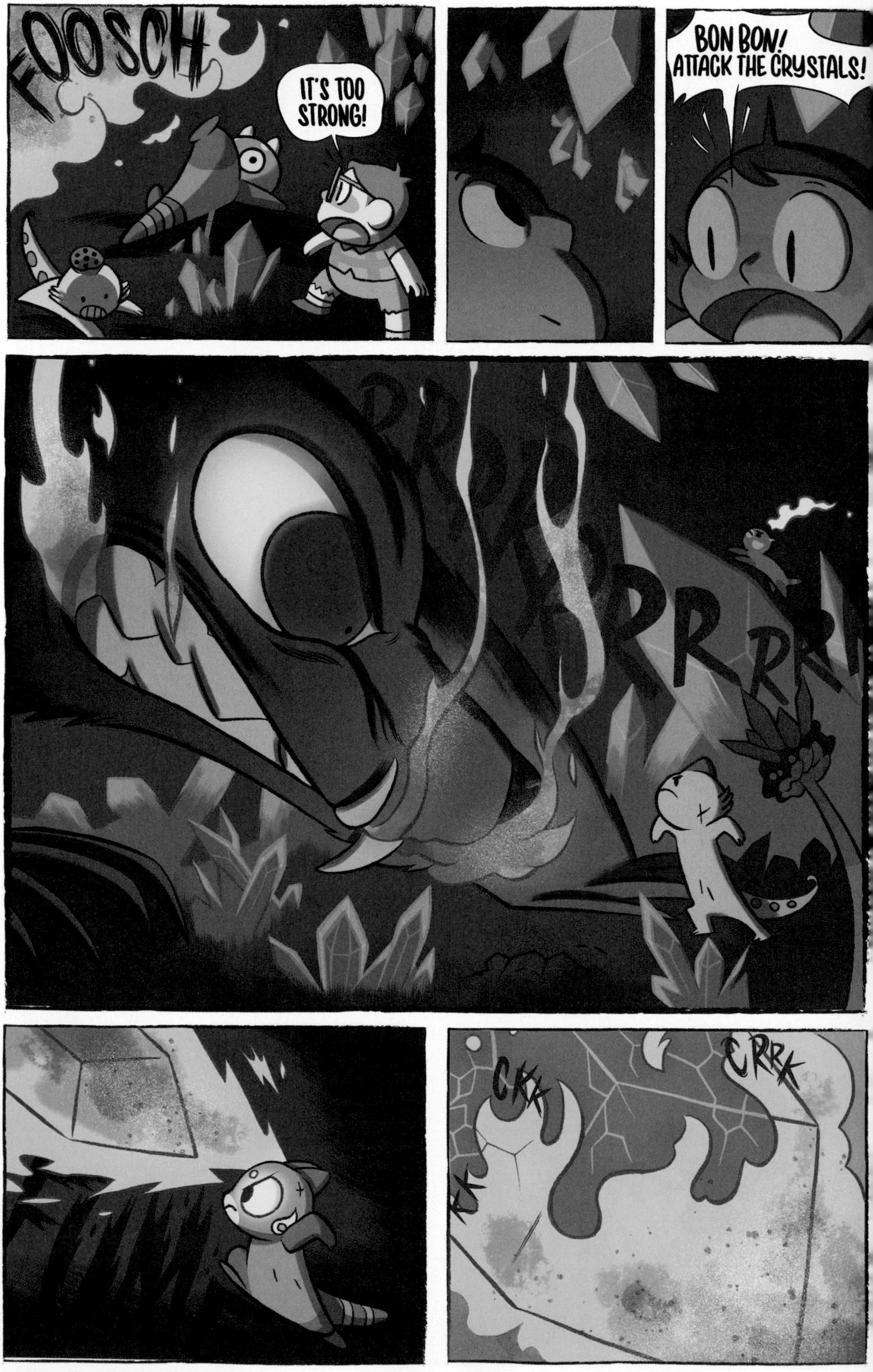
FOOSCH
IT'S TOO STRONG!
BON BON! ATTACK THE CRYSTALS!
RRRRRRR
CRRK

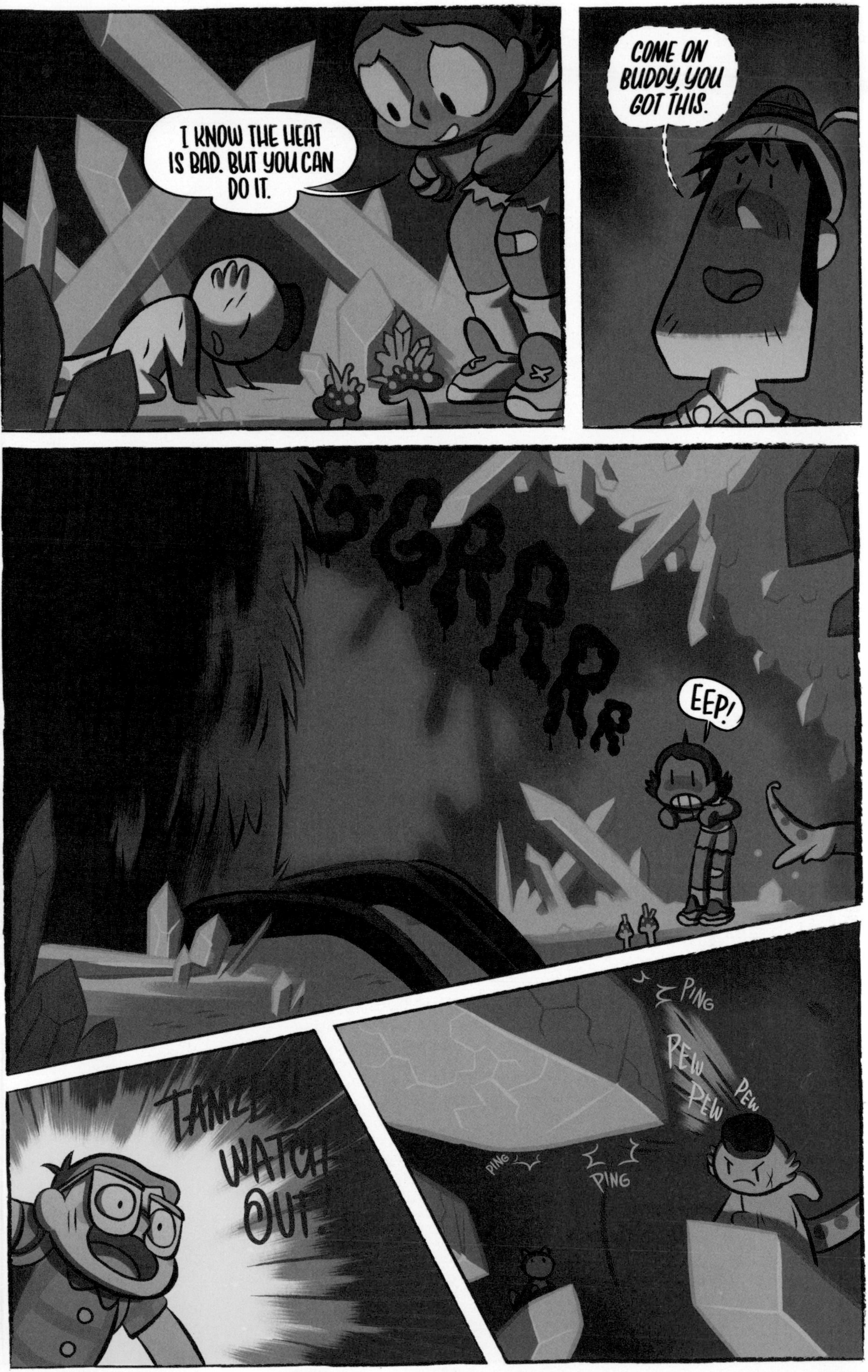
I KNOW THE HEAT IS BAD. BUT YOU CAN DO IT.
COME ON BUDDY, YOU GOT THIS.
GRRRRR
EEP!
PING
PEW
PEW
PEW
PING
PING
TAMZE WATCH OUT!

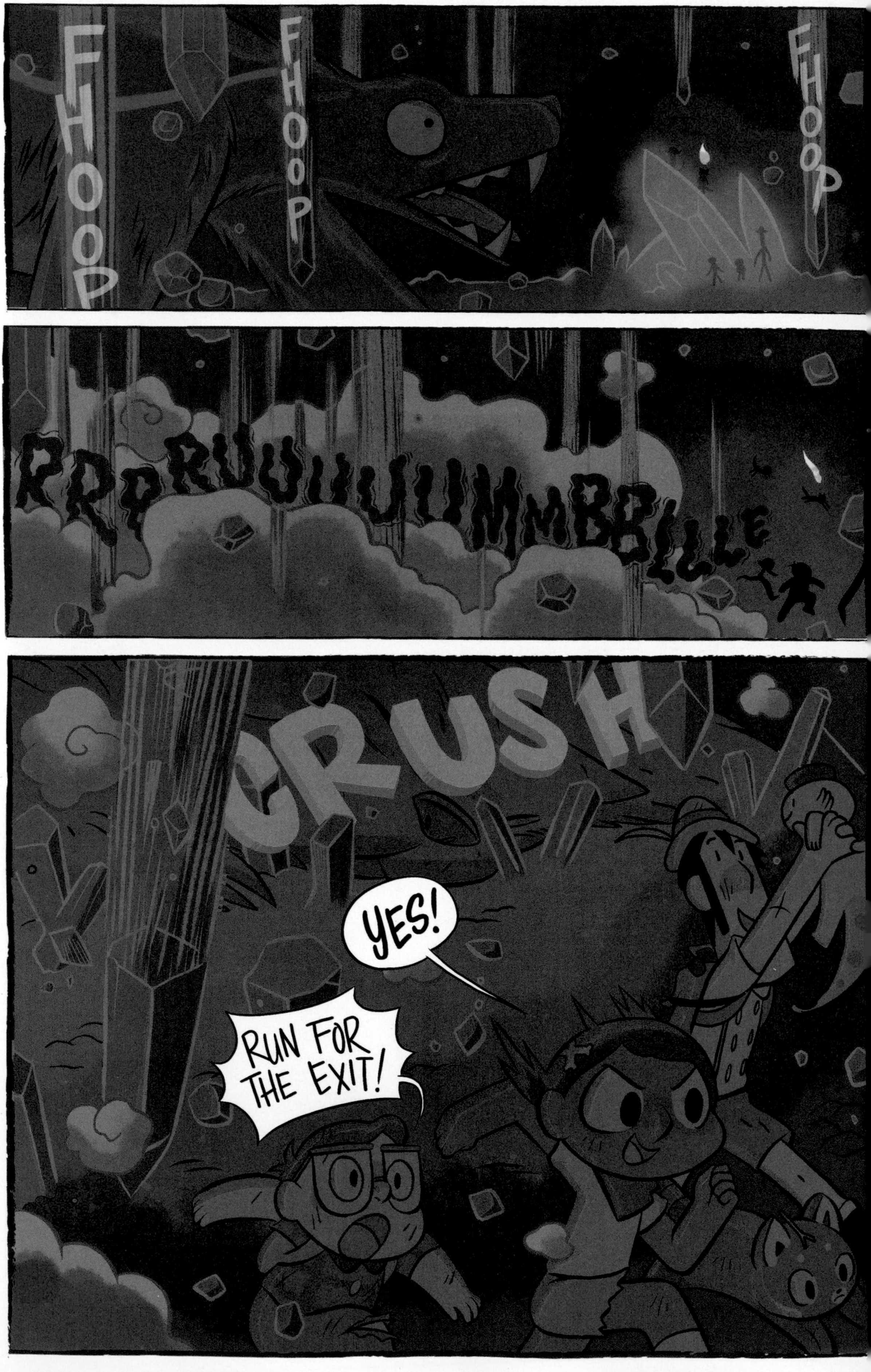
FHOOP
FHOOP
FHOOP
RRRRUUUUUMMBBLLLE
CRUSH
YES!
RUN FOR THE EXIT!

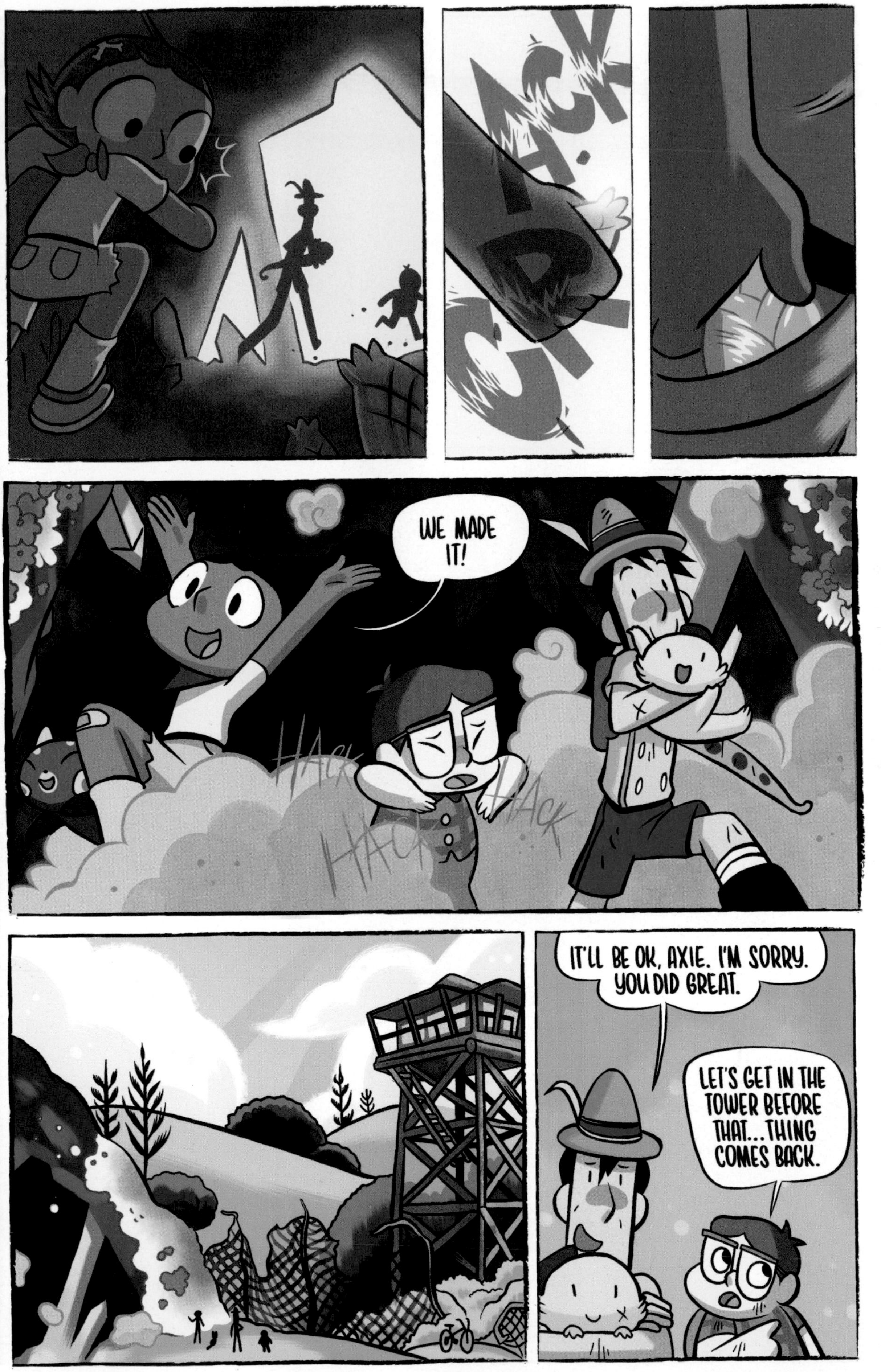
CRACK
WE MADE IT!
HACK
HACK
HACK
IT'LL BE OK, AXIE. I'M SORRY. YOU DID GREAT.
LET'S GET IN THE TOWER BEFORE THAT...THING COMES BACK.

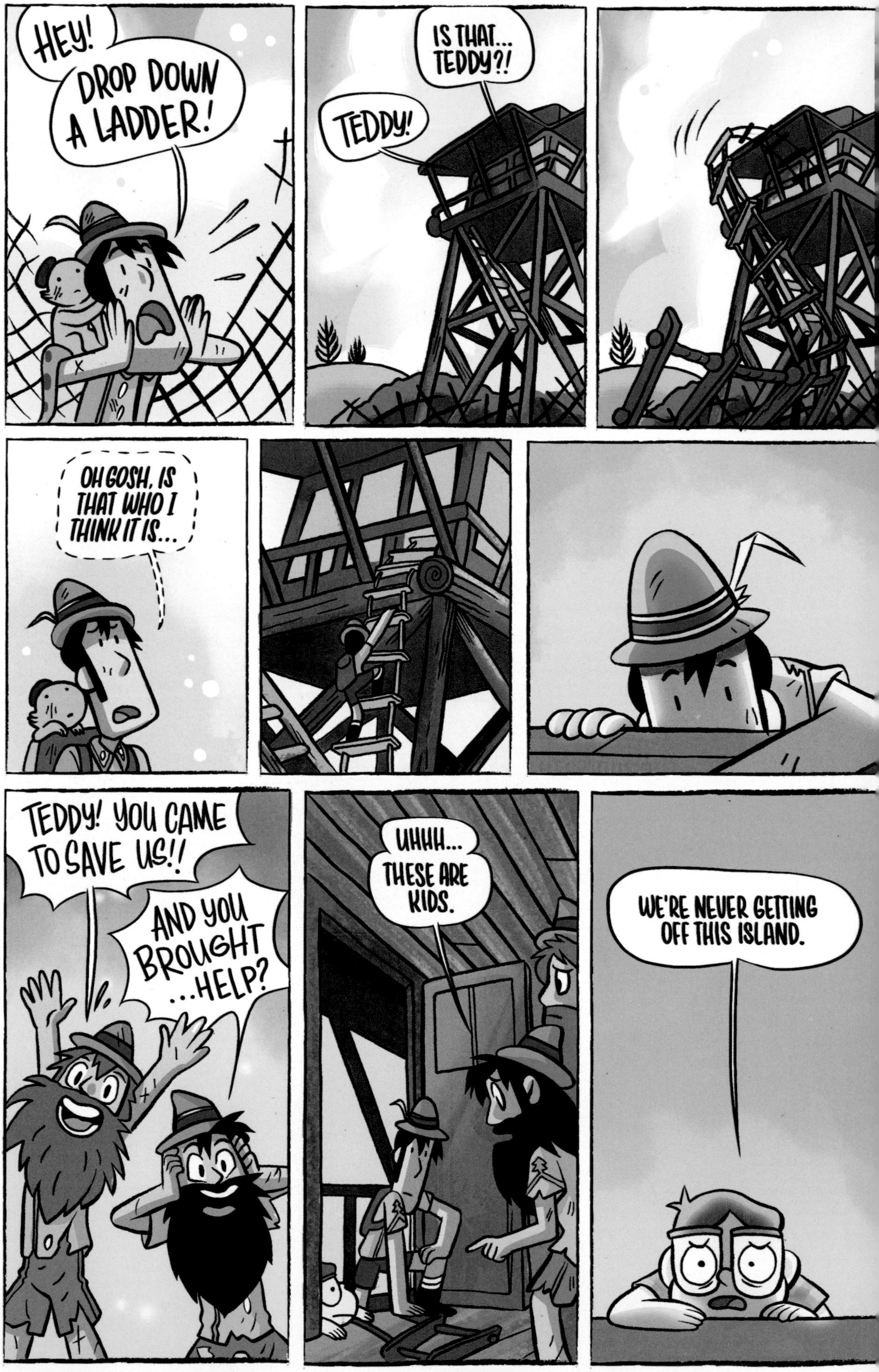
HEY!
DROP DOWN A LADDER!
IS THAT... TEDDY?!
TEDDY!
OH GOSH, IS THAT WHO I THINK IT IS...
TEDDY! YOU CAME TO SAVE US!!
AND YOU BROUGHT ...HELP?
UHHH... THESE ARE KIDS.
WE'RE NEVER GETTING OFF THIS ISLAND.

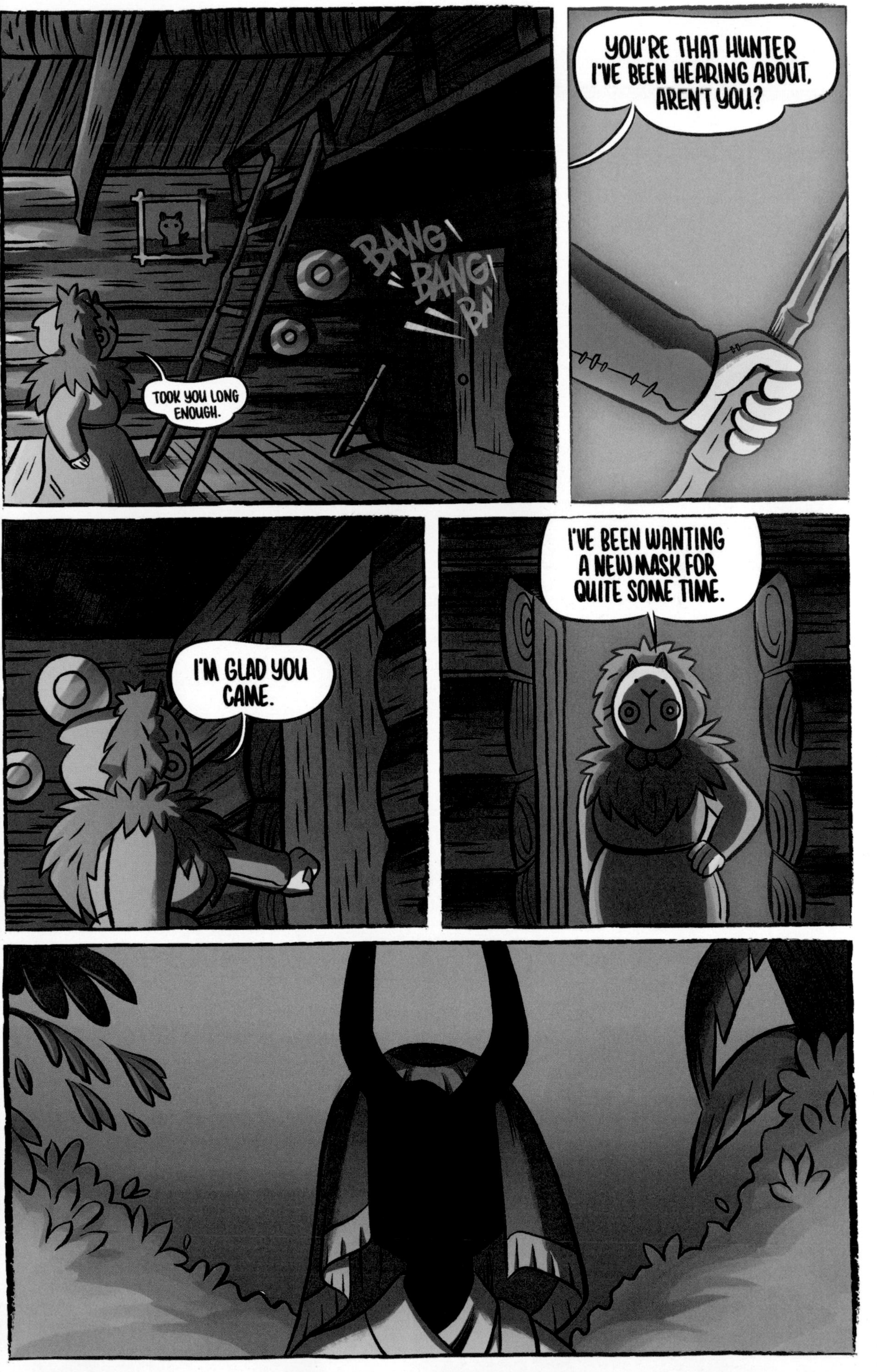
BANG
BANG
BA
TOOK YOU LONG ENOUGH.
YOU'RE THAT HUNTER I'VE BEEN HEARING ABOUT, AREN'T YOU?
I'M GLAD YOU CAME.
I'VE BEEN WANTING A NEW MASK FOR QUITE SOME TIME.

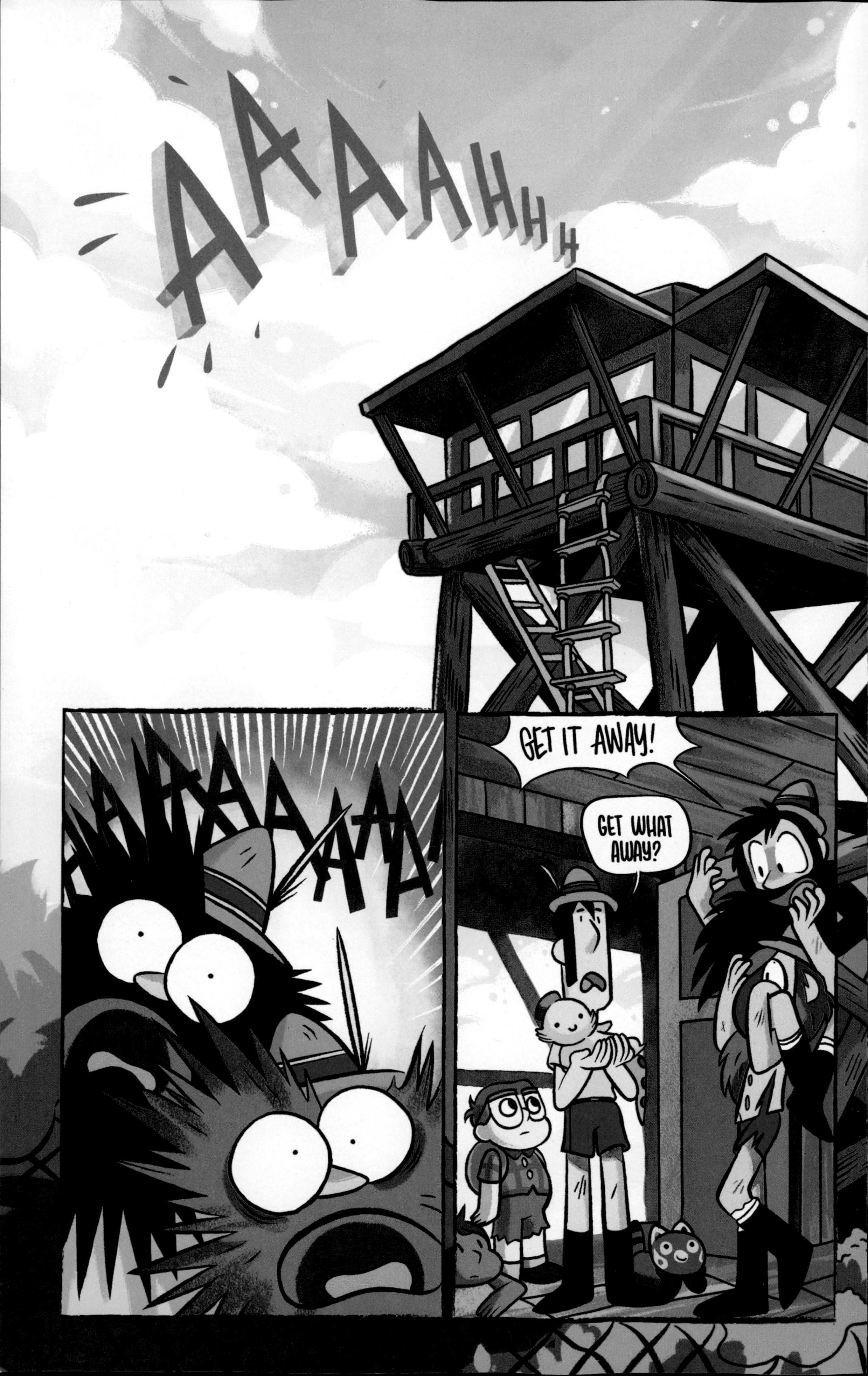
AAAAAHHHH
GET IT AWAY!
GET WHAT AWAY?

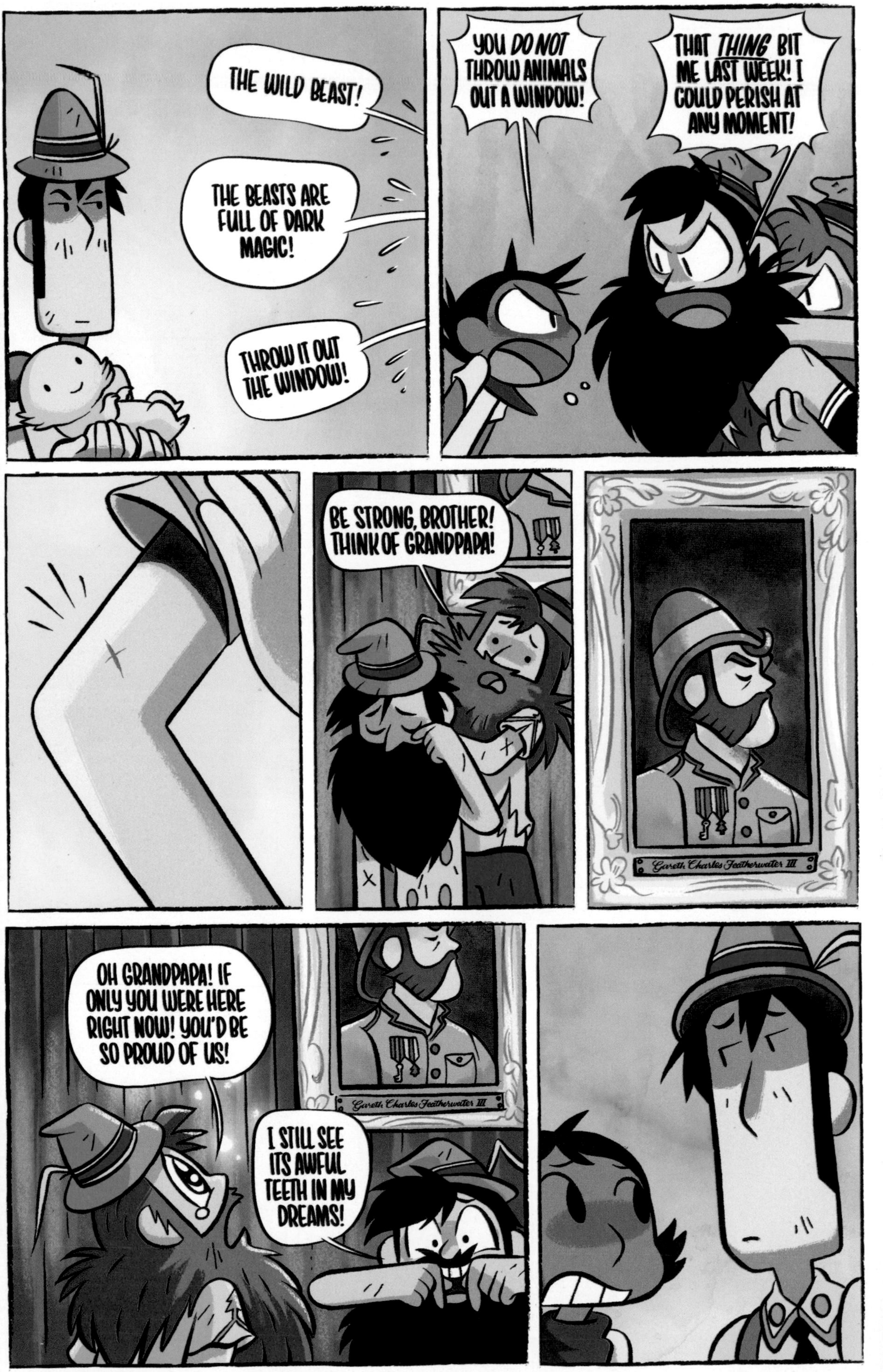
THE WILD BEAST!
THE BEASTS ARE FULL OF DARK MAGIC!
THROW IT OUT THE WINDOW!
YOU DO NOT THROW ANIMALS OUT A WINDOW!
THAT THING BIT ME LAST WEEK! I COULD PERISH AT ANY MOMENT!
BE STRONG, BROTHER! THINK OF GRANDPAPA!
Gareth Charles Featherwater III
OH GRANDPAPA! IF ONLY YOU WERE HERE RIGHT NOW! YOU'D BE SO PROUD OF US!
Gareth Charles Featherwater III
I STILL SEE ITS AWFUL TEETH IN MY DREAMS!

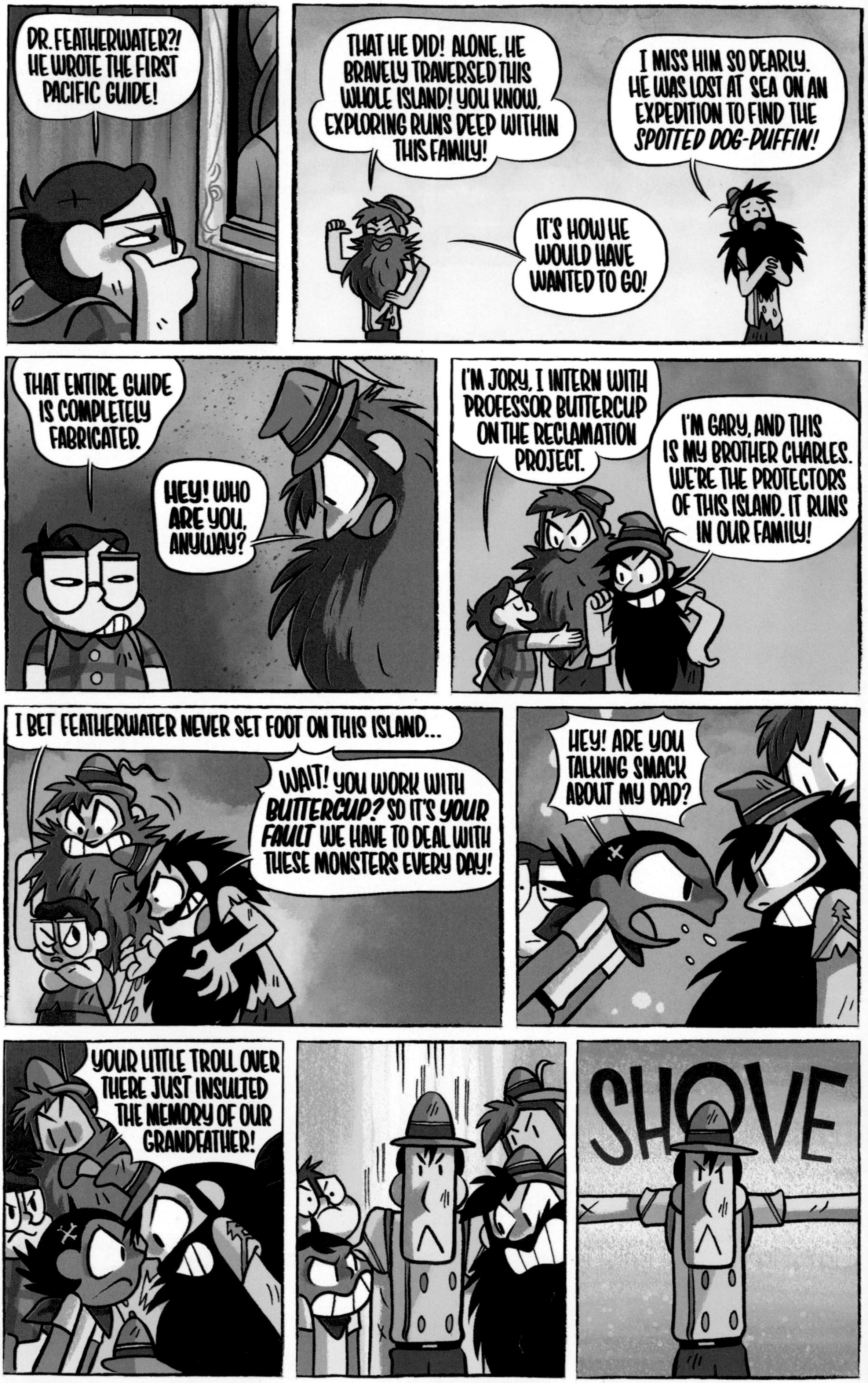
DR. FEATHERWATER?! HE WROTE THE FIRST PACIFIC GUIDE!
THAT HE DID! ALONE, HE BRAVELY TRAVERSED THIS WHOLE ISLAND! YOU KNOW, EXPLORING RUNS DEEP WITHIN THIS FAMILY!
I MISS HIM SO DEARLY. HE WAS LOST AT SEA ON AN EXPEDITION TO FIND THE *SPOTTED DOG-PUFFIN!*
IT'S HOW HE WOULD HAVE WANTED TO GO!
THAT ENTIRE GUIDE IS COMPLETELY FABRICATED.
HEY! WHO **ARE** YOU, ANYWAY?
I'M JORY, I INTERN WITH PROFESSOR BUTTERCUP ON THE RECLAMATION PROJECT.
I'M GARY, AND THIS IS MY BROTHER CHARLES. WE'RE THE PROTECTORS OF THIS ISLAND. IT RUNS IN OUR FAMILY!
I BET FEATHERWATER NEVER SET FOOT ON THIS ISLAND...
WAIT! YOU WORK WITH ***BUTTERCUP?*** SO IT'S ***YOUR FAULT*** WE HAVE TO DEAL WITH THESE MONSTERS EVERY DAY!
HEY! ARE YOU TALKING SMACK ABOUT MY DAD?
YOUR LITTLE TROLL OVER THERE JUST INSULTED THE MEMORY OF OUR GRANDFATHER!
SHOVE

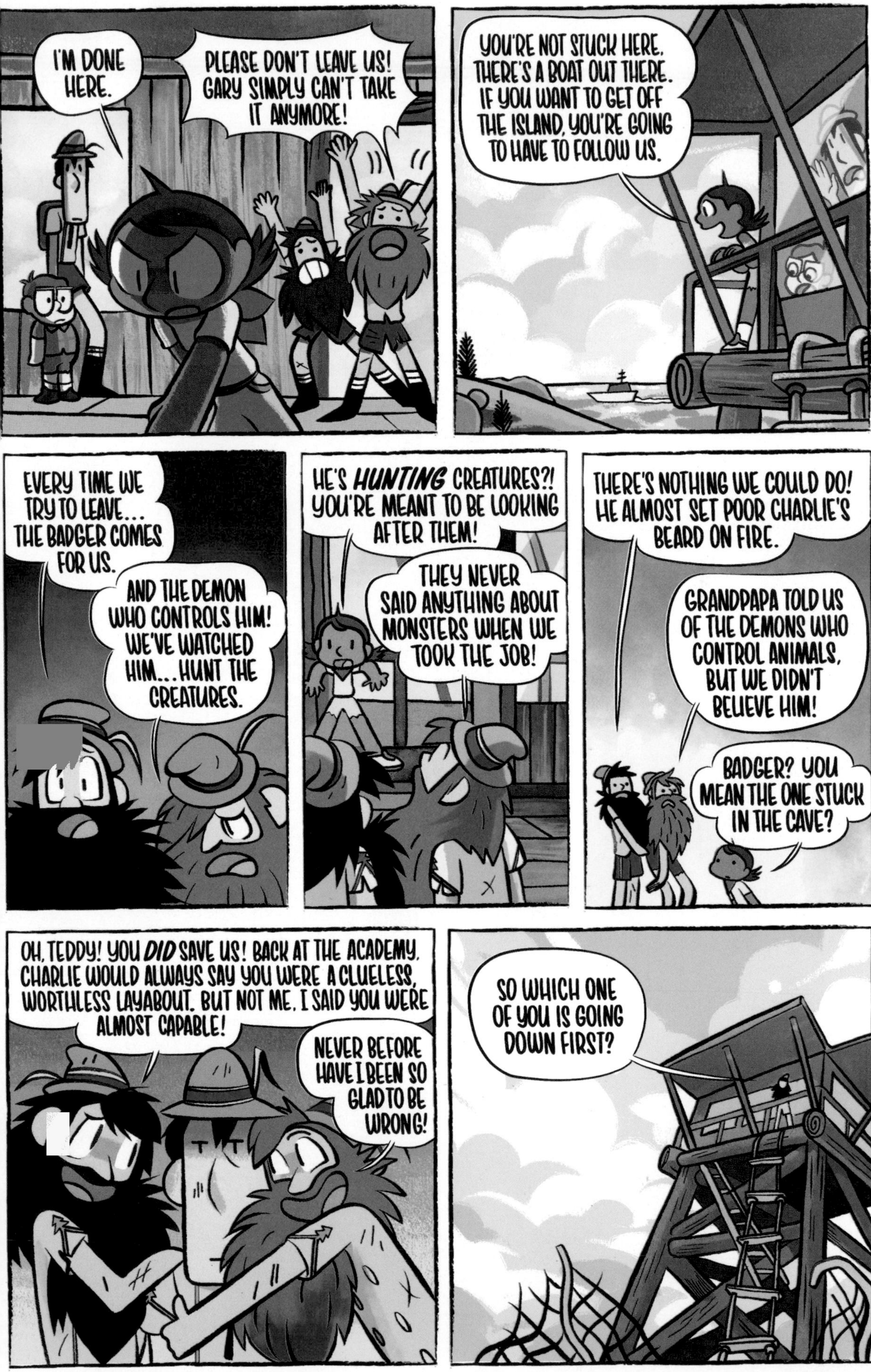
I'M DONE HERE.
PLEASE DON'T LEAVE US! GARY SIMPLY CAN'T TAKE IT ANYMORE!
YOU'RE NOT STUCK HERE. THERE'S A BOAT OUT THERE. IF YOU WANT TO GET OFF THE ISLAND, YOU'RE GOING TO HAVE TO FOLLOW US.
EVERY TIME WE TRY TO LEAVE... THE BADGER COMES FOR US.
AND THE DEMON WHO CONTROLS HIM! WE'VE WATCHED HIM... HUNT THE CREATURES.
HE'S *HUNTING* CREATURES?! YOU'RE MEANT TO BE LOOKING AFTER THEM!
THEY NEVER SAID ANYTHING ABOUT MONSTERS WHEN WE TOOK THE JOB!
THERE'S NOTHING WE COULD DO! HE ALMOST SET POOR CHARLIE'S BEARD ON FIRE.
GRANDPAPA TOLD US OF THE DEMONS WHO CONTROL ANIMALS, BUT WE DIDN'T BELIEVE HIM!
BADGER? YOU MEAN THE ONE STUCK IN THE CAVE?
OH, TEDDY! YOU *DID* SAVE US! BACK AT THE ACADEMY, CHARLIE WOULD ALWAYS SAY YOU WERE A CLUELESS, WORTHLESS LAYABOUT. BUT NOT ME. I SAID YOU WERE ALMOST CAPABLE!
NEVER BEFORE HAVE I BEEN SO GLAD TO BE WRONG!
SO WHICH ONE OF YOU IS GOING DOWN FIRST?

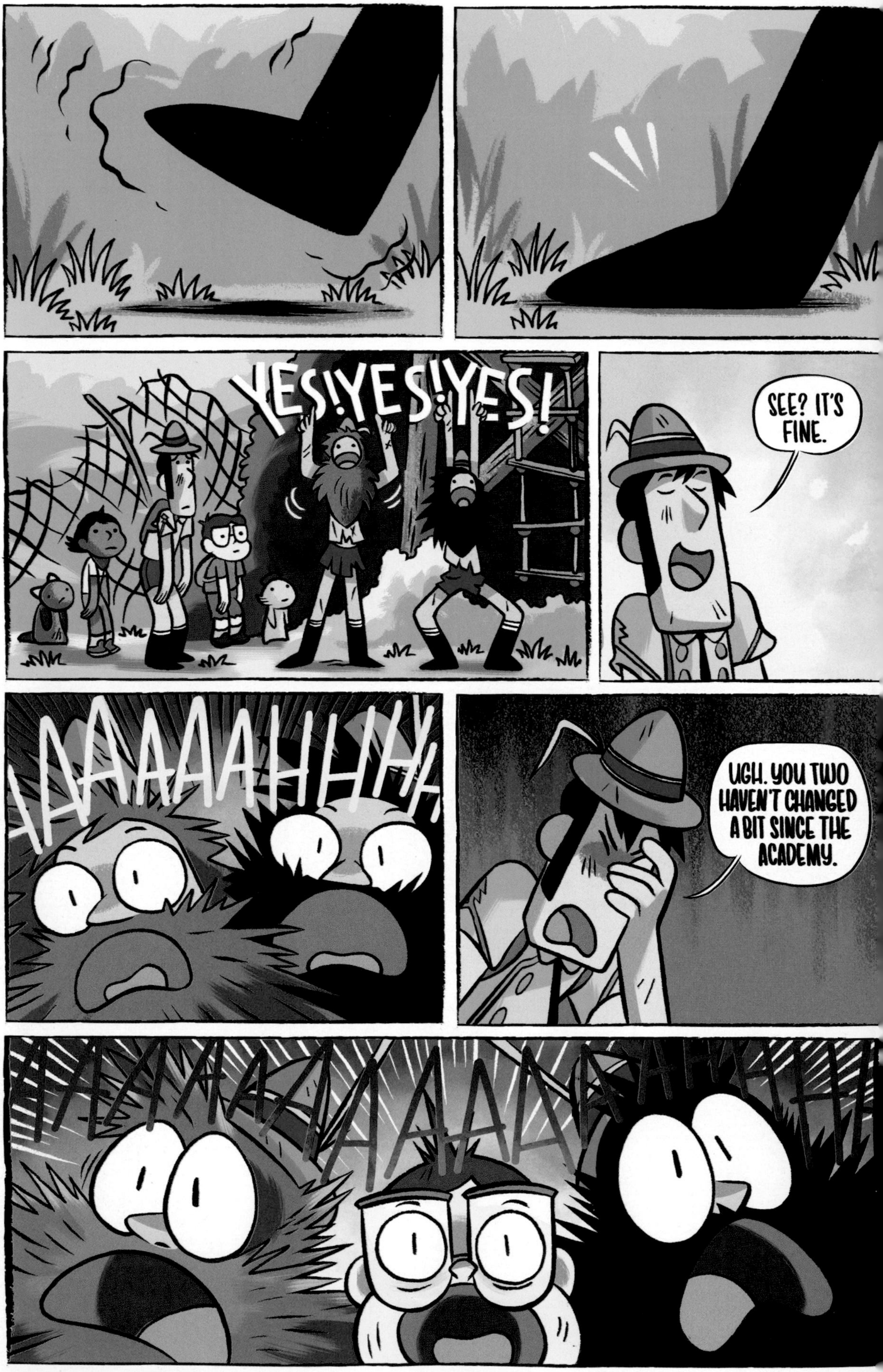

YES!YES!YES!
SEE? IT'S FINE.
AAAAAHHHH
UGH. YOU TWO HAVEN'T CHANGED A BIT SINCE THE ACADEMY.
AAAAAAAAAAAAAHHHH

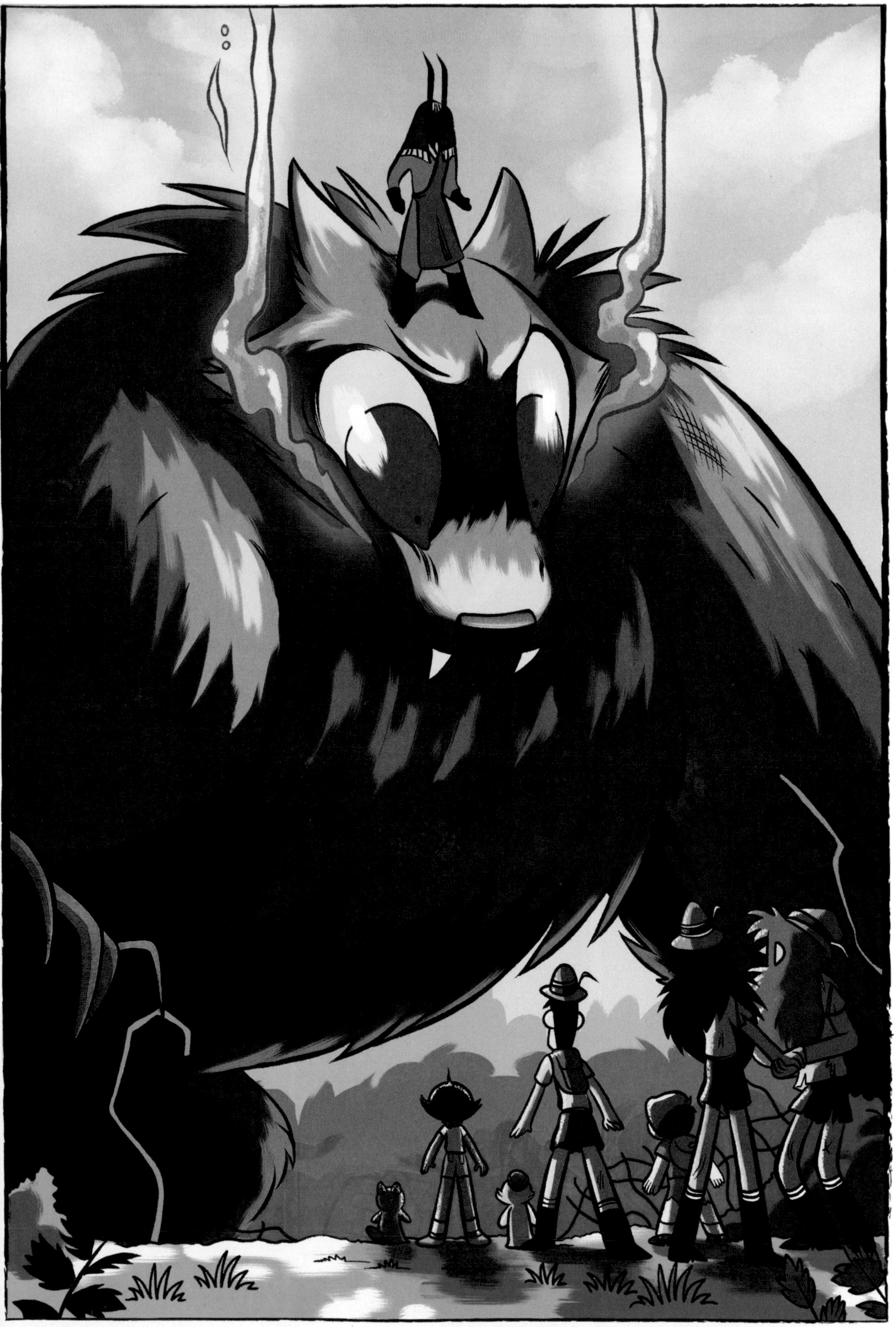

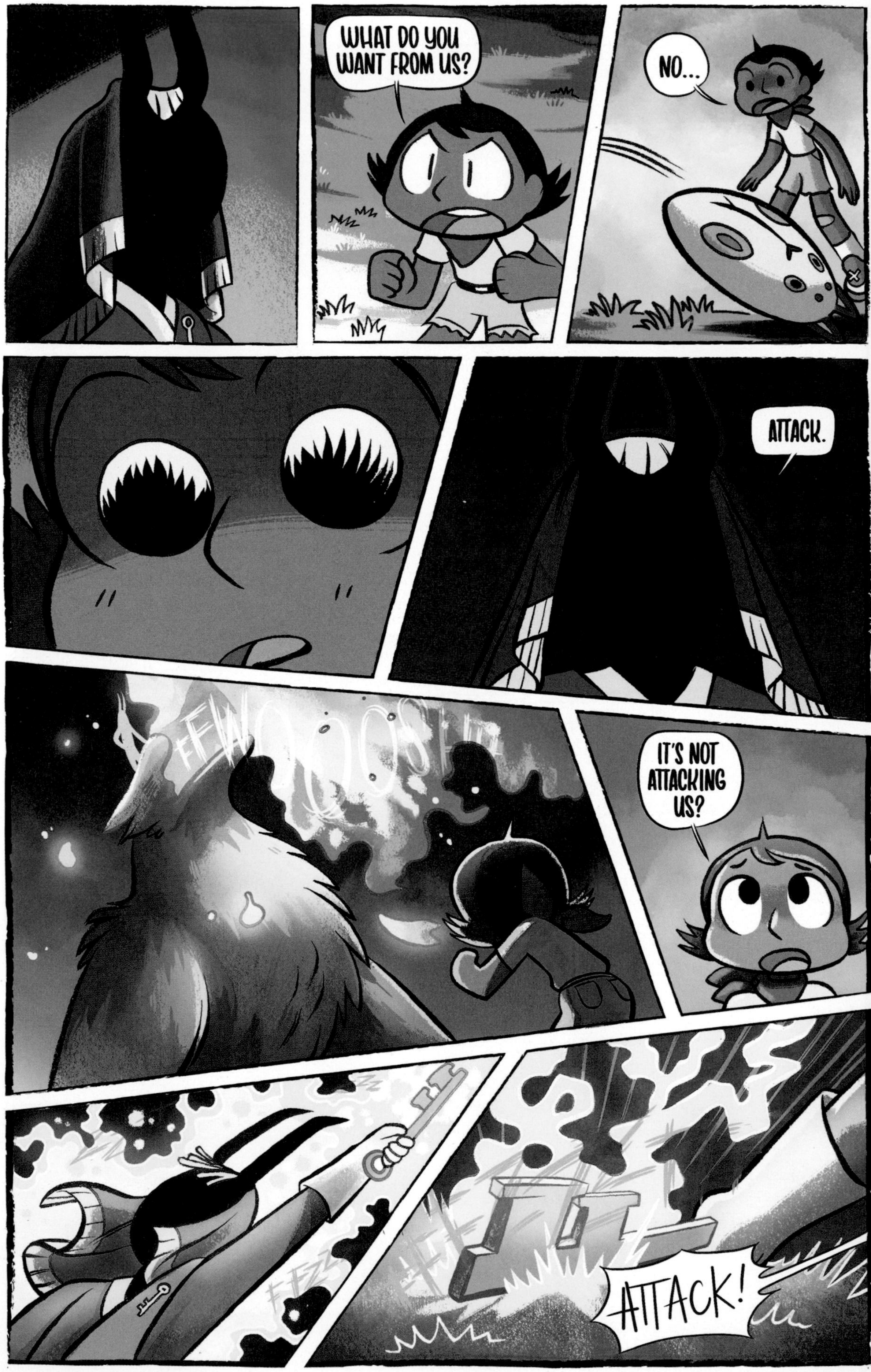
WHAT DO YOU WANT FROM US?
NO...
ATTACK.
FFWOOOSH
IT'S NOT ATTACKING US?
ATTACK!

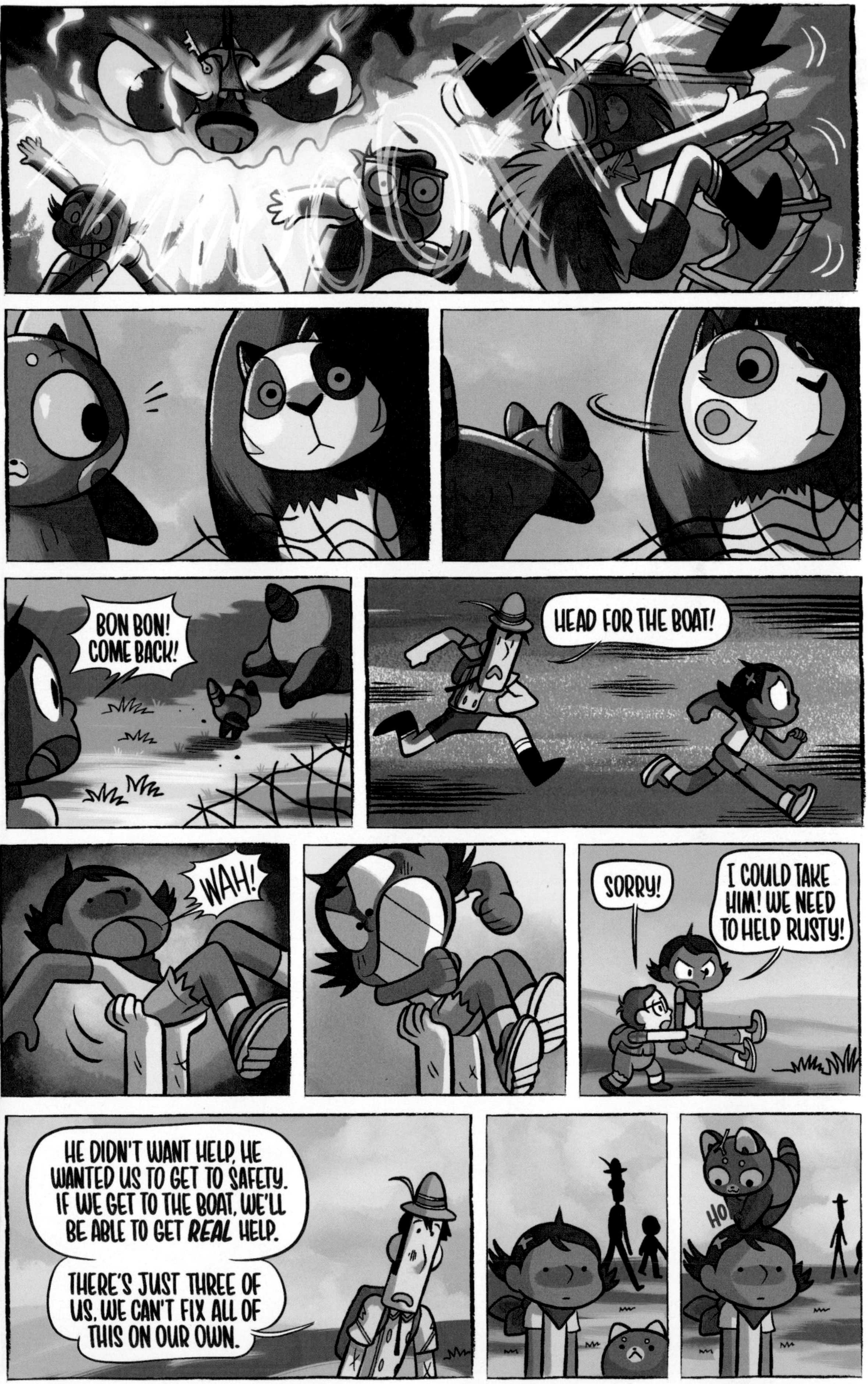
BON BON! COME BACK!
HEAD FOR THE BOAT!
WAH!
SORRY!
I COULD TAKE HIM! WE NEED TO HELP RUSTY!
HE DIDN'T WANT HELP, HE WANTED US TO GET TO SAFETY. IF WE GET TO THE BOAT, WE'LL BE ABLE TO GET REAL HELP.
THERE'S JUST THREE OF US, WE CAN'T FIX ALL OF THIS ON OUR OWN.

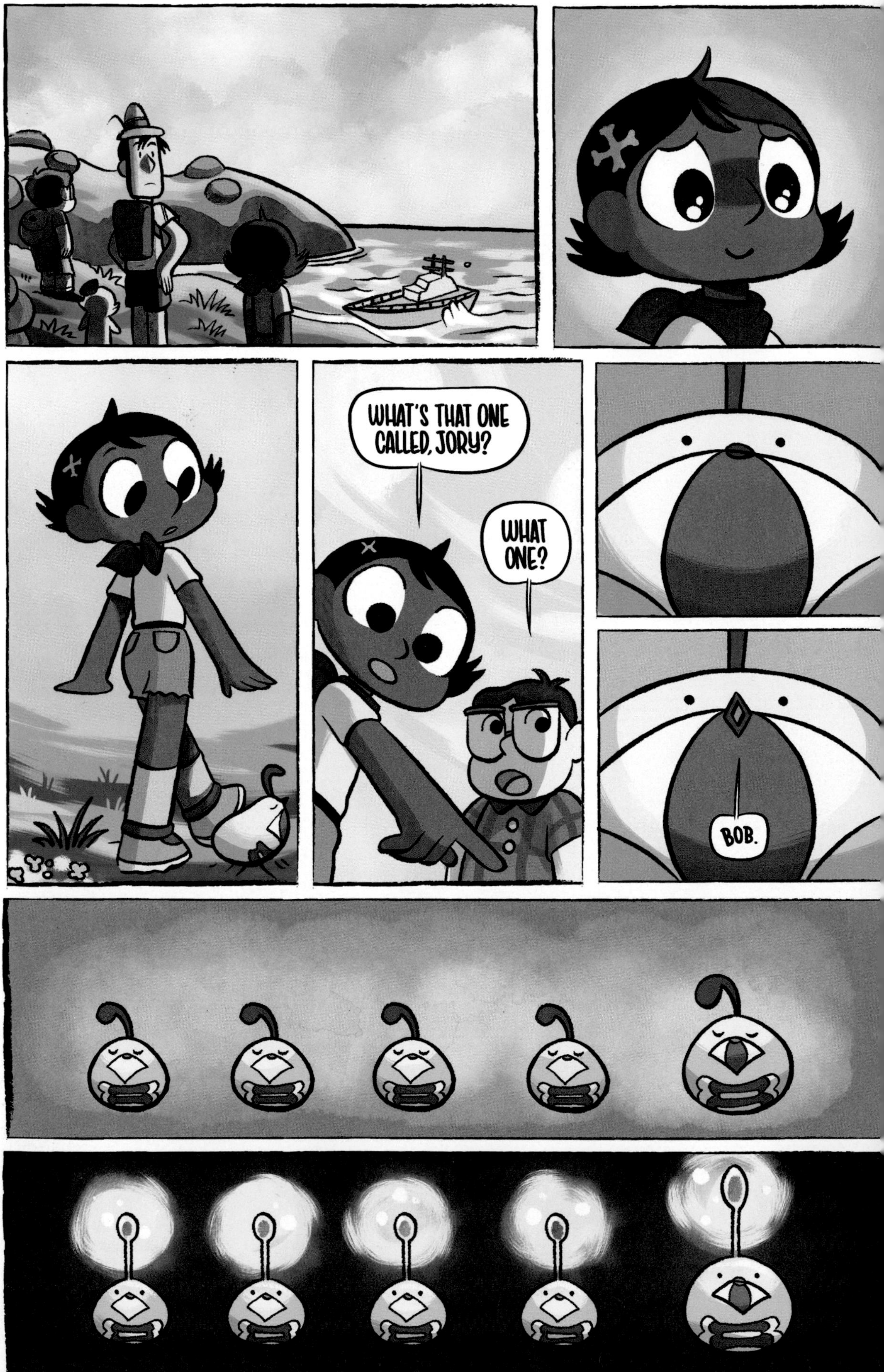
WHAT'S THAT ONE CALLED, JORY?
WHAT ONE?
BOB.

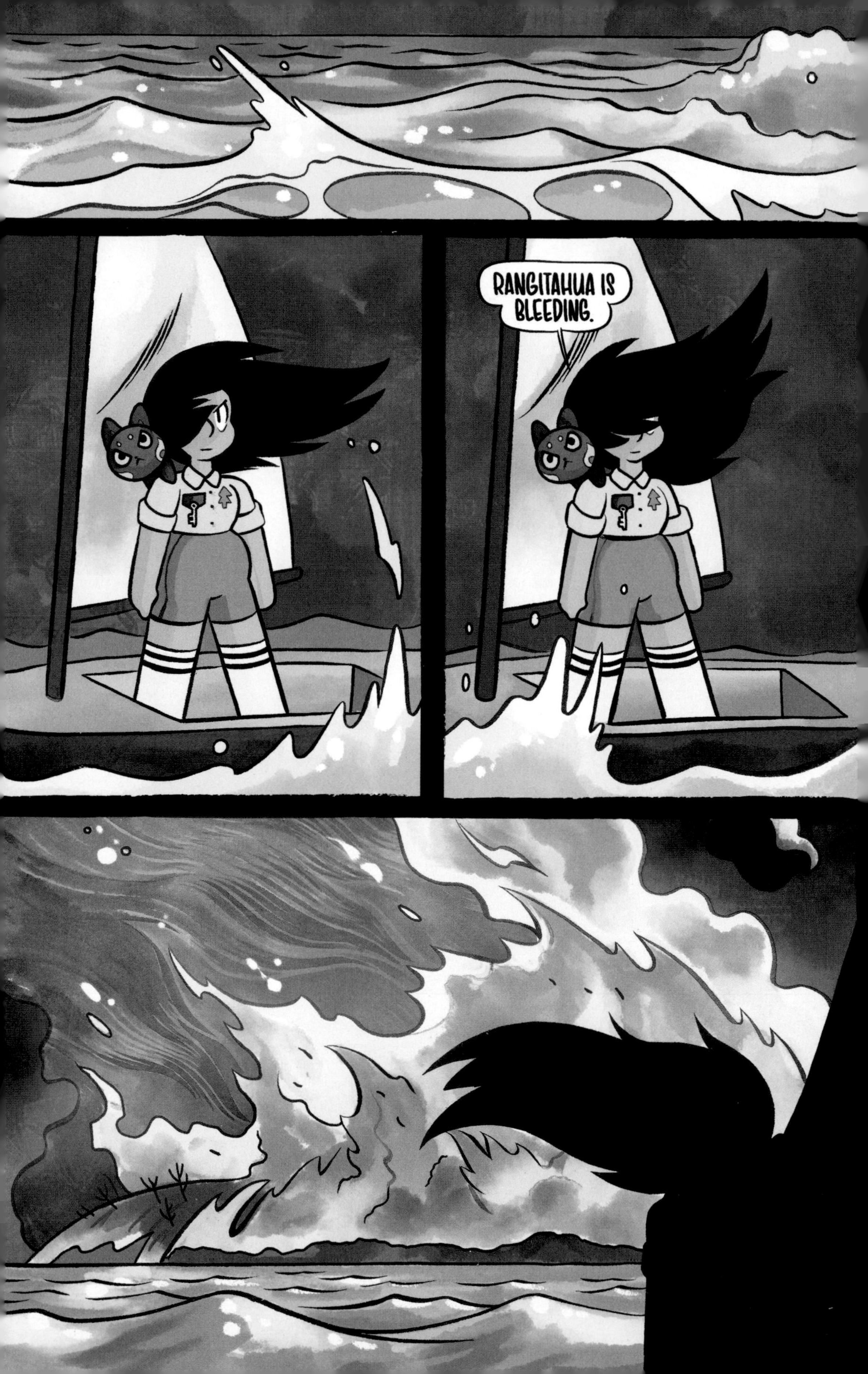
RANGITAHUA IS BLEEDING.

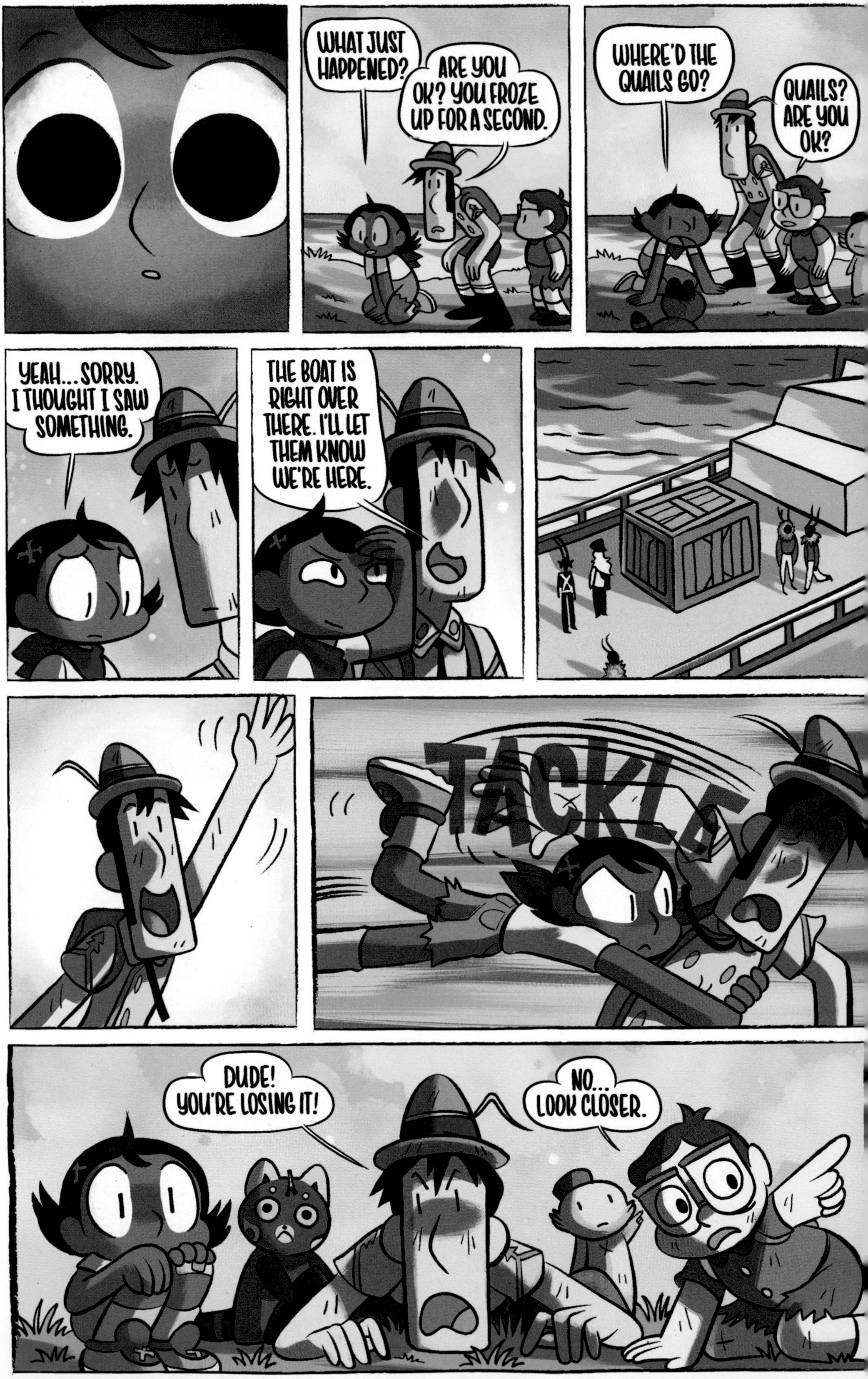
WHAT JUST HAPPENED?
ARE YOU OK? YOU FROZE UP FOR A SECOND.
WHERE'D THE QUAILS GO?
QUAILS? ARE YOU OK?
YEAH... SORRY. I THOUGHT I SAW SOMETHING.
THE BOAT IS RIGHT OVER THERE. I'LL LET THEM KNOW WE'RE HERE.
TACKLE
DUDE! YOU'RE LOSING IT!
NO... LOOK CLOSER.

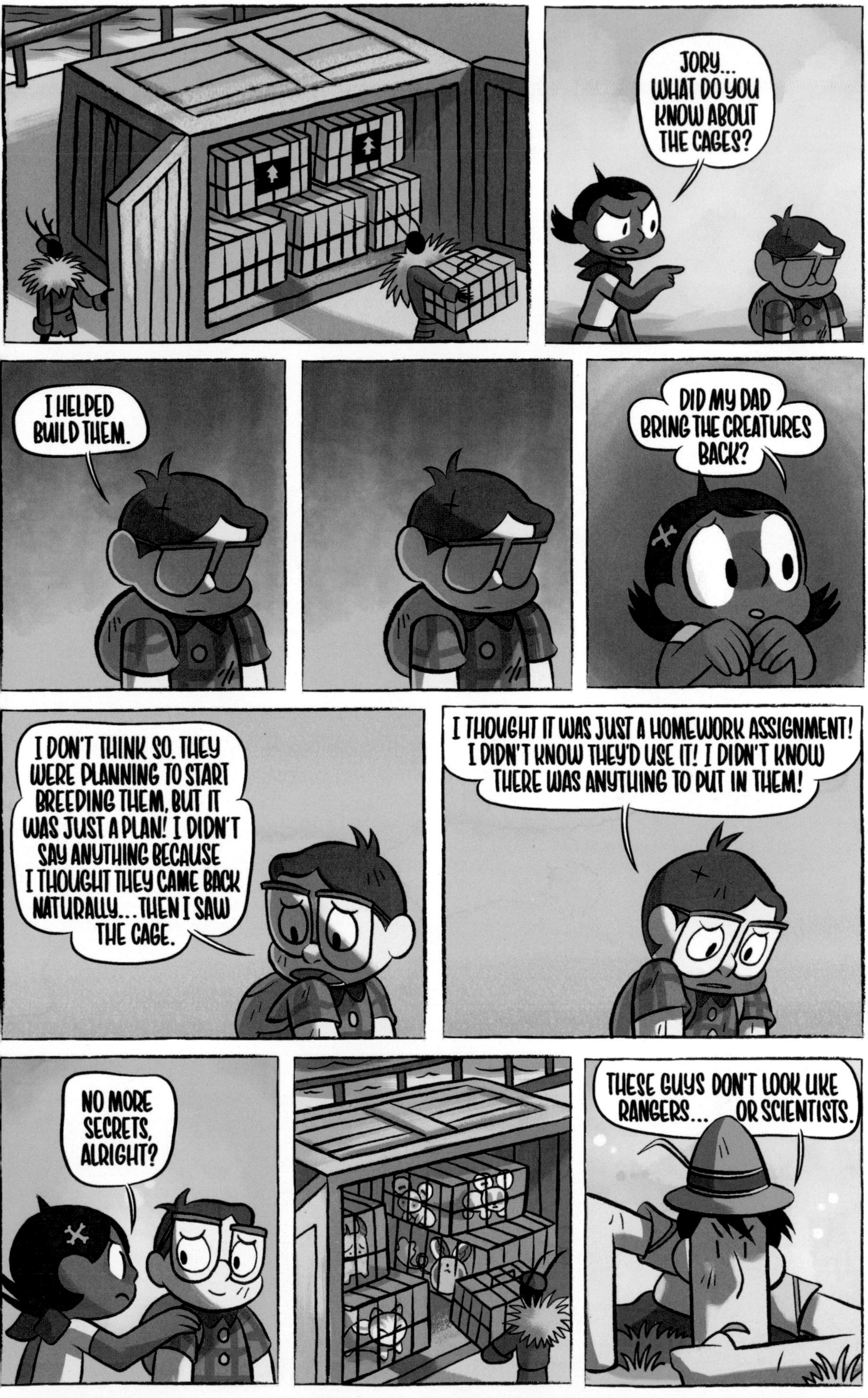
JORY... WHAT DO YOU KNOW ABOUT THE CAGES?
I HELPED BUILD THEM.
DID MY DAD BRING THE CREATURES BACK?
I DON'T THINK SO. THEY WERE PLANNING TO START BREEDING THEM, BUT IT WAS JUST A PLAN! I DIDN'T SAY ANYTHING BECAUSE I THOUGHT THEY CAME BACK NATURALLY... THEN I SAW THE CAGE.
I THOUGHT IT WAS JUST A HOMEWORK ASSIGNMENT! I DIDN'T KNOW THEY'D USE IT! I DIDN'T KNOW THERE WAS ANYTHING TO PUT IN THEM!
NO MORE SECRETS, ALRIGHT?
THESE GUYS DON'T LOOK LIKE RANGERS... OR SCIENTISTS.

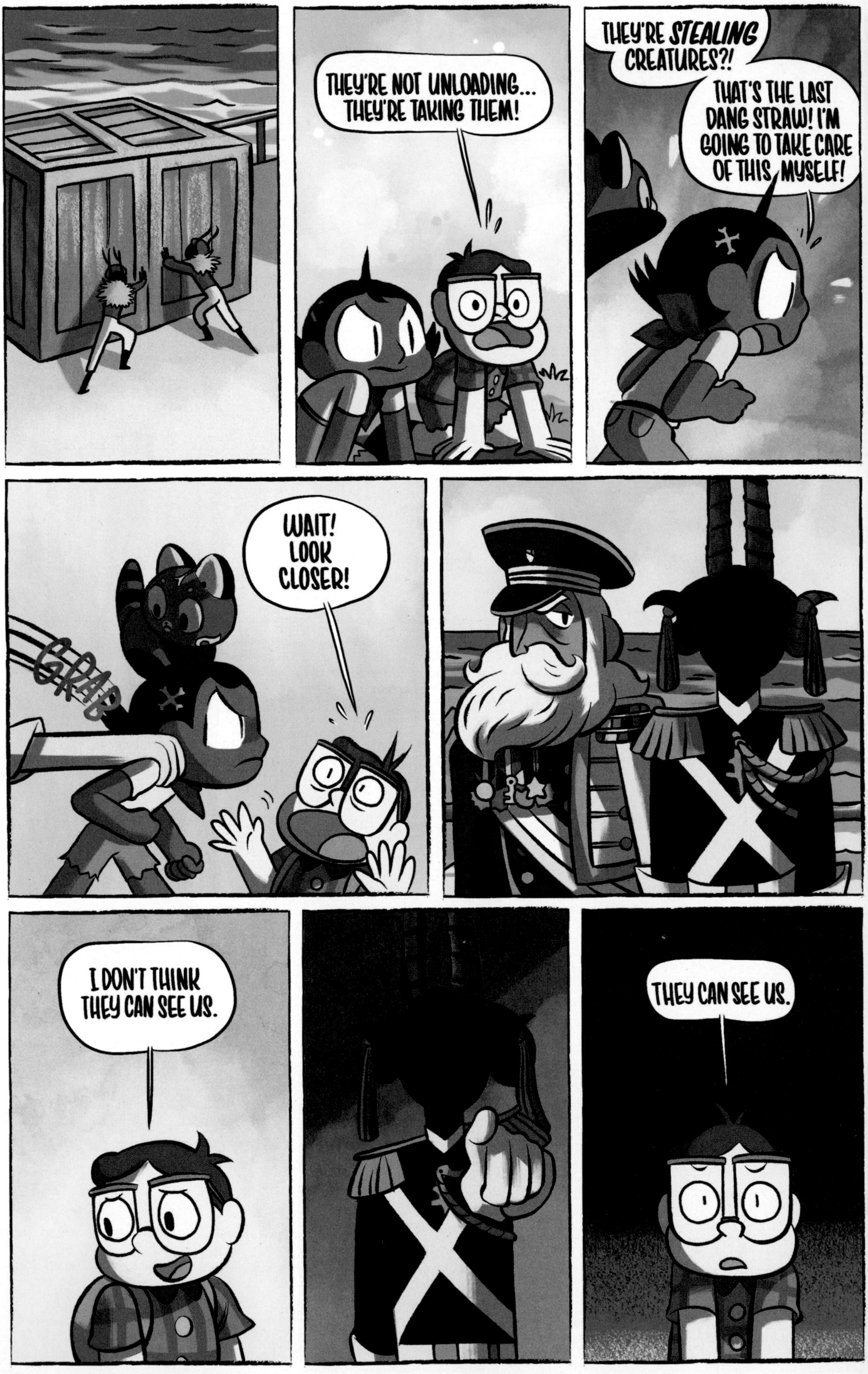
THEY'RE NOT UNLOADING... THEY'RE TAKING THEM!
THEY'RE *STEALING* CREATURES?!
THAT'S THE LAST DANG STRAW! I'M GOING TO TAKE CARE OF THIS MYSELF!
GRAB
WAIT! LOOK CLOSER!
I DON'T THINK THEY CAN SEE US.
THEY CAN SEE US.

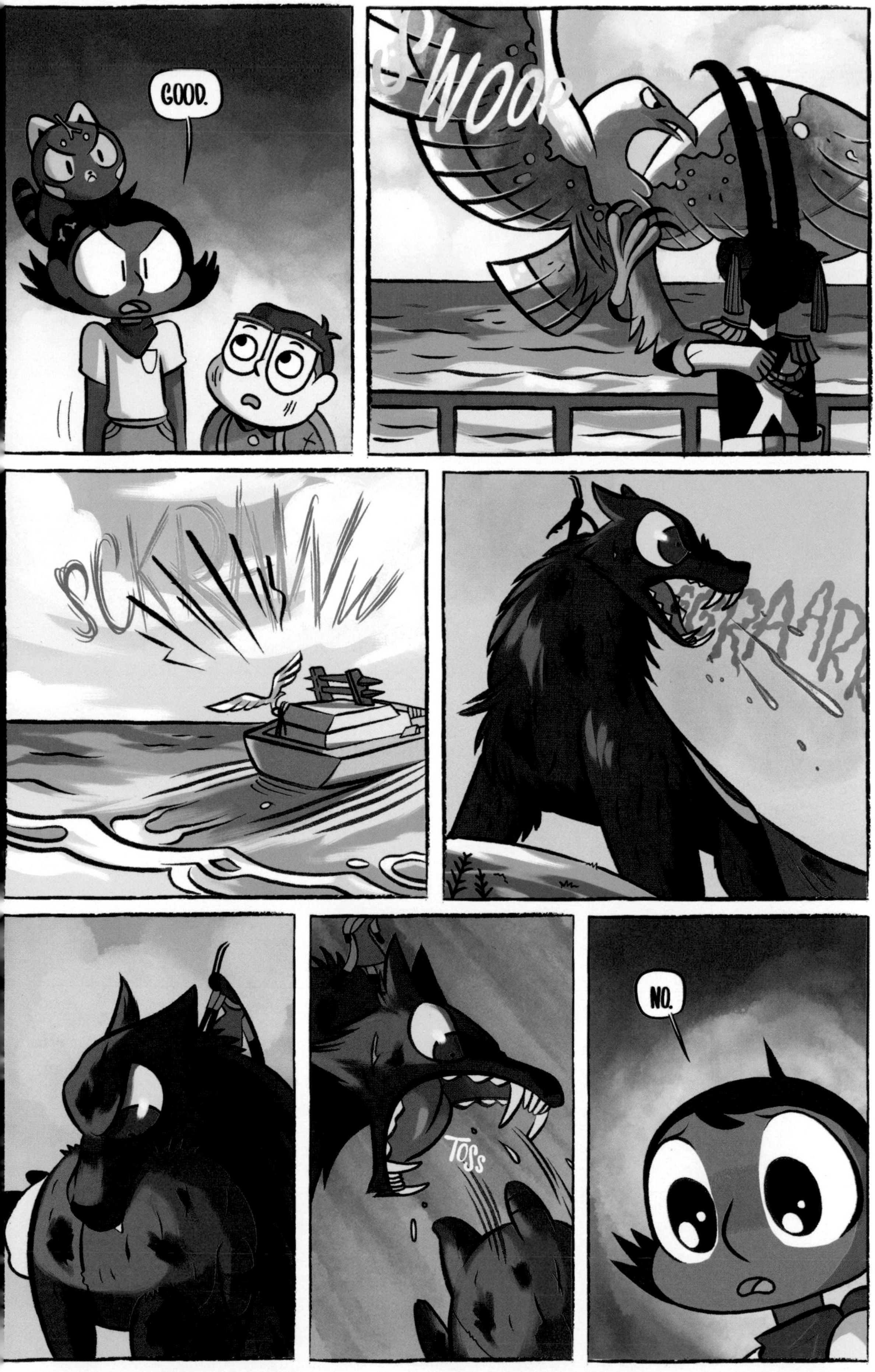
GOOD.
SWOOP
SCKRAW
GRAARR
TOSS
NO.

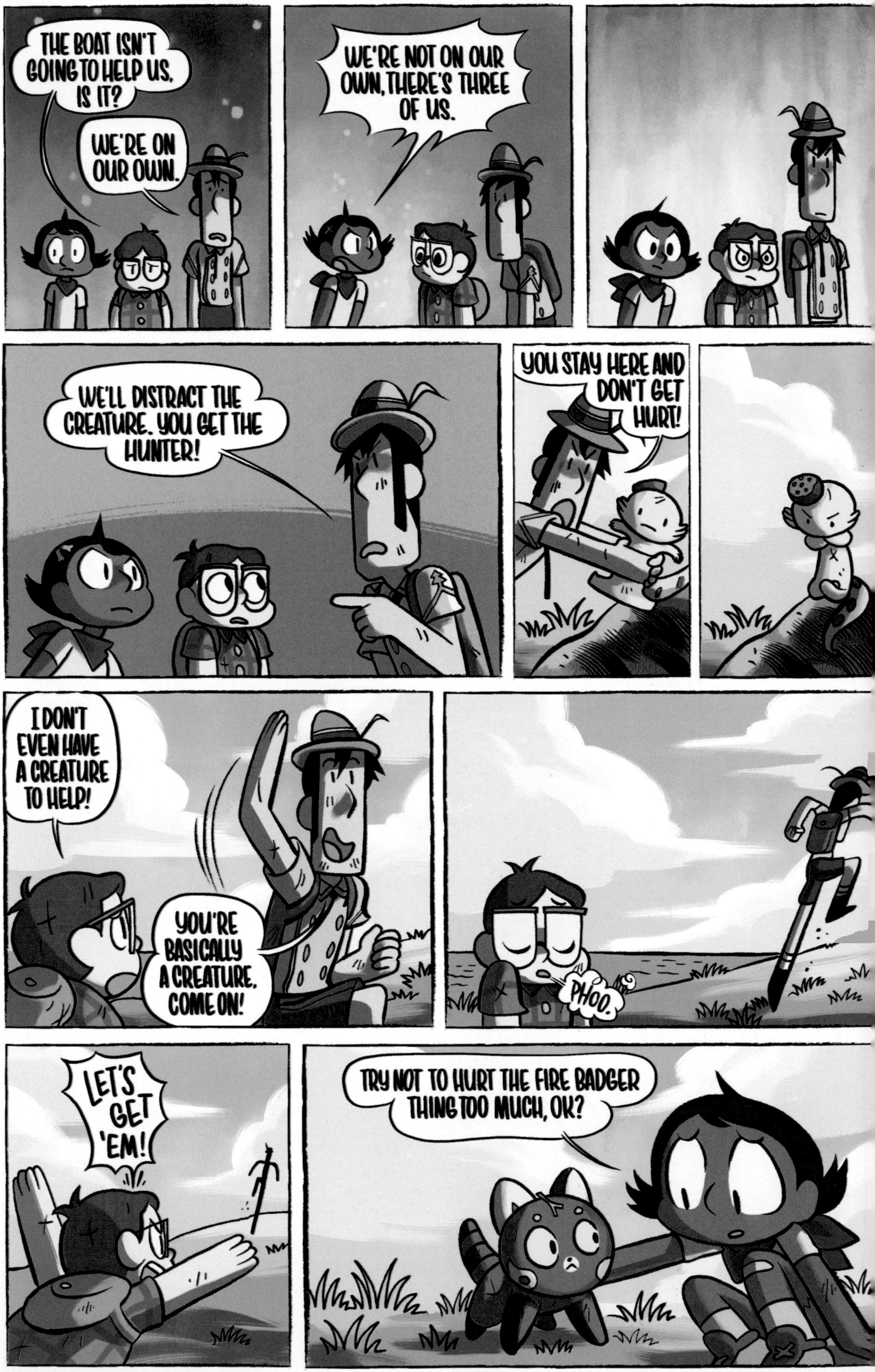
THE BOAT ISN'T GOING TO HELP US, IS IT?
WE'RE ON OUR OWN.
WE'RE NOT ON OUR OWN, THERE'S THREE OF US.
WE'LL DISTRACT THE CREATURE. YOU GET THE HUNTER!
YOU STAY HERE AND DON'T GET HURT!
I DON'T EVEN HAVE A CREATURE TO HELP!
YOU'RE BASICALLY A CREATURE. COME ON!
PHOO.
LET'S GET 'EM!
TRY NOT TO HURT THE FIRE BADGER THING TOO MUCH, OK?

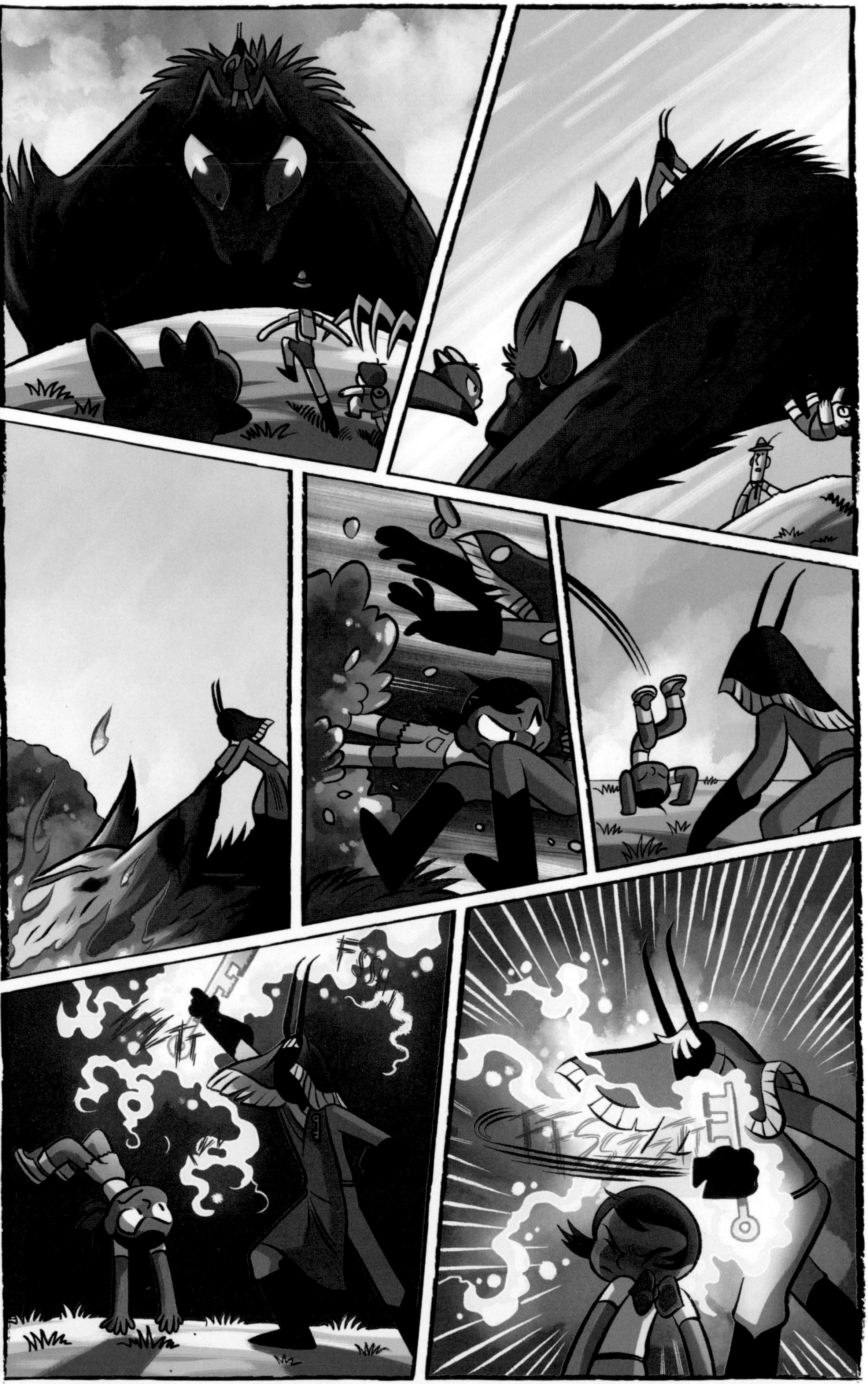

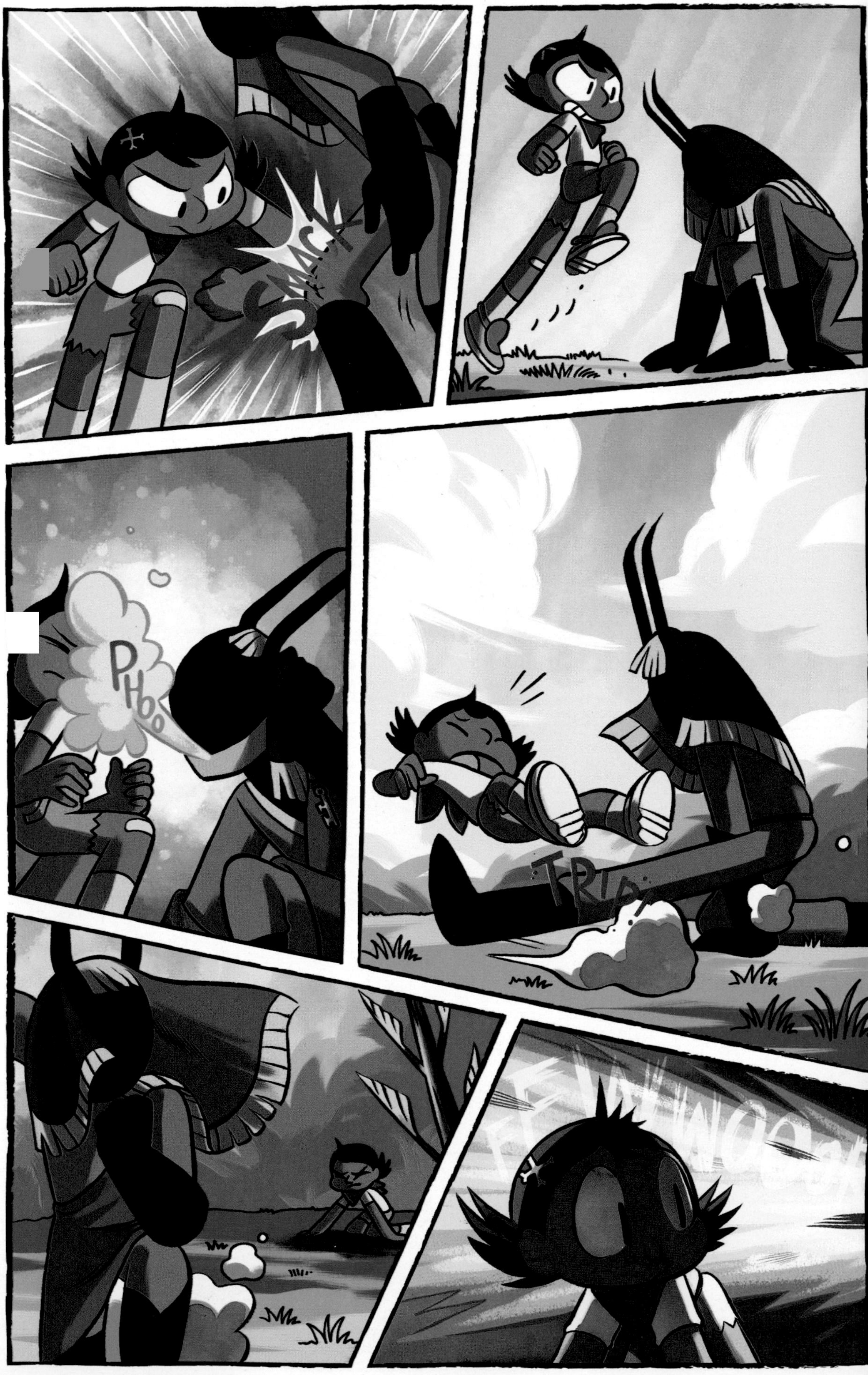
SMACK
PHoo
TRIP

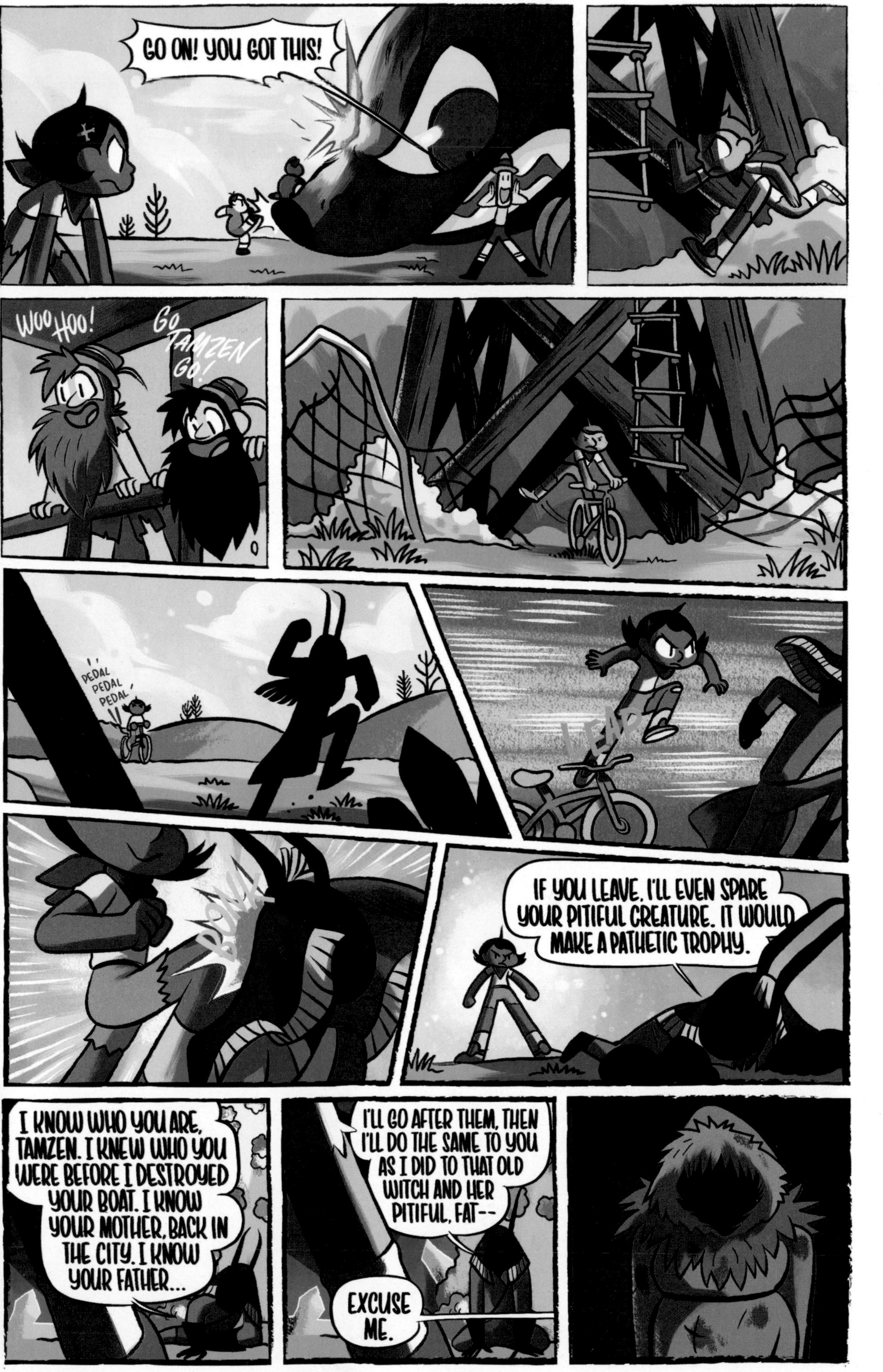
GO ON! YOU GOT THIS!
WOO HOO!
GO TAMZEN GO!
PEDAL PEDAL PEDAL
LEAP
BONK
IF YOU LEAVE, I'LL EVEN SPARE YOUR PITIFUL CREATURE. IT WOULD MAKE A PATHETIC TROPHY.
I KNOW WHO YOU ARE, TAMZEN. I KNEW WHO YOU WERE BEFORE I DESTROYED YOUR BOAT. I KNOW YOUR MOTHER, BACK IN THE CITY. I KNOW YOUR FATHER...
I'LL GO AFTER THEM, THEN I'LL DO THE SAME TO YOU AS I DID TO THAT OLD WITCH AND HER PITIFUL, FAT--
EXCUSE ME.

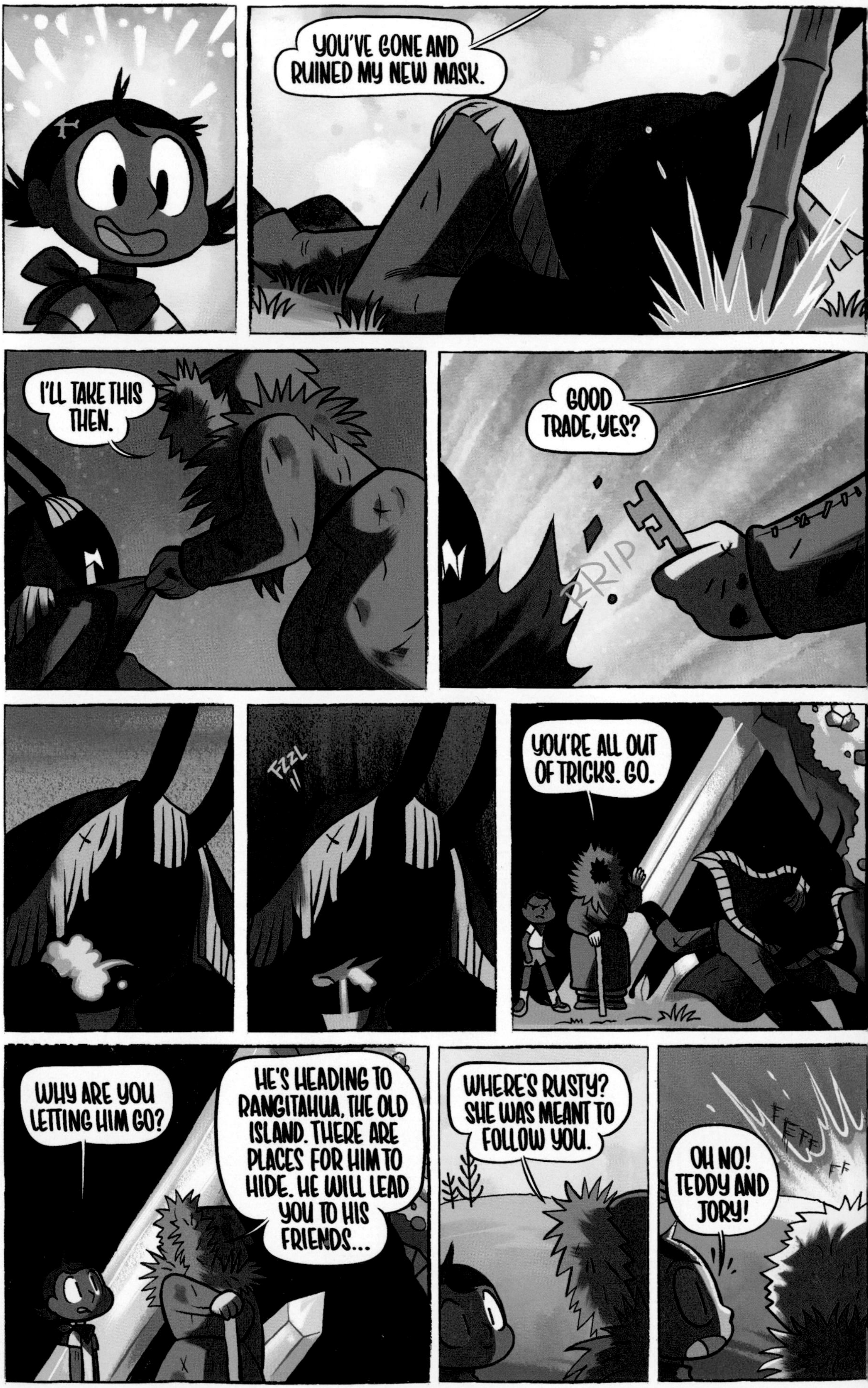
YOU'VE GONE AND RUINED MY NEW MASK.
I'LL TAKE THIS THEN.
GOOD TRADE, YES?
RRIP
FZZL
YOU'RE ALL OUT OF TRICKS. GO.
WHY ARE YOU LETTING HIM GO?
HE'S HEADING TO RANGITAHUA, THE OLD ISLAND. THERE ARE PLACES FOR HIM TO HIDE. HE WILL LEAD YOU TO HIS FRIENDS...
WHERE'S RUSTY? SHE WAS MEANT TO FOLLOW YOU.
FFFF
FF
OH NO! TEDDY AND JORY!

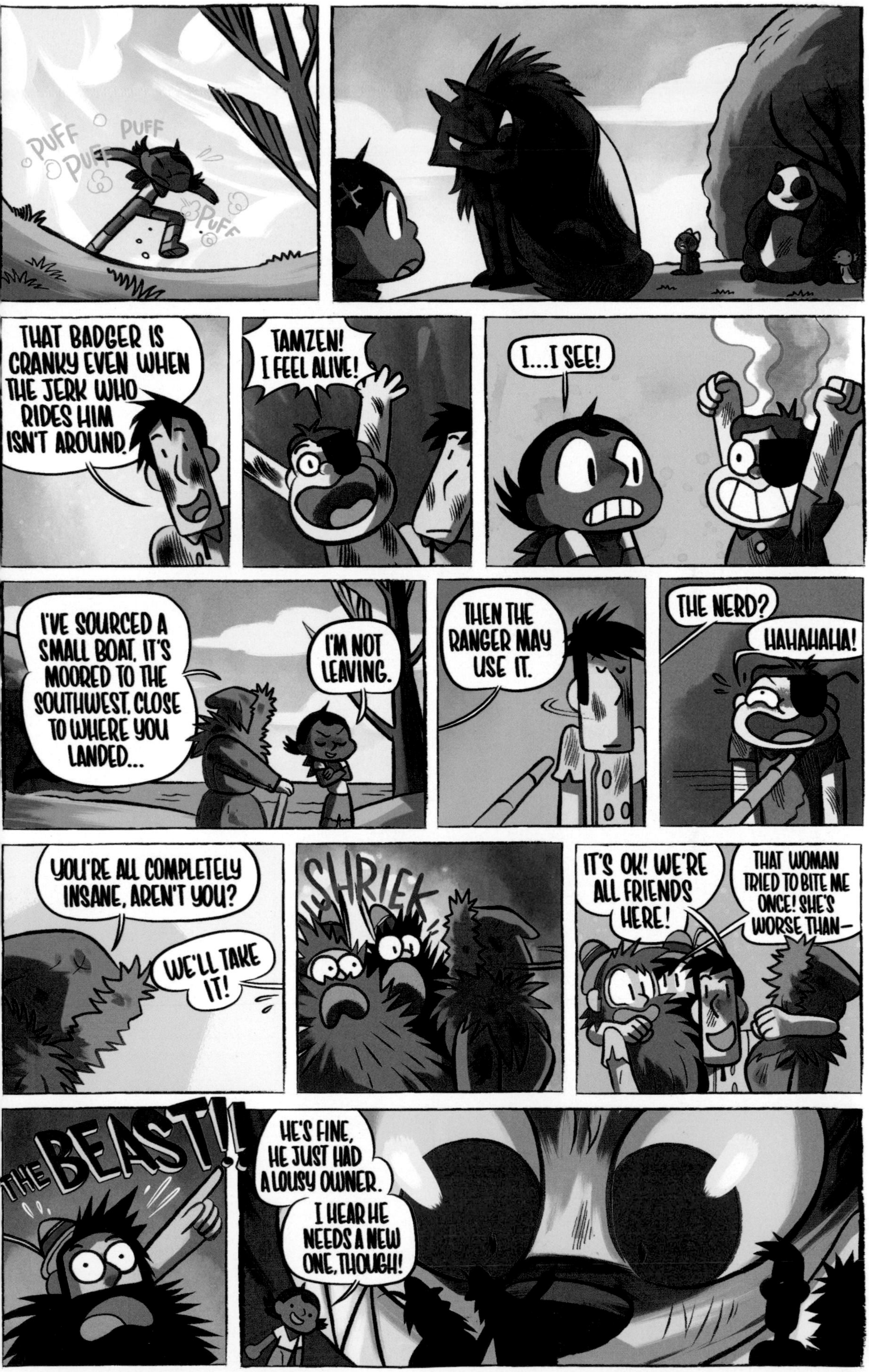
PUFF
PUFF
PUFF
PUFF
THAT BADGER IS CRANKY EVEN WHEN THE JERK WHO RIDES HIM ISN'T AROUND.
TAMZEN! I FEEL ALIVE!
I...I SEE!
I'VE SOURCED A SMALL BOAT, IT'S MOORED TO THE SOUTHWEST, CLOSE TO WHERE YOU LANDED...
I'M NOT LEAVING.
THEN THE RANGER MAY USE IT.
THE NERD?
HAHAHAHA!
YOU'RE ALL COMPLETELY INSANE, AREN'T YOU?
WE'LL TAKE IT!
SHRIEK
IT'S OK! WE'RE ALL FRIENDS HERE!
THAT WOMAN TRIED TO BITE ME ONCE! SHE'S WORSE THAN—
THE BEAST!!
HE'S FINE, HE JUST HAD A LOUSY OWNER.
I HEAR HE NEEDS A NEW ONE, THOUGH!

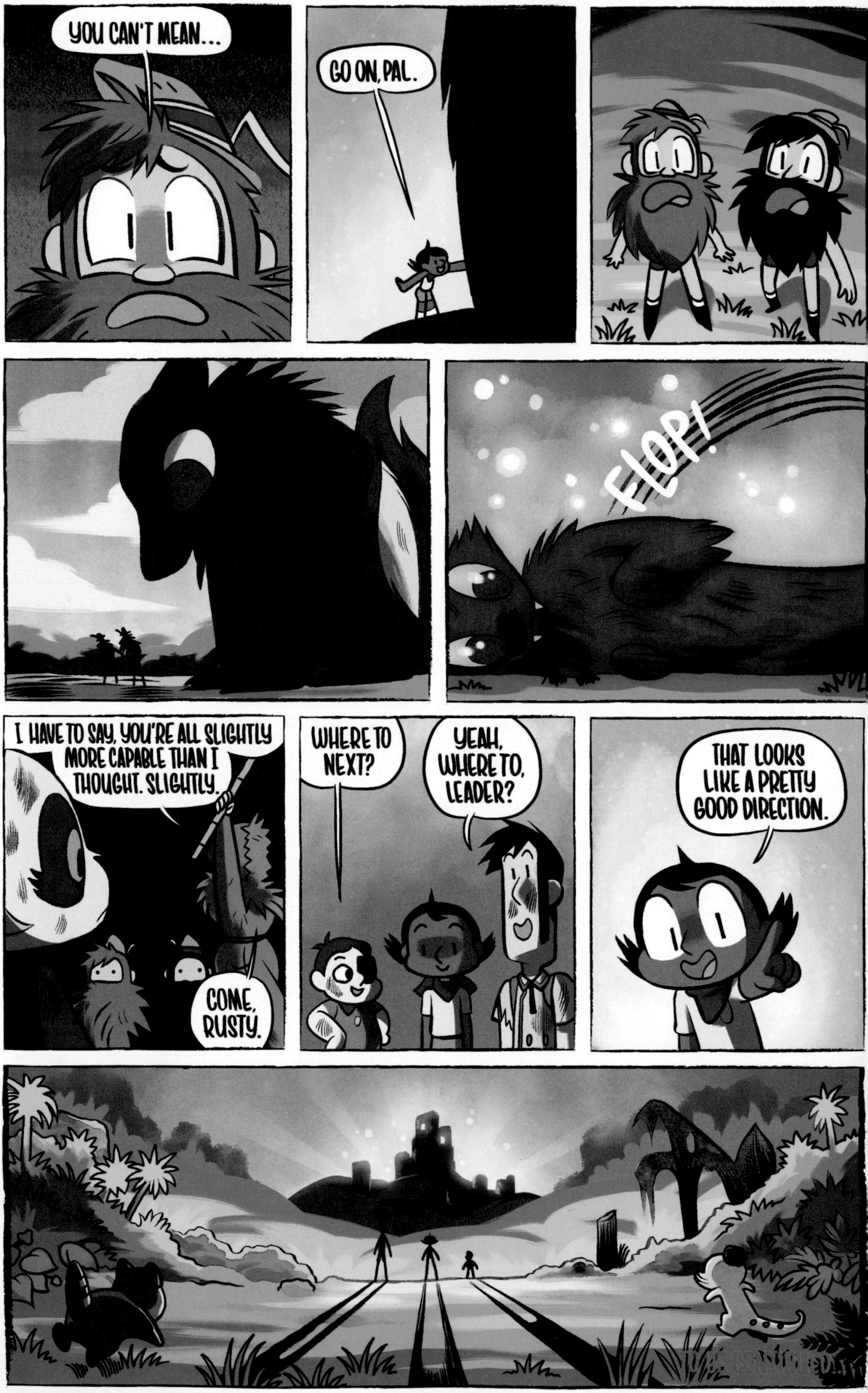
YOU CAN'T MEAN...
GO ON, PAL.
FLOP!
I HAVE TO SAY, YOU'RE ALL SLIGHTLY MORE CAPABLE THAN I THOUGHT. SLIGHTLY.
COME, RUSTY.
WHERE TO NEXT?
YEAH, WHERE TO, LEADER?
THAT LOOKS LIKE A PRETTY GOOD DIRECTION.

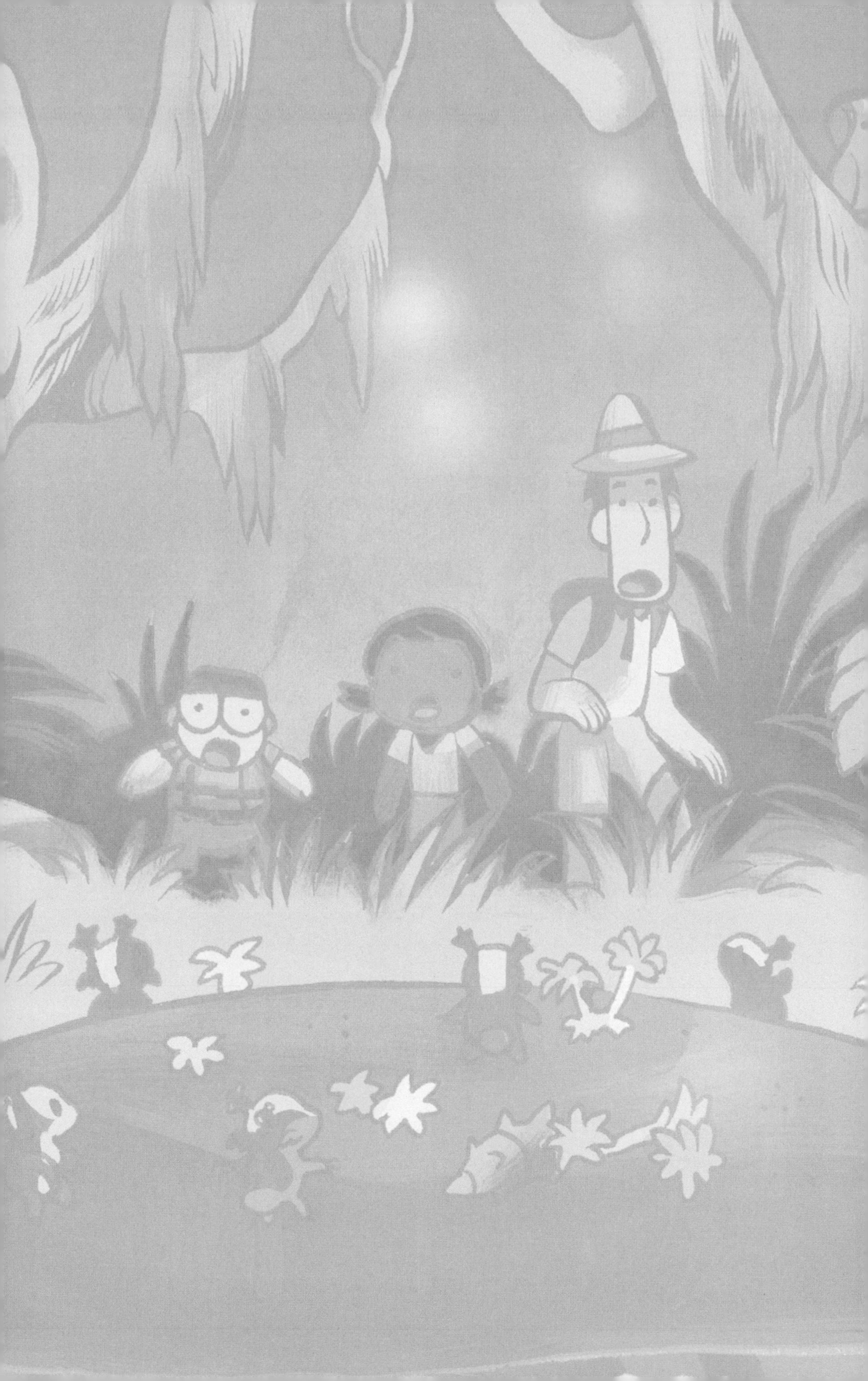

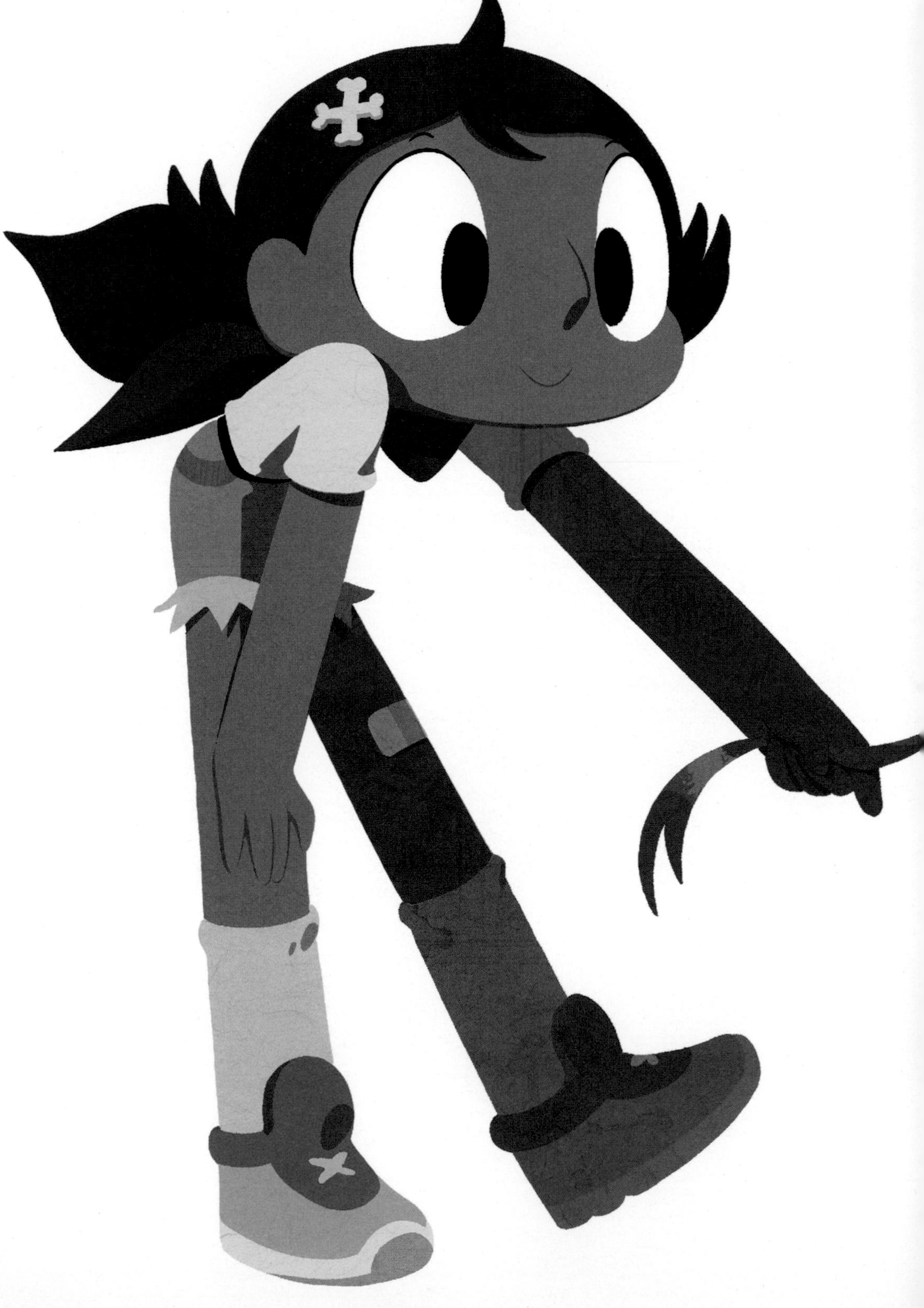

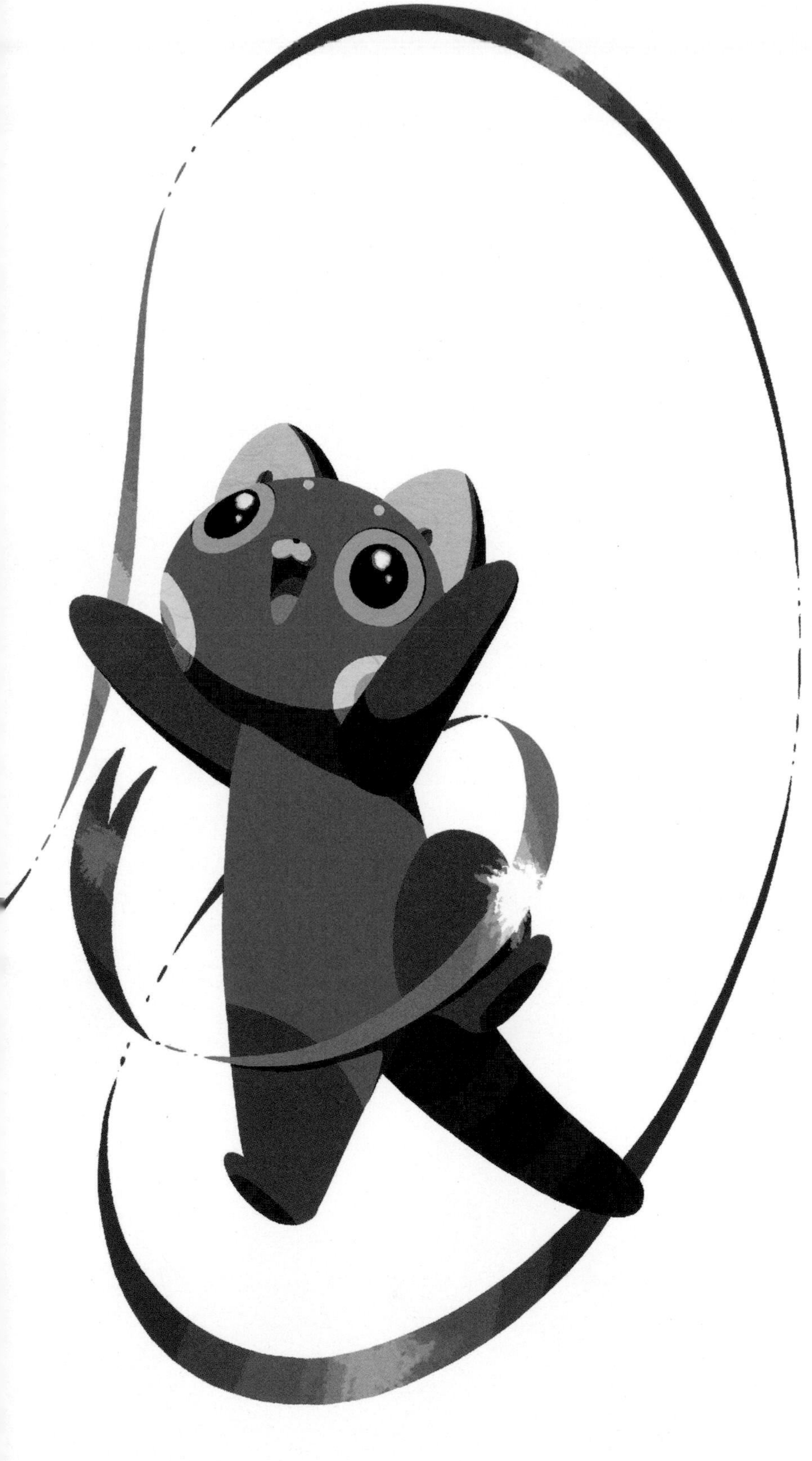

Cover by
Becky Dreistadt

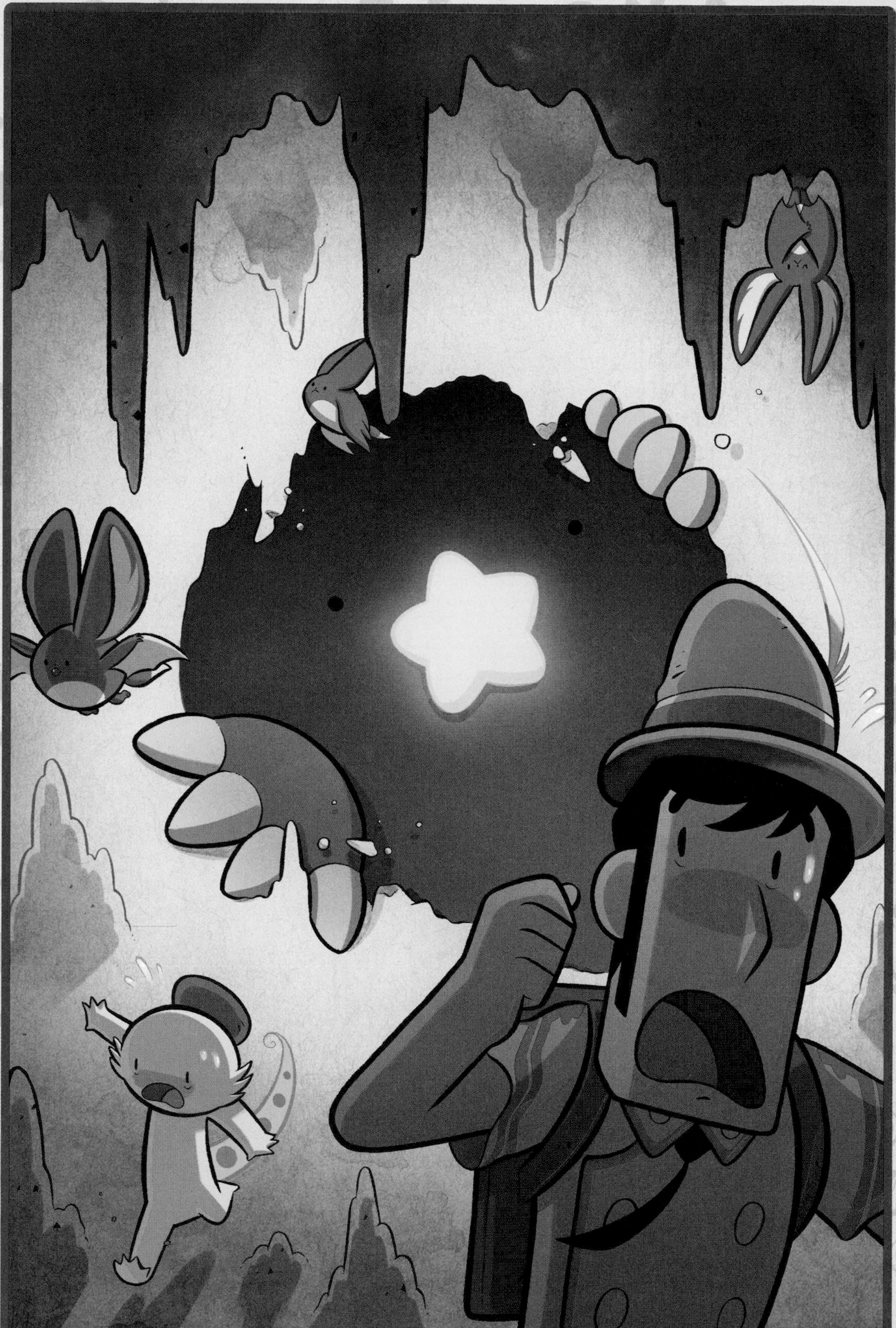

Cover by
Becky Dreistadt

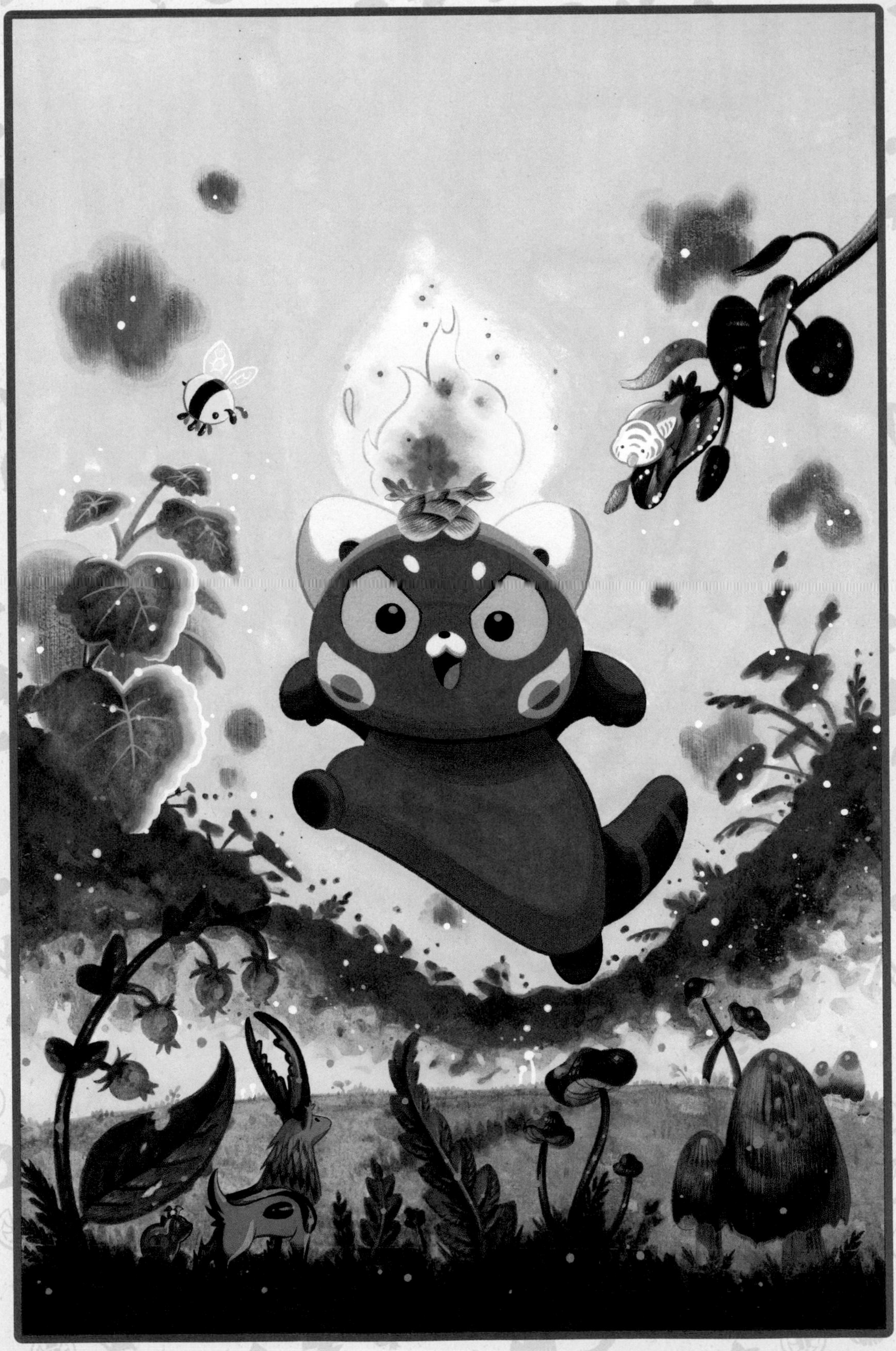

Cover by
Becky Dreistadt

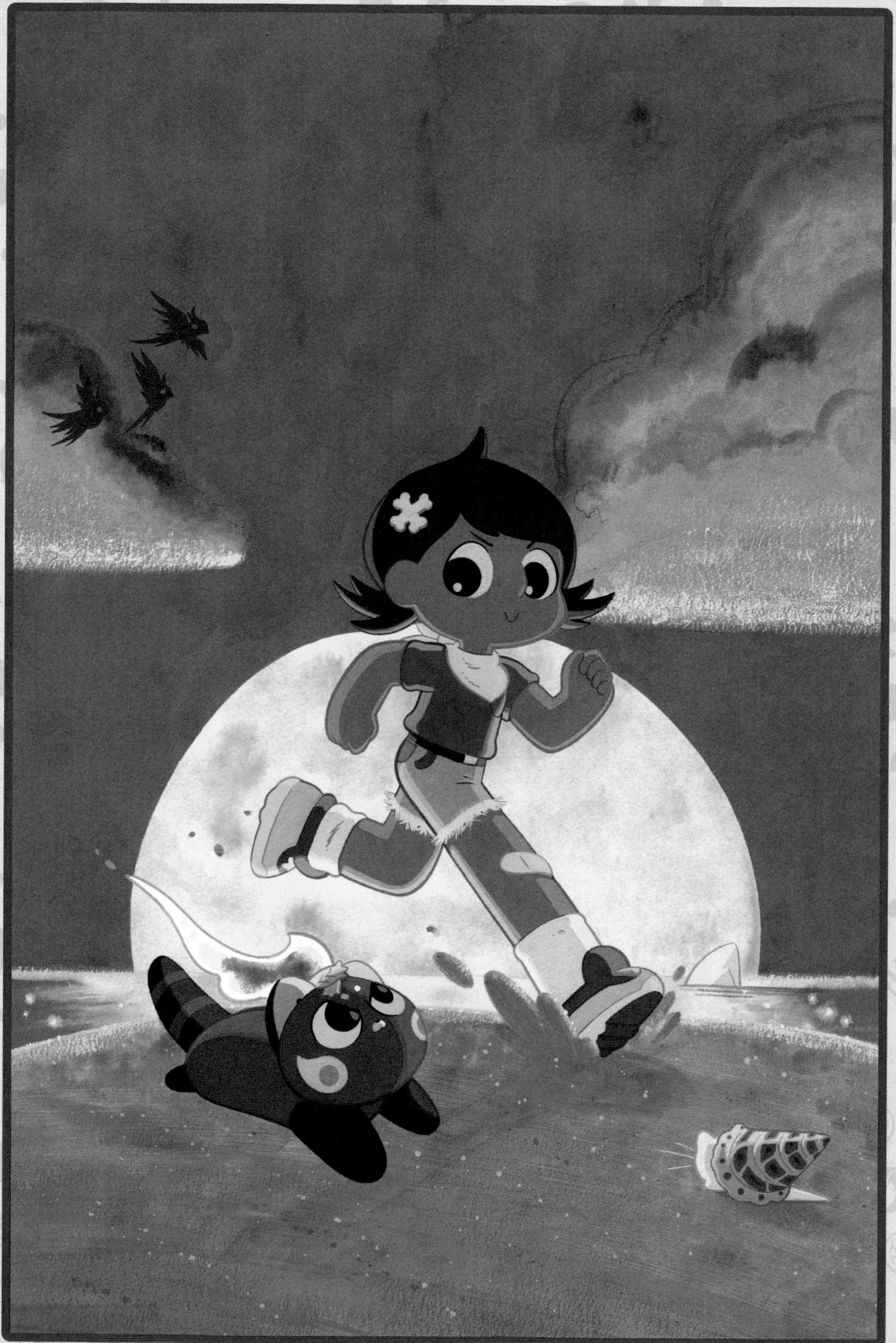

Cover by
Becky Dreistadt

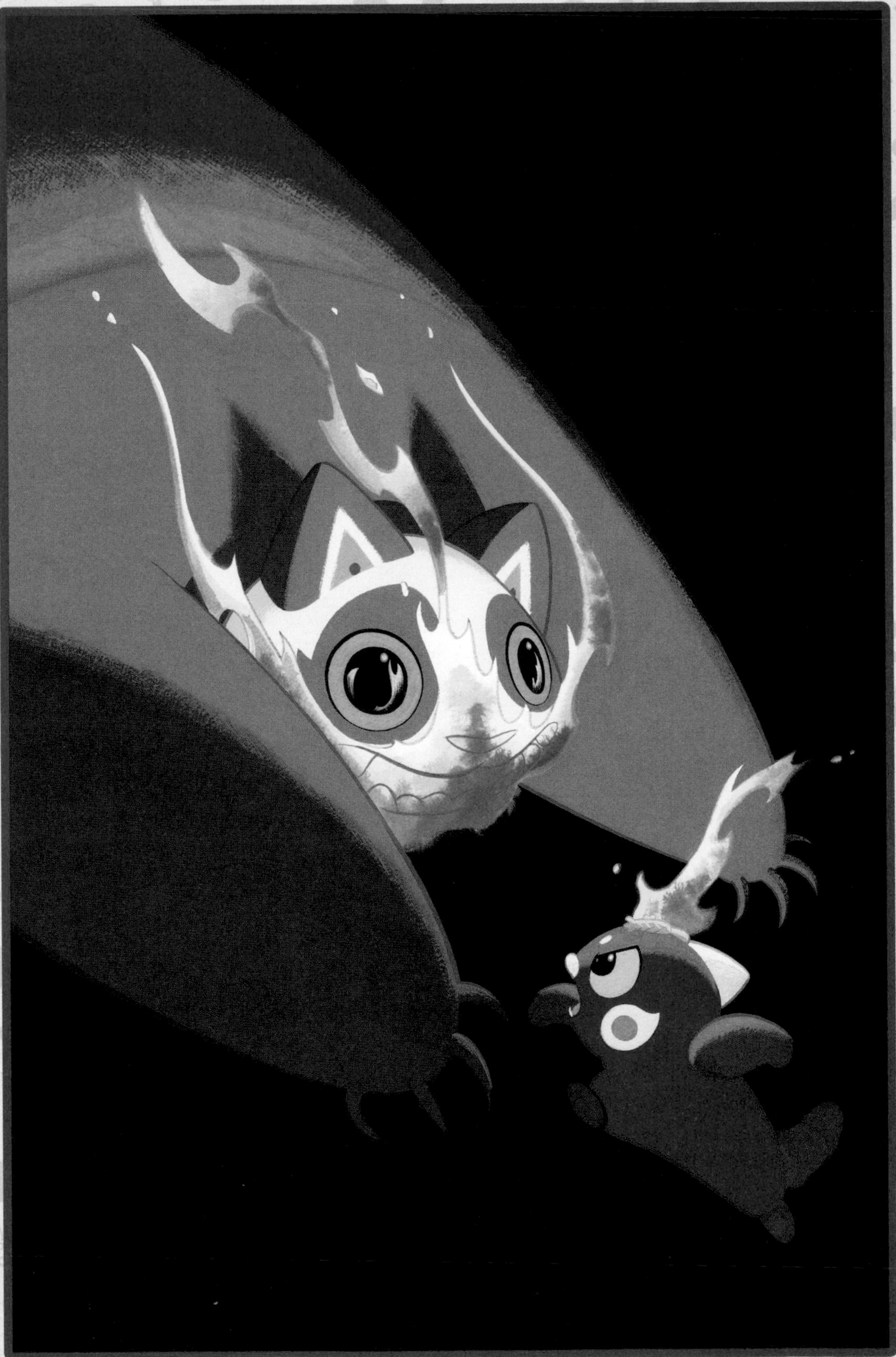

Cover by
Becky Dreistadt

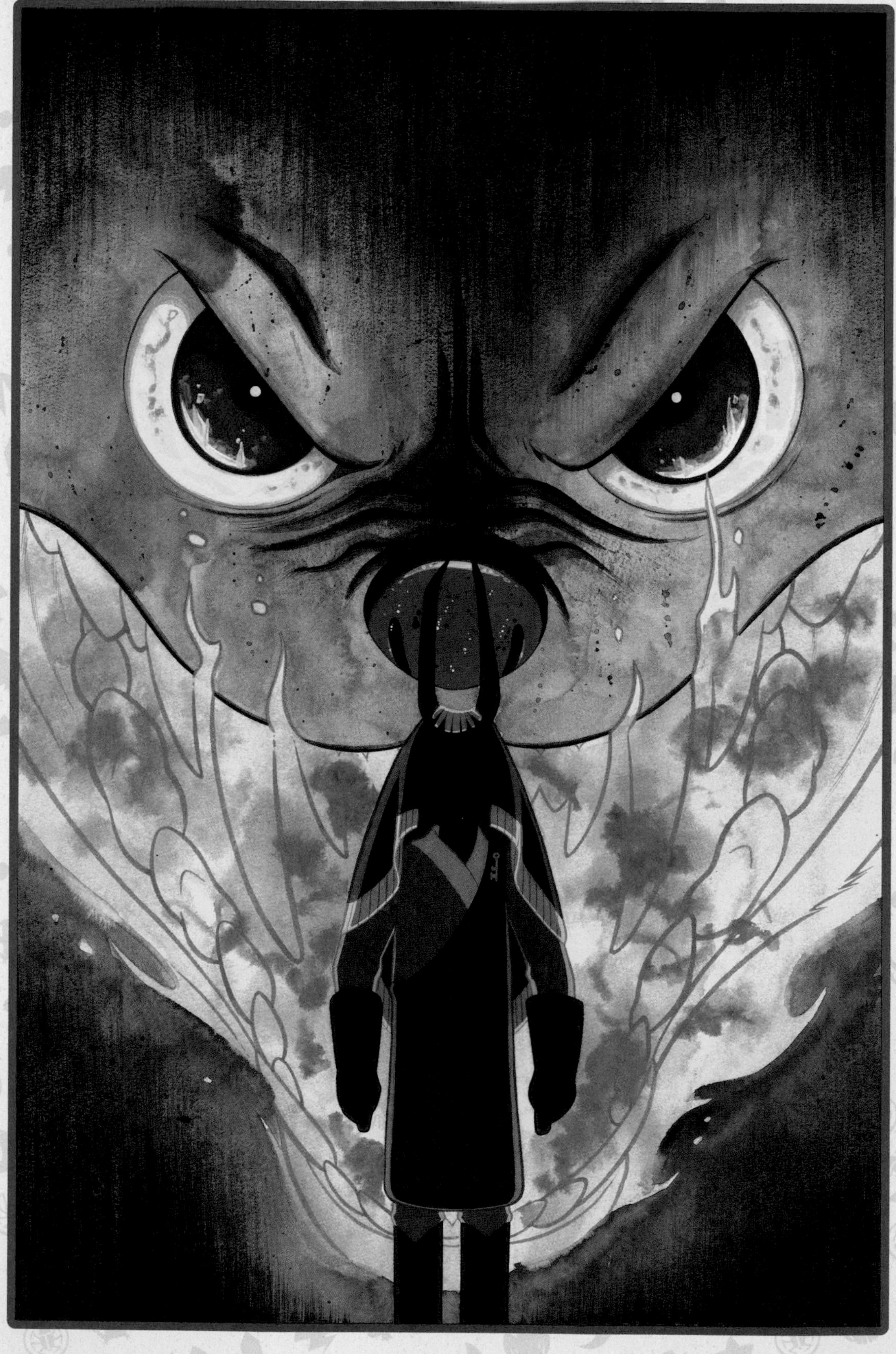

Cover by Becky Dreistadt
with inks by Kelly Bastow
& colors by Tracy Liang

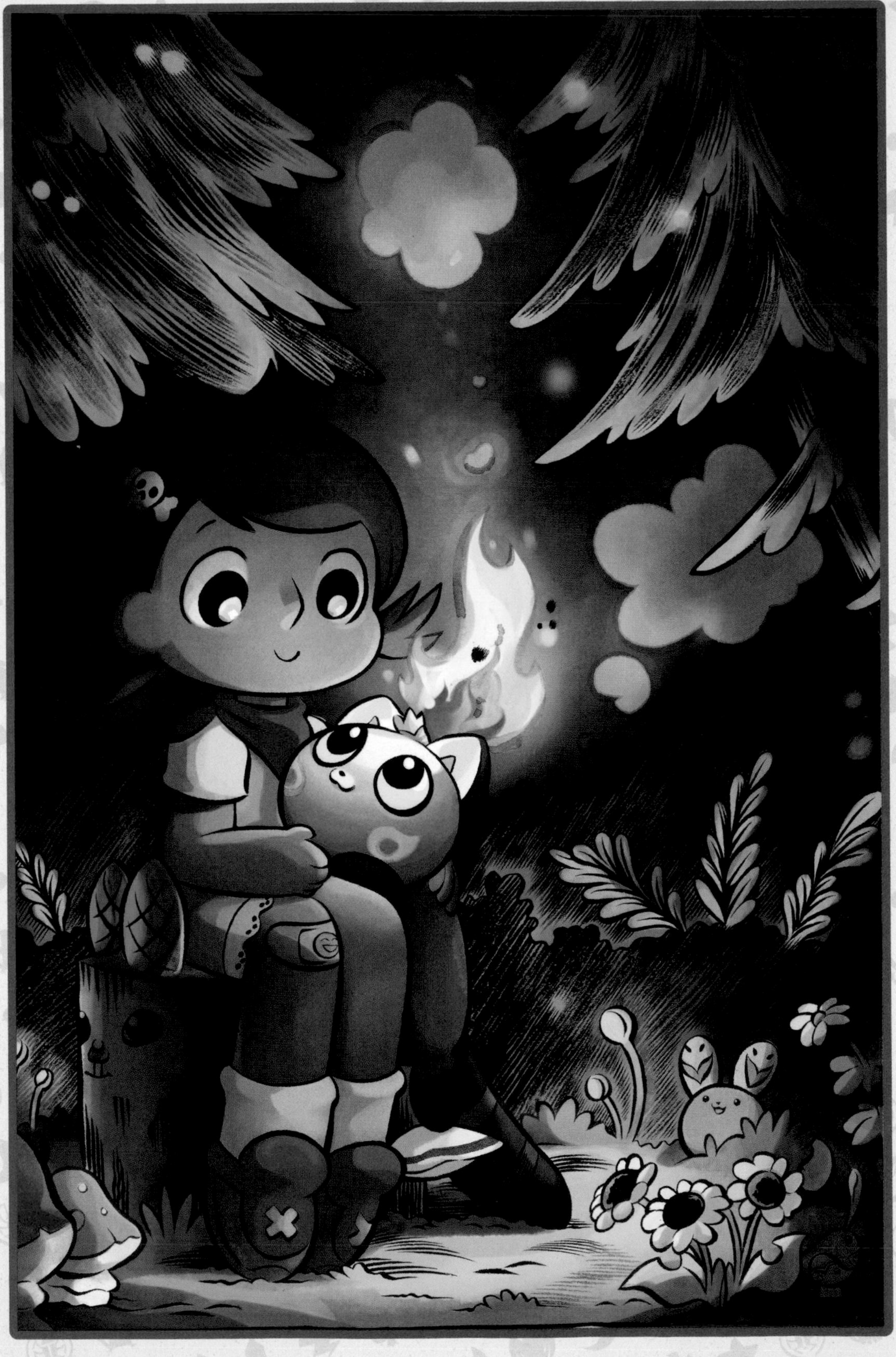

Cover by
Becky Dreistadt

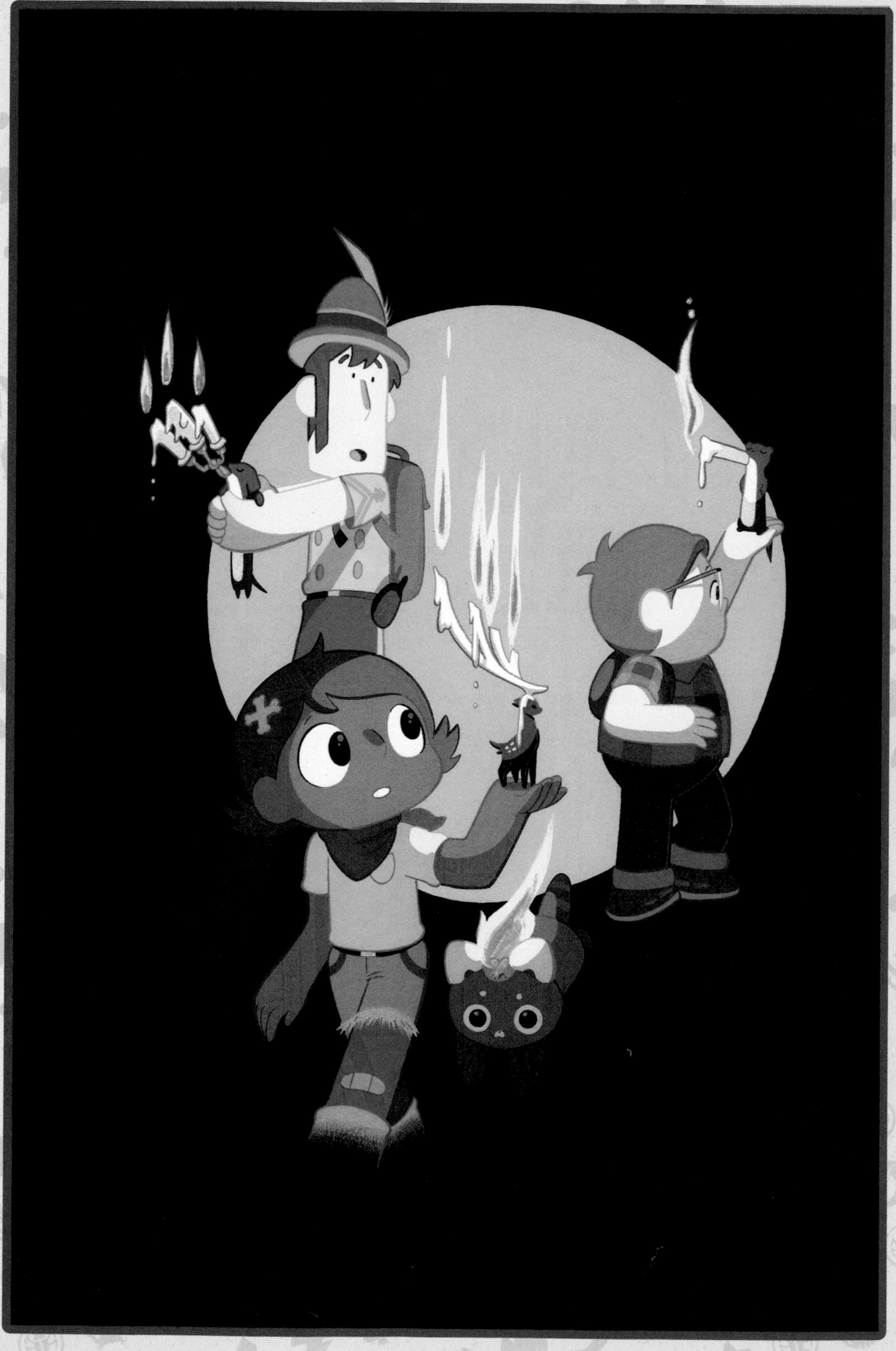

Cover by
Becky Dreistadt

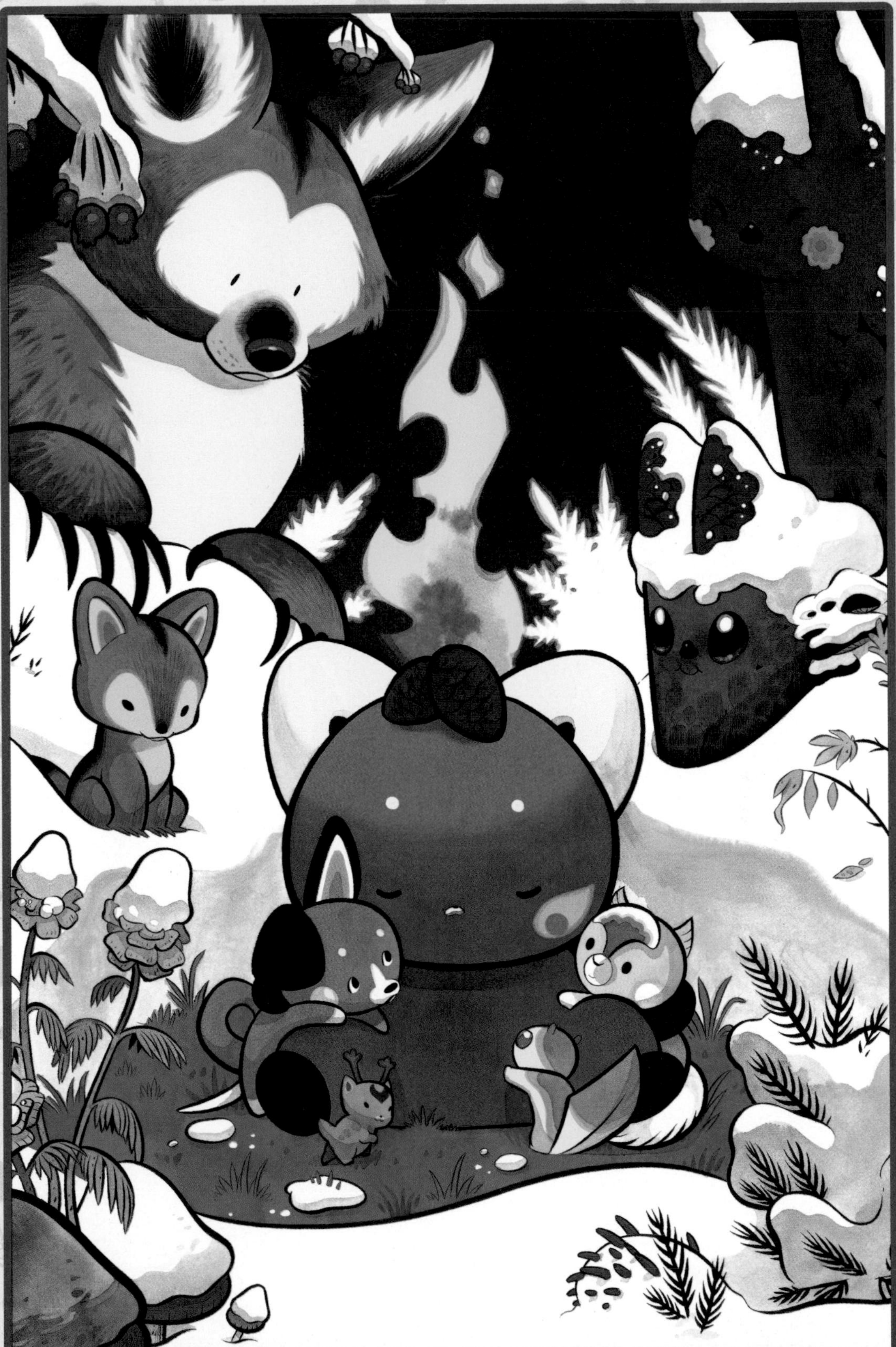

Cover by
Becky Dreistadt

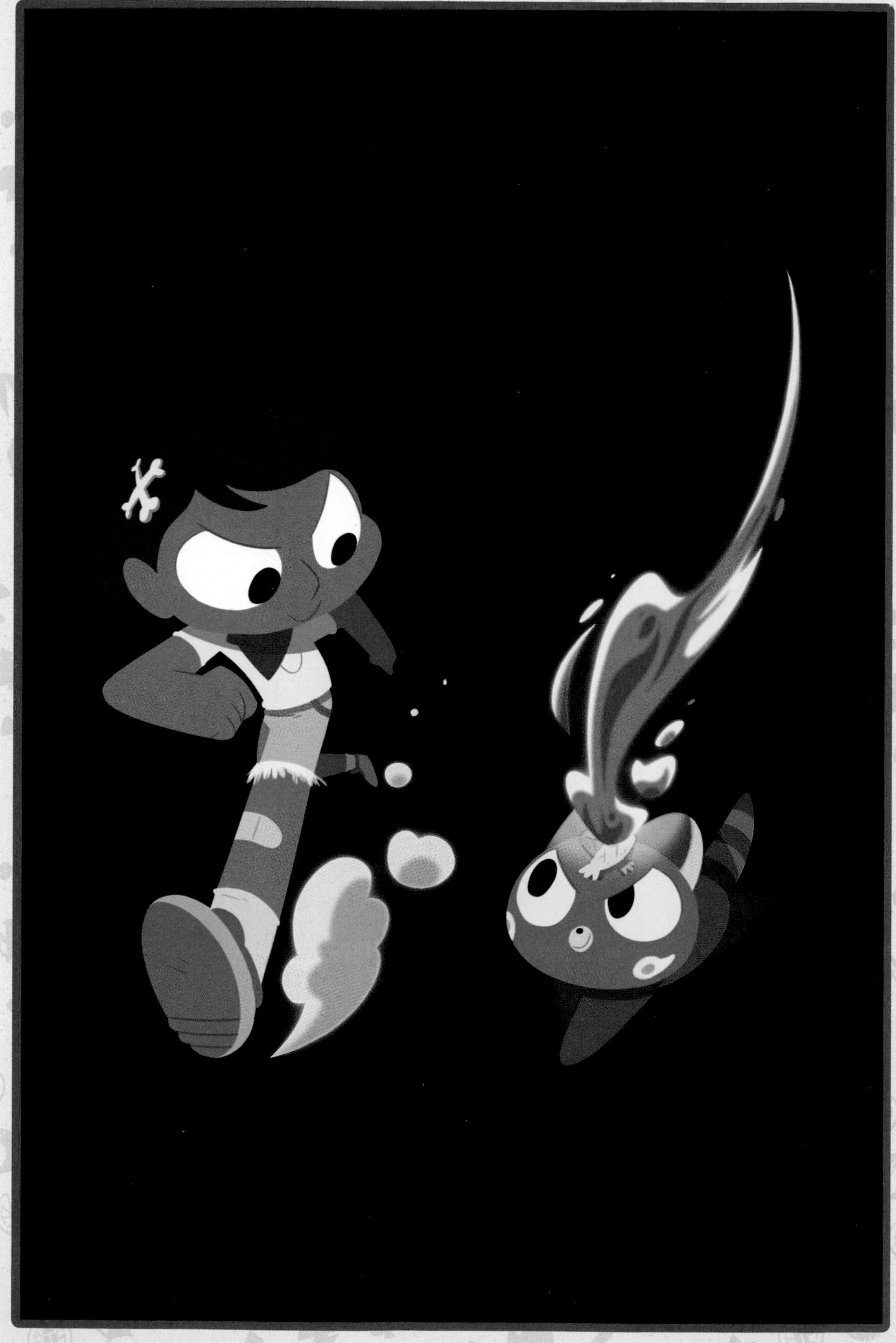

Cover by
Joy Ang

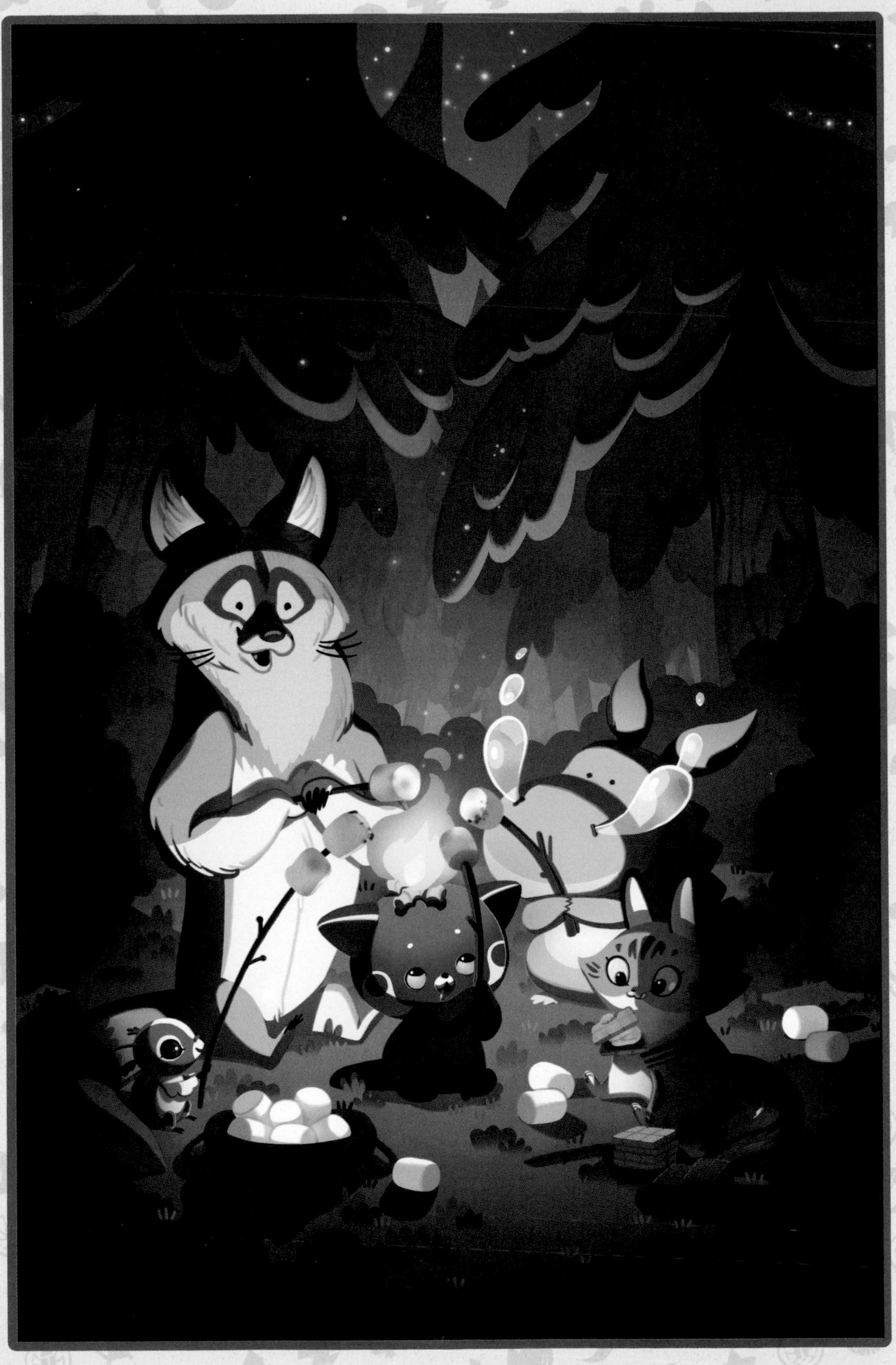

Cover by
Missy Peña

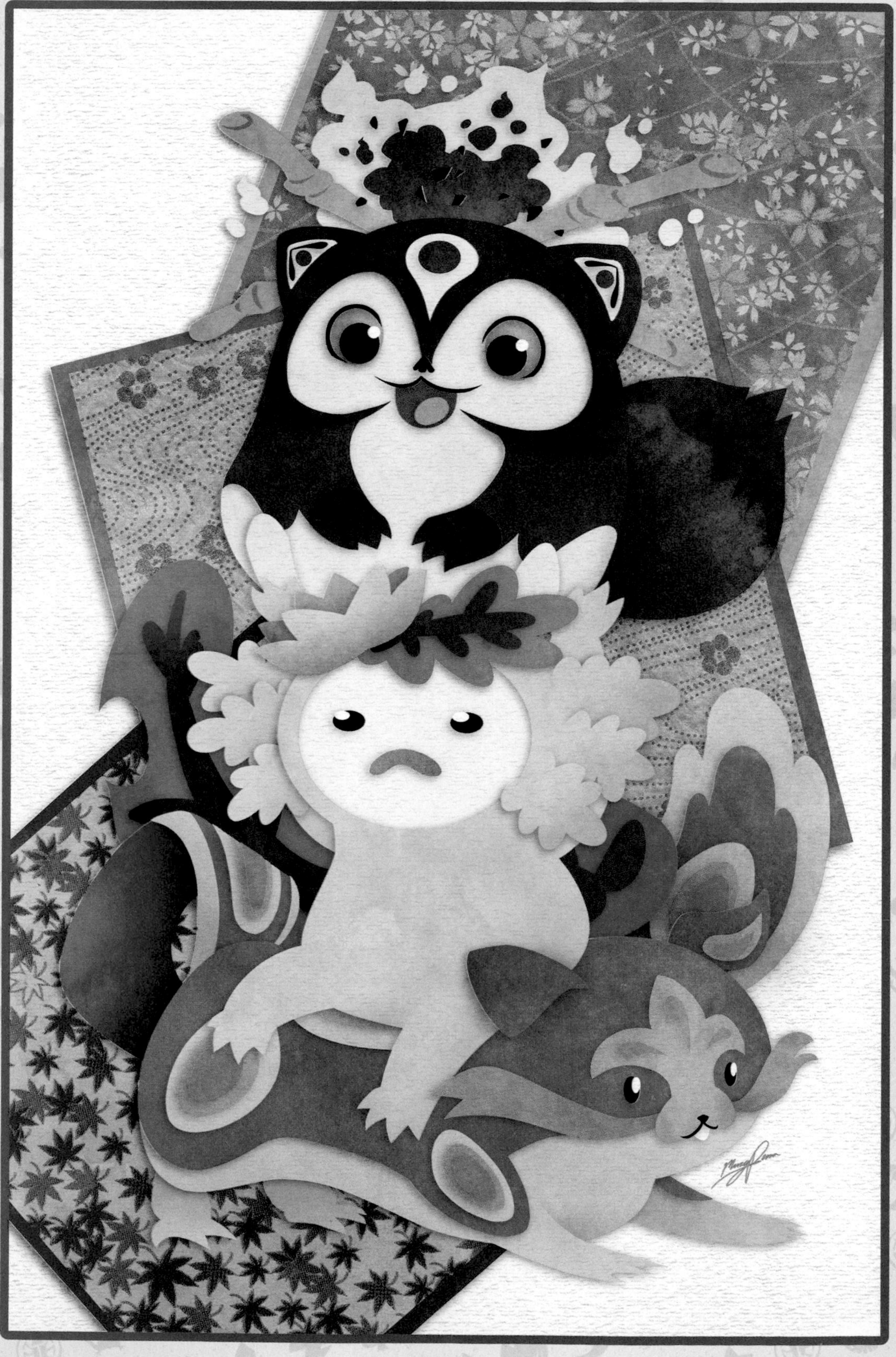

Cover by
Amanda Visell

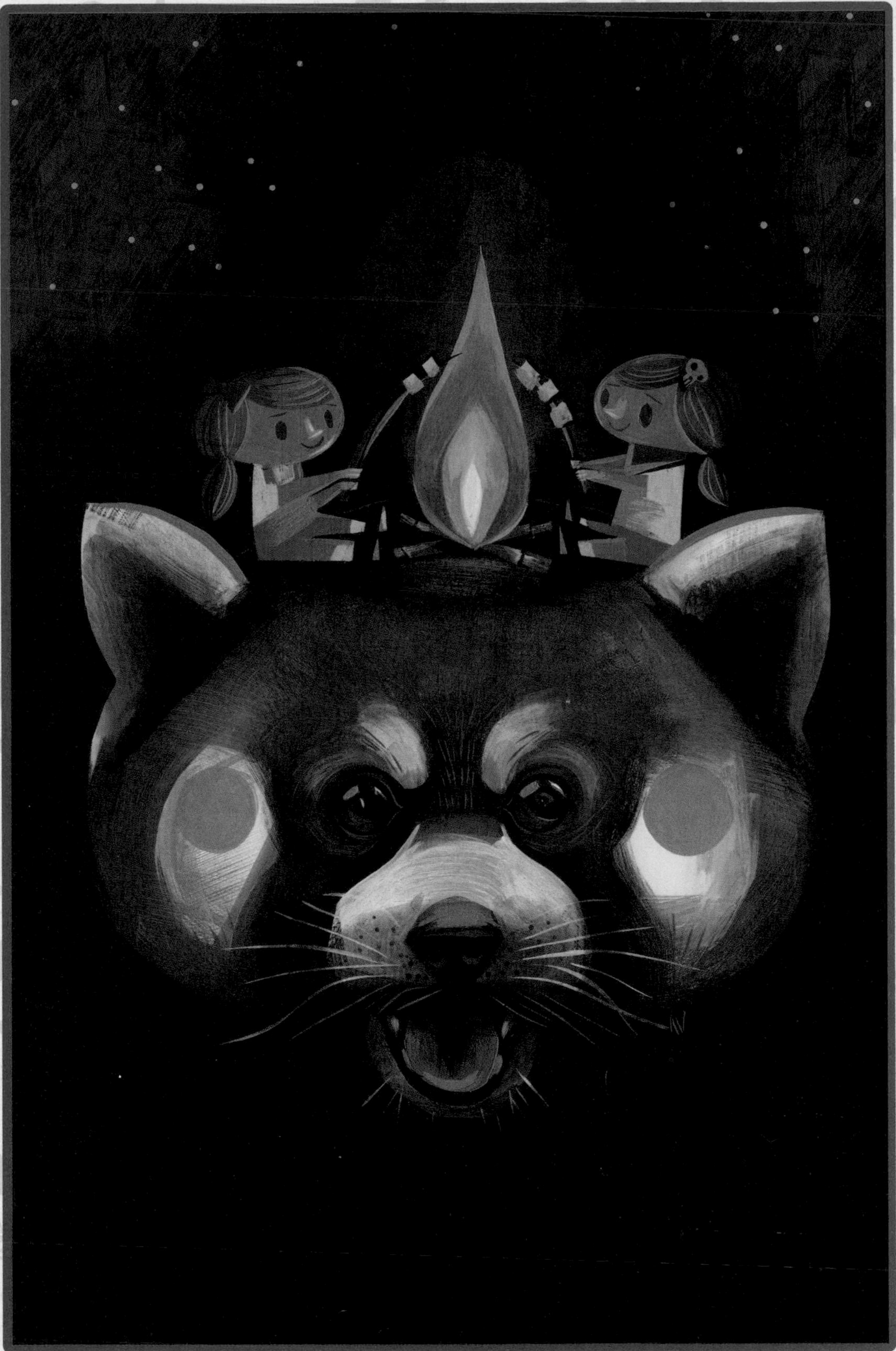

Cover by
Katy Farina

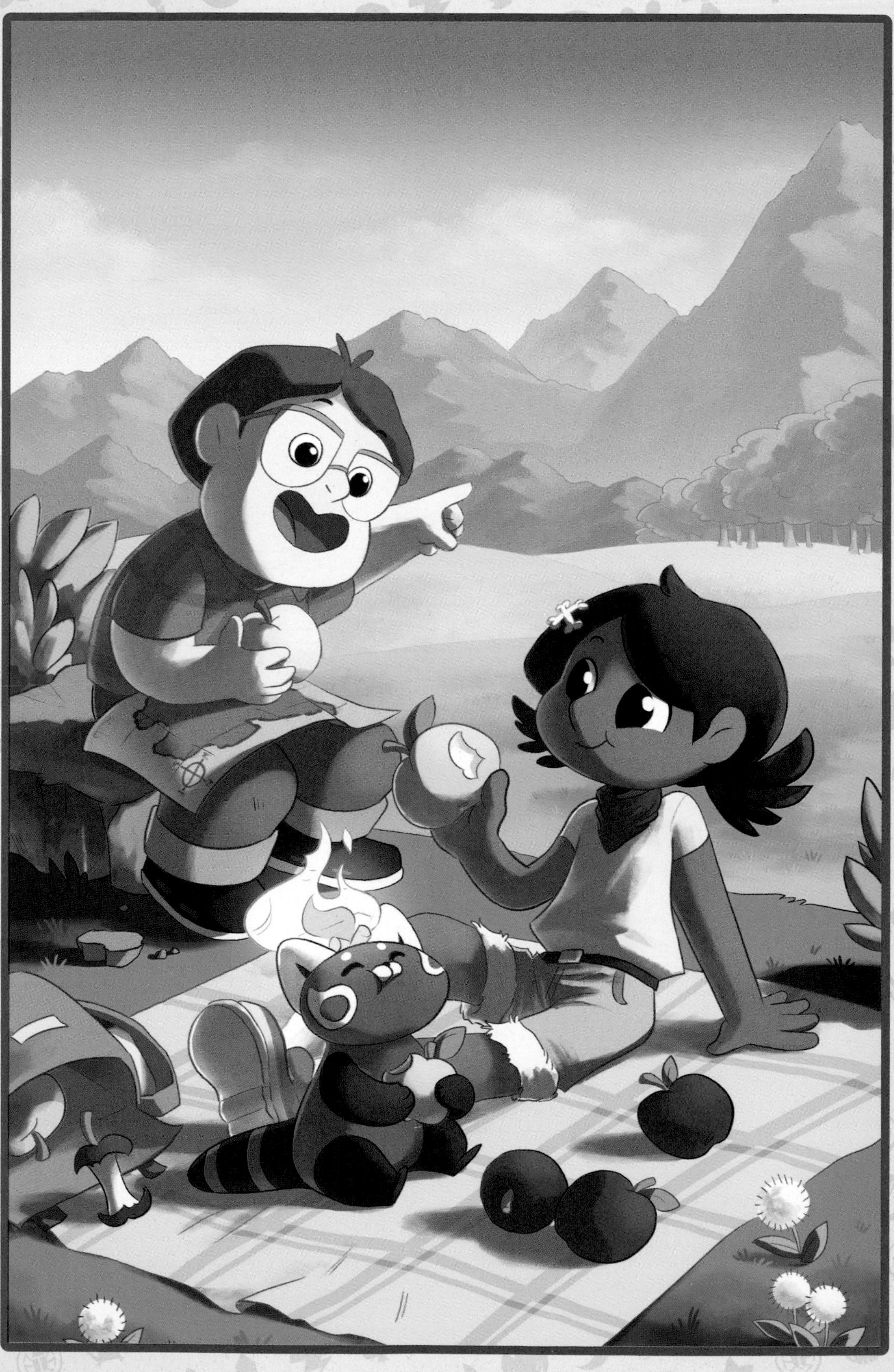

Cover by
Maggie Rudy

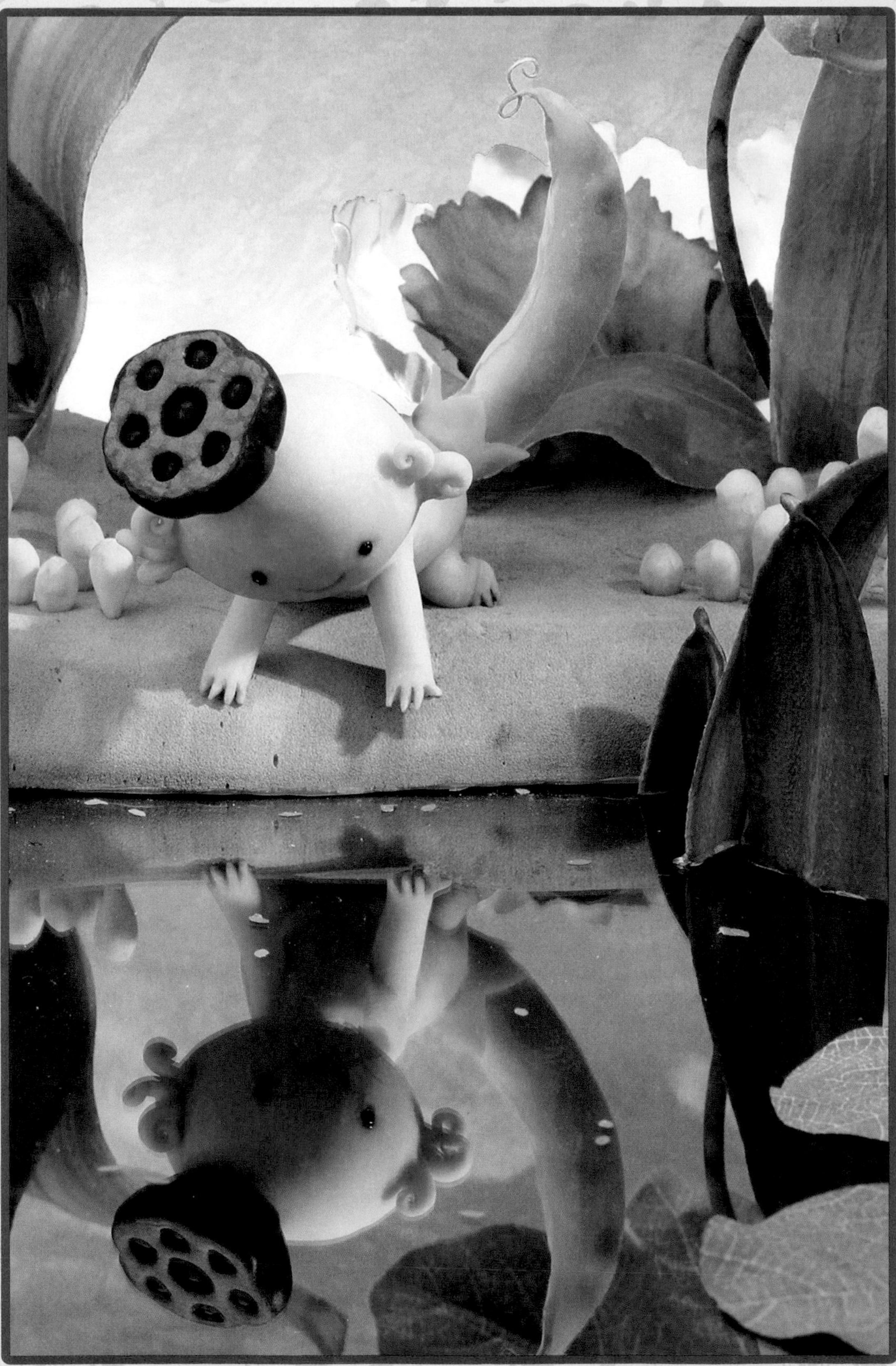

Cover by
Kevin Jay Stanton

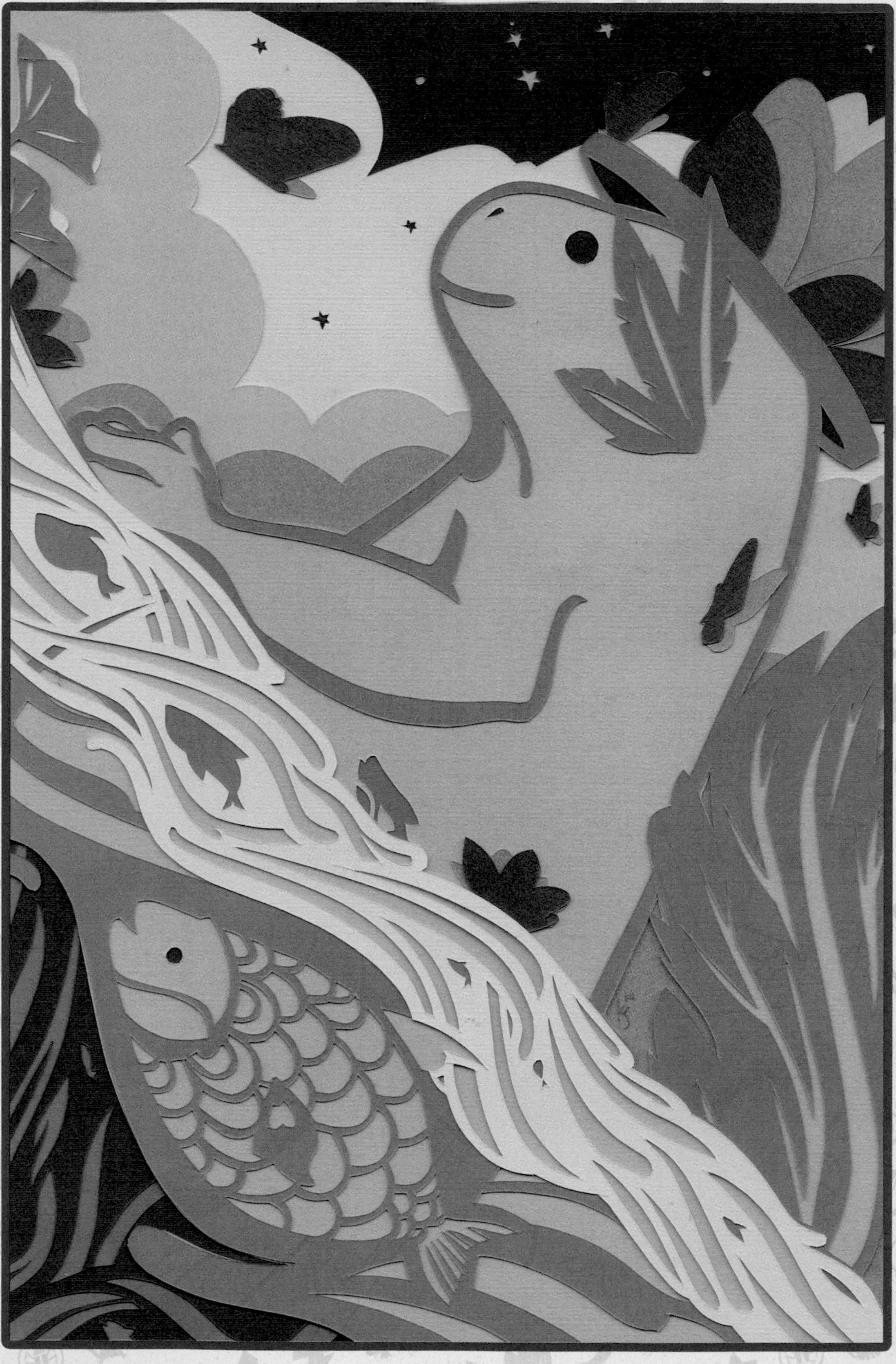

Cover by
Teagan White

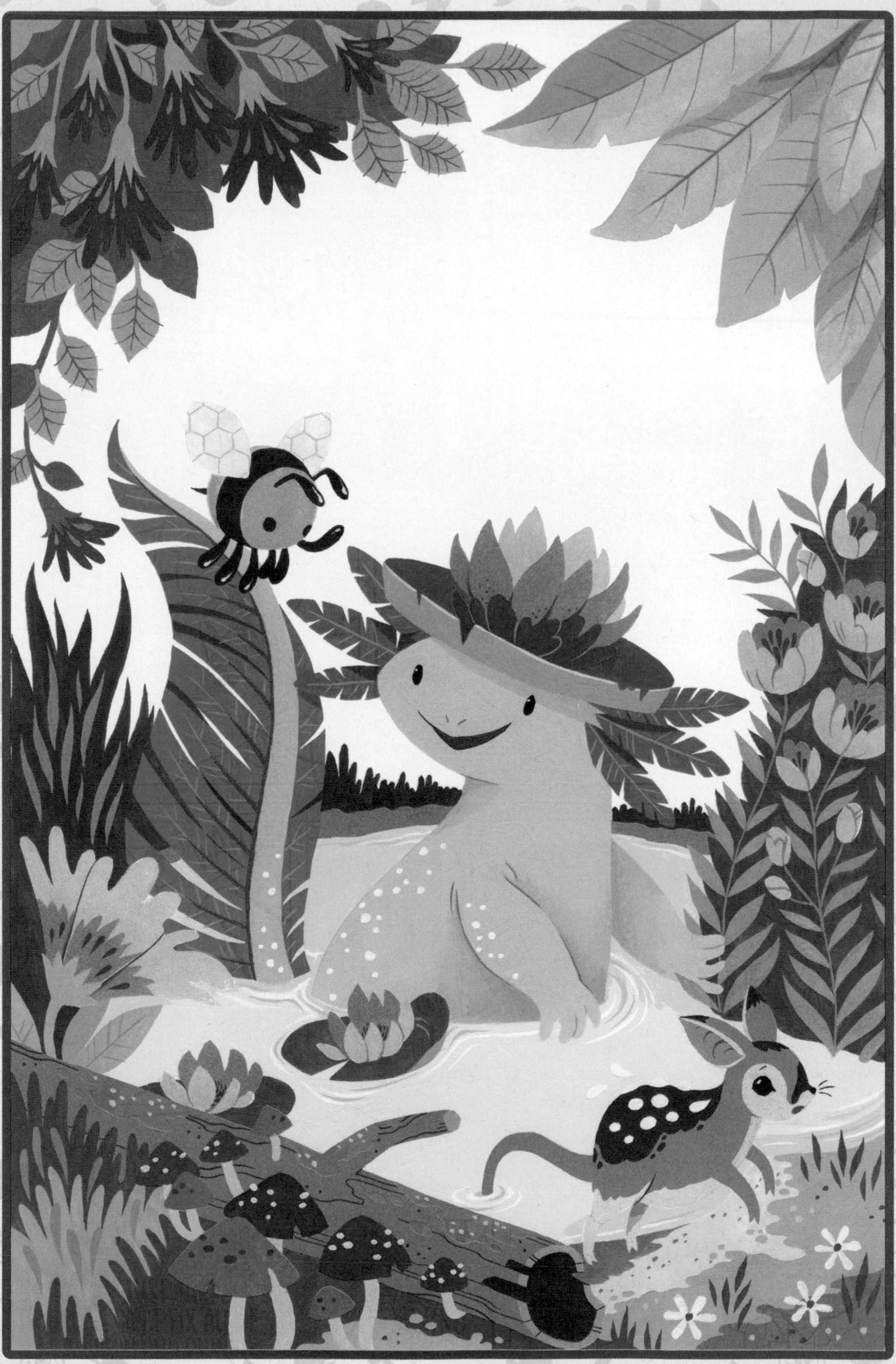

Cover by
Katy Farina

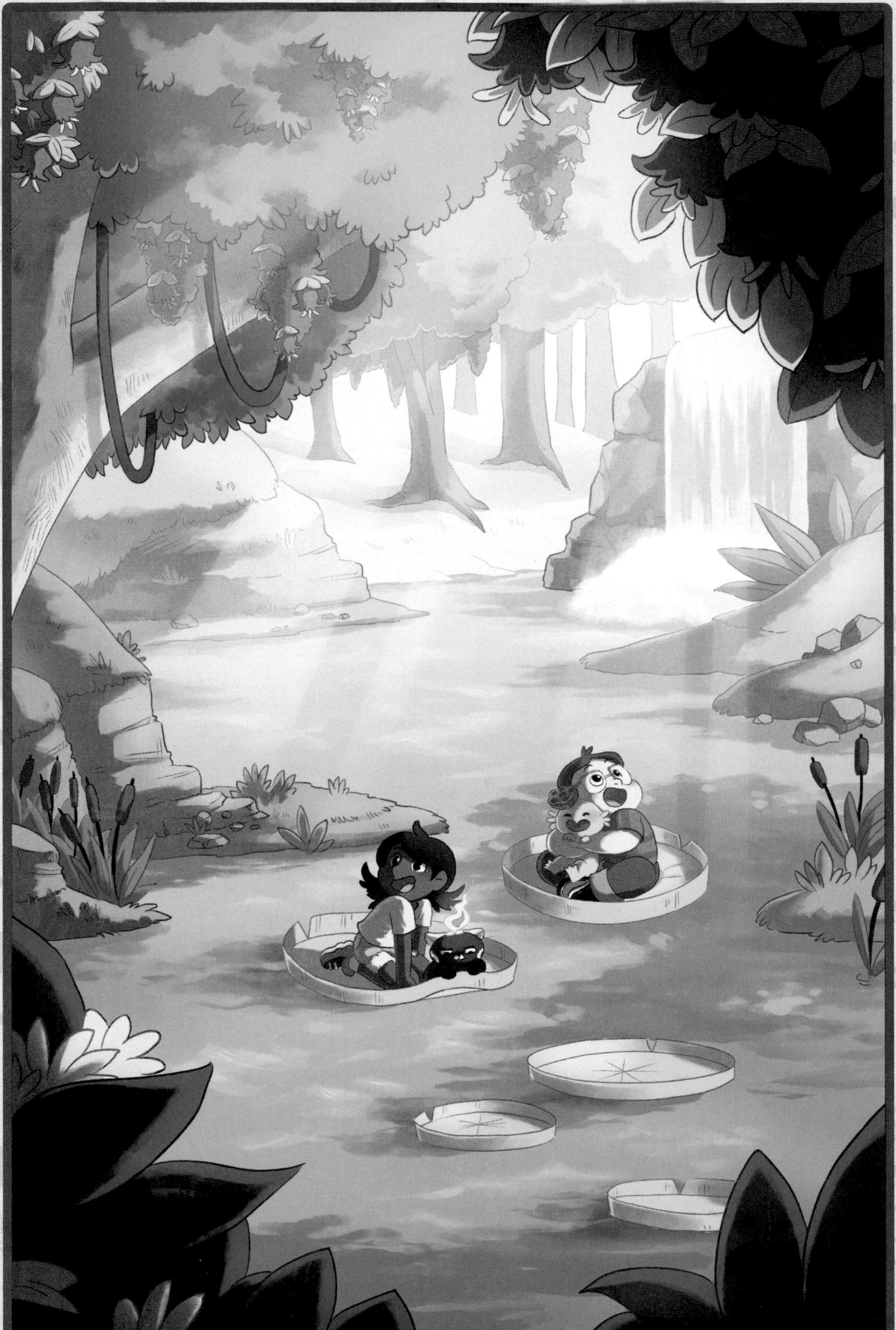

Cover by
Derek Sullivan

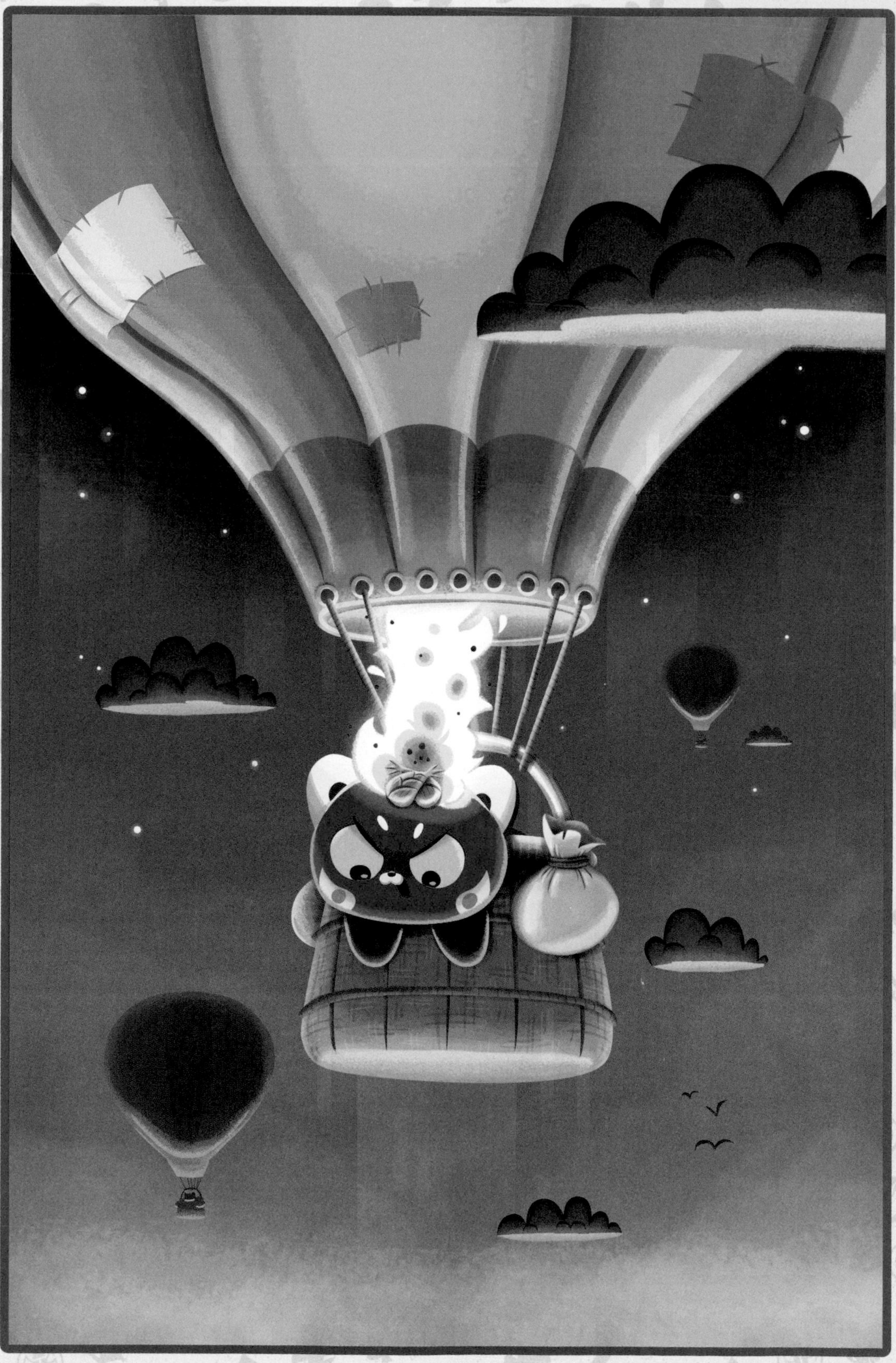

Cover by Katy Farina

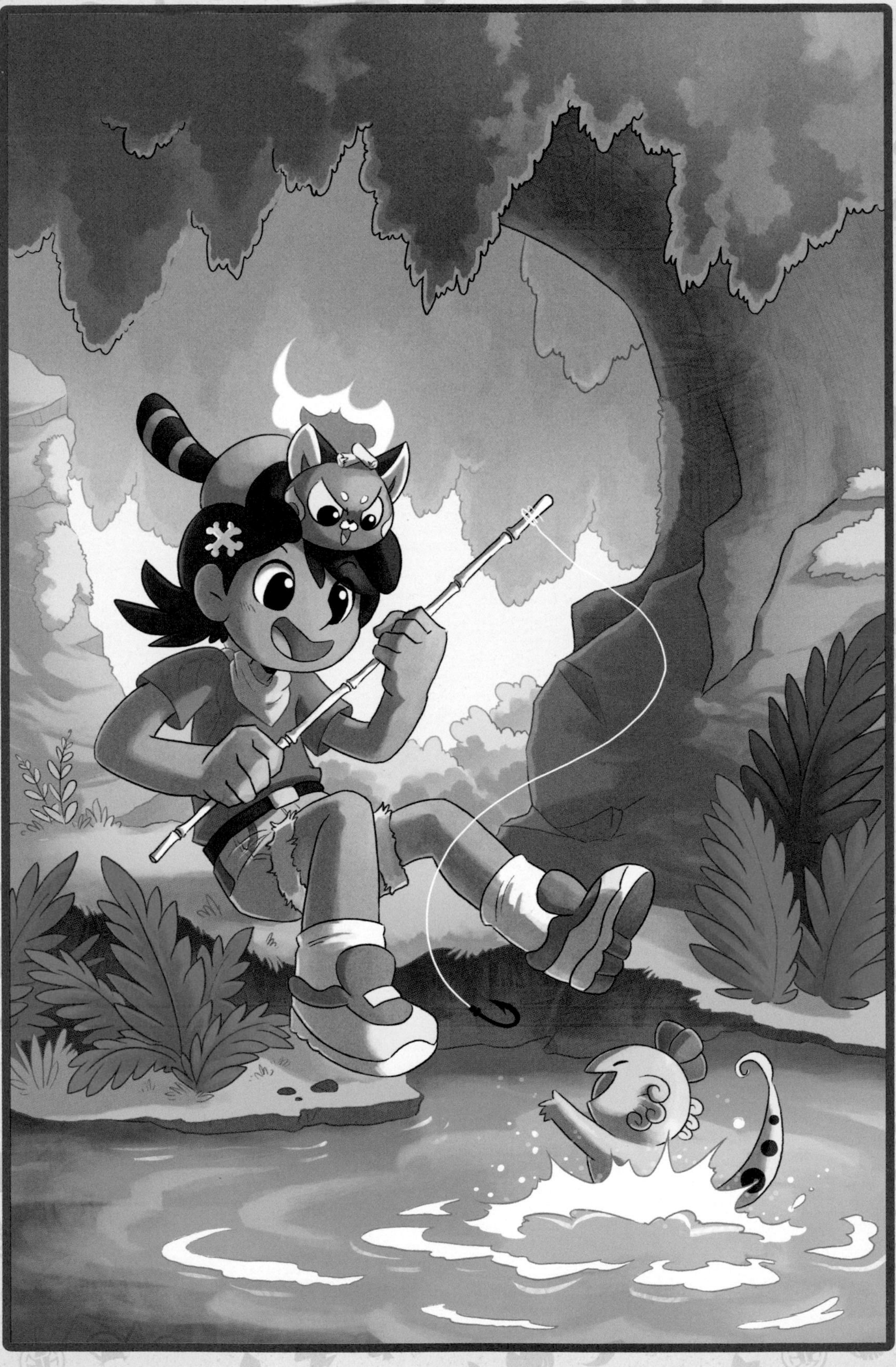

Cover by
Maryanna Hoggatt

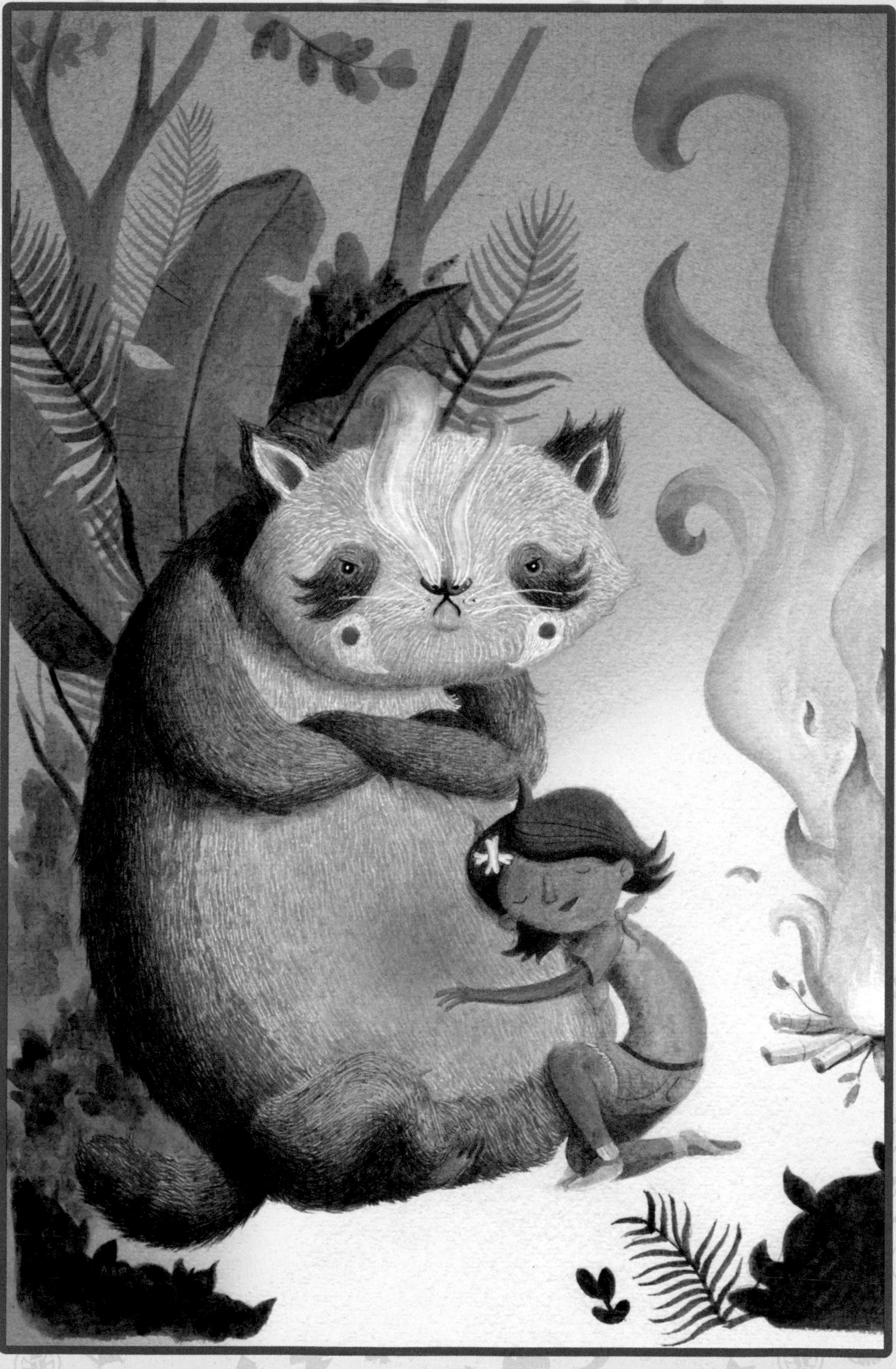

Cover by
Amélie Fléchais

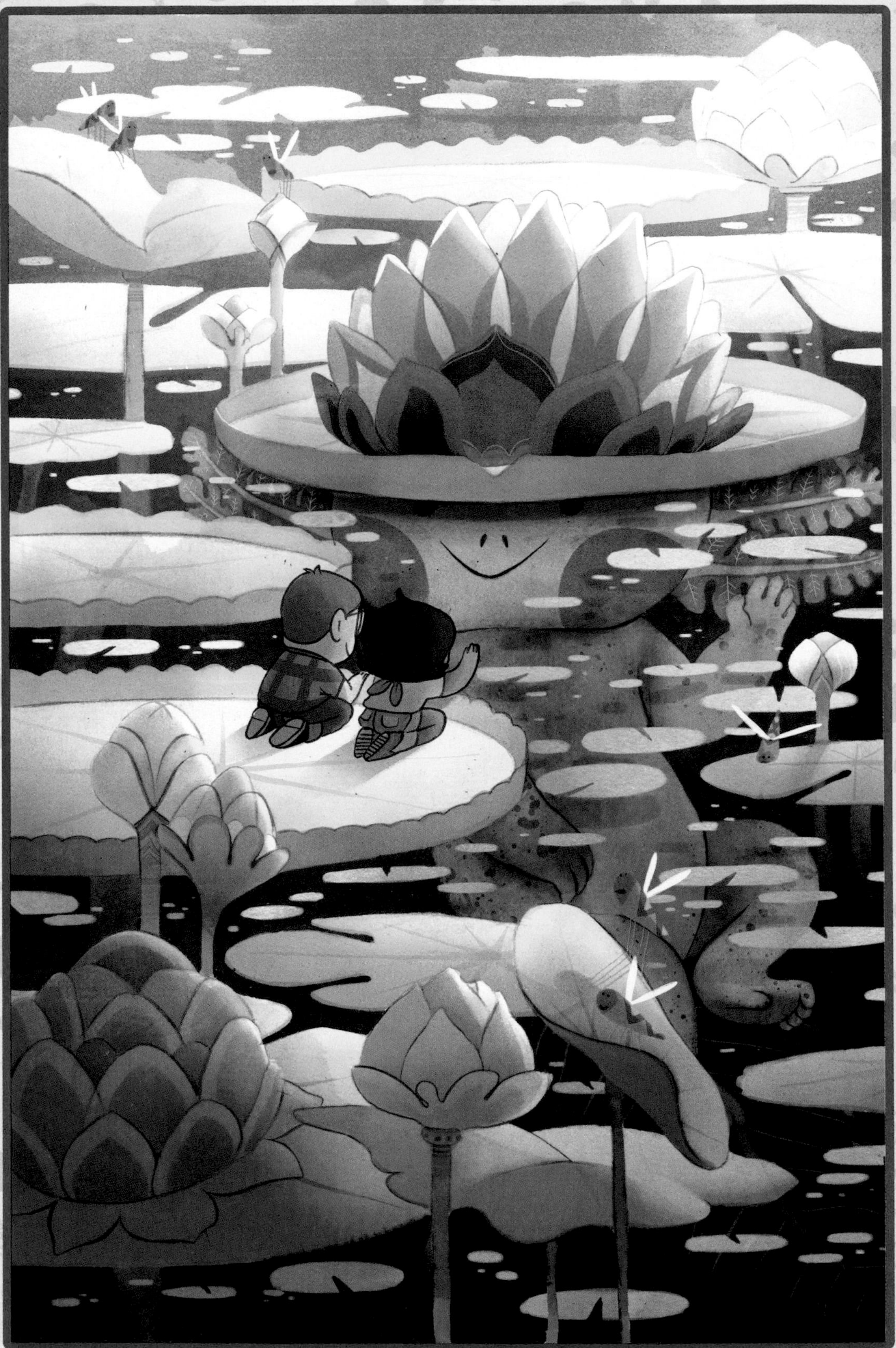

Cover by
Lorena Gomez

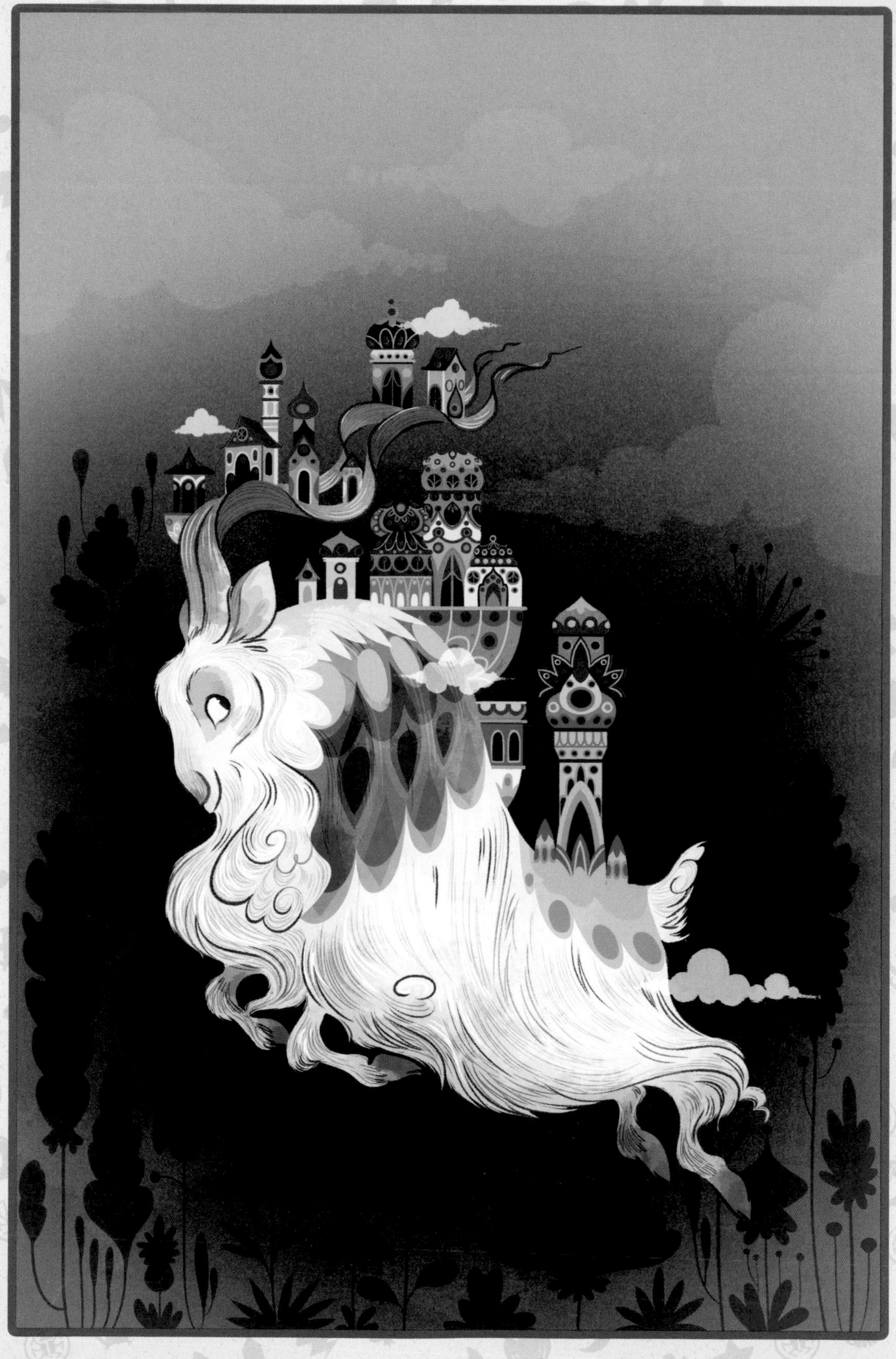

Cover by Tony Cliff

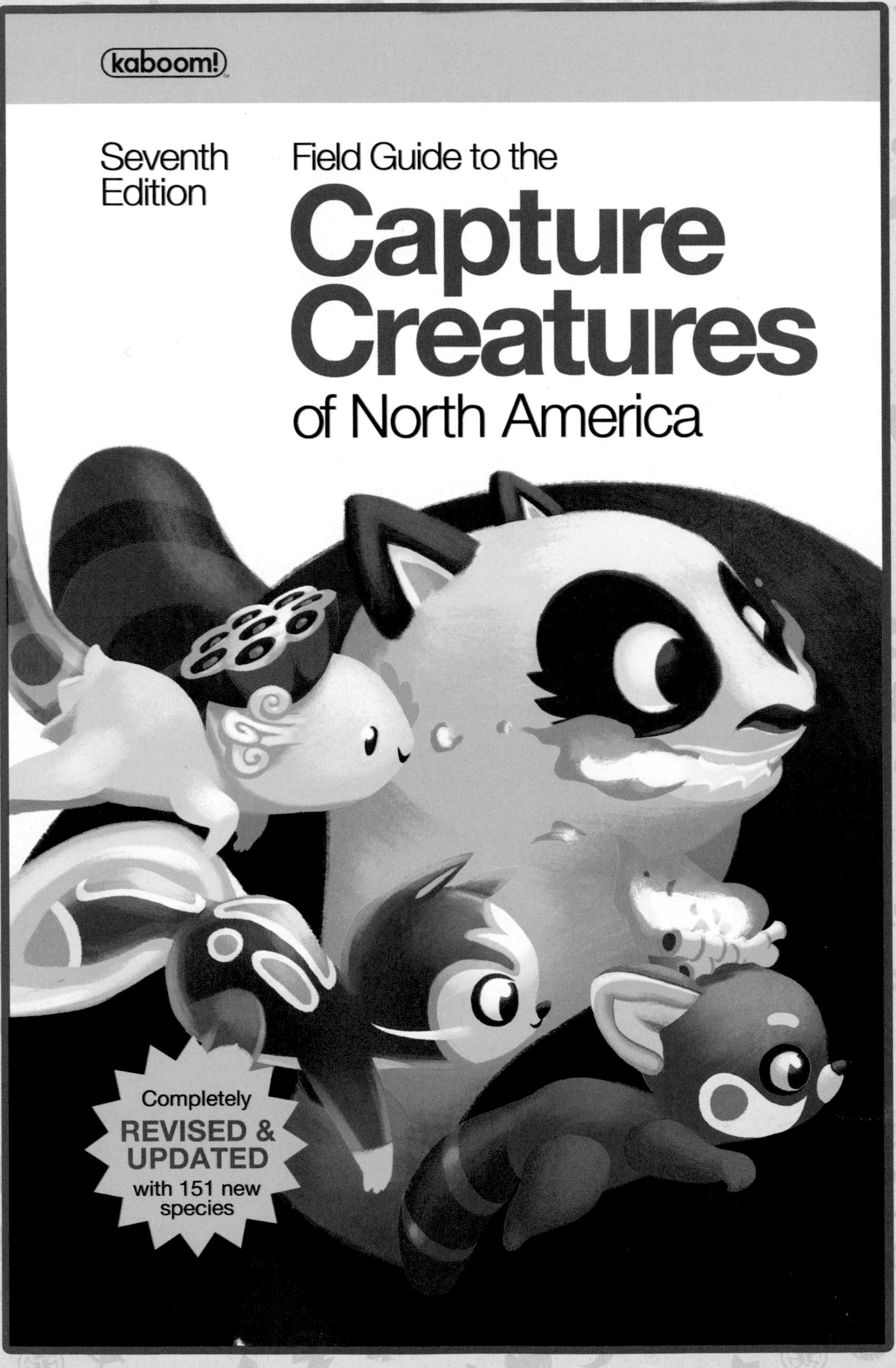
kaboom!
Seventh Edition
Field Guide to the
Capture Creatures
of North America
Completely
REVISED & UPDATED
with 151 new species